children of Magic Moon

Book 2

wolfgang and Heike Hohlbein

STORY	Wolfgang and Heike Hohlbein
TRANSLATION & ENGLISH ADAPTATION	Barbara Guggemos with Stafford Hemmer
DESIGN	James Lee
LAYOUT	Courtney H. Geter
COVER DESIGN	Anne Marie Horne
COVER ILLUSTRATION	Yoseph Middleton
EDITOR	Kara Stambach
SENIOR EDITOR	Jenna Winterberg
CREATIVE DIRECTOR	Anne Marie Horne
PRE-PRESS SUPERVISOR	Erika Terriquez
DIGITAL IMAGING MANAGER	Chris Buford
PRODUCTION MANAGER	Elisabeth Brizzi
MANAGING EDITOR	Vy Nguyen
EDITOR-IN-CHIEF	Rob Tokar
PUBLISHER	Mike Kiley
PRESIDENT AND C.O.O.	John Parker
C.E.O. & CHIEF CREATIVE OFFICER	Stuart Levy

First TOKYOPOP printing: October 2007

10 9 8 7 6 5 4 3 2 1

Printed in the USA

Library of Congress Cataloging-in-Publication Data

Hohlbein, Wolfgang, 1953-
[Märchenmonds Kinder. English]
Children of magic moon / Wolfgang and Heike Hohlbein ; translation & English adaptation Barbara Guggemos with Stafford Hemmer.
p. cm. -- (Children of magic moon ; Bk. 2)
ISBN 978-1-59816-453-4
I. Hohlbein, Heike. II. Guggemos, Barbara. III. Hemmer, Stafford. IV. Title. V. Series: Hohlbein, Wolfgang, 1953- Magic moon (Series) ; Bk. 2.
PT2668.O3795M3713 2006
833'.92--dc22

2006010395

I

For all those who have not yet
forgotten how to dream . . .
Because machines
have no dreams.

★ ★ ★ ★ ★ ★ ★ ★ ★ ★ ★ ★ ★

As it had begun in the hospital, that was the logical place for it to continue. *Not that there is anything logical about this story,* Kim thought. *No, definitely not.*

In the meantime, with a mixture of puzzlement and curiosity, he gazed at an ambulance's flashing blue light, which was reflected in the windowpanes of the building across the street. Of course, Kim much rather would have checked out the ambulance firsthand—or, more precisely, the reason it was parked a little more than thirty feet from the entrance to the University of Düsseldorf's Medical Center, waiting for a tow truck. An ambulance that itself had been in a traffic accident—that bordered on the ridiculous.

Aunt Brigit once again had been roped into keeping Kim company until Mom and Becky were done at the hospital and they all could go home together. She had assured Kim that no one was seriously hurt in the accident—so there was no need to feel guilty for grinning at the idea of ambulance attendants being accident victims. Kim pulled out the last piece of chewing gum from the packet that Aunt Brigit had bought him, stuck the gum in his mouth, and pitched the wrapper toward the curbside trash can, missing by less than than two feet. He took a quick, covert look around for his aunt. No trace of her, so it would seem. Then, he spotted her short black hair in the crowd of onlookers gathering around the crumpled ambulance, hindering both police and paramedics in the performance of their duties.

Here we go again, Kim thought, irritated. *Typical adults—always lecturing that "you just don't do that sort of thing," and that "it's not right to stand around and gawk when there's been accident," and topping it off with—to quote Aunt Brigit—"this isn't a circus; it's a serious matter." Then, they go ahead and make an exception for themselves.*

Kim felt a little disgruntled. Not that he had anything against his aunt—actually, he was quite fond of Aunt Brigit. Even so, nice as she was, she still was an adult: The way she acted was so typical of adults. *Disgusting!*

Kim wasn't in a particularly good mood. He hated it when people treated him like a small child. Every time Becky went to the hospital for an exam, he had to go, too. His aunt always tagged along as his bodyguard. How did this differ from the way small children were treated? Could someone please explain that to him? Kim had objected bitterly many times, but his father wouldn't budge on this point. All because once, on one single occasion when Kim had stayed home alone, he'd had a few friends over who'd made a little bit of a mess. It wasn't fair. Just because that dumb, wobbly TV stand was so unbalanced, even the tiniest bump from a soccer ball could make it tip over and crack the TV screen . . . It wasn't Kim's fault that the TV stand was so unstable. Besides, his parents had been talking about buying a new TV for months—and now, they'd done it. The place of honor in their living room now was occupied by a monstrous thirty-six inch TV—just what his father always had wanted . . . and what his mother always had opposed, arguing that the old one still worked fine. His father should have thanked him, not punished him. It wasn't fair.

But then, whoever heard of adults being fair to kids?

Now tired of the chewing gum, Kim spit it out, sending it sailing in a high arc. It landed about the same distance from the trash can as the wrapper had, but on the other side this time. Across the street, his aunt briefly glanced in his direction. Kim shoved his hands in his pockets and glumly turned away. She was checking whether her ward still was where she'd left him. After all, there was always a chance that he might sneak over to the accident site and take a peek, the way she had. *Of course, then I'd suffer inevitable emotional trauma,* he thought sarcastically. After all, the sight of a smashed bumper was obviously too much for the fainthearted to handle. *Yeah, sure.*

Kim's fingertips touched a couple of coins in his pocket. He hesitated for a moment before pulling them out and quickly counting up his money. Almost two euro; maybe it was enough for him to go to the café across the street and treat himself to a cola. It would be at least another hour or more before his mother and Becky got back. For the hundredth time, Kim asked himself why a ten minute exam always ended up lasting three or four hours—and for the hundredth time, he couldn't come up with an answer. It seemed to be an ironclad rule that everything in a hospital took a long time, even if it could go fast, in principal. He also wondered—this, too, for the hundredth time—why his sister still had to go in for checkups every six weeks, even though she was back to normal.

Maybe the doctors still hadn't figured out what had happened. But, of course, how could they have? There were only two people in the world who knew the reason, and neither of them would betray the secret to anyone. Not to mention the fact that no one would believe them, anyway . . .

Involuntarily, Kim's thoughts returned to that day, long ago, when it all began. Maybe the surroundings triggered something, for it was right here, in this very hospital, where he'd seen Themistokles for the first time; and over there, across the street, where Themistokles had smiled at Kim a second time, through the window of the café where he'd been sitting. That was the place where he'd had the feeling that his sister's illness wasn't really an illness but something completely different, and that—

Kim broke off that line of thought.

It was over. Long ago. Not forgotten, but over and done. He and Rebecca had caught a glimpse—actually, a bit more than a glimpse—of a strange and different world: the world on the other side of sleep, where reality became dreams and dreams became reality. They had both experienced the oddest and greatest adventure of their young lives. But that was over and done.

For Kim, this thought wasn't painful. Sometimes, when his mind drifted back to Magic Moon and its inhabitants, he did feel slight regret that he'd never see them again: Themistokles, the kind old wizard with his white beard and gentle eyes; Gorg, the good-natured giant; Gorg's friend, Kelhim, the bear; Rangarig, the golden dragon; Prince Priwinn; Ado; and all the others he'd met and made friends with on his fantastic journey. But he felt no bitterness or anger. Kim knew that he hadn't lost Magic Moon. A part of that magical world always would be inside him, and he sometimes sensed that world filling him—like a gentle, warm light that shone brighter as the real world around him became darker and more depressing.

What Kim and his sister had experienced was more than a glorious adventure. The two of them had received a gift that most other kids possessed, as well, but only a very few were conscious of: faith in the power of fantasy, as well as certain knowledge that something else existed beyond what could be seen and touched—that their world, in fact, made up only a very tiny part of what most people would call reality.

Sometimes, Kim wondered what all those super-smart adults with their all-knowing computers and books would say if they heard the truth. Sometimes, the temptation to tell them was great.

But he didn't. What he and Rebecca had experienced would remain a secret between them—and, of course, Themistokles.

Kim studied the shiny coins in the palm of his hand; then, with a disappointed sigh, he slipped them back into his pocket. The café was definitely beyond his means. Maybe he could talk Aunt Brigit into buying him a soft drink. Not only was she nice but also extremely generous—most of the time, at least.

Kim was about to turn back around and send his aunt a "one more minute and I'm going to die of thirst" look over the heads of the crowd, when he saw a distorted reflection in the large windowpane of the café. For a fraction of a second, there was a brief flicker, like the flashing blue light of the ambulance. But it was very clear, and it wasn't a formless spot of light but the outline of a human figure.

A figure he knew!

It was a white-haired, bearded, old man, slowly raising his left hand toward Kim in a desperate, beckoning gesture. Kim stared at him, stunned. Then, with a barely suppressed cry, he whirled around, his eyes wide in disbelief.

There was no one behind him, no one who could have been the person reflected in the pane. Of course, *somebody* was behind him. In fact, a number of somebodies stood around, curiously gaping at the crashed ambulance. More than a few of those people now turned toward Kim to give him strange looks. Kim realized he actually had screamed, and now he was standing there with wide eyes and his mouth gaping open. He was as white as a ghost. One woman turned toward him and lifted her hand as if she were going to put it on his shoulder, but she stopped in mid-movement.

"Are you all right?" she asked. When Kim didn't react, she repeated the question.

Kim just nodded without saying anything, and he contorted his features into what he hoped was a smile. Still very upset, he looked back and forth from the large windowpane to the empty space directly behind him, where an old man with a long white beard should have been standing—an old man reflected in the glass, not wearing a suit or an overcoat like the other men but cloaked in a wide black robe, holding in his right hand a staff that was as tall as a man and carved with a coiled snake, its mouth agape.

The old man wasn't there.

He wasn't there now; that was absolutely clear. He couldn't have been there before, either; Kim had turned around so fast that no one could have disappeared into the crowd in so short a time.

Nevertheless, Kim had clearly seen such a man in the windowpane.

"Are you sure you're all right?" the woman asked doubtfully. "You're as white as a sheet!" She took a step closer, and this time, she actually did put her hand on Kim's shoulder. Her touch was light and warm, and she smiled in a friendly manner. She genuinely seemed concerned.

Nevertheless, after a brief hesitation, Kim pushed away her hand and once again forced a smile. "I'm fine," he finally managed to get out. "There's nothing wrong. I was just . . . startled." He tilted his head in the direction of the windowpane behind him. "It was just a reflection, you know."

From the expression in the woman's eyes, it was clear that his explanation either made no sense to her at all or she didn't believe him. "A reflection?"

"Just an illusion," Kim hastily reassured her. "Everything's fine. Really."

The woman looked at him sharply for a moment—but then, she shrugged, turned around, and disappeared into the crowd. Kim remained where he was, immobile and expressionless, as if he'd been frozen in place.

This calm was only on the surface, though. Inside his head, his mind was reeling. The few words he'd spoken just now had used up almost all his strength.

Everything's fine?

Suddenly, it was all Kim could do to keep himself from bursting into hysterical laughter at what he'd said.

In fact, nothing was as it should be! Although reason told him that this was impossible, another, much louder voice barged into his thoughts, telling him that yes, he had indeed seen the figure. Neither the figure nor its gesture of beckoning to Kim had been imagined—nor the desperate, almost terrified expression on the old man's face.

But if none of it had been imagined, then Kim had every reason to say that nothing was as it should be anymore.

For the figure in the mirror was none other than Themistokles, the wizard from Magic Moon.

"Are you all right?"

It was the third time that Kim had heard this question. The very slight nod that he gave in response didn't seem to convince Aunt Brigit any more than it had the other lady. Once his hands and knees had stopped shaking and his heart had stopped racing, Kim had made his way through the halted traffic to the ambulance—and thus, to his aunt. An annoyed frown had swept across Aunt Brigit's features when she'd first caught sight of him. But then, obviously alarmed, she'd hurried over to him.

"Nothing's wrong," said Kim. "It's just . . ."

"What?" His aunt put her hand on his shoulder and regarded him intently. At the last moment, Kim resisted the temptation to brush away her hand.

"I feel a little . . . strange," he said finally.

Aunt Brigit gave him another very serious, searching look before removing her hand from his shoulder to put it on his forehead. "You don't have a fever, at any rate," she noted soberly.

"No, that's not the problem," Kim said hastily. "I just feel a little sick to my stomach. Maybe I'm coming down with the flu."

"Possibly," his aunt said. Then, she asked, "Have you eaten anything at all today?"

"Of course," Kim replied. "You know Mom doesn't let me out of the house without breakfast."

"Without breakfast?" Aunt Brigit gave him an incredulous look. "It's almost four now!"

"I wasn't hungry," Kim said. "And it's not that—"

"Nonsense," Aunt Brigit said, interrupting him. With a tone of voice that brooked no contradiction, she said, "We're going to that café across the street right now, and you are going to eat a piece of cake—or even better, a couple of pieces."

Kim gave up. He knew it would be useless to raise any sort of objection. Still, he made one more attempt: "Mom and Becky will be getting back soon and—"

"They'll find us," his aunt said briskly. "Besides, we'll have a perfect view of the entrance from over there. And I have the keys to the car, remember? Anyway, I could use a cup of coffee right now. So, come on."

"Um . . . what happened?" Kim asked, gesturing at the ambulance.

Someone finally had turned off the blue light, and the two attendants had gotten out of the vehicle. One of the attendants was standing with his hands in his pockets, shaking his head at the ambulance's bashed fender. Like most of the people here, Kim had witnessed the accident: Moving rather slowly, but with screeching brakes, the ambulance had jumped the curb, plowed through several flowerbeds, and then smashed into one of the stone posts flanking the entrance gate. The impact hadn't been loud at all. There had been only a soft crunch. Even so, the entire fender and one side of the hood were bashed in, and the bumper was pushed so far back into the car that the tire was slit open.

Luckily, the back of the ambulance had been empty and the attendants had been wearing their seatbelts, so no one had been hurt. The only reason the driver had switched on the blue light was to keep the cars behind him from driving into the wrecked vehicle, which now pointed sideways, blocking one side of the street.

"What made it do that?" Kim asked curiously.

For a moment, his aunt looked at Kim with undisguised suspicion, as if she were considering the possibility that he might have been faking the nausea in order to sneak a look at the accident. But then, she apparently concluded otherwise. Shrugging, she pointed at a small group of people who had retreated deep into the archway and were talking in an excited manner. Kim saw the second ambulance attendant in his white uniform and a tall, dark-haired boy standing between two uniformed policemen. Something about the boy was odd, but Kim couldn't quite put his finger on it.

"That boy over there," Aunt Brigit began, "just ran into the street. The ambulance driver had to swerve to keep from running over him, and then the driver lost control. At least, that's what I heard."

Kim stood up on his tiptoes to get a better view. The two policemen, the ambulance driver, and the boy were standing in the shadow of the arched, stone gateway, so he couldn't see them distinctly. Even so, something about this boy was . . . well, peculiar. His face seemed strangely empty of expression, as if he were detached completely from everything happening around him. One of the two policemen was talking to him, gripping his shoulder, shaking him. The boy didn't respond. It almost seemed as if he took no notice at all.

"Shock," was his aunt's diagnosis. Naturally, she'd noticed Kim's curious gaze. "That's very common. It will probably be a while before the poor kid has any recall of what happened. Oh well." She added with a sigh, "They'll take care of him. That's what a hospital's for, right?" Then, turning around, she pointed at the café across the street. "Come on. Let's go—before I remember that I gave you strict instructions not to gawk."

Kim obeyed, but not without taking one last, intent look at the boy. Why did he feel like he knew the boy from somewhere? No, not that he *knew* him—Kim was quite sure he'd never seen the boy's face before—but an inner voice still told him that he ought to know who this boy was. It was strange.

Strange—and very disturbing.

Surprisingly, once Kim forced down the first few bites and followed up with a glass of cola, the cake tasted delicious. Coca-Cola and cheesecake—a combination bordering on culinary anarchy! As Kim's trembling subsided, his inner agitation eased, as well. After a while, the confusion in his mind also cleared, and he gradually came to the realization that he'd probably just imagined the figure in the window.

Kim even came up with an explanation for it. It was so simple. Now, he felt really silly for not thinking of it right away: This place—the café where he'd seen Themistokles standing in front of the window, and the hospital on the other side of the street—this was where everything had started. The memories here were overwhelming. For a moment, they had affected his ability to tell what was real. What else should he have expected? Kim had thought he'd be over those memories at some point, but that wasn't the case. There were things that people never got over. That included his adventure in Magic Moon.

The first piece of cake just whetted Kim's appetite, and when Aunt Brigit offered to order a second piece for him—not without another almost horrified look at the peculiar composition of his meal—he didn't turn her down. The truth was, except for five pieces of chewing gum, Kim hadn't eaten a thing since breakfast. There was nothing particularly unusual about this. Kim was the exact opposite of a gourmet. He regarded food as a necessary evil. He didn't like regular mealtimes and ate only when he truly was hungry. Right now, he was hungry, and the food tasted wonderful to him.

As Kim sat there eating the cake, he watched the action in front of the hospital entrance. Traffic on the street was jammed completely. A tow truck had fought its way through to the wrecked vehicle by weaving in and out of traffic and even driving on the sidewalk for part of the way. But in front and behind the wreck, countless cars had formed a barricade, completely blocking the street. At first, there had been just a few rubberneckers who had slowed down and held up the cars behind them; but soon, the traffic had come to a complete stop. The traffic jam extended to the end of the block and beyond. Not without a certain degree of malicious pleasure, Kim watched as one of the two policemen bravely but vainly tried to bring order to the chaos.

Moving away from the chaotic mix of automobiles and pedestrians, Kim's gaze shifted to the green-uniformed policeman who just now was emerging from the entrance gate to make his way back to his patrol car. He was alone.

"Is something happening?" asked Aunt Brigit, following the direction of Kim's gaze.

Kim looked at her for a moment, confused, and then he realized from the way she was looking at him that something probably was not quite right about his own expression. "No," he said. "Why?"

"You're staring so hard at that policemen."

Kim shrugged, ill at ease, and gained some time by stuffing his mouth with a huge piece of cheesecake. "Heezalone," he muttered with a full mouth.

"What?"

Kim swallowed the bite of cheesecake, suppressed a cough with great effort, and then quickly drank the rest of his Coke. His aunt ignored the mournful look that he cast at his now-empty glass.

"He's alone," he said once again. "I thought they were going to take the boy with them; he's the one who caused the accident."

Aunt Brigit shrugged. "They probably just took down his name and address," she replied. "He didn't commit a felony, after all. Or maybe they kept him at the hospital. He didn't look quite well somehow." She broke off, glanced at the archway again, and then added, "Your mother and Becky are coming. There they are."

Kim ate one last bite of his cheesecake and was about to stand up, but Aunt Brigit gestured that he should stay where he was. "Go ahead and keep eating. There's enough time. They've found us—see?"

She raised her hand and waved; on the other side of the street, Kim's mother waved back. She and Becky walked toward the café, weaving their way through the cars that were idling bumper to bumper in both lanes. After a few moments, they showed up at the table.

"What's going on outside?" Kim's mother asked, shaking her head. "It looks like traffic has come to a complete stop."

"An accident."

Aunt Brigit pointed at the bright-yellow tow truck, which had hitched up the ambulance in the meantime and now was trying to tow it off the street without demolishing a half-dozen other vehicles in the process. Kim observed the action with almost scientific interest. The tow truck moved forward and backward, an inch at a time, without changing its position to any appreciable degree. Meanwhile, the two policemen started bellowing directions at the other drivers—an exercise as fruitless as it was loud. *Maybe they ought to pour cement over the whole street, just as it is,* Kim mused, *including all the cars that blocked the tow truck.* Once the cement was set, they could just mark new lanes on it. Probably, that would take less time than the other useless attempts to end the chaos.

Dismissing this absurd thought, he exchanged a quick look with his sister, who had sat down on one of the chairs opposite him and was looking hungrily at what remained of his cheesecake. Kim hesitated briefly then pushed the plate over to her. He was full, in any case.

"Don't eat that, Becky," Aunt Brigit said with a stern look in Kim's direction. She pushed the plate back. "I'll order a new piece for you." She raised her hand, beckoning the waitress.

"We really should get going," Kim's mother objected.

"Get going?" Aunt Brigit laughed softly, but without much humor. "Until this traffic jam lets up, you'd need a tank to get out of our parking spot. Sit down and have a cup of coffee."

Kim's mother thought it over for a moment. A glance out the window finally convinced her that her sister probably was right. Sighing, she sat down. When the waitress arrived, she ordered a cappuccino, along with a glass of orange juice and a piece of cake for Rebecca.

Aunt Brigit turned to the little girl. "So, how did it go?"

It was no secret that Rebecca wasn't thrilled about the regular hospital visits. In fact, in recent months, she'd strongly objected to them. The past couple of times, Mom and Aunt Brigit practically had to drag her there. Kim didn't quite understand this. He knew that nothing painful was being done to his sister. The doctors just wanted to be sure that she'd fully recovered from her week-long coma. True, it had happened quite some time ago, but the doctors wanted to check Rebecca for potential complications.

"It went great," Mom replied, answering for Rebecca. "And that was our last appointment—at least for this year."

Kim wasn't the only one who looked up, surprised. "Last appointment?" Aunt Brigit repeated.

"They don't want to see her again for another six months," Kim's mother confirmed. "The professor himself examined her again today. He says he's very pleased with her health. There's no reason for her to keep coming in every few weeks. There will be two or three more exams at six month intervals, and then we'll finally have this behind us for good."

"That's wonderful!" Aunt Brigit exclaimed. "How about that, sweetie pie?"

"Sweetie pie" glared at her. Kim wasn't quite sure why. Part of it probably was that she hated that name. But something else seemed to be going on, as well. Rebecca had never been particularly talkative—but since they'd entered the café, she hadn't said a single word. Overall, she seemed rather subdued—too quiet for Kim's taste. It was as if something were bothering her, or she'd seen something that had frightened her deeply. . .

"Dumb hospital," she said finally. "I hate it."

Aunt Brigit looked at her, shocked, while Mom hardly could keep from laughing.

Eventually, Aunt Brigit also managed a smile. "Well, now it's behind you," she said. "Half a year is a long time, you'll see."

Rebecca gave her another dark look before turning her attention to the piece of cake that the waitress had just brought. On the street outside, the tow truck finally had freed the ambulance and was now stuck in traffic itself. Kim watched as a young woman in a sporty convertible caught sight of a tiny open space in the traffic just ahead of her. She deftly maneuvered her car backward and forward a couple of times, until she crunched into the bumper of the car ahead. The driver of that car got out and immediately flew into a rage.

Kim was picking aimlessly at the last of his cheesecake, when he noticed a mounted policeman at the other end of the street. The policeman was trying to find a gap in the pile of steel wide enough for his horse to pass through. Actually, there was nothing unusual about this: In Düsseldorf, policemen still were seen on horses now and again. Sometimes, that was the only way they could get through the congested streets. Still, there was something about this sight that caught Kim's attention. Once again, he had a feeling that the image he saw held meaning for him, but he didn't know what the significance was.

"This is going to be fun." Aunt Brigit sighed. "How are we ever going to get out of here?"

"What in the world happened?" Kim's mother asked once again.

"Not much, really," Aunt Brigit replied. "A boy ran in front of the ambulance. The driver had to swerve and rammed into the entrance gate. No one was hurt."

"A boy?"

Aunt Brigit nodded. "Yes. He was acting strange in my opinion. Completely unresponsive afterward, you know . . . as if he were dreaming. And he was wearing such odd clothes."

Kim choked on his cake, started coughing, and sprayed cake crumbs on his aunt and sister. Rebecca shrieked and, without a moment's hesitation, grabbed a little piece of cake and threw it at him. Aunt Brigit flew back in her chair, surprised. The piece of cake missed Kim by a hair and landed on the dress of a fat woman sitting behind him. Startled, the woman jumped up, nearly knocking a fully laden tray out of the hands of a waitress rushing by. With a cry of surprise, the waitress leaped aside just in time, spilling coffee out of the cups. At this point, Rebecca used her fork to fling a second piece of cake, which managed to land right in the middle of her brother's face.

Under other circumstances, Kim would have been delighted with the pandemonium that had broken out so suddenly. But at the moment, he hardly was aware of it. He didn't even feel the whipped cream that had smacked into his right cheek and was starting to slide down his chin.

"He was wearing such odd clothes!"

That was it! That was what had been gnawing at him the whole time! Why hadn't he figured it out at first sight?

Because it's impossible, replied a quiet voice inside his head. *Because it's totally out of the question, as you well know.*

In addition to the voice of reason, there also was another, much louder voice at the moment—and he just knew that the second voice was right. The image reflected in the window, the boy wearing strange clothing who looked as if he were dreaming, the angry expression on Rebecca's face, and the strange uneasiness he'd felt ever since they'd arrived here . . .

There was only one explanation, even if it seemed impossible. That simply had to be it. But at the same time, that couldn't be it. No way in the world.

He had only one choice—he had to see for himself.

Kim jumped up so quickly and suddenly that he tipped over his chair and knocked his cake plate off the table.

"Kim!" his mother cried. "Where are you going? Come back!"

But he didn't even hear her. He'd already spun around and rushed out of the café. When Kim's mother finally recovered enough from her surprise to chase after him, Kim already had disappeared through the hospital entrance on the other side of the street.

For the first time that day, Kim was glad that he'd been to the hospital so often, because by now, he knew the grounds like a second home. Not that he was giving a moment's thought to what he did now, but it was advantageous that he didn't have to ask the gatekeeper where they'd taken the boy. Aside from the fact that Kim probably wouldn't have received any answer to this question, he also would have lost valuable time—time that he didn't have. If his mother wasn't chasing after him, then Aunt Brigit certainly was—guaranteed. And she was in extremely good shape.

Thank goodness Kim had a kind of home turf advantage. He raced through the arched gateway, peeled off to the left, blew past a bewildered hospital attendant, and cut across the closely mowed lawn to the white-tiled, concrete box that housed the emergency room. Before, when they'd visited Rebecca at the medical center, he'd often looked out the window and watched the admitting procedure. They definitely would've brought the boy here first. That would have happened not all that long ago. All in all, it couldn't have been more than ten minutes since the policeman had emerged from the gateway.

Glancing back over his shoulder, Kim was relieved to see no sign of his aunt, and no one else was following him, either. The only one in sight was the attendant, who stood there as if struck by lightning, staring at the tall blond boy who had committed the grave sin of running across the carefully manicured lawn, leaping from time to time over "Keep Off the Grass" signs.

Right before he reached the admitting station, Kim returned to the gravel pathway and slowed to a trot. He was bathed in sweat, coughing from the exertion. The building's automatic doors, which were controlled by infrared sensors, slid apart so slowly that Kim almost ran into the glass. The strong reek of disinfectants billowed toward Kim as he rushed into the hospital lobby. Memories forcefully were awakened by the sight of the gleaming tiles; white-clad nurses and doctors; cold plastic chairs; and uninspired, framed prints on the walls, which—together with the artificial flowers in plastic buckets—vainly tried to cheer up the gloomy atmosphere. Suddenly, he felt small and lost here. He should not have come. It was completely crazy—the boy *couldn't* be who Kim thought he was. In a few minutes, an absolutely furious Aunt

Brigit would appear behind him and read him the riot act, and that—together with the unpleasant talk that his father inevitably would have with him that evening—was all he'd accomplish. Even if the boy was here, how could Kim find him?

Kim stopped in the doorway to give his wheezing lungs an opportunity to recover, so that he would enough at least have breath to speak. Then, he walked over to the huge counter that dominated the entire right half of the room. A half-dozen nurses were sitting behind glowing green computer monitors, apparently oblivious to his presence.

Kim cleared his throat in an exaggerated manner; after, he'd done that three times in a row, one of the young women actually did look up at him. Initially, she appeared somewhat baffled by his sweaty, bedraggled appearance. Then, she smiled in a friendly manner and stood.

"What can I do for you, young man?" she asked.

A good question, Kim thought. He would have given anything for a good answer. He hemmed and hawed before saying the first thing that came to mind. "My brother," he said, breathing hard. "I'm looking for my brother. He was just brought here—just now. The accident, I mean . . ."

He began to stammer and finally broke off completely as the nurse looked at him inquiringly. "Your brother? What's his name?"

"Thomas," Kim replied, saying the first name that popped into his head.

"And last name?"

Kim was at a loss to answer, but this time Lady Luck—or, more precise, a second nurse—came to his aid. Peering up from her monitor, she gazed through her glasses, looking first at Kim and then at her colleague.

"The boy who was almost run over in front of the entrance gate?" she asked.

Kim nodded vigorously.

"He's not here."

Before Kim could fully register the acute disappointment that filled him thanks to these words, she added, "They've taken him to the pediatric ward."

From her position behind her computer, she leaned forward and looked intently at Kim. Her glasses reflected the monitor's green light. It looked as if little columns were scrolling down her eyes.

"The pediatric ward?" Kim asked just to make sure.

"You can't go there right now," she said, "but it's good that you're here. Your brother didn't say a single word. We don't even know what his name is. Maybe you can help us—"

"I'll give all that information to the doctors over there," Kim interrupted, whirling around.

"Hey!" protested the nurse. "You can't just—"

But of course Kim could. And he did, too.

With a few quick strides, he crossed the lobby and ran into the glass door, which again parted at a snail's pace. Then, he stumbled out onto the walkway. The pediatric ward was at the other end of the large, medical center campus, but Kim covered the mile in absolutely record time. He was completely out of breath when he reached the six-story pediatric building, but he felt sure that this sprint had left his aunt behind, as well as any other pursuers.

Staggering from exhaustion, he entered the building and took a quick look around. It was much quieter here than in the admissions office. Instead of a counter, there was a pane of glass with a small, round, metal-rimmed hole in it—and no one behind it. The opposite wall had two elevators.

The doors of one of the elevators were closing at that very moment, and Kim was just in time to catch a glimpse of laced-up, calf-high, brown suede boots.

Darn! Exactly one second too late!

Kim already was heading toward the second elevator, planning to jump in, when he realized that it wouldn't do him any good. Instantly changing course, he made a sharp right turn, ran to the stairwell, and raced up the stairs, taking them two or three at a time. On the second floor, he arrived just in time to see the light above the elevator door go out.

Without breaking his stride, he spun around and charged up the flight of stairs, the next, the one after that—and finally, the fourth flight of stairs.

By the time Kim reached the sixth floor and saw the elevator doors open, his prospects for becoming the hospital's youngest heart attack patient weren't bad.

He was dizzy. As he sank against the door separating the stairwell from the hallway, coughing and drenched in sweat, he felt a violent wave of nausea. At that very moment, the strange boy stepped out of the elevator, accompanied by an orderly. They quickly turned right and walked in the opposite direction; so, thankfully, the orderly didn't see him. The boy didn't see him, either; but Kim got a fleeting look at his face—still as vacant and expressionless as it had been at the entrance gate. The stranger was dressed very oddly indeed, as Aunt Brigit would have put it. His feet were clad in calf-high, skin-tight, laced boots made of tough but velvety suede, and his pants and the wide-cut tunic that he wore over them were made of the same material, only somewhat thinner. The tunic and pants were held together by a wide belt with a bright brass buckle. He also wore a short, diagonally cut cape across his shoulders. The burgundy leather cape didn't quite reach his belt.

Kim stood there, dumbstruck, as the boy and his escort slowly made their way down the hallway, eventually disappearing into a room at the far end.

Impossible, he thought, over and over. It was hard to tell what ached more: his heart or his lungs. He was shivering as if it were freezing cold. Kim's thoughts whirled madly as he tried to come up with a logical explanation for the unexplainable.

Behind him, a door closed. Startled, Kim spun around and quickly retreated into the stairwell. Holding his breath, he pressed against the adjoining wall and listened to the steps approach—and then, to his great relief, pass by without any hesitation. He kept listening until the sounds faded away completely. Kim's heart still was pounding wildly; however, it was more from excitement than from physical exertion.

For a long time, he simply waited there until, finally, footsteps sounded from the end of the corridor. This time, it wasn't the previous click-clack: It was a soft, almost silent footstep, typical of the rubber-soled shoes worn by nurses and other hospital attendants. Summoning all his courage, Kim stepped out into the hall.

The orderly who had accompanied the boy was walking in Kim's direction. He was alone, but his right hand carried what Kim eventually recognized as a narrow leather sheath. There were two loops on it, obviously for hanging the sheath from a belt. The handle of a slender dagger, bound also in leather, jutted out of the sheath.

The man stopped and looked at Kim inquiringly. "What are you doing here?" he asked in an unfriendly tone of voice. "Visiting hours are over."

"I know," Kim replied, secretly surprised at his own composure. "I just wanted to get my parents. They're with my brother. He had an operation this morning."

The level of distrust reflected in the orderly's eyes didn't change one iota. "What room is he in?" he asked.

"Seven-oh-nine," Kim replied, taking a wild chance.

"That's up one level. You're on the wrong floor," the man replied. "This is the sixth floor." He pointed at the elevator. "I'm going up. You can come with me."

Kim shook his head. "I'd rather not," he replied. "I don't like elevators. I got stuck in one once. Besides, I can go faster on foot. Thanks, anyway."

With that, he turned around; walked back into the stairwell; and after a final hesitation, actually started to climb the stairs.

He had reached the landing when he heard the door to the stairwell open beneath him. Obviously, he hadn't allayed the man's distrust completely.

Kim stood still and listened. A few seconds went by. Then, the door closed again. A few moments later, he heard the whirring sound of the elevator moving. Kim instantly turned around and ran back down the stairs.

One last time, Kim's inner voice of reason tried to hold him back; but when he stood outside the door to the boy's room, he decided to go ahead with his utterly insane plan. The boy probably was not alone in the room. Even if he were, then it would be a few minutes before someone came by to check on him, at best. Nevertheless, Kim ignored the whispering in his head, just as he had previously. Conquering his fear, he turned the door handle softly but with determination.

The room was dark and silent. The curtains were closed, so Kim could make out the boy's figure only as a dark shape against the white bed linen. It appeared he was lucky for a change—the boy was alone.

Walking over to the bed, Kim saw that the orderly had dressed the boy in a white hospital gown. His neatly folded clothes rested on a stool on the other side of the bed, and the contents of his pockets were spread out on the small dresser beside the bed. Obviously, the orderly had been looking for some kind of identification or papers. If Kim was right about this boy, the orderly would be looking for a long time; where this boy came from, there was no such thing as identification cards.

Kim quietly leaned over the bed and studied the stranger's face. When he'd entered the room, Kim had thought the boy was sleeping because he was lying so still and showed no reaction to Kim's presence. But that wasn't the case: The boy's eyes were wide open, staring at the ceiling.

"Hello," Kim whispered.

No reaction. Not a single muscle moved on the boy's face; his expression remained vacant, as well. Even when Kim bent down so that his face almost touched the boy's, the boy's dark eyes looked straight through him. The boy didn't see Kim any more than he'd seen the ambulance that almost ran over him or the men who had brought him here. Nevertheless, Kim once again tried to speak to the boy.

"Do you understand me?" he asked.

No answer.

Kim gnawed on his lower lip and hastily glanced at the door before he continued: "I know who you are. You can trust me. Everything here must be very scary for you, but . . . but you don't need to act as if you're sleeping. I know where you come from. Did Themistokles send you? Or Prince Priwinn?"

At the sound of these two names, something lit up in the boy's eyes; then, just as quickly, it faded away. Kim couldn't tell whether a spark truly had been there or whether he'd seen it because he'd wanted to see it.

The boy obviously was conscious, but he seemed totally unaware of his surroundings.

Disappointed, Kim moved away from the bed, stood up straight, and was about to turn toward the door. Then, he stopped to look at the belongings laid out on the dresser and stool. Quickly walking over to the dresser, he took a closer look at the contents of the boy's pockets.

He didn't find anything helpful. The only things the boy had were a ball of string with a fishhook attached; two worn flints; and a tiny, three-holed flute, which wasn't quite as long as Kim's little finger. Kim wondered what kind of music could be played on this mini-instrument. The mouthpiece looked as if it were made for a dwarf. Maybe it was.

Kim held the flute in his hand, uncertain what to do. Then, he closed his fist around it and turned toward the stool. Despite everything he'd seen and found so far, he thought maybe it was just a coincidence—a very, very unlikely coincidence. What Kim now needed was evidence.

That's what he found as soon as he turned to the boy's clothes.

The boy's shirt, pants, and boots were made of that fine, almost indestructible leather that he remembered so well. The belt buckle was fashioned from shiny brass. When Kim picked it up to take a closer look at the skillfully engraved design in the metal, suddenly, it seemed as if a bucket of ice-cold water was pouring down his neck. On the belt buckle there was a horse's head extending from a half-moon. When he looked at it more closely, the crescent turned out to be an elaborate "C." Kim stared at the belt buckle for a whole minute, stunned and disconcerted.

Then, the door behind him flew open and a group of hospital staff members stormed into the room, led by the orderly he'd encountered by the elevator and the bespectacled nurse from the admissions office.

"What are you doing here?!" an angry voice cried. One hand gripped his shoulder, roughly pulling him away from the clothes, while another hand wrested the boy's pants from Kim's grip and tossed the garment back on the stool.

Someone was shaking his shoulder, and voices were questioning him, louder and louder: "Who are you? What are you doing here?"

Kim stood very still. He offered no resistance when someone grabbed his arm and forcefully dragged him from the room. At the last second, his eyes fixed on the belt buckle. In the dim light of the hospital room, the buckle—and the emblem it displayed—glowed with an inner fire.

The design wasn't just a pretty picture: It was a coat of arms.

He'd seen this coat of arms before—countless times, in fact. It was the coat of arms of Caivallon, the homeland of the proud Steppe riders of Magic Moon.

II

That evening, Kim's father came home from work unusually late. Kim wasn't quite sure if this was a good thing. While it gave him a short reprieve until the expected fireworks, the waiting period wasn't exactly pleasant.

He barely could recall what had happened in the hospital after being discovered. The orderly who had dragged him out of the hospital room had shoved him into the chief medical officer's office, and the only thing he could remember after that was his mother showing up some time later, completely out of breath and passionately demanding to speak with the authorities. She had managed to get a meeting and took her son under her wings—although with an all-too-familiar look at Kim that promised a swift reckoning. That hardly had bothered him, however. His thoughts had been totally focused on the nameless boy's belt buckle and what it signified. Even if everything else had been coincidence, that definitely hadn't. There was no doubt at all that the boy was a Steppe rider from Caivallon, the vast, grassy plains in the heart of Magic Moon—a land that didn't even exist, according to most people that Kim knew, and whose inhabitants couldn't live in this world.

Later, after Kim had calmed down a little and returned to his senses, he remembered that the uproar eventually had caught the attention of the chief physician himself—and that had been lucky. Dr. Halserburg knew the Larssen family quite well. After all, Rebecca had been his patient for quite some time.

It was due to his intervention (combined with the eloquence of Kim's mother, who had spoken with the tongue of an angel) that the hospital authorities finally decided not to call the police.

Kim didn't understand what all the excitement was about. He had entered a room where he wasn't really supposed to be and had looked at a boy's clothes. Other than that, what had he done?

The hospital staff, however, viewed things differently. Their faces looked grim when Kim's mother finally managed to calm the professor enough to let Kim go. In particular, the nurse with glasses—the one who had given Kim information in the admissions office—watched him leave with unconcealed anger.

When they'd finally left the grounds of the university medical center, at least one problem had been resolved: the traffic jam. A sporty red convertible with a bashed hood stood on the side of the road; a short distance away, a police patrol car was parked with its blue light flashing but its siren turned off. Here and there, passersby still were standing around in small groups, talking—rather excitedly, for the most part. Kim could make out only a few isolated words, but from what he picked up, he concluded that something must have happened after he'd run into the hospital.

Even that failed to arouse his interest. It was almost as if he were dreaming—like that odd boy. Kim's thoughts were chasing each other in wild circles; again and again, he asked himself: *What has happened in Magic Moon?*

What had caused him to see a reflection of Themistokles' face? And what had caused a Steppe rider from Caivallon to show up here?

On the way home, as Aunt Brigit was driving the car across the Rhine Bridge—which was clogged as usual—Kim's mother had tried to start up a conversation. Of course, she'd wanted to know what in the world had gotten into him. What was the explanation for his strange behavior, and so forth and so on.

Kim hadn't answered any of her questions. What could he have said, anyway? That he had seen a wizard and a boy from a world that existed only in his dreams—a world where he'd flown on the back of a dragon and fought mighty battles? Ridiculous. If he had said that, he would've found himself back in the hospital in no time flat—in the locked wing of the psychiatric ward, to be precise.

While Kim valiantly tried to act as if he'd suddenly gone deaf and was unable to hear his mother's words, he glanced at Rebecca's face several times. But Rebecca looked away. She was the only person in the world he could talk to about his experience—after all, they'd been to Magic Moon together. But Becky still was quite young, and despite the adventure they'd shared, their sibling relationship was, well, typical: like cats and dogs.

Aside from that, even if he'd wanted to talk with Becky about Themistokles and the young Steppe rider, it would've been impossible in the car, directly in view and—more importantly—earshot of his mother and aunt! He had to wait until they were alone.

They'd arrived home relatively quickly, but there was even less opportunity for a private moment together then.

Kim had been the first to get out of the car—almost as soon as Aunt Brigit had parked it on the driveway. He hastily opened the front door and was heading up to his room when his mother called him back with a sharp tone of voice. She pointed at the large dining room table—the traditional place in the Larssen house where problems were discussed, conflicts were resolved, and, when necessary, judgments were handed down. Kim felt sure that there definitely would be a judgment on this day. . . .

However, he hadn't protested. Instead, he'd slumped down into a chair, stony faced and uncomplaining. Now, he sat there, waiting. He spent a brief moment trying to think up some logical excuse for his behavior but soon gave up the attempt. Whatever he might say would sound just as ridiculous as the truth.

The expected court martial was delayed for a time. While his mother took Rebecca up to her room, Aunt Brigit rummaged around in the kitchen and put on a pot of coffee. Every so often, she swept through the dining room, casting baleful looks in his direction. Kim sat like a poor criminal on a courtroom defendant's bench, nervously playing with his fingers. Finally, Kim's mother came back and sat down. Aunt Brigit trundled in with a tray containing two cups of coffee, a sugar bowl, and a glass of hot milk and honey.

Yuck! The mere sight of the milk was enough to turn his stomach, but Kim reached for the glass, anyway, taking a giant gulp—not because he was thirsty, but because this would placate his aunt, who was a health nut. (Everyone had some flaws.)

"Well?" said his mother, opening the discussion.

"What?" Kim played dumb, which—at least, according to his sister—wasn't all that hard for him.

His mother's expression darkened. "You know exactly what I mean," she said. "What happened? Why did you break into that room?"

"I didn't break in," Kim said, indignantly defending himself. "I—"

"Fine. Have it your way," said his mother, interrupting him. "But those were the words that the hospital administration lady used."

Kim looked at his mother, perplexed. *The nurse with the glasses?* He hadn't noticed that she'd used such a strong expression. He hadn't picked up on anything, because his thoughts had been far away. A whole world away, to be precise.

"We're not accusing you of anything," his mother continued. "Just the opposite. I know you, and I know you wouldn't do something like that without a good reason. You're not a little kid, after all. You're almost a grown-up."

"So, we very much would like to hear this reason," his aunt added. She took a sip of coffee. "If your mother weren't so well acquainted with the chief physician, you would be in all kinds of trouble right now. Do you realize that?"

Kim nodded. He barely could restrain himself from bursting into hysterical laughter. All kinds of trouble? His poor aunt had absolutely no idea how much trouble he was in already.

"What did you want from this boy?" asked Mom, continuing to probe. "The orderly who caught you swears up and down that you were trying to steal his things."

"That's ridiculous!" Kim cried out.

Mom nodded. "That's exactly what I said, too. The professor believed me, thank goodness. If he hadn't, we might be sitting in a police station right now. But the orderly still insists you were holding those things in your hand when he came in. Is that true?"

Kim reluctantly nodded. In addition to the orderly, about a half-dozen other people had caught him with the boy's belt in his hand. There was no point in disputing that.

"So why?"

"I just wanted to . . . look at them," Kim said evasively.

"All right. But why?"

"I . . . I don't know," Kim said in a quiet voice. "They looked so strange. And I thought . . . I thought I might know the boy."

Aunt Brigit's eyebrows shot up, and his mother also looked at him with reawakened mistrust.

"From where?"

"Nowhere," Kim replied hastily. "I was wrong. I just thought I knew him."

"And so ten minutes after you see him, it occurs to you that you might know him?" his aunt asked. "This occurs to you so suddenly that you jump up and run off as if a pack of hounds were after you?" She tilted her head from side to side, weighing the possibility.

No, the only excuse that occurred to Kim wouldn't convince anyone here.

"Well?" his mother said, trying again.

This time, Kim said nothing, and after a while his mother realized that she wasn't going to make any progress—at least, not at the moment. With a deep sigh, she shook her head, took a sip of coffee, and then said with a gesture of resignation, "All right. Let's drop this for now. We're all upset. Go to your room and wait there. Maybe you'll tell your father more."

Kim went upstairs as quickly as he could without running, closed the door behind him, and leaned against it with his eyes shut. His heart started pounding again. Just now, the fear that he'd felt registered. Instead of relaxing, his hands started to shake again. He kept seeing the boy's pale face, as well as the gold-colored belt buckle with Caivallon's coat of arms. The orderly also had held a dagger in his hand when he left the hospital room—undoubtedly, the boy's weapon. Daggers, swords, and bows were the traditional weapons of the Steppe riders of Magic Moon.

It's impossible! For the last time, Kim tried to listen to the voice of reason. If this boy was here, then that meant . . . something unimaginable had happened.

Then, his thoughts returned to the face he'd seen in the windowpane.

Kim now was certain that it hadn't been his imagination. The man he'd seen was Themistokles, the wizard from Magic Moon. His face hadn't been as kind, wise, and gentle as usual; instead, it resembled a mask of horror—the countenance of a man who had seen something incomparably worse than death. Something incomparably worse.

Something was poking his right leg. Kim frowned and stuck his hands in his pocket. His eyes widened in astonishment when he saw what he pulled out.

It was a tiny cylindrical piece of wood with three holes hardly bigger than pinholes—the flute he had found among the boy's belongings. He had no memory of putting it in his pocket. Obviously, when the orderly had come storming in, Kim had stuck it in his pocket instinctively.

An ice-cold shiver ran down his back. It was unimaginable what would have happened if the man had searched him and found the flute! In that case, no one would have believed that he hadn't gone into the hospital room to steal something!

Kim guiltily slipped the flute back into his pocket. Then, he pulled himself away from the door, locked it, went over to his bed, and lay down on it with his hands folded behind his head. There wasn't a thing he could do about it—his thoughts kept returning to the land of dreams.

Magic Moon . . .

That was so long ago, even though sometimes it seemed as if it had happened only yesterday. He had come to terms with the fact that he probably never would return to the realm of fantasy. Of course, there always had been a very tiny glimmer of hope that he might find a way back there. He'd often dreamed of it. But he had thought it was impossible.

Now, though, it appeared that a pathway did exist—not necessarily for him, but for the inhabitants of that world . . . a way for people of Magic

Moon to come here. For some reason, the young Steppe rider had entered the world of humans; however, it seemed that he'd done so at a terrible cost. He'd probably done so for the same reason—which Kim couldn't even imagine, but which he was certain was terrifying—Themistokles had attempted to contact him.

Why? To warn him?

Or to ask for his help?

Themistokles already had come here once before to ask for Kim's assistance (although it turned out later that the inhabitants of Magic Moon had helped Kim more than he'd helped them). Even back then, it hadn't been easy for Themistokles to contact Kim. However, he'd managed it with his magical powers, showing Kim the way there, via the Shadowy Mountains, where Kim had—

Kim had a truly electrifying thought.

He jumped out of bed and crossed the room. His knees were trembling from excitement as he stood before the small bookshelf where he kept his model collections and science fiction and fantasy books. Arranged in a neat row in front of the well-thumbed pocket novels, there were the models: a flying saucer that Kim had constructed from two cup saucers (his mother still was puzzled about their disappearance), a six inch long golden dragon made of tin, two Perry Rhodan armored spacecrafts, and . . . the Viper.

Kim's hands shook so hard that he almost dropped the Viper fighter when he picked up the model from its plastic mount.

The large, foot long model, with its swept-back wings, was much more than a toy. The Viper was the ship in which he had so often fought against the Cylons and Maahks and Cantaro in his fantasies. It was the ship in which he'd explored the depths of the galaxy in his dreams, and he'd carried out daring rescues from the surfaces of hellacious, storm-battered planets.

It was the ship that had taken him to Magic Moon.

For a long time, Kim simply stood there, staring at the model spaceship. During that time, a decision ripened within him. He knew it was absolutely crazy and practically had no chance of success. But he had no choice: Themistokles and perhaps all of Magic Moon faced danger—he knew that, now—and they needed his help. Kim was the only person in this world who could help them.

He checked to make sure that the door to his room was locked securely. Then, he carried the model back to his bed and sat on the blankets, his legs crossed. His eyes narrowed and, after a while, small beads of sweat appeared on his forehead; he focused all his thoughts on this one wish: to sit in the cockpit of the Viper again and find his way back to Magic Moon. He could do it. He'd done it before and could do it again if he truly wanted.

As he sat like that, his room got darker. It was as if the world were shrinking into a tiny, bright spot in the center of a vast ocean of darkness, which contained only him and the Viper—then ultimately, only the Viper. It seemed to him as if the spaceship slowly were beginning to increase in size . . .

When Kim awoke, he was surrounded by darkness. An eerie green glow provided a bit of light. It hung in the air like a sinister magic charm, changing the shape of things in a most unpleasant, indescribable way. Something was jabbing Kim through his shirt, digging painfully deep into his chest. His neck and shoulders hurt so much that, at first, Kim didn't even dare to move.

I've done it! That was his first thought. *I'm back!*

It was exactly like before. Even though Kim had no memory of the flight this time, he seemed to have crashed over an impassible part of the land, just as he had the first time he'd flown the Viper. The soft ground under him had to be the marsh on the far side of the Shadowy Mountains. This blackness was the darkness that prevailed in those sinister forests, pierced only by the greenish-blue glow of cold-burning marsh gas. The object jabbing Kim's chest so painfully was undoubtedly the wreckage of the Viper, which had once again faithfully transported him before its mechanical systems failed—here, where technology was as useless as magic in the everyday world.

Clenching his teeth and bravely enduring the pain in his neck and shoulders, Kim propped himself up, squinted his eyes, and looked around, expecting to see a huge black rider emerge from the darkness at any moment. This time, he was prepared. He wouldn't fall for Baron Kart's tricks or Boraas' lies again.

But no black rider or sinister despot appeared; the only thing Kim could do was sit there, feeling incredibly stupid.

The trees surrounding him were his furniture; the forest shadows were the darkness of his own room. Kim wasn't lying on marshy ground but on his bed, and his neck hurt because he'd fallen asleep in a ridiculous position. He must have sprawled there for a long time, judging by the dim light outside his windows. For the eerie magical glow, that was from his computer monitor, which was switched on, displaying the usual green script. Kim was right about only one thing: The poking in his chest was a result of the Viper wreckage. In his sleep, he'd slumped forward and crushed the plastic model with the weight of his body.

For a long time, Kim simply sat there, staring at the remains of his skillfully constructed model—now, a pile of plastic parts with flaking paint. The model wasn't just broken: It was completely wrecked, as if a giant had stomped on it, trampling over it so that not a single piece would remain intact. Kim's eyes filled with tears. The Viper had carried him to that strange, faraway world. Losing it pained him—like the loss of a good friend. Trembling, he took two of the larger pieces in his hands and tried to fit them together in the dim light of the computer monitor—of course, repair was impossible. Except for the three or four larger pieces, the model had broken into countless fragments, which were bent and twisted out of shape. Even if Kim could rebuild the Viper—which wasn't the case—he would have needed months to re-create something from this mess that would resemble the original Viper in any way.

After a while, he stood up, sniffled, and brushed his face with his lower arm to wipe away the tears. Gently, almost protectively, he gathered up the plastic pieces, carried them to the waste basket, and then backed away. No. He just couldn't bring himself to throw the wreckage in the trash. Instead, he carefully laid what was left of the model on his desk and went back to the bed to gather up the last of the little pieces.

That was hard, because the room was almost completely dark, and the pale glow of the monitor provided only enough light for him to make out vague contours and shapes. So, Kim went back to the door and reached for the light switch. He hesitated once again.

His gaze idly wandered over the desk, stopping at the computer monitor. That was odd: He couldn't remember turning it on. No, he was certain now that he hadn't. *Strange. Very strange. A little unsettling.*

Kim gave this some serious thought for a while, but then he rejected the idea that occurred to him: No matter how skewed reality seemed today, Magic Moon and Themistokles the sorcerer definitely hadn't a thing to do with his computer's weird behavior. In the land of dreams, not even cigarette lighters worked. So, there absolutely was no chance that a computer would function. He looked at the flickering green letters on the screen for a few more seconds. What did this image remind him of? He shrugged his shoulders, turned off the machine, and turned on the light in his room.

The white brightness of the florescent light banished the dull fear that had settled in Kim's soul. He looked at the clock. It was after seven. His father probably had been home from work for a long time now. Kim was surprised that no one had knocked on his door, yet—a polite prelude to the thunderstorm assured once his old man found out what Kim had done at the hospital.

Mulling this over, Kim turned off the light again, opened the door, and stepped into the hallway.

It was very quiet in the house. He faintly heard his parents' voices against the background of television babble; they were talking in the living room. So, his father actually was home already.

Kim braced himself for the confrontation that lay ahead. He took a deep breath, full of determination—then, turned on his heels even before he took one step.

Instead of going downstairs to the living room, he continued down the hall, stopping in front of Rebecca's room. Maybe before facing his father, he could have a private talk with her.

He listened. Not the slightest sound came from her room, but that didn't mean anything: When the kids bought their own radios and CD players, Dad had realized that family harmony would be enhanced greatly by soundproof doors.

Kim knocked.

No answer.

Knocking again, this time somewhat louder, he held his breath and turned his attention downstairs, listening for any indication that the noise might have set off alarm bells with his parents. Again, his knock went unanswered. Finally, he cautiously turned the door handle.

The door was unlocked—Rebecca wasn't there. The bedcovers were pulled back, but the only thing on the bed was Kelhim: the tattered, one-eyed teddy bear. That was strange, because Rebecca hardly went anywhere without her teddy bear. In fact, she sometimes took him into the bathtub with her. Like Kim's room, Rebecca's also was almost completely dark. The only illumination came not from a computer screen but from the lighting in a large terrarium on the low cabinet by the window. The eerie, bluish-white glow made things look as unreal as the computer light had in Kim's room.

Kim stood in the doorway for a moment, feeling disappointed, and then he turned toward the terrarium. The previous Christmas, Rebecca had received that thing, together with its cold-blooded inhabitants—two reddish-green dwarf iguanas, both about the size of a hand. Meanwhile, Kim had asked for the computer. Becky never missed an opportunity to tell Kim she thought his computer was dumb. For his part, Kim made no attempt to conceal his opinion about how boring the two mini-lizards were.

But suddenly, something about them fascinated him: It was as if the glass tank with the cold bluish light magically attracted his gaze.

He took a step closer and squatted down. As usual, one of the two animals had crept under a piece of bark, so that only the tip of its tail was visible—was it Rosie or Rosa? He had never figured out how his sister could tell the two lizards apart. The other animal had climbed halfway up the little plastic tree that occupied the right half of the terrarium.

Kim blinked in astonishment. The animal hung there in a comical position. It had climbed a little way up the tree and wound itself around the trunk, firmly gripping the plastic surface with its tiny claws. Its mouth was half-open and unmoving; its glittery eyes stared right through Kim. It resembled a snake wound around a staff. Kim doubted whether the animal understood what was on the other side of the glass—if it saw him at all.

Still, it gave him the creeps. He quickly stood up, left the room, and went downstairs.

His parents still were sitting in the living room, talking. When Kim walked in, they broke off their discussion. Dad looked at him for a moment with an expression Kim couldn't interpret, and then he nodded at an open seat on the couch.

Kim obediently sat down. His gaze wandered to the TV. The sound was turned almost all the way down, but scenes from a science fiction movie flickered on the large, flat screen: Huge spaceships raced at low altitude across the scorched surface of a barren planet, where men and women in ragged clothes desperately defended themselves against the attacks of a giant robot army. It wasn't a particularly well-made film, as its special effects were primitive. Kim had a practiced eye for these things. In spite of this, he was surprised. Science fiction and fantasy stories were his great passion. He would have known if this kind of film had been scheduled to broadcast. His habit of always taking the TV guide first had led to fights with his parents on more than one occasion—particularly when he forgot to return it or gave it back only after clipping out everything that interested him.

His father loudly cleared his throat. Kim winced, feeling slightly guilty. He tore his gaze away from the flat screen . . . but not entirely. Out of the corner of his eye, he continued to follow the story, which was rather stupid, although it did hold his interest somehow.

"If you would deign to grant me a few minutes of your valuable time, I would be eternally grateful," his father began.

Kim sighed to himself. When Dad took this tone, things were really serious. Kim pretended, at least, that the film on TV didn't interest him.

"Sure," he said, embarrassed. "What do you want?"

The expression on his father's face turned from a rainstorm to a full-fledged hurricane. "Don't play dumb," he said sternly. "You know exactly what information I want from you. I should have called you down an hour ago, but your mother didn't want me to wake you." He inserted a pause here so that his words could sink in.

Kim took a quick peek at the TV—inconspicuously, he hoped. The screen now showed a close-up of one of the robots. The thing was built so amateurishly that Kim thought he himself could make a better one. The face wasn't a mechanical copy of a human face, but it resembled one of those scary masks worn by ice hockey goalies. Only one detail was really good: No eyes were visible behind the narrow slit in the upper third of the mask; instead, flickering green script filled the space there. The sight was very unsettling because, without knowing why, the image gave Kim a definite feeling of unpleasant familiarity.

"So, what happened this afternoon?" Dad asked, when he finally realized that his silence wouldn't produce a response.

"I don't know," Kim admitted. "I had this feeling I knew the kid. I . . . I just had to go there, you know?"

"No, I don't know," Dad replied. "I don't understand. Why did you have to take off like a madman, without saying a single word to your mother?"

"Well, I—"

The doorbell saved Kim from having to stammer out another excuse, which probably would have made his father even angrier. His parents exchanged surprised looks: Obviously, they weren't expecting any visitors. Dad shrugged his shoulders, stood up, and quickly walked out of the room.

Confused, Kim stared in the direction his father had gone; then, he took advantage of the opportunity to watch a little more of the movie on TV. Since he'd last looked, the robots had overrun the human defenders and were now beginning the final assault on the humans' fortress—a huge tower of multi-faceted blue crystal, with an increasing number of ugly holes made by the robots' laser weapons.

Dad came back, and he was not alone. A policeman in a green uniform and the chief physician from the hospital accompanied him. The policeman—a gray-haired man, maybe fifty years old—looked so much like a detective that his job title might as well have been tattooed on his forehead in red letters.

Disconcerted, Kim stared at the doctor in particular with an exponentially growing feeling of discomfort—until his father caught his attention again with an exaggerated clearing of his throat.

"We have visitors," he said unnecessarily. "You already know Dr. Halserburg. And this is Chief Inspector Gerber from the Criminal Investigations Bureau," he added, gesturing at the gray-haired man. He shot a quick, reassuring look at Mom, who had turned several shades paler at the sight of the policeman and now sat stiffly upright in her armchair. Then, he turned back to Kim. "The inspector has a few questions for you, son."

"F-for me?" Kim stammered. He stared at the detective, mystified. "But I didn't do anything—"

"No need to get upset, son," Inspector Gerber said, interrupting him. A friendly, seemingly genuine smile appeared on his face, in stark contrast to the impression he made otherwise. Without waiting to be invited, he sat down in the chair across from Kim and continued: "We're not here to accuse you of anything. I'd just like to ask you a few questions."

"Questions?" Kim echoed. "But I don't know anything."

"Well, that remains to be seen," Inspector Gerber said, smiling. Suddenly, the smile didn't seem so genuine. Kim felt he'd have to be very, very careful about what he said.

"Can I offer you a . . . a cup of coffee?" asked his mother, hesitantly interrupting. It was obvious how uncomfortable she felt having a policeman in her house! From the quick look she gave Kim, it appeared he would be grounded for at least a month.

Dr. Halserburg shook his head, declining the offer, while Inspector Gerber nodded. "Yes, thank you—if it's not too much trouble, that is."

"No, not at all."

Mom stood up and quickly disappeared into the kitchen. However, she left the door open so she could follow everything that was said. On TV, the image of the ice hockey robot reappeared. Its glowing green eye looked at Kim attentively.

"I'm sure you can imagine why we're here, young man," Inspector Gerber said, resuming the conversation.

Kim swallowed nervously. He wanted to answer, but the only reply he could manage was a shake of his head.

The policeman pointed at the doctor. "Dr. Halserburg told us what happened this afternoon at the medical center."

"I didn't steal anything," Kim said, defending himself. "I was just in the room. I didn't—"

"Sure, okay," Inspector Gerber said, interrupting him with a reassuring gesture. "But even if you had, that would hardly be a reason for a detective to show up here."

"Why don't you just come out and say what you want from my son," Kim's father interjected. His voice sounded a bit sharper than the situation warranted. Obviously, he was nervous, too.

Inspector Gerber turned to look at Dad for moment without saying anything. "Just information, that's all," he finally replied.

"It's about that boy, isn't it?" Dad guessed. He sat down, as well, but without bothering to offer Dr. Halserburg or the policeman a seat.

Gerber nodded. "Among other things."

"Among other things?" Kim's father repeated incredulously.

Now, the professor spoke up. "I'm truly sorry if we're upsetting you or your son," he said. "But Kim may be our only chance to get answers to some questions that we have been working on for a long time now. We and the police, as well." He gestured at the inspector before continuing, addressing Kim. "See, Kim, this boy that you were so fascinated with is not the first . . ."

"Not the first *what?*" Dad asked sharply.

Mom appeared in the kitchen doorway and looked at Kim and the professor with a mixture of curiosity and bewilderment. On the TV, the robot's glowing green eye followed the scene.

"Not the first kid we've found in this condition," Dr. Halserburg continued. "You saw him, Kim. There's nothing wrong with him—physically, I mean. But he's catatonic."

"Cata . . . what?" Kim asked.

The doctor gave a fleeting smile. "In laymen's terms: unresponsive," he explained. "He's breathing, his heart is beating, and he reacts to external stimuli—pain, cold, heat—but that's all. If you were to put him in a corner, he simply would stand there until his legs gave out."

"And what does that have to do with my son?" Dad wanted to know.

"This boy is not the first one we've found in this condition," Inspector Gerber repeated. "During the past few weeks, in Düsseldorf alone, we've found almost a dozen kids in this state. And the strange thing is—no one seems to miss them. They have no ID on them, can't talk—"

"And they're all dressed rather strangely," Dr. Halserburg added. "Like the boy this afternoon."

"On top of that," said Inspector Gerber, "the ambulance driver claims the boy appeared suddenly, as if out of nowhere."

"What?" asked Dad.

Inspector Gerber shrugged. "Those were his words. He claims the boy was just suddenly there. He didn't run there from anywhere. I have a hard time believing that, but the man is willing to swear to it on a stack of bibles. As I've said, we're not here to investigate the cause of the accident; our main purpose is to find out where these kids come from—who they are and what's wrong with them."

"Are they sick?" Kim asked, instantly wishing he'd held his tongue.

Dr. Halserburg hesitated for a moment. "That's a concern," he said. "There's nothing wrong with them . . . at first glance. But they seem to be . . . well, in some sort of trance. We're faced with a riddle. And, of course, they're getting weaker all the time. We're already having to feed some of them artificially, and I don't know how long that can go on."

"We have to find out where they come from," Inspector Gerber said. "No one recongizes them. And so far, you're the only one who seems to know anything about them."

That isn't the only thing, Kim thought. Inspector Gerber might be unaware of this, but from the look in the doctor's eyes, Kim knew that the physician hadn't forgotten what had happened to Rebecca back then by any means. An icy chill ran down his spine.

"It's similar to how your sister was," Dr. Halserburg said, as if he had read Kim's thoughts. The doctor's voice took on an urgent tone. "If you know anything at all, Kim, you need to tell us. No matter what it is. I give you my word of honor that we'll keep everything confidential."

He gave the detective an inquiring look. Inspector Gerber nodded.

"I-I-I don't know anything," Kim stammered. "Really. I . . . I was wrong. I thought I knew the boy, but that . . . that's not the case and—"

"This afternoon," Dr. Halserburg said, "you were as white as a sheet. People don't react that way when they don't know anything."

"Dr. Halserburg is sure you know this boy," Inspector Gerber added.

"Well, I don't." Kim refused to budge.

The detective looked at him intently as he reached into his coat and pulled out a transparent plastic bag. Rolled up inside of it was a heavy leather belt with a shiny brass belt buckle. "This is what you had in your hands when they surprised you," he said. "Could you tell me what this is?"

"A belt," Kim replied.

Inspector Gerber's eyes flashed, but he kept himself under control. "We're aware of that," he replied tersely. "But it's a very unusual belt, isn't it? I've never seen anything like it. And our lab says that the brass has a degree of purity beyond our ability to produce."

"That's right," Kim replied. "It doesn't come from this world, either."

"What?" exclaimed Inspector Gerber. Surprised and curious, he leaned forward. The robot on the TV screen did the same. "You'll have to explain that to me."

"That boy . . ." Kim said with a strong voice, "there's no way he can have ID on him. He comes from another world, and there's no such thing there."

"What?" Inspector Gerber's face stiffened.

"There's a world where fairytales are real," Kim said. It was the first time he'd talked about it. "See, people can go there only when they're dreaming. At least that's the way it used to be. I went there once, and my sister did, too; but that was a long time ago and—"

"That's enough!" Inspector Gerber said, interrupting him. He made no attempt to hide his anger anymore. "If you're trying to pull my leg, kid, you'll have to come up with something better. Why don't you just come out and say the boy is from Mars?" He angrily wagged his finger at Kim. "We can deal with this another way if we have to."

"I don't think so," Dad coolly told the inspector.

Inspector Gerber's head swung around. "You—"

"You, sir," Kim's father said, coldly interrupting the policeman, "seem to be a little confused about this point: My son is still a minor, Inspector. Not to mention the fact that he hasn't broken any laws. Even if he had, though, you have absolutely no right to speak to him in that tone of voice."

Inspector Gerber swallowed a couple of times. He looked as if he would blow his top, like an overheated steam kettle. But then, he crammed the belt back into his coat pocket and stood up.

"Fine. Have it your way," he said. "You'll be hearing from me. Your son will, too."

"Gentlemen," interjected Dr. Halserburg, "Please. It doesn't help anyone if we fight." He sighed, shook his head a couple of times, and turned toward Kim again.

"We don't mean you any harm," he said. "Truly. These kids are the only issue. They're sick. They could die. Do you want that?"

"No, of course not," Kim replied emotionally. "But . . . I can't help you. Even if I wanted to—"

"So you don't want to," Inspector Gerber said pointedly.

"Nonsense," said the doctor, his voice also sharp. "I know this boy. Do you really believe he wouldn't help us if he could?"

"I don't believe in anything," Inspector Gerber said angrily. "That's my job."

Kim's mother came out of the kitchen, carrying a tray of coffee cups, but Dad waved her off. "No need for that," he said frostily. "These gentlemen were just about to leave."

Inspector Gerber looked at Dad, his eyes flashing, but he restrained himself and made no reply.

Dr. Halserburg suddenly looked very sad. "Perhaps you could give this some more thought, Kim," he said, reaching into his coat pocket. "I'll give you my home phone number. If you have anything to say to me, give me a call. I promise I won't tell anyone—not even the police," he added, glancing sideways at Inspector Gerber, who glared back at him.

"I'll walk you to the door," Dad said, standing up. He escorted the men out. The robot on the TV screen departed, as well. Kim stood up but immediately sat back down when he met his mother's gaze.

The battle between the robots and the men in the crystal fortress still raged on the TV screen, but Kim barely watched. *"Those kids might die, Kim. We just want to help them."*

Did they think he didn't want to help?!

Kim felt afraid—terribly, horribly afraid. He was certain now that something unimaginable had happened in the world of Magic Moon. He had to go there, no matter what!

The front door closed, and then his father came back into the living room. His features were composed, but his eyes blazed with barely suppressed anger.

"Satisfied?" he asked.

Kim looked at him, not knowing how to answer.

"You've done a lot of things," his father continued, livid, "but up until now, we've never had the police in this house. What are you planning next?"

"Please," Mom said. "Don't be so hard on him. You can see how sorry he is."

"Is that what I see?" Angrily, her husband walked over to the table and lit a cigarette—something he did very rarely. "The only thing I see," he said, coughing after the first puff and energetically waving his hand before his face, "is that our son has managed to get himself in a huge amount of trouble. Us too! You heard the detective. He doesn't believe a word Kim said. And frankly . . . I don't, either," he added, casting a grim look in Kim's direction.

"But I told the truth," Kim said, defending himself. "I don't know who this boy is!"

His father was about to deliver a furious retort, but he thought better of it at the last moment. He took another puff on his cigarette, which was followed by another coughing spell.

"Okay," he said once he caught his breath again. "Whatever you say. I'm sick and tired of this secretive game. Go to your room. Maybe between now and tomorrow morning, you'll reconsider the wisdom of this behavior."

Kim looked at him sadly before turning around to run upstairs to his room.

III

Kim stayed awake for a long time that night, tossing and turning, but he did drift off to sleep, eventually. He had curled up on his bed for an hour or more, listening to the muffled sound of his parents' voices without being able to make out their words.

Not that he really needed to understand them. Even if Kim hadn't possessed a well-developed imagination, it would have been easy to guess what his father and mother were discussing. Dad's voice sounded loud and very upset, while his mother's voice got quieter and quieter, soon becoming inaudible. Under these circumstances, Kim placed all his bets on his mother's diplomatic skills. She always had managed to calm down her husband whenever he got hot under the collar because of something Kim had done.

She seemed to have succeeded once again, because when Kim suddenly sat up with a start and looked around in his room later that night, the voices from the first floor were silent and the house was quiet—so quiet that it was almost eerie.

At first, Kim just sat there, blinking the sleep out of his eyes. He was a little surprised that he'd fallen asleep at all, given everything that had been flitting around in his head. But the day had been pretty exciting, after all. No wonder he was tired.

Kim yawned, swung his legs over the side of the bed, and rubbed his eyes with both hands. He had fallen asleep fully clothed. He still felt a little groggy but knew it would be a while before he could get back to sleep. Besides, he had better things to do than waste his time in bed. He just had to find a way back to Magic Moon.

But he had no idea how.

Moving slowly, he stood up, looked around his room, and headed toward the light switch by the door. Then, he changed his mind. His father had a habit of working late into the night. If Dad were to see a light shining from Kim's room, he might stop what he was doing and come in to make sure everything was all right—or perhaps to resume the interrupted confrontation. Instead of switching on the light, Kim turned on his computer and pushed a button to make the color screen turn white. The light the monitor emitted was more than enough for him to find his way around.

Sighing, Kim sat down at his desk, looked at the crushed wreckage of the Viper for a while, and halfheartedly set about gluing at least the largest pieces back together. He didn't expect much of this effort; but, dammit, he had to do something. Even doing something pointless seemed better than doing nothing at all.

When he bent forward to glue the rear engine to what was left of the back of the spaceship, Kim felt a stabbing pain in his right thigh.

Wincing, he dropped the plastic piece on the desk and reached in his pocket. He retrieved the tiny flute he'd taken from the hospital. This time, he didn't put it back right away but thoughtfully cradled it in his hands for a long time. *Is it possible that . . . ?*

It couldn't hurt to try. The idea seemed a little ridiculous and, besides, it would be too easy. Nevertheless, he put the little instrument to his lips, tried to cover the tiny holes with his fingertips, and blew hard.

At first, he heard nothing at all. Then, the flute produced a faint, discordant sound that made Kim flinch in surprise, nearly dropping the instrument. The tone was so shrill that his teeth hurt and the glass on his computer screen started to vibrate.

Dumbfounded, he stared at the little flute; then, he closed his fist around it again, looking around the room.

Nothing.

His room was still his room, and the darkness outside his window was normal. What did he expect? That the ground would open up and an elevator to Magic Moon would suddenly appear?

Shaking his head in disappointment, he stuck the flute in his pocket and was about to turn his attention back to the Viper, when he heard a noise coming from the first floor.

Surprised, he looked up at the little clock in the upper right corner of the computer screen: It was almost four in the morning. Even for his father, that was an unusual hour to be awake. Besides, when Dad stayed up that late, he was careful not to crash around like a bull in a china shop, which was what the noises from below sounded like.

Kim stood up and went to the door. He opened it as quietly as he could and listened intently to the sounds outside.

The crashing and banging was coming from the living room. It truly did sound as if someone were dragging out all the pots, pans, and cans from the kitchen. What in the world was going on down there?

Cautiously, Kim opened the door all the way, stepped into the hall, and looked left and right. It was dark—not the least bit of light came from either the first floor or from his parents' bedroom at the end of hall. The crashing and banging downstairs grew louder. Then, Kim heard a strange, unidentifiable rattling sound.

His heart pounding, Kim moved toward the stairs, stopping at the top landing. The living room door was open. Apparently, the curtains hadn't been closed, because he saw pale, grayish light shine through the rectangular doorway. Then, after his eyes got used to the dim light, he saw dancing shadows. Someone was moving about in the living room—and it wasn't his father.

He tiptoed a little farther, stopped again halfway down the stairs, and glanced back at his parents' bedroom. His bravery worried him a little—all the more so when he remembered a discussion he'd had with his father not too long before—about the difference between courage and foolishness.

If there really was a burglar down in the living room, then it probably was not very smart for Kim to go downstairs and confront him alone. On the other hand, though, whoever heard of a burglar making that much noise?

Kim crept farther, reached the living room door, and then—holding his breath—he peeked around the corner.

He was very glad that he had moved so quietly.

The living room was in shambles: All the furniture was upended, some of it broken to pieces. The TV, Dad's stereo tower, and the electronic wall clock now were a pile of smoldering debris, as if someone methodically had smashed them to bits. Kim could see through the open door that the same thing had happened to the appliances in the kitchen. Not only was the window wide open, but the glass was smashed also, and the curtains had been ripped down. A harsh, bright light shone into the room from somewhere outside, giving Kim a distinct view of the devastation. He saw the figure standing in the midst of the chaos, swiveling its head from right to left, as if looking for more things to pound and smash to bits.

No, this definitely was not Kim's father.

It wasn't a human being at all—at least, not any kind that Kim had ever seen before. For a long time, he just stood there, gaping at the angular, six and a half foot giant in the devastated room.

Kim doubted his sanity.

Although Kim could see only a dark silhouette against the harsh light, there was absolutely no doubt: the massive, angular shoulders; the giant claws (one, slender and equipped with extremely agile, dexterous jointed fingers; the other, a terrifying steel claw with razor-sharp edges useful for tearing and slashing); the face (shaped like a goalie's mask); and the narrow, eye slit (with glowing green letters racing behind it). This was the robot from the previous night's science fiction movie! As if sensing Kim's presence, the figure swiveled its angular head and looked at him.

Kim woke up from his trance. With a startled cry, he whirled around. Instinctively, he started to head for the front door; but suddenly, in mid-stride, he turned back. Rebecca and his parents! He had to warn them! This colossal intruder hadn't come here just to chat! No matter what corner of the galaxy he came from, if he surprised Kim's parents or sister in their sleep, it would be a close encounter of the lethal kind! It was quite odd that the din hadn't awakened them already.

As Kim rushed past the living room door, a terrific blow struck the wall, causing the house to shake down to its foundations. A steel fist smashed through the masonry, grabbed at Kim's arm, and ripped off a piece of Kim's jacket. He threw himself to the side at the last moment.

He tripped, banged against the banister, and stumbled up the first five steps. Another even harder blow completely collapsed the wall. Obviously, the giant robot wasn't one for using doors but preferred to take the more direct route.

Fear lent Kim additional strength. He bounded to his feet, rushed up the stairs, and yelled for his father at the top of his lungs. His shouting must have been audible two houses away—to say nothing of the infernal noise the robot made as it forced its way through the living room wall. Despite all this, nothing stirred in the house. No light went on in his parents' bedroom, and no one responded to his cries.

Kim reached the top of the stairs; cast a quick, harried glance back over his shoulder; and cried out a second time, even more shrilly. The robot's slender right hand was no longer empty.

A white needle of light flashed in Kim's direction.

The laser beam missed Kim by a fraction of an inch, burned a fist-sized hole in his bedroom door, and set the stairs and carpet on fire.

Blindingly bright firelight illuminated the hallway; within a fraction of a second, the air was piping hot and barely breathable.

Kim whirled around, covered the distance to his parents' bedroom in two giant strides, tore the door open—and ran, full tilt, into an invisible barrier.

The collision was so violent that Kim bounced off the barrier and landed on his butt, confused. His head roared, and the flashes of light before his eyes no longer came merely from the bright flames filling the hallway. Kim managed to pull himself up just as the stairs behind him trembled from the steel giant's weight. Once again, he approached the door. He could see his parents' bedroom; but when he extended his hands, his fingers met with hard resistance, as if he were standing before a massive glass wall.

That's precisely what it was. When he looked more closely, he noticed flashes of light in the glass, caused by the reflection of the flames. He also could see the shadow that suddenly appeared behind him.

For a second time, Kim simply dodged to the side; and for a second time, the robot's laser gun missed by a hair. The harsh beam hit the glass wall, effortlessly penetrated it—without even damaging it—and blasted the bedroom wall across from the door. The armoire, carpeting, and some of the curtains immediately caught fire. But in the bright light, Kim could see that the room was empty. The bedspread had been pulled back, but his parents weren't there.

He had no time to feel anything like relief, because the robot wasn't satisfied with torching his parents' bedroom: It was intent on Kim. A third laser blast flashed from the robot's hand, leaving a smoking trail in the floor before slicing off a good six feet of the banister and leaving another hole in the wall.

Summoning all his strength, Kim clenched his teeth, rolled over the smoldering track in the wood left by the laser beam, and shot to his feet. With one leap, he crossed the hall and tore open the door to Rebecca's room.

He wasn't surprised when he crashed against an invisible glass wall here, as well. It was as if a giant aquarium enclosed Kim, and he was trapped there with a berserk robot, which was determined to end the night with a barbeque.

When Kim got back on his feet this time, the robot was almost at the top of the stairs. It lifted its giant iron foot, preparing to step onto the hallway floor. At the same time, it aimed its laser weapon at Kim again—so close now that it would have to be blind or stupid to miss. Kim had the feeling that this creature was neither blind nor stupid.

Fear gave Kim a desperate idea: As the weapon in the robot's hand swiveled around, Kim leaped across the hallway, pulling the large mirror off the wall next to the bathroom and holding it in front of his head and chest.

The robot's laser gun fired another blast of blinding white light, which hit the mirror directly in front of Kim's heart.

Kim fully expected to fall down dead. But instead of passing through the mirror, the laser beam bounced off and shot back in its original direction. In front of the robot's feet, the wooden step turned to glowing red smoke before disappearing.

A half-second later, the step that was now deprived of its support collapsed under the robot; the robot disappeared as well, plunging downward with a thunderous crash. The whole house shook when it hit the floor.

Kim just stood there, gasping for breath, relieved that he still was alive. Then, he cautiously sank down on his hands and knees and crawled toward the collapsed stairs. The robot had fallen to the floor below. It was surrounded by a pile of splintered wood, some of which was burning. But it didn't seem out of action by any means—quite the opposite. Just as Kim peeked over the edge and looked down at the robot, it started to move again. Its right arm swung wildly back and forth, and an unpleasant, shrill howling issued from its interior. It slowly raised its head and looked up at Kim with its eerie, glowing green eye.

Kim quickly crawled a few feet backward, stood up, and frantically looked around. His victory had been short-lived. He was trapped. The flames in the hallway spread faster and faster. His parents' bedroom and Rebecca's room were inaccessible, as clearly evidenced by the two bumps on his forehead, and the bathroom didn't have a window. The only place left to flee was his room. With a little luck, he might climb out the window and escape across the garage roof before the whole house went up in flames.

Kim hastily opened the door and recoiled in fright, ducking his head as flames hurtled toward him. The laser beam that had punched a hole through his door had blasted his desk, turning it, the computer, and the Viper wreckage into a smoking pile of debris. Here, too, the flames already had spread to the walls and carpet.

Kim coughed, shielded his face with his hands, and blindly groped his way over to the window. With tears streaming from eyes, he pulled the curtains aside, opened the window, and groaned with disappointment when his hands again pushed up against a massive invisible barrier. Here, too—right behind the window—was a wall of glass as hard as steel.

Gasping for breath, Kim turned around and surveyed his room. The heat and the brightness made his eyes tear up, and he hardly could breathe. As if that weren't enough, over the crackling of the flames, he heard loud crashing and banging on the first floor. Clearly, his green-eyed persecutor hadn't given up. There was no way to tell what the robot was doing, but Kim felt sure that it would reappear in a few moments to deliver the final blow.

Unsure what to do, Kim staggered from the room and turned in a circle, searching for a way out. Most of the hallway already was on fire, and the thick smoke was suffocating him. Every breath he took was painful. Even if the robot didn't reach him, he was going to burn to death in a few moments.

Again, that terrible crashing and banging sounded from the first floor. Coughing, his eyes streaming tears, Kim walked to the staircase. He watched in horror as the robot gathered all available pieces of furniture and stacked them in a pile at the bottom of the collapsed stairs. In few more minutes, it would finish building a new stairway, which it easily could crawl up to check whether its victim were still alive—and then, if necessary, the robot could take corrective action.

In despair, Kim stumbled back into his room, picked up a chair and used all his strength to smash against the glass wall outside his window.

The chair broke into pieces. The glass wall didn't.

He needed something stronger to break it. But what? There were all sorts of things in his room, but nothing that looked capable of breaking a pane of armored glass. All the same, he grabbed a piece of the broken chair, raised it over his head, and repeatedly struck the glass as hard as he could. Nothing happened . . . except that his arm started to hurt after a few blows, and he couldn't catch his breath. The room was filled with so much hot smoke that Kim felt like he was breathing fire. He staggered back into the hallway—and looked straight into the robot's glowing green eye slit, which appeared directly above the stairway landing. The tiny glowing letters within the slit flared up in triumph. A powerful iron claw dug into the tiles as the heavy giant pulled its body upward.

Sheer desperation filled Kim with courage: All at once he lunged at the robot, drew his leg back, then kicked it so hard that its metal head rang like bell. The robot tottered, but it didn't tip over backward and break apart as Kim had hoped. Instead, it swung out its claw. Kim had to jump back quickly to save himself.

It was all over! The house now burned like a bonfire, and the iron colossus would reach Kim in a few moments. If Kim couldn't shatter the glass wall, he'd be killed.

Then, something occurred to him: There was one more way to make the glass burst. . . .

Kim kicked the robot a second time, leaped back into his room, and pulled the tiny flute from his pocket. He was so excited that he dropped it. For a moment, he blindly groped for it on the carpet, which was covered with ashes and smoldering wood. Then, he lifted it to his lips and blew into with all his might.

A shrill screech sounded, so intense that Kim closed his eyes in pain. His head felt like it would burst, and his teeth ached as if someone were pulling them out, one at a time.

But when Kim raised his eyes and looked at the window, all the panes had broken, and the glass outside was no longer invisible, instead having turned into a spider web of splits and cracks.

Kim took a deep breath, steeled himself for renewed pain, and again placed the musical instrument to his lips, when a steel hand grabbed his shoulders and swung him around with unbelievable force.

Shoved by the colossus, Kim cried out, hit the wall, and helplessly stumbled toward the hallway. The steel claw aimed for Kim's face, narrowly missing only because Kim lost his balance and fell backward into the hallway.

He immediately tried to turn over, but the robot took one trampling step forward and his giant steel foot caught Kim's pant leg, effectively nailing him to the floor. Kim cried out and tried to break loose, but the material of his jeans restrained his efforts.

Moving in an almost leisurely manner, the terrifying figure turned all the way around, stared down at Kim, and lifted its other foot to stomp him to death.

No longer reflecting on his actions, Kim put the flute to his lips and blew into it with all his might.

The sound was so intense that it almost split open his head. He cried out from the pain, threw his head back in agony, and then blew into the tiny mouthpiece once again. His bedroom window shattered; right after that, the invisible wall behind his parents' bedroom door collapsed, raining shards of glass.

Something struck the glass behind Rebecca's door with enormous force, causing it to explode. A long, reddish-brown shadow flew through the air like a bolt of lightning and crashed into the robot. The giant killing machine skidded several yards before crashing into the wall with a metallic shriek.

Kim's eyes widened in disbelief when he saw what had attacked the robot: Something reddish-green and scaly—with horrifying claws and teeth; eyes like cut rubies; and a wildly thrashing, muscular tail—now crouched in front of the robot, eying it warily. The creature looked like a salamander—or at least, would have looked like a salamander if it weren't ten feet long from its muzzle to the tip of its tail, with shoulders as tall as a German shepherd . . . a very large German shepherd.

The robot turned around in a flash and sized up its new opponent with its green eye. Kim watched as it repeatedly tried to raise the hand carrying the laser weapon, but the arm refused to do its bidding. The other arm still functioned, though—and that one had the terrible steel claw on the end.

"Watch out!" Kim shouted when he saw the robot fake a movement toward the left before suddenly striking out in the other direction. Kim had no idea whether the giant lizard heard or understood his warning. In any case, it was superfluous: With a degree of speed incredible for a creature that size, the animal dodged the blow and simultaneously charged the robot, flicking out its long, pliant tongue.

Before the robot even knew what was happening, the lizard's tongue had wrapped itself around the robot's arm. The lizard turned, lashing out with its tail.

A noise sounded—like the sound of a hammer the size of national monument striking against a giant anvil.

With a dry, grating sound, the robot's arm broke off right under the shoulder joint. All at once, the giant spewed blue and reddish-orange sparks. Suddenly, the narrow eye slit filled with red flames instead of green light. The giant figure tottered, caught itself for a second, and then fell backward to the ground floor for the second time. This time, Kim clearly heard the sound of metal breaking apart.

Kim stared at the large reddish-green lizard, stunned. It was somehow familiar to him—as crazy as that idea seemed. It . . . might be—

Kim had no time to finish this line of thought, because he wasn't out of danger—not by any means. The robot might be beaten, but the house still was burning; flames had engulfed almost the entire hallway. Yellow and red tongues of fire leaped up under the lizard's body. The lizard didn't seem to notice this, though. Probably, its thick, scaly armor protected it from the heat.

Kim had no such protection, however. He started to feel the heat more and more with each agonizing breath. Coughing, he stumbled to his feet, looked around, and noticed with horror that flames now filled the doorway to his room. The area was a glowing inferno that looked more like the interior of a blast furnace than the room he'd lived in for fourteen years. His parents' bedroom also was burning. The only path left was through Rebecca's room.

Kim coughed, took a big step so as not to trip over the lizard's tail, stumbled through the doorway—and jumped back with a startled cry.

Rebecca's room was on fire.

It wasn't even Rebecca's room, anymore. It wasn't a room at all.

Stretching out before Kim was an apparently infinite expanse of land, colored in gloomy brown and black hues. It was devoid of all vegetation except for a few crippled trees and strange, bushy growth that resembled braided barbed wire. The doorway he'd walked through wasn't a doorway, either, but a jagged hole in a huge, shiny glass wall that stretched as far as the eye could see.

Something was touching his hip. Kim turned around and, startled, reflexively took a step back when he saw the giant lizard. It had drawn up next to Kim. The coldly glittering, fist-sized reptilian eyes bored into Kim, directly meeting his gaze.

"Ssso, young man?" hissed the lizard. "What are you waiting for? To sssee it return?" Impatiently moving its huge, triangular head, the creature took a step toward Kim. Its tail swished from side to side. "Climb up," it hissed. "We mussst leave as sssoon as posssible. Thisss one wasssn't alone."

Kim made no move to climb onto the lizard's back. He didn't do anything at all—at least, not right away.

He simply stood there, looking back and forth between the giant talking lizard and the surreal landscape stretching before him. Very, very slowly, realization dawned: This was one of the two iguanas from his sister's terrarium. Only, it wasn't a dwarf iguana, and the eerie marshland was no longer the interior of the terrarium.

With a sudden flash of insight, he realized where he was. This wasn't his parents' house—not even the same city or the same world. Kim had found the road that he'd been seeking so desperately.

He was in Magic Moon.

Hours later, Kim wasn't so sure that this bleak, monotonous world the lizard was carrying him through was what he'd thought. In truth, he'd lost his sense of time, as well. He didn't know whether he'd been sitting on the giant lizard's scaly back for twelve hours, two, or a full two hundred. In any case, however, he sensed it had been a long time.

The huge reptile trotted over the marshy ground at a steady pace. Without heed, it splashed through pools of water, plowed through thorny underbrush, and wove its way through the sparse trees, its flat body untouched by low branches—which brushed its rider instead.

Before long, Kim's face was bruised and full of bloody scratches. His sweater—and much of the skin under it, as well—hung in shreds. His back and lower body ached unbearably. A couple of times, Kim had asked the lizard to stop for a while or to be more careful as it ran, but the lizard apparently had lost its ability to understand human speech.

Hour after hour, it trotted, wading across creeks and crossing through small patches of forest. It crawled through marshes full of huge mud holes, where bubbles rose up through the slime and—upon reaching the surface—burst open, giving off foul-smelling gas. It had grown dim but not completely dark. The sky still glowed with an eerie gray color, although Kim couldn't see the moon or stars. At some point later on, the sky brightened, but—like the strange night—it wasn't exactly bright. The day was held in suspense, resembling a rainy November evening, even though the sun shone in the sky.

Despite his uncomfortable position and the complete turmoil reigning in his mind, Kim had fallen asleep on the back of his peculiar, scaly taxi. When he opened his eyes again, his surroundings had changed. Marshy wasteland still stretched before him, where trees and bushes grew from hard black wire; but the sky was lighter, and here and there, Kim saw green and red spots in the midst of the marsh's gloomy hues.

Kim's uncommunicative mount had become markedly slower. No sooner had Kim noticed this than the lizard came to a complete halt and wagged its head, as if sending a coded signal. Kim understood and stiffly climbed down from its back.

Every single bone in his body ached. Groaning, he straightened up, carefully took a step, and gritted his teeth as his back and sore rear end reacted with violent pain. The iguana stood a short distance away, silent but very attentive, its large, glittery eyes trained on Kim. Kim returned its gaze . . . but not for very long. Although this creature undoubtedly had saved his life, he didn't feel particularly comfortable around it. The reptile seemed so alien and bizarre to him that it made him shudder.

Kim nevertheless forced out a smile when he turned to face the lizard directly. "I was starting to think you would never get tired," he said. "How far have we come?"

"Thisss is not a ressst break," replied the iguana. "Thisss isss asss far as I go. You are now sssafe."

Kim glanced back in the direction from which they'd come. "You mean they won't come here?" he asked.

"They wouldn't dare," the iguana assured him.

Then, it uttered something that sounded like a crocodile trying to laugh. "But if they do, they'll be in for a sssurprise. Let them come. I'll rip them to piecccesss."

Considering how the iguana had handled the robot, Kim was more than ready to believe that.

"So, anyway . . . thank you," he said. "For everything you've done. Without you, I'd be dead now."

"That isss correct," the scaly creature hissed, closing one eye and coldly assessing Kim with the other. "And?"

"Oh . . . well, nothing," Kim murmured. "I wouldn't have liked that. That's all."

The iguana didn't dignify that with an answer but abruptly turned around and started back. Kim couldn't say why, but he felt sure that the iguana was as uncomfortable in his presence as he was in its. Even though this seemed a little unjust to him, he was relieved that it was leaving.

Nevertheless, he called the lizard back one more time.

"Rosie?"

He had no idea which of the two iguanas this was, but the creature stopped and turned its massive head toward him.

"Why do you call me that?" it hissed in a slightly annoyed tone of voice.

"I beg your pardon," Kim said hastily.

"I mean—don't take this the wrong way—but to me, you two look exactly the same. If you're not Rosie, you must be Rosa."

"My name isss Lizzzard," snarled the iguana. "Your sssissster callsss me Rosssie. A sssilly name."

"Lizard, I'm s-sorry," Kim stammered hastily. "There was no way I could know that."

"Well, now you know," hissed the iguana grumpily, licking its lips with its long, slithery tongue.

Kim wondered whether it might be hungry, but he decided he really didn't want to know the answer.

"Where are you going?" he asked.

"Away," Lizard replied. "My realm endsss here. You mussst continue your journey by yourssself."

"Alone?" Kim asked in a soft voice. He looked around, uncomfortable. Although the terrain was no longer quite as desolate as before, it wasn't inviting, either. "What direction should I go, then?"

"You'll find the way," Lizard replied. "You wanted to go to the land of dreamsss, didn't you? You're there."

"Here?" Kim asked, bewildered. "You must be wrong. This place is . . ."

He broke off, confused. The terrain was anything but a dreamland. It was more like a realm of nightmares.

"This isn't the land of dreams," he said finally.

"But it isss," Lizard replied. "Jussst not *your* dreamsss. Did you think everything isss basssed on you, warmblood?"

Kim looked at the lizard, completely taken aback. It took a moment before he understood what he'd heard—and, above all, what it meant.

"Wait a minute!" he said. "Are you saying that . . . that this place right here . . . that this is *your* Magic Moon? Your dreamworld?"

"Do you have sssomething againssst that?" Lizard inquired menacingly.

"No, not at all," Kim hastily assured him. "I . . . I was just surprised. That's all. I thought that . . ."

"What?" Lizard asked when Kim halted in mid-sentence.

Kim looked at the giant scaly creature, very disconcerted. It was hard for him to continue speaking. How often he had watched the two iguanas sitting behind the pane of their glass prison, looking frozen stiff. He'd thought they were just small, dull-witted animals that he didn't even consider pretty. Kim shuddered again.

"I didn't know you had dreams, too," he said.

"Well, we do," Lizard retorted crossly. "And now I'm going. Jussst go ssstraight. That will get you where you want to go."

"Wait!" Kim said quickly.

Lizard stopped again, annoyed, and stared at him with one eye. Moving independently, the other eye looked in another direction, scanning the marsh.

"What now?"

"Just one more question," Kim said. "What do you iguanas dream about?"

Lizard openly stared at Kim until its gaze made him jittery. Then, the iguana made a noise that sounded like another laugh. Maybe it was; then again, maybe it wasn't.

"Freedom," Lizard said.

Kim made no reply. Stunned and at a loss for words, he stood there, unmoving, until his scaly rescuer disappeared from view among the bushes.

IV

Kim continued walking in the same direction that Lizard had carried him throughout the day. Rather arbitrarily, he decided that this direction was south. (Later, he found out that it truly was south, for the sole reason that he'd wanted it to be so.) Eventually, he was so tired that he stretched out on a patch of half-dry ground and immediately fell asleep. When he opened his eyes again, it was dark. For the first time since he'd crossed over into Magic Moon, it actually was nighttime. The sky was black, not that gloomy, suffocating, cottony gray of a streetlight glowing through fog in the far in the distance. Although large bubbles of gas still were rising from the marsh, releasing unpleasant odors, the wind brought a hint of pleasant coolness.

Kim awoke with a start when he felt something touching him. He looked around, but the darkness surrounding him was so deep and absolute that he couldn't make out anything at first. He almost wished he could have the foggy gray light of the Lizard's dreamland back again. Then, his eyes got used to the pale starlight, and he saw shadowy outlines.

Kim wasn't sure seeing things was so great. He had indeed been awakened by something touching him; that something still was crouched next to Kim's right leg, alternately eyeing his face and his tennis-shoe-clad foot.

Kim had to force himself not to turn away his head in disgust. The creature that had nibbled on his toe was a big as a cat but nowhere near as cute. To be precise, it was the ugliest creature Kim had ever seen: small and primitive, sporting an indefinable color that fell somewhere between slime green and mud brown. Even though scales covered every part of its body that didn't consist of quills, barbed hooks, or razor-sharp claws, it had a shiny, moist, sticky appearance. The smell this creature gave off was enough to take one's breath away. Its bleary, oversized eyes looked over Kim with an expression that reflected both cunning and malice. A row of small, needle-sharp teeth flashed in its gaping mouth, from which saliva dripped onto the ground. The creature studied Kim from head to toe, looking as if it were trying to decide where to take its first bite.

"Uh—hello," Kim said hesitantly. Cautiously, he sat up. Bravely, he tried to suppress his disgust, forcing himself to smile. "Who are you?"

The revolting little thing drooled a great deal, but it didn't reply. Kim swallowed a couple of times to control the nausea triggered by the sight of this creature; then, he sat up all the way, drawing his knees close to his body. The dull eyes of the disgusting creature registered disappointment when the tennis shoe was withdrawn, but it still didn't move.

Kim tried again. "Do you understand me?" he asked. "I mean, do you understanding what I'm saying? No? Come here."

Although the mere sight of the animal turned his stomach, he leaned forward and reached out his hand. After all, there was nothing the creature could do about its appearance. In its eyes, Kim probably was not much prettier, although he may have been more appetizing—in the literal sense. Kim knew that someone's character shouldn't be judged by appearance—necessarily. Then again, there were exceptions.

The little monster looked at Kim's face out of one eye for a moment, directed its other eye at Kim's outstretched hand, and finally sniffed Kim's forefinger like a dog registering a scent.

Then, it chomped down.

"Ow!" Kim yelled, jumping to his feet and quickly pulling back his arm.

However, the disgusting little thing had bitten down on his finger and had no intention of letting go.

Kim cried out in pain and fury, hopping about like a madman—sometimes on his right foot and sometimes on his left—flailing his arm this way and that. The animal didn't loosen its grip in the least.

"You rat!" he shouted. "Ow! Let go right now!"

But the animal had no intention of doing so—quite the contrary. In addition, it started to work on Kim's hand with all four claws, wrapping its long tail—which was full of sharp, pointy quills—around Kim's lower arm.

Kim cried out, twirled his arm around in front of his face like a threshing machine—and finally managed to shake off the little monster. It sailed through the air with a whistling sound and landed in a bush several yards away . . . only to come scuttling back on its short little legs.

For a moment, Kim stared at the animal in wide-eyed disbelief, torn between anger and astonishment at this living pincushion that had the temerity to attack an opponent Kim's size.

Then, the animal was at Kim's feet. It bit him so hard that his toe felt the pain despite the protection of the tennis shoe. He jumped back, again letting out a shriek. Without thinking, Kim gave the animal a kick that sent it rolling, head over heels, while he lost his balance and landed flat on his seat.

When the animal charged again, Kim was ready. He made a fist and tensed his muscles to deliver a blow that would crush the creature on the spot.

As if sensing the danger, the monster broke off its attack at the last moment, cocking its head to the side instead. Its eyes flashed with malice but also reflected caution.

"Come on! Try it!" Kim said. "I've been waiting for someone like you."

The disgusting little thing made an unpleasant hissing sound and drooled again. Its tiny little claws dug into the marshy ground.

"What are you waiting for?!" Kim asked, daring it to come closer. "Come get it or get out of here!" He reached for a rock.

"Hungry!" said the animal.

Kim's eyes widened. "What?"

"I'm hungry," repeated the miniature monster. "You're big, and I'm very hungry."

Kim swallowed, stared down at the spiny creature at his feet, and then looked at his forefinger. The little beast's tiny teeth had left a double row of bleeding, needle-sized dots on his skin. The wounds burned as if someone had rubbed them with salt.

"Just a piece," begged the animal. It snuffled audibly and repeated in a sobbing voice, "I'm hungry!" Its eyes actually filled with tears.

"I'm inedible," Kim said hastily, sticking his bleeding finger into his mouth. "I taste horrible!"

"You're lying," said the sentient pincushion.

"Oh?" Kim asked warily. "Why do you say that?"

"You're eating yourself!"

Kim blinked in astonishment, took his finger back out of his mouth, and suddenly had to laugh. The animal licked its lips and crept a little closer, drenching Kim's right pant leg in slobber from his knee up to his pocket.

"Hey!" Kim protested. "Watch what you're doing there!" He tried to push the creature aside but seeing its eyes light up greedily at the last moment, he withdrew his hand.

"Now, listen," he began. "I have something against being eaten. Get it?"

"Not eaten entirely," the disgusting little thing assured him. "Just a piece—a very small piece." Its eyes suddenly reminded Kim of a helpless fawn begging a human for a lump of salt lick. "One finger—that's all," it begged. "Or just a half a finger?"

"No!" Kim yelled, not knowing whether to laugh to be angry. "Not even a quarter of a finger! Not even my fingernail! Is that clear?"

Kim stood up and curled his right hand into a fist because his finger still hurt like the dickens.

"Maybe a toe?" the little animal asked hopefully.

Kim was about to explode with anger, but then he couldn't help it: He sputtered and started laughing so hard that he couldn't catch his breath. Still chuckling to himself, he squatted down in front of the little animal and looked at it, shaking his head as he wiped the tears out of his eyes with his left hand.

"Is something wrong with you?" asked the animal. "Why are you screaming like that?"

"I'm not screaming," Kim assured him. "It just sounds like that when I . . . Who are you, anyway?"

"Who am I?" The little animal appeared serious as he pondered the meaning of this question. "I," it finally said, "am I. Who else would I be?"

"Serves me right," Kim murmured. "Ask a dumb question, get a dumb answer." He sighed. "My name, anyway, is Kim. Maybe you've heard of me before?" he added hopefully.

"No," replied his conversation partner. "And I haven't tasted you yet, either. I would remember the taste—definitely."

"Oh yes, definitely," Kim agreed, standing up again. "I have to go now. I have a long road ahead of me. It was nice to meet you."

With that, he turned around and quickly strode off. It still was deep in the night, but Kim wasn't the least bit tired anymore. Besides, he couldn't have gone back to sleep in any case—not in a place where people likely would be eaten if they didn't watch out.

Finding a way through the marsh turned out to be harder than Kim expected. He kept stumbling over roots that he didn't see in the darkness, and he kept stepping into holes that suddenly opened up in the marsh. Twice, he banged his head against a tree trunk that suddenly popped up out of nowhere. He was getting disheartened. One look at the sky told him that daybreak wouldn't be for a long time yet.

All in all, the terrain through which he stumbled seemed more and more sinister to him. The marsh extended as far as the eye could see, and all the trees and bushes looked sickly and crippled.

What had he expected? This area might be part of Magic Moon, but it was the Land of the Armored Animals. Actually, he should be glad that his sister Rebecca had asked for a terrarium and iguanas and not some long-legged, hairy spider . . . or a fish.

When Kim happened to turn around a little while later, he saw a tiny, shadowy figure quietly scurrying behind him. Kim abruptly stopped and frowned in annoyance, peering into a familiar pair of bleary, overly large eyes.

"What's going on?" Kim asked. "Why are you following me?"

"Hungry!" the little animal begged obstinately.

Kim sighed.

The monster looked at him guilelessly. "Maybe an ear?"

"No!" Kim yelled as loud as he could. Furious, he walked toward the animal, but then he changed his mind at the last moment. "Wait a minute," he said. "You're hungry, you say?"

The little animal nodded vigorously and scurried toward him.

"Listen," Kim said. "There are lakes and ponds all around here, right? I'm sure there are fish in them. Do you like fish?"

"Of course."

"And you're familiar with this area?" Kim asked.

"Sure."

"In that case, I have a suggestion," Kim said. "As soon as it's light, I'll catch you a big, juicy fish. I promise."

"A big one? Just for me?"

"For you alone," Kim assured him. "I won't take even a single scale. In return, you'll show me the way out of here. I'm looking for . . . people like me. Do you understand?"

"Like you?" the little monster repeated.

"Exactly," Kim replied. "Beings like me, who don't want to be eaten. Do you know where I can find them?"

"Of course. It's not much farther. But first: the fish."

Kim sighed. "Can't we wait until it's light?" he asked. "I mean, you appears to see very well in the dark; unfortunately, I don't."

"I noticed," the animal replied. "You almost fell into a snapper's hole."

Kim judiciously decided not to ask what a snapper was. He probably wouldn't have liked the answer.

"So, is it a deal?" he asked. "I'll get you the fish first thing in the morning, and you'll show me the way out of here."

"It's a deal." The animal sneezed.

Kim stood up straight again; but before he continued on, he turned once more to his companion. "If we're going to travel together, then you need a name," he said. "What should I call you?"

The spiny little animal looked at him, disconcerted, and Kim finally understood.

"Okay, okay," he said hastily. "I'll think one up." Suddenly, his whole face lit up in a grin. "You're as ugly as the night—did you know that? I think I'll call you Chunklet."

"Chunklet?"

"That's short for 'Little Chunk of Vomit.' Somehow fits you," Kim replied, laughing to himself. "Okay?"

The animal thought it over briefly, nodded, and scurried off. Chunklet passed over Kim's feet with small, tripping steps, smearing green slime all over Kim's tennis shoes and ankles.

Kim took advantage of the first light of dawn to braid a fishing line out of grass stems and thin branches. That was easier said than done, but Kim was good with his hands; after a little experimenting, he produced about ten feet of braided line suitable for his purposes. After all, he wasn't planning to catch a whale—just something large enough to satisfy the voracious appetite of his companion.

The fishhook presented a somewhat bigger challenge, but eventually he solved the problem by taking apart his belt and bending the tongue over a rock. He whetted the hook as sharply as he could. Chunklet sat next to him the whole time, watching him with bulging eyes, not saying anything else—for which Kim was grateful. One of the reasons Kim had started making the fishing line this early was that he'd become hungry, also. More important, as the hours had gone by that night, the disgusting little thing never ceased telling Kim how hungry it was. It had continued to beg him for an ear, a finger, or a toe. Kim was at the end of his patience and didn't know what else would shut up the miserable chatterbox.

His four-legged companion led him to a small but obviously deep pond. As soon as Kim cast his homemade fishing rod, a silver shape shot up from under the surface of the murky water and tugged on the line so violently that Kim almost tumbled into the pond headfirst.

Nevertheless, he held onto the line with an iron grip and, to his astonishment, caught a very big fish. The water splashed and bubbled as his catch put up a stubborn fight. More than once, Kim was afraid he'd lose his strength and have to let go. The whole time, Chunklet excitedly ran back and forth in front of him, greedily licking his pimpled lips and sprinkling Kim with spittle and green mucus. Finally, things calmed down at the other end of the fishing line.

Gasping from the exertion, Kim pulled his catch out of the water. It truly was a huge fish, almost as long as Kim's arm and weighing close to fifteen pounds. Its eyes seemed confused; it was looking at Kim almost reproachfully. *Maybe,* Kim thought with a feeling of consternation, *this is the first fishing rod that's ever existed in this world.*

Banishing this thought, he pulled the fish onto the bank with a last-ditch effort. When the fish started to flop around violently with its tail and fins, Kim picked up a rock.

"What are you doing?" Chunklet wanted to know.

"I'm releasing him from his suffering," Kim replied. "That's how fishermen do it. Or should I wait until he dies a painful death of suffocation on land?"

Chunklet didn't reply but watched Kim attentively as he did what he had to do. Finally, breathing hard, Kim stood up again, feeling queasy. He often had gone fishing with Dad before but always had left this unpleasant task to his father.

"You killed him," Chunklet said reproachfully. Of course, this didn't keep the little terror from immediately opening his mouth wide and biting off a huge piece of the fish.

"You did want it, didn't you?" Kim retorted, irritated.

"Yes, but not all of it," Chunklet replied with a full mouth. "One piece would have been enough." He swallowed, bit off another piece from the fish's flank, and looked at Kim with his head cocked at an angle. "Would you have killed me, too, last night?" he asked.

Kim was a little embarrassed. "Um, why are you asking that?"

Chunklet pointed at the rock that Kim had just put down again. "You had a rock in your hand then, too."

"That—well, that was c-completely different," Kim stammered.

"In what way?"

"Well, I . . ." For a moment, Kim vainly searched for the right words. "Well, um . . . what that was about was . . . well, you were so ugly, and I was afraid."

"Oh," said Chunklet, taking another bite of the fish.

Kim gaped in astonishment. The fish was about three times as long as the spiny little monster, but Chunklet had already consumed a good part of it.

"I understand. You kill ugly animals."

"No," Kim replied. "I . . . I didn't mean it that way. That was, well, before I knew that you could speak."

"You mean, if I hadn't said anything, you might have killed me?"

Kim sighed. He began to feel more uncomfortable. "No, not at all," he murmured. "I mean, well, I . . ."

All at once, he felt very small, mean, and petty. This tiny thing truly had disconcerted him.

Not just to change the subject, he asked, "Can I have a piece of your fish?" He suddenly was aware of how hungry he was.

Chunklet raised all his quills, crouched down like a cat ready to attack, and looked at Kim with flashing eyes. "You said I could have it all for myself," he scolded.

Kim sighed. "It was just a question. The fish is so big!"

"So?" retorted Chunklet. "You said so. You can't take it back!"

"Okay, fine," Kim said with a dismissive wave of his hand. "Here's an idea: You eat until you're full, and I'll take what's left over. Okay?"

Chunklet grunted an answer that Kim didn't understand and stuck his nose deeper into the fish, smacking his lips and swallowing in gulps. Kim stood there for a while, shaking his head, slightly repulsed. Then, he turned around and walked away so he wouldn't have to watch, anymore. Unfortunately, he was unable to close his ears. Chunklet grunted like a whole family of pigs.

Kim slowly walked around the little lake, taking in the scenery. It was getting increasingly brighter. The first light of morning mixed with the gray of dawn, and the marsh no longer looked as threatening. Kim even spotted some wildflowers sprinkled among the drab marsh plants; far in the distance, on the horizon, he thought he saw a strip of real grass. Evidently, Chunklet truly had kept his word and had led Kim to the edge of the eerie marshland.

He wondered what part of Magic Moon this might be. The land was big—very, very big. If he was unlucky, he might wander for weeks before finally reaching the crystal palace of Gorywynn . . . assuming that actually was his destination.

Kim became painfully aware of how little he actually knew. He'd seen the reflection of Themistokles' face and found a boy wearing Steppe riders' clothing and their coat of arms—and that was about the extent of his knowledge. He didn't know what had happened in Magic Moon or why he was here.

But he wasn't going to find the answers by standing around, racking his brains. The only thing he could do was look for the way to Gorywynn. Maybe later on, he'd come across a more reliable guide.

He waited until he was sure that Chunklet had eaten his fill, and then he returned. His eyes popped open in amazement.

That disgusting little thing still was crouching where Kim had left him—but the fish had disappeared. In its place was a spine with hundreds of curved, needle-thin fish bones attached. All the flesh was gone.

"That can't be!" Kim exclaimed.

Chunklet grinned at him, licked his lips, and belched loudly.

At a loss for words, Kim glanced back and forth from the animal to the bones. "You . . . you're not going to tell me that you . . . that you ate it all by yourself?!" He gasped incredulously.

"I did," replied Chunklet. "It tasted good." He looked at Kim with his head cocked to the side. "Sorry that there's nothing left over for you. But I thought to myself: Because it's dead, anyway, I can eat all of it. If you want, we can continue on our way now."

"Sure," Kim murmured, still standing there, stunned. "Sure. Whatever you say."

"Well, off we go." Chunklet took a step, suddenly stopped, and looked thoughtfully at the fish skeleton. "Actually, it would be a shame to leave it there," he said—and, with a single bite, gulped down the remains.

They walked for another half hour toward the strip of green on the horizon. The sun rose over the marsh—but down below, it never got completely light. The short, densely growing trees swallowed up most of the sunlight, and what escaped was consumed by fog that rose from the ground with the first light of day. Dampness settled on Kim's skin like a sticky film, but it no longer had the power to curb Kim's optimism: They obviously were approaching the edge of the marshland.

Most of the time, Chunklet went ahead; but sometimes, he also ran next to Kim or a few steps behind. The longer Kim looked at the little creature, the less disgusting he found it. Of course, Chunklet was ugly and continued to be so. But Kim began to wonder why he'd felt such disgust at the initial sight of the creature.

They now arrived at the edge of the marsh, and Chunklet stopped. His goopy-eyed gaze turned toward the gently undulating, sunlit meadow that extended before them, which was interrupted by a few trees or bushes only here and there. Kim saw the edge of another forest a couple of miles away—but it was a completely different kind of forest than the one in the marshy area.

"So, here we are," said Chunklet. He looked at the sky before turning back to Kim. "If you're looking for people like you, just go straight ahead." The little animal hesitated for a moment. "What you did there with the fish was good," he said finally. "Do you think you can do that again?"

"Why not?"

"I could guide you a little farther," Chunklet continued. "You have a rather long way to go. You might get lost. Or do you happen to know your way around here?"

Kim suppressed a smile. "No," he confessed. "I could use a guide—if that guide agrees to my payment."

"One fish a day?"

"Minus the portion that I eat." Chunklet seemed disappointed and Kim hastened to add, "I'm a poor eater. Honest. I can't eat anything close to my own weight in food."

"Definitely?" Chunklet asked, wanting to be sure.

"Yes, definitely," Kim replied. "Usually, I eat much less than that."

He didn't know exactly why, but suddenly, he was hoping that the little creature would accompany him farther. It didn't matter to Kim whether Chunklet was ugly.

"All right," Chunklet said after thinking it over for a while. "Wait here a moment." With that, he turned around and disappeared behind a bush with light, weasel-like steps.

He was gone for a long time. So long, in fact, that Kim started to wonder whether Chunklet had played a practical joke on him as a way of saying goodbye and simply abandoned him here. He waited quite a while longer before resolutely walking toward the bush.

As soon as he'd covered half the distance, however, the dry branches parted and a fantastically beautiful red, yellow, and orange-striped creature stepped out.

Kim's jaw dropped open and his eyes widened in amazement. Standing before him was the most beautiful creature he'd ever seen. It was no bigger than Chunklet; but whereas Chunklet had needle-sharp quills and slimy scales, this creature had a gorgeous coat of feathers. Velvety soft paws and a long, bushy tail like a Persian cat's were concealed beneath the rustling feathers that surrounded its body like a fluffy coat, and a pair of large, soft doe eyes looked up at Kim from the pretty little face, instantly putting him under its spell. In its gently waving feather stole, it looked like a magnificent lionfish that Kim had once seen in a movie.

"Wh-who are you?" Kim murmured as he squatted down with a smile and stretched out his hand to the magnificent creature.

The little animal looked at him almost disdainfully for a second—and it bit down hard on Kim's finger. "Actually, I'm not hungry," it said. "But there's always a little room for dessert."

Kim jumped to his feet with a puzzled cry, stuck his bleeding finger in his mouth, and stared at the creature with wide eyes. "Ch-Ch-Chunklet?" he stammered.

"It's a silly name; but as far as I'm concerned, we can stick with it. Somehow, it fits."

"But how? How can that be? I-I mean—"

"That I'm as ugly as the night? I know that," Chunklet said. "It's true. But the night is over, isn't it?"

"Hm," Kim said, which was relatively profound, considering all the commotion inside his head.

"Exactly," Chunklet said. "So, let's go. It's a long way, and I believe a certain fish is waiting for us."

It took a long time—a very long time—before Kim calmed down and got used to the prickly creature's astonishing metamorphosis. He didn't even try to understand it. Long ago, he'd experienced things in this land that were even more wondrous—but few of those things had come as a greater surprise.

They set off across the grassland. The forest that Kim had seen was farther away than he'd thought, because they walked for a good two hours before they finally reached its edge. The entire time, Chunklet flitted ahead of him, his velvety soft cat paws not making the least noise. More than once, he vanished in the tall grass, only to suddenly reappear like a gaily colored, feathery bouncing ball.

Along the way, they talked about this and that: Chunklet curiously asked who Kim was and where he came from, and Kim patiently replied. Kim also asked various questions but got only a few answers. Apparently, up until now, the featherball never had been outside his home territory of the marshland. Nevertheless, he knew that Kim's destination was in the south—the direction that they were going.

When they reached the edge of the forest, they took a rest break. Kim was exhausted. Chunklet (who Kim was too spent to rename, despite the silliness of Chunklet's moniker in view of his fantastic metamorphosis) swore up and down that he would: one, hold the first watch; and two, abstain from taking a bite out of Kim as a late breakfast. So, Kim stretched out under the shade of a tree and fell asleep almost immediately.

When Kim awoke, the sun was already high in the sky. He'd slept away almost half the day, but he felt so rested and refreshed that his annoyance quickly disappeared. Nearby, they discovered a brook with crystal-clear water. (It would seem that in Magic Moon, people always found a source of water when they were parched.) After Kim quenched his thirst, they continued on their way.

As it turned out, the forest wasn't very deep. The underbrush soon thinned, and the ancient tree trunks were spaced farther apart, allowing easier passage. However, the ground began inclining slightly. More and more often, they encountered hard, gray boulders and rocky outcrops in the lush moss, and Kim had to climb over them or take big detours several times. This usually happened when he disregarded Chunklet's warning, believing that, with his larger body size, he'd overcome obstacles that were too big for the little fellow.

Finally, they reached the edge of the forest, and now Kim saw why walking had become increasingly strenuous. The forest grew like a natural rampart along the rim of a steep rock wall that plunged into the depths far below. The foot of the rock wall marked the beginning of gently rolling hills with fields, meadows, and patches of forest—interspersed with lighter-colored villages and isolated houses and farmsteads.

Getting down there presented some difficulties, but Kim still was jubilant. Villages and farms: That meant he finally would be able to ask someone what had happened in Magic Moon, and why Themistokles had called for his help.

"What now?" Chunklet asked.

Kim sighed deeply and pointed to the cliff at their feet. "We have to climb down there," he said. "But don't worry—we'll manage it somehow. If you'd like, I'll carry you."

"Excellent," Chunklet said, immediately hopping onto Kim's shoulders. The contact was so gentle that Kim hardly felt it, except for the feather coat tickling his cheek.

"Or we could use the bridge," Chunklet suggested.

"What bridge?"

A slender velvety paw pointed to the left, past Kim's nose. "That one over there. You're as blind as a bat."

Kim chuckled. It seemed that Chunklet's character hadn't changed as fundamentally as his appearance. Kim obediently looked in the direction indicated and did see something like a filigree web far in the distance. It rose up next to the cliff, as thin as a spider web, but definitely too angular to be natural in origin.

Apparently, he wasn't the first to arrive here. Someone had constructed something resembling a giant fire escape along the rock wall. The way there seemed far, but Kim preferred to walk a few miles rather than climb down an equal distance along an almost vertical rock face.

With the multicolored feather duster on his shoulders, he set off.

The sun had long since passed its zenith by the time they'd reached the ladder, and Kim accepted the fact that he'd have to spend another night under the open skies. His energy was waning already—he'd be lucky if he reached the foot of the cliff before dark. Even Chunklet's featherlight weight gradually started to feel burdensome. Of course, the little twerp had no intention of getting down voluntarily.

Kim was astonished when he got closer to the strange structure. It actually was suspended on the rock wall like the ladder of a fire escape. Its very size was astonishing—indeed, even frightening. It was truly gigantic. The individual steps were the usual height—but so wide that twenty men could have walked down them, side by side. The entire structure consisted of ancient, rusted iron that already had holes in several places. Individual rungs were missing here and there, and the wind that continually blew along the rock face carried reddish plumes of rust. Kim couldn't figure out what purpose this strange structure served, or why anyone would have taken the trouble to build it only to let it fall into disrepair.

Kim hesitated for a considerable time before placing his foot on the top rung. Then, he cautiously put his full weight on it, mentally preparing for the whole thing to collapse under the weight of his body and planning to jump back with lightning speed. But nothing of the sort happened. The tread didn't even wobble. The only thing that wobbled was Kim when the full force of the wind hit him. He extended his arm and grabbed onto the railing. Some of the rusty iron crumbled under his fingers, but he was able to get a firm hold.

Chunklet cried out when the wind struck his feather coat, puffing it up. The creature nearly was blown off Kim's shoulder. He desperately clung to Kim's hair, but his soft little paws no longer had any claws. The wind picked him up like an oversized downy feather, and he inevitably would have plunged into the depths if Kim hadn't reached out instantly with his free hand and held tight to the fluffball.

"Whew!" Kim said. "That was close."

"You might say," Chunklet gasped. His voice had become squeaky and shrill, and Kim could feel his little body under the downy coat trembling like an aspen leaf.

Very cautiously, Kim proceeded down the steps, always keeping his left hand on the rusty iron railing and always putting down one foot completely to secure his footing before lifting up the other foot.

The descent was perilous in the extreme. It turned out that the ladder was in truly bad condition. All too often, Kim had to skip over treads that were rusted so far they consisted of nothing but paper-thin, rust-colored mesh—or were missing entirely. In one place, a whole section of the stairway disintegrated into red dust, leaving nothing beneath them but a huge, yawning chasm. Kim moved hand over hand along the rusty railing on the edge of the stairway, anxiously closing his eyes and gritting his teeth. He made it. But afterward, once he finally reached an intact rung, he felt so exhausted that he had to sit down and catch his breath.

As they approached the foot of the stairway, the sun already had entered the final section of its daily path across the sky. The shadows got longer and a cool breeze blew from the south—something Kim very much welcomed, as his whole body was bathed in sweat. Chunklet had contributed to this: After the little feather duster almost was blown off Kim's shoulder the second time,

Kim promptly had stuffed him under his shirt. Even though Kim barely felt Chunklet's weight, the downy feathers had made him sweat.

Kim halted suddenly, stood up straight, and squinted, focusing on something down below.

"What's the matter?" Chunklet squeaked, his snout curiously poking out of Kim's shirt. The red feathers on the back of his little head tickled Kim's chin.

"I'm . . . not quite sure," Kim said hesitantly. "I think someone is standing there, down below."

His feathery companion also looked down, and Kim could tell from the renewed tickling of the downy feathers that Chunklet was nodding.

"That's right," he squeaked. "There's something . . . funny about him."

"In what way?"

Kim had figured out a long time ago that Chunklet's eyes were much sharper than his own.

"Don't know," replied the creature. "Just funny. Better be careful."

That information wasn't particularly helpful to Kim, but he decided to heed Chunklet's warning, anyway.

Now alert, he slowly continued the descent, finally sidling over to the middle of a rung. Down here, almost on the ground, the wind was no longer so strong that he had to hold on continually. From this position, he had a full view of the figure he'd seen from above.

It was a man: a very tall, broad-shouldered man, wearing dark clothing. He was standing there, completely motionless, his back turned to them. He didn't move even when they got closer, and Kim's steps should have been audible. The man just stood there, motionless, his right arm raised halfway, stretched out as if reaching for some invisible support. Fear now joined the sense of caution that Kim already felt.

Although they were quite close to the man now, Kim couldn't see who he was, because the sunlight was fading rapidly; down at the foot of the huge rock face, it was already dusk. The figure over there formed a black silhouette against a insignificantly lighter background. But he seemed too big—too massive.

Under Kim's shirt, Chunklet cleared his throat. "Kim?"

"What?" Kim didn't take his eyes off the eerie figure.

"It's getting dark," Chunklet said.

"I know," Kim replied.

"Well, I was thinking you might prefer that . . . that I not be under your shirt when I . . ." Chunklet's voice trailed off.

Suddenly, Kim was in an extreme hurry to get the featherball out from under his shirt. Kim put the creature on the rung beside him.

"Thank you," Kim said.

Then, he turned his attention back to the silhouetted figure. The man still had not moved. Even if Kim's pounding footsteps on the echoing iron stairway had somehow escaped his notice, he would have to be deaf not to hear their voices. All of sudden, Kim was no longer sure that this was even a man . . .

He cautiously stepped off the last rung of the stairs, walked all the way around the figure, giving it a wide berth, and then approached it from the side.

Strange!

This giant, broad-shouldered figure, which had to be at least six foot six, was made entirely of iron, now rusted and scarred. Its right hand was slender, with thin, nimble-looking fingers frozen in a grabbing gesture. The left hand had a terrifying iron claw resembling a mechanical digger—smaller, of course, but probably not much weaker.

Kim's heart began to pound wildly when he realized where he'd seen such a figure before. . . . Nevertheless, he cautiously continued his approach. Mentally prepared to see the iron figure whirl around at any moment, he was ready to leap back and immediately take flight. Kim circled around the immobile giant until he could see its face—or more precisely, the place where its face should have been. . . .

Kim breathed a sigh of relief. What he saw was similar to the robot that had attacked his family home. But where that robot had a fearsome goalie's mask with a glowing green eye, this figure had a gaping hole that allowed a direct view of the inside of its head, which was completely empty. Kim could see where the iron had rusted through in the back.

"What *is* that?" Chunklet asked. His voice had changed a little.

"I'm . . . not sure," Kim said. "I was thinking I once had seen someone like him before. But now . . ."

He shrugged his shoulders, leaving his sentence unfinished, and he approached the iron man—still very cautious but now a little less fearful. Moving carefully, he stood on his tiptoes; shot a final, quick, wary look at the giant's motionless digger claw; and then peered up at its head.

A shadow leaped toward him, scratched his face, and flew off, squawking and beating its wings. Kim cried out. He stumbled backward, regaining his balance at the last moment. Startled, he looked up. A small black bird flew up in the air and started circling over Kim, scolding him.

Proceeding even more cautiously, Kim stood up on his tiptoes and looked up at the huge iron head a second time.

Yes, the head was empty. Not only that, but a doleful "cheep, cheep, cheep" came from the metal armor. Up in the sky, the bird continued its angry scolding of Kim. Evidently, the bird had used the vacant cavity as a nesting site, and now it was worried about its young.

"That's strange," Kim murmured as he stepped back from the figure.

"What's strange?"

"This thing." Kim said, pointing at the iron giant. "It's completely empty."

"Maybe someone ate it and left the shell behind," Chunklet surmised. "It looks rather hard."

Kim smiled but immediately turned serious again. "Not likely," he said. "You would break your teeth on what was inside there."

He shook his head, took a few steps backward, and thoughtfully looked around. It occurred to him only now what a strange position the empty shell stood in. The outstretched fingers of its half-raised right arm seemed to point south. Or were they really outstretched? Actually, when Kim thought about it, the fingers were spread as if frozen while grasping at something. What had the giant wanted to grab: something that was attacking him or the whole broad country that stretched before them?

Kim shuddered at the thought. He took another look around.

After a while, he detected a second immobile shadow standing not very far away. Another robot—it, too, was empty like the first one but not in nearly as good condition. Its body had countless jagged holes and deep dents. One arm was missing, and someone must have taken its hollow head and played soccer with it, because it lay several yards away, completely bashed in. This robot wasn't the last one they found, either.

Once they really started to search, Chunklet and Kim found almost a dozen of the huge, rusted-out figures, all standing or lying in the vicinity of the stairway—some destroyed almost to the point where they were unrecognizable, others almost undamaged but empty and inert. That wasn't all they found.

On the ground between the figures, huge amounts of ruined equipment piled up: bent iron rods, rusty gears bigger than Kim himself, and components of mysterious machines with functions that Kim couldn't identify. Reddish-brown fragments, scarred and sharp-edged, crumbled to dust at the slightest touch. It was like walking through a huge junkyard that had been abandoned hundreds of years before.

How weird, Kim said to himself, chilled by the thought. He was now glad that darkness was descending rapidly and they had to be off. They headed south so they could follow daylight for at least another half hour.

V

They caught up with the day again when they came out of the shadow of the rock face. The sun had changed into a red fireball now only a finger's width above the horizon, and the shadows had grown longer. But Kim had carefully studied the terrain while atop the giant staircase, and he'd seen a little farmstead very close by.

With a little luck, he might reach it before the onset of darkness, or soon thereafter.

He set off quickly—perhaps more quickly than necessary, and it definitely was not mere restlessness and hunger for information that drove him to hurry in this way; the cluster of frozen, hollow iron figures and the pile of rusty parts had frightened and confused him deeply. They just didn't fit in this world, any more than a winged dragon would have fit in Kim's homeland. The more he thought about it, the stranger the huge staircase on the cliff seemed to him. Who in this land would build such a staircase? And above all: Why? No matter how long or how often he thought, he just couldn't make sense of it. It really was high time for him to see Themistokles and his friends again, so he could ask them some questions . . . a great many questions.

Chunklet's voice penetrated Kim's thoughts: "What about that fish you promised me?" Turning his head as he walked, Kim saw something reddish-orange and fluffy flitting alongside him through the calf-high grass.

"It's going to get dark soon, and you're so blind, you'll never catch anything at night."

Kim searched his memory for a moment, and then he recalled seeing a creek that meandered through the grass; it wasn't far from the cliff—not quite halfway to the farm.

"Okay, okay," Kim said. "There should be a creek around here somewhere. We just need to keep going straight ahead." Without stopping, he put his hand in his pocket, pulled out the fishing line and improvised hook, and carefully unwound it.

They did reach the creek shortly thereafter and, just as in the morning, the fishing line started to tug in Kim's hands the second he threw one end in the water. The fish he pulled out this time was larger than the first one, and the feather duster leaped onto it with enthusiastic grunting almost as soon as Kim removed the hook.

Although Chunklet had much better table manners during the daytime, his appetite wasn't diminished one whit. Under Kim's astonished gaze, Chunklet shortly devoured a fish that weighed several times more than he did. He didn't pause until he got to the tip of the tail, whereupon he looked up at Kim with a sheepish expression on his face.

"Oh," he murmured. "I didn't leave anything for you. I . . . I completely forgot you wanted some of it, too. Sorry."

Kim magnanimously waved it off. The sight of the white fish meat reminded him that he hadn't eaten anything for two days. His stomach growled so loudly that he was prepared to eat even raw fish. But the house he'd seen wasn't too far away. He was sure he could get something to eat there.

"That's all right," he said. "Go ahead and eat until you're full. I'm . . . not that hungry."

"You really are a poor eater," Chunklet murmured, and then he gulped down the tip of the tail and the fish bones, as well. He belched—but with more reserve than the previous night. (Actually, it was just a small burp.)

"Shall we continue on?" he asked, licking his lips with great satisfaction.

Kim stood up, but he hesitated to wade across the creek, even though it wasn't quite six feet wide and couldn't be more than a foot and a half deep. "I think I can find my way on my own from here," he said. "You don't have to accompany me any farther. That is, if you'd rather not," he added hastily.

Chunklet looked at him almost reproachfully, and then he turned around and looked back at the rock face. The cliff already was immersed in darkness, a huge shadow behind which the world disappeared.

"Go back up the staircase?" the critter murmured, shuddering. "And at night, too?" He shook his head. "I think I'll stay a while yet. Actually, it's very nice here."

"Maybe later, you'll find an easier route back home," Kim said.

He felt . . . odd. Indeed, he'd started to feel sympathy for this strange creature; honestly, he didn't care what shape Chunklet took when the creature sat in front of him.

"That's possible," Chunklet said. "But I could escort you a little farther. I mean, just to make sure that you really do get to your destination." Suddenly, he chuckled. "Maybe you could catch another fish for me? Later, I mean."

Kim laughed. "All right; it's a deal. Afterward, I'll give you my fishing gear, too. Maybe you'll learn how to use it."

So, they set off. The countryside they walked through changed constantly. Sometimes, they crossed meadows full of colorful wildflowers. Other times, they fought their way through thorny underbrush or felt their way through patches of forest where night already had descended. Then, it was dark for good, and the next time Kim turned to his companion, he saw a spiny monstrosity creeping through the grass instead of a reddish-orange featherball.

"Listen," he said. "When we get to the farmstead, it might be better if . . . I mean, maybe you sh-should . . ." Kim started stammering, finally breaking off.

"What?" asked Chunklet.

Kim took a deep breath. "I mean, maybe it would be better if no one sees you," he said. "If you know what I mean."

Chunklet made no reply. After a few moments—during which they continued walking side by side in an uncomfortable silence—he said in a clearly audible voice, "Hungry."

Kim stopped. "That's impossible," he replied. "You just gobbled up a fish that—"

"Not me," Chunklet said, interrupting him. "I mean that thing over there!"

By the time the critter had finished his sentence, he was shouting. When Kim whirled around and looked at the forest behind him, he, too, screamed in terror, reflexively raising his hands.

An absolutely gigantic shadow rose up behind them.

At first, Kim thought that one of the iron statues had recovered from paralysis and followed them, but then he saw that the shape was even bigger and bulkier than the robots—and furry, as well. The low growling that registered in his ears a second later was unnecessary information: He already knew what had emerged so suddenly from the darkness behind them.

It was a bear!

Chunklet shrieked and vanished into the underbrush with lightning speed. After that, the bear took a lumbering step forward to rise up on its hind legs, growling furiously. Kim saw starlight reflected in a single, glittering eye.

He jumped back with a cry of horror when the powerful bear swiped at him. The blow missed, but the force of the air knocked him off his feet, causing him to fall on the grass. Quickly rolling over, he protectively threw his arms over his head and simultaneously jumped to his feet. The bear growled and shoved him in the chest so hard that it nearly cracked Kim's ribs. He would have fallen again if he hadn't grabbed onto a tree as he reeled back.

However, he didn't hold on for long.

He let go almost immediately; seconds later, the terrifying bear claws gouged half inch marks in the tree trunk, precisely where Kim's face had just been.

Kim staggered away from the giant black bear. The beast followed him, growling, forepaws extended, lurching from side to side with a tottering gait that wasn't nearly as slow or clumsy as it looked.

Kim's foot caught on something. He stumbled and struggled to maintain his balance, his arms whirling about wildly; then, he tumbled between the trees and fell flat on the ground. The bear caught up to him with a single, powerful stride and opened its jaws. Finger-length teeth like small, curved daggers flashed in the moonlight.

Then, suddenly, a spiny little ball shot out of the darkness, landing on the bear's neck and attacking the animal with teeth, claws, and quills—all at the same time.

"Hungry!" shouted Chunklet. "You're a big, giant brute, but I have a big, giant appetite, too!"

The bear bellowed in surprised rage and tried to reach the prickly ball on his neck with his paws. Chunklet clearly was no match for this huge animal. His claws probably didn't even penetrate the bear's thick fur. But the unexpected attack had distracted the bear. Maybe Kim had enough time to run away.

He quickly jumped to his feet, ran a few steps, and then stopped again. The bear still was trying to reach the back of his neck with his claws, all the while bellowing so loudly that the whole forest trembled. He angrily stomped about. Now that Kim could get a good look at him in the moonlight, he saw that this truly was a huge beast—bigger than a grizzly and weighing a least half a ton.

Perplexed, Kim turned all the way around and looked more closely. In the same instant that the shaggy giant's shaking finally rid him of the tiny tormentor on his shoulder, Kim saw that the bear had only one eye—and an ear was missing, as well.

Chunklet soared in a high arc and landed in the bushes; he immediately turned around and rushed toward his oversized adversary with bared teeth. The bear growled, bent forward slightly, and raised its right paw to deliver a killing blow to the tiny animal.

Kim shouted at the top of his lungs, "Chunklet! Stop!"

The little creature actually did stop in his tracks and looked over at Kim with a puzzled expression. The bear turned his huge head to look at Kim with his one eye.

"Stop!" Kim cried again. "He won't hurt me. And you, Kelhim," he added with a smile. "You ought to be ashamed of yourself for scaring us like that. Haven't you learned that your kind of humor is a little uncouth sometimes?"

Smiling, he walked up to the giant bear, stopped in front of him, and spread his arms out for a hug.

Kelhim cocked his head, assessing the boy with a long, pensive look. He didn't move, and for a fraction of a second, Kim started to have doubts. What if he had made a mistake and was standing across from a wild beast instead his old friend? But then, he took closer look and saw that it was Kelhim. Kelhim, the magical talking bear, formerly his companion in the battle against Boraas' black hordes—and one of the best friends Kim had ever had. There was no doubt at all.

"Getting a little old, are you?" Kim teased. "Maybe you should think about coming up with some new tricks. You acted as if you wanted to eat me the first time we met, too."

Chunklet conspicuously cleared his throat. "Excuse me," he said to Kim uncertainly, "but are you sure you know what you're doing?"

"Absolutely," Kim replied firmly, stepping even closer to the giant bear.

Kelhim growled, raised his paw, and simultaneously lowered his head. His scarred nose wiggled like a snuffling dog's.

"Come on, old boy," Kim said. "Say something."

Kelhim growled again, raised his paw a little higher—and swiped.

This time, he didn't miss.

Kim suddenly felt as if he'd been hit by truck. The blow knocked him off his feet and sent him far over the forest clearing. He tumbled, head over heels, through the air. The fact that he landed in a bush was the only thing that saved him from breaking his neck or several bones. The bush absorbed most of the force of the fall.

Nevertheless, he continued to lie there, stunned. He struggled for several seconds against black, foggy unconsciousness, which threatened to envelop his thoughts. Groaning, he turned over. He tried to prop himself up but sank back down with a cry of pain when his battered shoulder gave way under his weight.

Red and black spots danced in front of his eyes. Kim saw the silhouette of the bear totter toward him like a distorted ghost in a nightmare, still standing on his hind legs with his forepaws outstretched. A deep, thoroughly angry growl penetrated Kim's ears.

"Kelhim," he groaned. "What . . . what are you doing? It's me! Kim!"

At that, the bear stopped for a fraction of a second. An almost thoughtful expression appeared in his eye; for a moment, Kim thought he saw a spark of recognition. But then it disappeared, and he again was looking into the eye of a voracious predator.

"Kelhim!" Kim gasped. "No!"

The bear roared, grabbed hold of Kim with one claw, shredding his shirt and a good part of the skin under it and lifting him up. His jaws opened wide; stinking, hot, carnivore breath blew into Kim's face. Resigning himself to his fate, Kim closed his eyes and waited for the ultimate pain that would end it all.

Suddenly, the bear's body shuddered from a violent blow; for a second time, Kim's body plunked to the ground.

Kelhim roared and turned around. Behind him, Kim could make out only a huge shadow. The bear's massive paws swung through the air and met with resistance from something that rang like a bell as blows rained down on it.

Kim hastily crawled away; stood up, groaning; and pressed his arms against his body. He could hardly breathe. He looked at Kelhim with tearful eyes.

The bear stubbornly struggled with that shadowy figure, which was almost as massive as he was. Time and again, the powerful bear paws swung through the air and pounded his adversary. But Kelhim's foe seemed invulnerable—he didn't stagger under the terrible blows. Kelhim, on the other hand, was struck time after time, and he seemed to feel each hit, because his growling sounded as if he were in pain.

Eventually, something unimaginable happened: Kim would never in his life have thought that anyone could stand up to this powerful beast, but in the end, Kelhim lost the fight, retreating, step by step, from the unknown attacker.

Kim felt dizzy. His shoulder started to throb and a numb feeling spread throughout the left side of his body. With the tips of his fingers, he gingerly touched the place on his shoulder where the bear paw had struck him. He whimpered in pain. The wound itself wasn't very deep and didn't bleed much, but Kim was afraid his arm might be broken.

"Stop that, you fool!" said a voice behind him. "Lie down. I'll see to your arm."

Kim obeyed—because he was too weak to deal with yet more terror. Groaning, he sank down, closed his eyes, and gasped in pain as the skillful—if not exactly gentle—fingers worked on his arm.

"This doesn't look very good," continued the voice. It seemed somehow familiar to Kim—but try as he might, he couldn't figure out where he'd heard it before. "Your arm doesn't look broken, but you're going to have the biggest bruise of your life from this. You must be completely insane, young man—running around this area at night, all by yourself."

Kim finally opened his eyes and looked at a friendly, bearded face. Once again, he had the feeling that he knew the person before him. The man also looked at Kim intently.

"Do you think you can stand up and walk?" he asked eventually. "My house isn't very far away. You can't stay here in the forest: Chonk has chased the beast away, but it will come back."

"Kelhim . . ." Kim groaned. "That was . . . Kelhim."

"Of course it was Kelhim," the bearded man said, shaking his head. "Everyone here knows that. Not many people have seen him that close up, though, and lived to tell the tale."

"Why did he . . . attack me?" Kim moaned.

The man's eyes widened in disbelief. "Why did he attack you, you fool?" he snorted. "Kelhim is the most terrible, dangerous predator this side of the mountains. Everyone knows that, and you're asking why he attacked you? Where are you from? From—"

Suddenly, he broke off. His jaw dropped open and his eyes widened so much in disbelief that they nearly popped out of their sockets.

"Kim?" he whispered. "Are you . . .?" He gasped and stared at Kim for another second, unable to control his emotions. Then, he fell to his knees. "You *are* Kim!" he exclaimed. "It's you! The savior of Magic Moon."

In the exact same instant Kim recognized him as well. "Brobing?" he said softly. "Are you . . . Brobing?"

It made him uncomfortable that the man was kneeling before him; so, despite his great pain, Kim reached out his arm and tugged on Brobing's shoulder to make him stand up. The man raised his head but didn't get up all the way.

"It-it's you!" he stammered joyously. "You came back!"

Now, Kim remembered, too. Brobing was the farmer whose homestead had been attacked by a troop of black riders during Kim's first visit to Magic Moon. Kim—together with Gorg, Rangarig, Prince Priwinn, and . . . Kelhim—had saved Brobing's life. It had to be more than mere coincidence that Kim had stumbled into him, of all people.

"You've come back," Brobing repeated. "So, everything will be all right now. I knew you'd show up one day. We all knew it!"

He was about to prostrate himself again before Kim, but this time Kim restrained him with a gesture.

"I don't understand," he said. "What . . . what's going on here? What are you doing here, and why . . . how come Kelhim attacked me?"

Brobing's face darkened. "He's become a wild animal, my lord," he said. "And that's not all that's happened. There are bad things going on in Magic Moon." He looked as if he wanted to say more but thought better of it, and he visibly restrained himself. "I'll tell you all about it later. Right now, the first thing I'm going to do is bring you home so we can take care of your arm. Don't try to stand up. Chonk can carry you."

Brobing turned his head and called into the darkness, "Chonk!" A figure walked toward them from out of the night.

Kim jumped up with a startled cry.

This was the giant shadow that had beaten Kelhim. He was more than six and a half feet tall and so broad-shouldered that he almost looked misshapen. His face was a flat, expressionless mask with a narrow slit for an eye. An eerie green light glowed behind the slit, and his body consisted entirely of iron. His right hand was shaped like a human hand—but larger; his left hand looked more like the claw of a mechanical digger.

Standing before them was an iron giant like the ones Kim and Chunklet had found at the foot of the stairway.

"Brobing!" Kim gasped, horrified. "Watch out!"

Brobing turned to look at the iron man first, and then, with an expression of slight surprise, at Kim.

"There's no need to be afraid, my lord," he smiled. "That's just Chonk. A good friend."

The farmer's house was farther away than Brobing's words had made it sound. Kim valiantly had tried to stand up and walk by himself but failed miserably. Not because of the pain, but because the whole left side of his body simply was numb. Kim's arm and also his whole leg refused to cooperate. So, Kim let Chonk carry him, even though the mere touch of the iron man was unpleasant. Brobing seemed to sense Kim's discomfort, because even though Kim hadn't commented on it, the farmer himself initially tried to carry Kim. That soon exhausted him. Brobing wasn't a weakling by any means, but Kim was big for his age, and it was a long way. Chonk, on the other hand, didn't seem to notice Kim's weight, and he carried Kim with an astonishing gentleness, considering his hard, angular exterior. The only problem was that his jolting, jerky gait nauseated Kim. Thank goodness they reached Brobing's farm before it got too bad.

The farmhouse was a simple but spacious two-story white building, with a thatched roof that extended almost to the ground. Behind it, only vaguely discernable at night, were the stalls and barns. Over the grating noise of the iron man's footsteps, Kim could hear cows and pigs—and the bark of a dog, which came running toward them, growling. The dog's howling changed to joyous barking, its tail wagging when it recognized the new arrivals. Brobing, who had lost his house and farm back when Kim had first known him, now had acquired a fine new home—and a much larger one, at that.

When Kim brought this up, the farmer nodded proudly. "A lot has changed since you left, young sir. We're much better off now—at least, in some ways."

Kim had no chance to ask the farmer what he'd meant by those cryptic words, because a door in the house had opened in response to the dog's barking; suddenly, a high-pitched voice cried out. A figure he soon recognized as Brobing's wife ran toward them, her hair streaming out behind her.

"Torum!" she shouted. "Did you—"

She halted abruptly, looked at Kim, at her husband, and then back at Kim, who still was lying in the iron man's arms. Something in her face changed. Kim had seen wild, almost desperate hope in her eyes when she'd come flying out. Now that look of hope faded, replaced by an expression of deep disappointment and grief.

"Jara!" Brobing called out. "Look who we found! Don't you remember?"

The woman looked at Kim again, and he saw by her expression that she had indeed recognized him—in fact, even more quickly than her husband had, earlier. But Kim saw no joy in her eyes over the reunion: only this deep, painful disappointment that he couldn't understand.

"This is Kim!" Brobing said excitedly. "Chonk was right when he thought he heard the bear! We came to rescue Kim from Kelhim just in time. The bear would have killed him, but he got off with a good scare."

"That's . . . good." Jara tried to smile at Kim, but he saw tears glistening in her eyes. "Are you injured, my lord?"

"Just a scratch," Kim said.

"He took a rather hard blow," Brobing said, setting the record straight. "Go get some water and clean rags from the house so we can put a cold dressing on his shoulder. And be a little more welcoming to our guest. You're acting as if you weren't at all pleased to see him again."

"But I am," Jara hastily replied. "It's just that . . ." She searched a moment for the right words; once again, Kim saw how hard it was for her to hold back her tears. "When I saw you and Chonk—when I saw Chonk was carrying a boy in his arms—I thought at first it might be—" She now lost her composure entirely. Jara broke off with a little sob, turned around, and ran back into the house as quickly as she'd run out.

Brobing's eyes followed her for a moment before turning back to gaze at Kim. He gave an apologetic smile. "Please excuse this, my lord," he said. "But my wife is crying for Torum, our son. He . . . he disappeared half a year ago. She must have thought he was the one we'd found."

"Disappeared?" Kim asked, suddenly alert. "What do you mean by that?"

"He's gone," Brobing replied sadly. "Like so many. He was almost your age, you know. He even looked a little like you." He sighed deeply, made an obvious effort to pull himself together, and furtively wiped his eyes with the back of his hand. Then, he resumed talking. "Let's go in the house. We can talk better in there. I imagine you're also hungry and thirsty—at least, you look as if you were."

Kim didn't object. The last thing that interested him just then was feeding his queasy stomach, but he understood that Brobing was suffering in his own way just as much as Jara was, and that it was difficult for him to talk about it, so he welcomed this distraction.

Chonk carried Kim into the house. He had to duck to avoid banging his huge iron head against the lintel. The wooden flooring creaked under his weight, and he was so broad-shouldered that Kim wouldn't have been surprised if he'd gotten stuck in the door frame—like a cork in the neck of a bottle. But the iron man deftly swiveled as he walked through doorway, carrying Kim to a wooden bench and carefully setting him down on it.

Kim breathed an audible sigh of relief when the iron claws withdrew. Chonk obviously enjoyed Brobing's absolute trust, and there was no doubt that he'd saved Kim's life. Yes—even if Kim didn't understand why, Kelhim definitely would have killed him if Brobing and his alarming companion hadn't shown up at the last minute.

The farmer still sensed Kim's discomfort, because he looked at Kim and back at the iron man, frowning; then, he pointed at the door and said, "Go outside, Chonk. Keep watch. The bear was a little too close to the house. I don't want him to surprise us while we're asleep."

Silent and obedient, the rust-colored giant turned and tromped out of the room. The whole house shook from his footsteps.

"He seemed eerie to me, too, the first time I saw him," Brobing said, smiling once Chonk was outside. "But you shouldn't be afraid of him: He can't hurt anyone, even if he wanted to . . . and he is very useful."

Brobing looked at Kim as if expecting Kim to ask a very particular question at this point. But Kim was silent. He was glad that Chonk had left, and he most definitely didn't want to talk about it. There were more important things to discuss. A thousand questions were on the tip of Kim's tongue, and he saw from Brobing's face that the farmer felt the same way.

Before he had a chance to ask even one of these questions, however, Jara and two servant girls came in, carrying bowls of steaming water and strips of clean, white cloth. They immediately set about tending Kim's injured shoulder and all the other little scratches and bruises that he'd accumulated during his journey through the marshland.

All this attention made Kim feel uncomfortable, although he secretly did enjoy having someone take care of him. His shoulder was massaged with fragrant oil and bound so tightly that the bandages initially hurt more than the contusion itself. All the other little wounds were tended as well. When the treatment was finally over, Kim felt noticeably better than before. Jara concluded her ministrations by bringing clean clothes: a short, sleeveless leather shirt as soft as silk, which was worn over the belt; pants made of the same material, but stronger; and soft, calf-high boots that fit perfectly, as if they had been made for Kim. All this reminded him of the young Steppe rider—and, thus, of the actual reason he was here.

"Don't you like the clothes?" Jara asked. She had noticed his look but incorrectly interpreted it. "They do fit, don't they?"

"Like a glove," Kim assured her. "And they are really very beautiful."

He again saw grief in Jara's face. "Did they belong to your son?" he asked softly.

Jara nodded. Her eyes filled with tears, but this time she didn't turn away. Instead, she steadily looked at Kim as she replied: "Yes, I sewed them for him myself. Last winter. He was . . . almost as big as you when he disappeared."

"When was that?" Kim asked.

"Half a year ago, my lord."

Jara gathered up the bowls and strips of cloth, as well as Kim's shredded pants and sweater, while one of the servant girls brought plates and silverware for the food that had been prepared while Jara was tending Kim's wounds.

"He went . . . to the north pasture to check on the animals. That was one of his regular chores, and he enjoyed doing it."

"So what happened?" Kim asked.

"I don't know," Jara whispered. Her tears dried up as quickly as they had started, but her expression remained vacant, as if she were focusing on a point far in the distance. "One evening, he just didn't come home. We searched for him everywhere, for weeks. My husband and Chonk even went into Kelhim's cave—"

Out of the corner of his eye, Kim saw Brobing give his wife a quick, dismayed look, but she didn't respond. Instead, she continued in a monotone voice, "because they thought the bear might have taken our boy."

"Kelhim?" Kim still couldn't believe it.

"He has killed many of us, Kim," Brobing said earnestly. "As I told you before: He's become a wild animal." He let out a sigh, and his face darkened as he was overcome by the memory. "We found many bodies, but Torum's wasn't among them. I don't think that Kelhim got our son; if he had, then that damned bear would be dead, even if it cost me my life."

His words, and especially his tone of voice, made Kim shudder. *Revenge?* He thought, confused. *That . . . that word that didn't belong here in this world.* But he didn't say anything. Instead, he patiently waited until Brobing's emotions were under control, allowing Kim a chance to speak again.

"Torum is not the first one to disappear like that, my lord."

"I didn't think so," Kim murmured.

Brobing glanced up in surprise, and his wife also gave Kim a startled look. Kim wished he had held his tongue, but it was too late to take back those words.

"Do you know something about this?" whispered Brobing. A wild hope flared in his eyes.

"I think that's the reason why I'm here," Kim said cautiously.

"Then, perhaps you've heard something about Torum?" Jara asked. "Do you know how he is? Where he is?"

Kim wished he could tell her that Torum was fine and that there was no reason for her to worry, but he couldn't. Magic Moon wasn't a place where a lie lasted for a long time—not even a lie told out of pity—and it *would* have been a lie. He didn't know where Torum was. The boy in the hospital had been wearing Caivallon's coat of arms, and definitely was not Jara's son. Kim hadn't forgotten the professor's words: *"They might die if we don't figure out what's wrong with them, Kim."*

"No," he replied sadly. "I haven't seen your son."

Jara looked at him for a moment. She smiled, but the tears once again streamed down her face. After a while, she stood up and left the room.

Distressed, Kim said nothing.

Brobing's expression also was filled with pain. "She used to be such a happy person," he said. "You knew her. But after Torum disappeared, Jara stopped laughing. Sometimes, I'm afraid her heart will break and I'll lose her, too."

"I think Torum is still alive," Kim now said to console the man. He was close to telling Brobing what he knew, but he held back because it would have led to more questions than answers.

"Did you forget?" Brobing asked. "We don't mourn our dead: We keep them in our hearts, and they remain alive in our memories. But someone who just disappears—that's something completely different. No one knows what happened to Torum and the others: where they might be, or whether they're alive, of if they're being held captive, have been sold into slavery, or are living free."

He stopped speaking. There was no need for him to say anything more, though, because Kim understood his point. What broke Brobing's and Jara's hearts wasn't just the loss of their son—it was the uncertainty. Was there anything worse than sitting around helplessly, imagining all the dreadful things that might have happened to a loved one?

"How many have disappeared?" he asked.

Brobing looked grave. "Quite a few," he said. "They simply walk away and don't come back, or they go to sleep in their beds and aren't there when the sun comes up. Nobody knows what happened to them. Everyday, there are more and more of them missing. Some people say that soon all the children will be gone."

"There has to be an explanation for this," Kim insisted.

Brobing looked at him and said nothing.

Kim suddenly understood that people here had been expecting him to answer this question, not ask it.

"When did it start?" he asked. "And where?"

"I don't know," said Brobing. "We live a long way from the towns and fortresses, my lord. Not much news gets through to us, and it arrives slowly. But I've heard that children are disappearing from everywhere in the land."

"And no one is doing anything about it?" Kim asked in disbelief.

"What are they supposed to do?" Brobing asked sadly. "Oh, they've searched for a long time—everywhere. Themistokles has used all his magical powers to find them, and other wizards have helped him. Nothing has worked. They've searched the entire land, and I've heard that Rangarig, the golden dragon, has flown over all Magic Moon, going as far as the burning plains to try to find a trace of the children. They haven't been kidnapped, if that's what you're thinking. No one could have fooled a wizard like Themistokles." He spread his hands out in a gesture of helplessness. "They're just . . . gone."

For a long time, Kim gloomily stared into empty space. For an instant, he thought he knew the answer to all the questions, but the thought slipped away as quickly as it had come.

"That's not all that's happened, is it?" he asked softly. He hadn't forgotten the farmer's words.

Brobing sighed. "No. I can't tell you what exactly, my lord, but there is something . . . happening. Everyone notices; no one knows what it is."

"I don't understand."

"People are changing, Kim," Brobing explained. "They're not laughing as much. Many have become hard and bitter. People are fighting, and last year a traveler said a war had broken out."

"War?" Kim exclaimed incredulously. "War in Magic Moon?!"

Brobing raised his hand soothingly. "Not a big war like the one against Boraas and his black riders," he said. "But there have been skirmishes—for reasons I don't know—between the Steppe riders of Caivallon and the Tarn King, Lord of the Eastern Marshland. Many have been wounded, some killed. If Themistokles hadn't intervened and settled the dispute, the outcome could have been much worse.

It was hard for Kim to believe this news. He'd met the King of Caivallon and knew the Lord of the Eastern Marshes even better. The Tarn King was many things—but most certainly not a warmonger.

"It's as if . . . we're losing something," Brobing murmured, unable to express it. "And we don't even know what."

Kim suddenly recalled the image he'd seen shortly before sunset: The iron man frozen in place at the foot of the ladder, stretching his hand toward the land as if he wanted to grab it.

"Is it the . . . iron men?" he asked.

Brobing seemed honestly surprised. "The iron men?" He shook his head and came close to laughing. "Oh no, my lord. You've got that wrong. They are our friends and servants. Without them, everything would be much worse, believe me."

"When I was here before," Kim replied, "children weren't disappearing. And there were no iron men, either."

"It's easy to blame a scapegoat," Brobing replied, "but that doesn't make it right."

Before Kim could answer, a dull pain shot through his bandaged arm, and he gritted his teeth, moaning.

"Is it bad?" Brobing asked him worriedly.

Kim shook his head and suppressed a whimper. "No," he got out. "But—dammit—I just don't understand what's gotten into Kelhim."

"I've already told you—he's become a wild animal."

"It's so hard for me to believe that," Kim replied. "Even though I experienced it firsthand. He's killed many people, you say?"

"Yes, that's right," Brobing confirmed sadly. "He's a predator. Some farmers have moved away because they're afraid of him. If we didn't have Chonk, we would have fled a long time ago, too, because our farm is very close to his cave. If our neighbors knew how close it was, they would have gone there to kill Kelhim. They've been trying to get him for a long time. However, in the forest, he's their superior, no matter how many of them there are."

Kim recalled the quick, dismayed look that Brobing had given his wife earlier. "You two know where his cave is, and you haven't told them?" he asked to make sure.

Brobing shook his head. "I ought to tell them," he said guiltily. "I know that. But I can't. Along with your friends, he once saved our lives. I can't hand him over now, even though he's dangerous."

"I just don't understand it." It made no sense to Kim. "Kelhim, a bloodthirsty monster! How did that happen?"

"That's one of the changes I was telling you about, my lord," replied Brobing. "The animals are losing their ability to talk. Some are becoming dangerous. The forests are no longer safe. After dark, no one leaves home without a weapon."

What had Brobing said in the forest? *"There are bad things going on in Magic Moon."* A cold shiver ran down Kim's back.

"I'll find out what happened here, Brobing," he promised. "Early tomorrow morning, I'll leave for Gorywynn to find Themistokles."

VI

He didn't leave for Gorywynn the next day. It seemed the two-day journey through the marshland had exhausted Kim's strength more than he was willing to admit, and he slept like a rock. At any rate, Brobing and his wife both said they'd tried to wake him up several times, but he wouldn't budge. When Kim awoke on his own, more than half the day was gone.

That was frustrating, but the meal and the chance to sleep on a soft bed had been good for Kim: He truly felt rested and refreshed for the first time in days. The hearty breakfast Jara gave him made up for the long time it took to prepare. Afterward, Kim turned to Brobing and asked to borrow a horse so that he could ride to Gorywynn.

The farmer turned him down, however. "It's too late," he said. The nearest town is by the river, and it's a good day's ride away, even if you don't stop to rest. You'll never make it there today."

"I can sleep out in the open," Kim said. The idea of losing another day made him uneasy. "I don't mind."

"I'm sure that's true," replied Brobing, "but it's too dangerous. Remember, there's Kelhim."

When Kim started to protest, Brobing gestured emphatically and continued with his voice slightly raised: "His territory includes all the land from here to the river. He rarely attacks during the day. If he does, though, you'll be able to get away. I'll give you Stardust, my best steed. But it's too dangerous at night."

Kim suppressed the retort on the tip of his tongue, mainly because he'd noticed the worried looks that Brobing and Jara had exchanged. They both truly were concerned about him. The last thing he wanted to do was add to their burden. They shouldn't have to worry about him.

"Would you like to meet Stardust?" Brobing asked abruptly.

Kim nodded enthusiastically. He loved animals—horses most of all. He quickly jumped up and followed Brobing out of the house. They went to one of the large stables behind the main building. Once again, Kim was struck by how much larger this farm was than the previous Brobing homestead. When the farmer noticed Kim's surprise, he said with unmistakable pride, "We traveled for a long time before we found a spot where we could settle, but we don't regret it. This location is beautiful."

"And you have more land," Kim added.

"Six days' worth of plowing in each direction," Brobing confirmed. "And just last winter, we discovered a source of bitter water."

"Bitter water?"

"You put it in lamps and it burns for hours," Brobing explained.

"Oil," Kim said. "You mean oil."

"Is that what it's called where you come from?"

Kim nodded, and Brobing continued with a smile: "Next year, I'm going to hire a couple of men to help me extract it and put it in jugs so we can sell it at the market in town."

"You must need a lot of hired hands to farm a property this size," Kim observed, but Brobing shook his head.

"Oh, no," he replied. "Just the two servant girls you saw, one man, and me, of course."

Kim found that hard to believe as he gazed at the long row of stalls and sheds, before looking out over the fields behind the farmhouse, which extended as far as the eye could see.

"How do you manage to do all this work?" he asked.

Brobing smiled again. "I might as well tell you—why not?" He laughed when he saw the bewildered expression on Kim's face. "I'll explain it to you later," he promised. "Let's go see Stardust first. I'm sure he's very anxious to meet his new master."

They entered the stable, which had at least thirty spacious wooden stalls arranged in two long rows on either side of the door. Although most of the stalls were empty, Kim estimated that Brobing owned at least a dozen horses: a small fortune in this region. It seemed the farmer's life truly had undergone significant changes since the last time Kim had seen him.

They headed toward the last stall. Brobing stopped a couple of steps in front of the door and swept his arm back in an expansive gesture, inviting Kim to look at the animal inside.

Kim's eyes widened with astonishment.

Every single horse in the stable was an impressive animal; Kim's practiced eye had noticed that, without exception, these were riding horses, not plow horses. But Stardust was by far the most impressive. The stallion was huge, with a coat as black as night, sprinkled with tiny white spots that looked like millions of stars. His large, intelligent eyes looked at Kim as if he knew him. After gazing for a while in amazement, Kim cautiously stepped a little closer. The horse lowered his head to let Kim gently stroke his nose.

"He's . . . wonderful," Kim said.

"I know," Brobing replied. "He's my fastest horse. I was going to give him to Torum."

"Then, I can't accept him," Kim said, unable to tear his gaze away from the magnificent steed. "I . . . I can't promise you that I'll bring him back. It's a long way to Gorywynn—"

"And the journey is full of danger," Brobing said, interrupting him. "That's why you need to take Stardust. I insist. I wouldn't want something to happen to you on the way, just because you're riding some worn-out nag."

"But if Stardust is supposed to go to your son—"

Once again, Brobing interrupted. (This time, his tone indicated that, inadvertently, Kim had come close to hurting Brobing's feelings.) "Don't you understand? I'm happy to give away this horse if it means I'll have some hope of getting my son back."

"I can't promise you that I'll find Torum," Kim said softly.

"I know that," Brobing said. "But if it's at all possible, you're the one who can do it. And you'll need all the help you can get. What does a horse matter?"

"A horse like this?" Kim now turned around and looked directly at Brobing. "He must be very valuable," he said.

"He is," Brobing confirmed, "but I'm a wealthy man. Without you, I wouldn't have any of this. Without you, I'd be dead—and my family would be, too."

Kim stopped resisting. They stayed in the stable for a while. Brobing waited patiently while Kim made friends with the magnificent stallion, continually talking to the horse so that he would get used to his new master's voice.

Finally, Kim cautiously climbed onto Stardust's back. The horse didn't object.

"I already can tell that you two are going to become good friends," Brobing said after Kim finally dismounted. "But let's continue on. I'll show you the farm—that is, if you'd like."

"Of course." Kim did want to see it—although maybe for different reasons than Brobing assumed. Without another word, he followed the farmer.

The next few hours passed quickly. Brobing proudly showed Kim his entire farmstead. It truly was impressive. In addition to twelve horses, the farmer had about one hundred pigs and cows, as well as a flock of goats. By his own laughing admission, he had no idea how many there were; he had never counted them. Brobing hadn't exaggerated back in the stable. He had become a very wealthy man, indeed.

"But how can you tend this huge farm?" Kim wondered again.

"Come. I'll show you." Smiling, the farmer gestured at the expansive field closest to the house. Kim followed him there.

Half of the field had been freshly plowed. A figure not far from the end of the last furrow moved toward the house, pushing a huge plow in front of him.

"Who is that?" Kim asked, surprised. It seemed very strange to him that the plow wasn't pulled by a horse or one of the oxen that lived in Brobing's stable. Above all, Kim had never heard of anyone pushing a plow in front of him.

He shaded his eyes with his left hand, hoping to get a better view of the lone figure in the field. It was large and had a dark, rusty red color; its movements were just as stiff and angular as its shape.

"An . . . iron man?" he blurted out, surprised.

Brobing nodded. "Chonk does almost all the work here on the farm," he said. "He plows the fields and brings in the harvest, shears the sheep, and slaughters the pigs and goats. And in his spare time, he does any repairs that are needed. He built most of the stables I showed you—did that all by himself. I really don't know what I would do without him. And you were afraid of him," he added, shaking his head.

Kim was silent. Brobing's words hadn't necessarily helped to allay the discomfort that he felt in the iron man's presence—quite the contrary.

"Why does he do it?" he asked. "I mean—what does he want in return?"

"In return?" For a brief second, Brobing looked at him, extremely confused, and then he understood what Kim's words meant. He burst into laughter.

"Nothing," he said. "I can tell you still don't understand. Chonk is not a hired hand. He belongs to me. I bought him three summers ago."

"Bought him?" Kim repeated uncomprehendingly. "You mean, Chonk is a . . . machine?"

"I don't know what a 'machine' is," replied Brobing, still smiling. "He's not alive, if that's what you mean. He's just made of iron. Iron men are made by the dwarves of the eastern mountains. They're expensive, but worth it—as you see. In two more years, I'll have this one paid off, and then I'll be able to get a second or maybe even a third one. You'll be amazed when you see what I can do with this farm."

"Why?" Kim asked.

Brobing looked confused. "What do you mean?"

"You're already a rich man," Kim replied. "You said so yourself. Isn't that enough? Why do you want to have more?"

"Why not?" Brobing asked, suddenly deflated. "I'm not taking anything away from anyone, am I? The land is big enough. Everyone could have a farm like this one, and there would still be enough room. I don't understand your question."

Kim didn't answer, because right then, he was strongly reminded of a topic he'd been studying in school. The biology teacher had even taken his class to the countryside so they could understand the topic. Kim walked a few steps into the freshly plowed field and squatted down. Lost in thought, he scooped up a handful of the turned soil and let it run through his fingers. The slight breeze blowing across the field carried most of the soil away in the form of gray dust.

"The ground is completely leached out," he noted. "You're plowing too deep. There's clay mixed in the topsoil, see?"

Brobing nodded. "We now have three harvests a year," he said. "That's hard on the soil. In an another year or two, we'll have to abandon the field."

"And then?" asked Kim asked gravely.

Brobing shrugged. "We'll plow a different piece of land," he said. "There's enough there."

"At some point, it's all going to be used up," Kim pointed out.

"Not likely." Brobing laughed. "But if it is, then we'll leave and build a new farmhouse somewhere else. Believe me, that's not a problem. Chonk will build me a new house in one night if I order him to."

Kim shuddered. He slowly stood up and gazed at the powerful iron man who approached with long strides, pushing the several hundred pounds of plow before him like a child pushing a doll carriage.

"At some point, there won't be any more land, Brobing," Kim said.

"Nonsense," the farmer objected. "Magic Moon is large, young sir—much larger than we can imagine. And besides, this isn't the only land there is."

"So you can make new land, eh?" Kim asked.

He intended for his words to sound sarcastic, but apparently they didn't, because Brobing nodded with complete seriousness.

"You've seen the steep wall that borders the marshes." The farmer pointed in the direction from which Kim had come. "A few years ago, the land between here and there was just barren rocks and mountains. The iron men carried off the debris and created fertile farmland. So you see, they can move mountains, if necessary. They can drain the marshes and create new living space."

"The marshes?" Kim thought of Lizard. "You don't mean that seriously, Brobing. That land doesn't belong to you."

"It doesn't belong to anyone," the farmer countered. "What else lives there besides a few snakes and lizards? But such a thing won't be necessary, believe me." He smiled again. "You aren't the only one who thinks that way. Some people say the iron men aren't good for us, but they're wrong. Look around! The first time we met, I was a poor man!"

"If you say so."

"And today," Brobing continued, "my family and I lack for nothing. I don't have to worry about storms or about bringing in the next harvest. Chonk takes all that off my back. Believe me—we're happy."

Kim refrained from replying. He suddenly recalled the expression of pain in Jara's eyes when she'd spoken of her vanished son, and he knew then that Brobing was wrong.

As they headed back to the house, the farmer suddenly stopped and looked to the west. Kim, too, squinted in the direction of the setting sun; he made out a tiny figure approaching the farm.

"Are you expecting visitors?" he asked. Without knowing why, he felt an odd unease.

Brobing shook his head. "Not really," he said slowly. "But sometimes—"

He broke off and stared hard at the approaching rider. Then, he cried out in surprise, "It's Jarrn!" He hesitated for a second before running into the house—leaving Kim standing there, completely forgotten.

Kim warily studied the approaching rider.

From Brobing's behavior, it was very clear that the unannounced visitor wasn't terribly welcome. Kim, too, felt strangely disquieted. For all that, however, the approaching rider hardly looked threatening.

"Comical" might be a better description, Kim thought.

As the stranger guided his pony into the farmyard and dismounted, Kim initially thought that he was a child. At the very most, the fellow came up to Kim's chin, and he would be that tall only if he stood on his tiptoes. He was dressed entirely in black: black boots, black pants and shirt, and a black cape that came down to his ankles, which flapped around his spindly body. His face reminded Kim of a half-starved vulture's. His hair, which was mostly hidden under the pointed hood of his cape, was black. His fingernails were black, too, for that matter.

"Who are you?" the little man asked crossly, stomping over to Kim and puffing up in a confrontational way.

"A good question," Kim replied. The dwarf's arrogant tone of voice irritated him. "Maybe I should ask that of you."

The dwarf's eyes flashed in anger. "I am Jarrn," he snapped. "I come here twice a year. But I've never seen you here before. Are you part of the farmer's brood?"

Kim barely restrained himself from giving in to the sudden impulse to grab the dwarf and shake him until he fell out of his absurd, draconian clothes. "That 'brood' of farmers, as you call them, are my friends . . . you twerp," he said, noticing with malicious pleasure how the dwarf's dusty face paled at the insult. "I'm a guest here."

"Well, I am, too," Jarrn said venomously. "Now, move out of the way so I can collect what's owed me." He raised his hand in order to shove Kim aside, but Kim didn't budge. "Move, boy," Jarrn threatened, "Or else—"

"Or else what?" Kim challenged, clenching his fists. He didn't recognize himself. This wasn't the way he normally behaved, getting goaded into a fight. But the mere presence of the dwarf irritated him, like Kim's rage was being induced by some sort of chemical coming off the black-attired figure.

The dwarf didn't answer.

Kim heard footsteps, and when he turned around, he saw that Chonk had let go of the plow and was striding across the freshly broken field. His green eye glowed in a threatening manner.

"What's going on?" Brobing's voice called from inside the house.

Kim turned his head and saw the farmer and his wife hurrying toward them. "Kim! Jarrn! What's going on here?"

"Nothing," Kim said sullenly.

Jarrn pointed his spindly forefinger in accusation. "This insolent bumpkin didn't want to let me in the house, Brobing. Is he a relative of yours?"

"He's . . . the son of a good friend," the farmer said. "Please excuse his behavior. He doesn't know who you are, and he's still young. You know how children are." As he said these words, he darted a conspiratorial look at Kim.

"Ah, yes," Jarrn rasped in a condescending manner, "I do know. That's why I detest them—almost as much as farmers' broods."

To Kim's utter surprise, Brobing laughed at these words—although the laughter did sound a little forced. Then, with a gesture, Brobing invited Jarrn into the house. "Please, come in. You must be tired and hungry. My wife can make something for you to eat."

"No time for that," Jarrn replied curtly. "I have to be on my way. I want to visit two other farms today. But I'll have a cup of wine while you're getting the money."

"The money?" Brobing blinked in surprise. "Already?"

"Don't you have it?" the dwarf asked, narrowing one eye mistrustfully.

"Yes, yes, of course," Brobing reassured him hastily. "It's all there. I just wasn't expecting you yet. Last year—"

"Last year was last year," Jarrn interrupted tartly. "If you don't have it, I'll come by again in a month. But I'm not going to wait any longer than that. If you don't have the money, then I'm taking him back with me." He pointed at Chonk, who was now very close, but approaching at a slower pace.

Brobing looked where the dwarf pointed. "I do have it," he said hastily. "Even more than that: I can pay the amount that is due in winter right now. That will save you a trip, Master Jarrn."

"You seem to be doing quite well," Jarrn said, without directly replying to the farmer's words.

"I can't complain."

Brobing only now noticed that Chonk had left his work. His face darkened. "What's gotten into you?!" he shouted. "Go back to the field, Chonk. Right now! It needs to be plowed by this evening!"

Chonk obeyed, but—Kim observed—only after the dwarf made a fleeting, almost imperceptible movement with his hand, which Brobing didn't notice.

They went into the house. Brobing and the dwarf sat down at the table where Kim had eaten the previous night. Kim briefly considered sitting down with them; but when he saw the visitor glaring at him, he decided to join Jara in the kitchen, instead. She already had started to prepare the evening meal.

Jara was standing at the hearth, stirring the contents of a huge cast-iron pot with a wooden spoon. A tantalizing fragrance drifted over. She smiled as Kim walked in and, with a nod of her head, indicated a stack of shallow porcelain bowls neatly arranged on a shelf. She smiled again when Kim took one of the bowls, and she gave him a large helping of soup.

"Who is that?" Kim asked, before tasting the first spoonful. He pointed at the front room.

"Jarrn?" Jara made a face, which answered his question—or at least, it was clear what she thought of the unexpected guest. "A dwarf from the eastern mountains," she said. "We bought Chonk from him. Until we own Chonk outright, he comes twice a year to collect his money."

"Why does Brobing put up with his rudeness?" Kim asked.

Jara smiled tolerantly. "I can tell you've never met any dwarves from the eastern mountains," she said. "They're the most impolite people you could imagine. I don't think anyone has ever heard a friendly word from them. But they're not evil. They're good craftsmen. Their forged metalwork is famous and prized throughout the land."

"If I were in your place, I would teach him some manners," Kim said.

Jara sighed. "Those people are not bad, Kim," she repeated. "Just impolite. But if you know how to handle them, you can overlook that. At least, Brobing can. I usually head into the kitchen when Jarrn shows up. He never stays long. Besides," she added with an audible sigh, "the iron man does belong to Jarrn until we've paid him off, which will happen next summer. Until then, he can reclaim Chonk at any time."

"And then, you'd be ruined," Kim guessed.

Jara smiled. "No. We would have to hire a few men. That would be expensive, but we wouldn't be ruined."

Kim finished eating his soup and went into the front room. Brobing handed the dwarf a bag chock full of gold pieces. Jarrn meticulously counted them, scribbled something on a piece of paper, and then stuck the bag and paper in his shirt with a dissatisfied grunt. "So, I'll just be back one more time, next summer," he said. "After that, Chonk will belong to you for good."

"I maybe could use a second iron man," Brobing said.

Jarrn shrugged his shoulders. "If we can agree on a price . . . There's a great demand—continually growing. We can't make as many as people want. Let's talk about that next year."

His scrawny hand reached for the cup of wine that Brobing had set down. The dwarf peered suspiciously at Kim over the cup's rim. "The son of a friend, you say?"

"Yes." Brobing again shot Kim one of those conspiratorial looks. "This is the first time he's been here. I don't think he's ever seen any of your people."

"First time, eh?" Jarrn's eyes narrowed. "Where do you come from, boy?"

"From New—" Kim started to say. But then, seeing a desperate look flare up in Brobing's eyes, he hastily corrected himself: "From a land that's very far to the west of here. I don't think you would be familiar with it, sir," he concluded politely.

"I know many lands," Jara replied, "but this is of no interest to me. I have to be on my way, now." He stood up. "Well, until next time. And make sure you have the money by then—all of it, and on time."

Brobing breathed an obvious sigh of relief when Jarrn left the house. The farmer didn't even bother to escort the dwarf to his horse or wait until Jarrn had ridden away, which would have been the polite thing to do. "A very eccentric fellow," he murmured, shaking his head. "Dwarves are known for their uncouth ways, but Jarrn is worse than any I have ever met."

Eccentric? thought Kim. No, he didn't find Jarrn "eccentric" at all. "Sinister" was more like it.

He couldn't get rid of the feeling that he'd see Jarrn again—sooner than he'd like.

The atmosphere was subdued during the evening meal. Although Brobing and his wife tried not to let it show, Kim sensed that they were depressed. He didn't ask them about it, but he assumed it had something to do with the dwarf.

After sundown, Kim went to his room. He told the farmers he was tired and, after all, he did need to get up very early the next morning. While that was the truth, it wasn't the real reason he voluntarily had gone to bed right after dark—he normally never would have dreamed of doing that. But from Brobing's and Jara's subdued manner, Kim concluded that they had things to say to each other in private and were just too polite to mention it to their guest. So, Kim went to bed early.

He rested in Torum's room for almost an hour, trying to sort out his thoughts; his hands were folded behind his head and eyes were wide open, staring at the white plaster ceiling.

It was in vain. Everything was so confusing and unsettling that the longer he tried to bring order to the chaos, the worse his head hurt. Eventually, he got up again and restlessly paced the length of his room. It wasn't late yet. Brobing and his wife, Jara, certainly would be up. Kim decided to do what he should have done in the first place: simply ask them what was going on. What was going on with Jarrn the dwarf and this iron man and the peculiar changes that were occurring to Brobing and his family and, in fact, all of Magic Moon? The farmer certainly knew more than he'd told Kim.

He quietly opened the door. As he stepped into the hallway, he could hear Jara's and Brobing's muffled voices coming up from the first floor. Kim couldn't make out what they were saying, but their raised voices alarmed him. Were they arguing? Kim stood still, listened for a moment, and then he tiptoed farther. He didn't feel quite right about eavesdropping on the couple after they'd been so friendly and helpful to him, yet he had the feeling it would be better if he did.

"I understand what you're saying," he heard Brobing say, "but he'll notice it. I told him it's a full day's ride to the river. What am I supposed to tell him when he finds out that it's not even one hour?"

Kim's ears pricked up. Brobing had lied to him? Why?

"He doesn't have to find out," his wife replied. "At least, not right away. Let him stay here a while yet, Brobing. Just one more day. Or two."

"Or a week, right?" Brobing sighed and Kim practically could hear him shake his head. "Jara, believe me. I understand you. I understand you all too well. Torum's loss breaks my heart, too. But Kim is *not* our son, and he never will be."

"Maybe he'll like it here," Jara insisted. "If he stays a while, he'll see how beautiful it is. We can give him anything he wants."

"He's not here because he *wants* something," Brobing said, using an almost gentle tone now. "You know that, Jara. You . . ."

Kim stopped listening. He crept back to his room as softly as he had come and closed the door behind him. He felt stunned. The little that he'd heard was enough. Brobing actually had lied to him—because Jara didn't want Kim to leave. But she seriously couldn't think that he'd stay here and replace her lost son! The thought made Kim angry. But only for a very short moment because, almost in the same instant, he understood why Jara felt that way. Brobing had said it himself: The loss of their son had broken her heart. People who were in despair sometimes did desperate things. Kim wasn't angry anymore; actually, he felt sorry for Jara.

Instead of going down to the front room as he had planned originally, Kim sat down on the bed and waited. He needed to get away—not early tomorrow morning, but this very night. Forget about Kelhim. When Jara got up, she would find a note on Kim's nightstand that said he'd left extremely early and very quietly so as not to disturb her or her husband.

He waited until it was quiet in the farmyard and the house. Kim's patience was put to the test because Jara and her husband continued to talk for a while. Kim estimated that it was close to midnight by the time he finally dared to get up. He listened with his ear pressed to the wooden door.

It was absolutely still. The only thing Kim heard was the blood rushing in his own ears. He gently opened the door a crack and listened again. Nothing moved.

Just as Kim was about to leave the room and tiptoe out of the house, he thought he heard a noise behind him. Startled, he turned around.

Nothing. He was alone. The room was dark, empty, and silent. Yet, something was there. He could still hear it—a peculiar creaking and groaning that he couldn't figure out.

With some trepidation, Kim closed the door and stepped back into his room. He began a thorough and, as it turned out, fruitless search. As he approached the window, he noticed that the noises were coming from the farmyard, not from his room. It was a very warm night, so the window was open. Complete silence had settled on the farm, so all outdoor sounds were magnified. Kim peered out, taking care to remain in the shadows so that no one below could see him.

It took a while for his eyes to get used to the silvery moonlight outside. Then, he was so shocked by what he saw that he almost screamed.

Next to the barn was a huge shadow, bigger—much bigger—than a human and, by moonlight, nothing more than an indistinct, ominous black shape. Kim's very first thought was that it must be Kelhim, coming to finish what he'd begun two days ago. Then, he saw the shape, while as massive as the bear's, was too angular and ungainly. Besides, Kelhim didn't have a glowing green eye! It was Chonk.

What in the world was the iron man doing out there in the middle of the night? The answer wasn't long in coming: A second, much smaller silhouette suddenly appeared next to the giant iron man. The figure had spindly arms and legs and a cloak with a pointed hood.

Jarrn.

The two of them were much too far from the house for Kim to understand what the dwarf was saying to Chonk, but Kim saw the small figure gesticulating wildly with both arms, time and again pointing at the house—and at the window to Kim's room.

A moment later, Chonk turned around with heavy, awkward movements and stomped toward the house.

Kim's heart jumped almost as high as his throat, pounding twice as hard and fast. His first instinct was to rush out of the house as quickly as he could. But almost immediately, Kim realized it was too late for that. Chonk wasn't very agile, but the barn wasn't very far away, either. The iron man would be in the house long before Kim had time to run out of the room, down the hall, and down the stairs. Besides, there was a risk that Brobing and Jara might wake up from that, and Chonk might harm them if they got in his way.

Kim waited, his heart pounding, until the iron man circled around the house and could no longer see his window. Then, acting quickly, he climbed onto the windowsill, took a deep breath, and jumped ten feet to the ground.

The impact wasn't as hard as Kim had expected. Nevertheless, he lost his balance, rolled over three or four times, and ended up on his hands and knees. Staggering up, he found himself looking directly into the grimy face of the dwarf, who stared at him in astonishment from under his pointed hood.

But Jarrn had the bad luck to recover one second later than Kim. He opened his mouth, but before he could cry out, Kim already had grabbed his collar and yanked him up so roughly that the cry turned into a mere gurgle.

Kim took a quick, desperate look around. Chonk had disappeared behind the house and probably was stomping up the stairs at this very moment. It surely would take at least a minute for him to reach Kim's room and discover that it was empty—probably another minute to retrace his steps. That was extremely little time—perhaps enough to reach the stable. Besides, what other choice did Kim have? He took off, dragging the furiously kicking dwarf behind him.

Jarrn gasped, spewing venom and gall, but Kim stubbornly kept a firm grip on him—tight enough so that he could breathe but not call out. With his shins kicked black and blue and one arm full of scratches, Kim rushed into the stable, ignoring Jarrn's wild flailing. He ran to the last stall in the long row.

Stardust raised his head and looked at him as he approached. Kim was elated to see that the steed already had on a saddle blanket, as well as a bridle. The saddle itself hung over the stall door. Kim had a lot of practice saddling horses, however. He needed barely a minute to put on the saddle and roughly secure it. During this activity, Jarrn remained pinned under Kim's left arm, where he continued to drivel, twist, and writhe.

Kim had opened the stall door and was about to swing up into the saddle when he found himself looking into a pair of watery, dark eyes, stared out at him from an absolutely hideous face.

"You owe me another fish," said a voice from on top of the saddle.

Chunklet sniffed in Jarrn's direction, making a sound unsuitable for polite company. "You're not planning to fob that one off on me, are you? I don't want him."

Kim breathed an audible sigh of relief. He had received quite a fright just then. Now, he was happier than he'd been for a long time.

"Chunklet," he said. "I have to leave." He prepared to swing up into the saddle, but Chunklet just sat there, refusing to budge.

"You still owe me something," Chunklet insisted.

"I can't do it right now," Kim groaned. But he realized there was no point in wasting valuable time arguing about a fish. "All right," he said. "I'll catch you your fish. Come with me."

Chunklet suspiciously considered the matter for a while before obediently creeping forward and grabbing hold of Stardust's mane. Kim finally was able climb into the saddle. He plopped the dwarf in front of him.

Jarrn still was flailing about, wilding kicking and scratching. "Let me go! Are you trying to break every bone in my body?" When Kim briefly loosened his grip on Jarrn's collar, the dwarf gasped.

"Not a bad idea," Kim muttered grimly, guiding Stardust to the stable door. "But first, we're going to have a nice long talk, just as soon as we're a few miles away from here. Go, Stardust!"

The horse leaped forward, but it stopped again so abruptly that Kim almost was thrown off. Chunklet, meanwhile, sailed over Stardust's head, turning a somersault in the air.

A massive shape suddenly had appeared in the stable doorway. Large, angular, and as black as night—it blocked their way. Its green eye flashed menacingly.

"Ha!" Jarrn cried. "You didn't count on that. Now, let's see if you can talk your way out of this!"

Chonk lumbered one step forward, shaking the whole stable. Stardust danced in place, and the other horses moved uneasily in their stalls.

"Get him, Chonk," screamed Jarrn. "Pull that rascal off the horse. I command you!"

Chonk took another step. His terrifying digger claw opened up, and the steel jags on it flashed like fangs.

Kim urged the horse forward, as if he wanted to ride right over Chonk. At the last moment, he pulled on the reins with all his might and threw himself back in the saddle. Stardust screamed in pain and surprise, rearing up. His whirling front hoofs struck Chonk's iron head, and it sounded like a large bell tolling. Kim could see the iron man shake under the impact of the hoofs. He tottered—but he didn't fall.

Stardust whinnied with fear and danced back.

Only through desperate wiggling was Kim able to evade the giant digger claw grabbing at him. Chonk began backing him into a corner. Stardust had to retreat, step by step. Although the iron man was slow and clumsy, there simply wasn't enough room to rush past him.

"Do it, Chonk!" Jarrn yelled. "Grab him!"

Kim did the only thing that he could think of: He grabbed Jarrn with both hands, lifting the dwarf high and throwing the little man at the robot as if Jarrn were a living cannonball.

Jarrn gave a blood-curdling yell, and Chonk instantly raised his arms to catch his master. He succeeded—with the wrong hand, however: the digger claw.

As Kim rushed past on Stardust's back, he heard a sound like a bear's jaw snapping shut, and Jarrn's furious yell turned into a pained rattling. By then, Kim was out of the stable and already racing into the night, bent over Stardust's neck.

VII

Kim had been planning to head south toward the river and the town that Brobing had mentioned. But the terrain became increasingly rugged, and once the initial excitement was over, Kim quickly realized that Jarrn—if he'd survived—surely would search for him there first. On top of that, Stardust started limping.

At first, Kim barely noticed it. He understood that the magnificent steed's gait was a little slower and no longer quite as smooth. Soon, however, Kim realized that Stardust hesitated slightly before putting down his right forefoot, then very quickly lifting it, as if he were in pain.

Concerned that the horse might have been injured during his attack on Chonk, Kim halted, climbed out of the saddle, and bent down. Despite the full moon, it was very dark. He couldn't see any wound—at least, not at first glance. But Stardust abruptly drew back his leg with a startled whinny; and when Kim examined it again—this time more carefully—he felt a sudden, stabbing pain. Withdrawing his hand in surprise, he saw a drop of blood glistening on his finger.

Very cautiously, Kim once again reached for Stardust's foreleg. The horse nervously was switching his tail from side to side and looking at Kim with his large, intelligent eyes. However, he didn't move—as if he clearly sensed that Kim had no intention of hurting him. Just below the horse's knee, there was a finger-length quill, as sharp as a needle, protruding from the animal's sensitive flesh.

Kim pulled out the quill, threw it away in disgust, and carefully searched the horse's leg for other quills. He didn't find any. On the other hand, Kim did find something else.

Kim was halfway under the horse's belly when he lifted his head and found a disgusting little face. It was Chunklet, who evidently had grabbed hold of the saddle belt at the last moment and clung to it until now. No wonder Stardust could barely walk: It was as if someone had strapped a large pincushion to his underside.

"Get down from there right now!" Kim ordered sharply.

Chunklet complied—simply releasing his grip. He would have fallen right onto Kim's face if Kim hadn't dodged in the nick of time.

Kim laboriously got back up on his feet, complaining and cursing all the way.

"Is something the matter?" Chunklet asked, before Kim stood up all the way up.

Kim looked at him, eyes flashing, about to fly into a rage; but then, he thought better of it and confined his reaction to an angry scowl. Without saying a word, he extended his hand toward the pommel—then stopped. He tightened all the saddle's belts and buckles.

"Come on," was all he said.

Chunklet leaped up onto Stardust's neck, where he clutched the horse's mane, just as he'd done earlier in the stable.

Kim hesitated. *Maybe Jarrn has pulled himself together and already is pursuing us.* Kim decided not to worry about that right now. He could handle that twerp. Luckily, Chonk couldn't run fast enough to catch up with them, even though Stardust was trotting slower now. *Maybe we should go to the town after all,* he reflected. That way, they could get food and other necessary provisions—and, above all, ask the way to Gorywynn.

As he was about to ride off, however, Chunklet spoke up: "I wouldn't recommend that direction."

"Why not?" Kim asked skeptically.

"Because it would take you right to the bear's cave."

Kim looked at Chunklet, startled. "Kelhim's cave? It's here?"

"Not here," Chunklet said, correcting him. "In this direction. See that forest over there? Ride that way and, in an hour, your old friend will have you for his dinner entree."

"You've been there?" asked Kim just to make sure. "You know where Kelhim's cave is?"

"The stench is unmistakable." Chunklet shuddered.

Kim thought it over for a moment. Then, he asked once again, "Are you absolutely certain you can find the cave?"

"Sure," replied Chunklet. Then, he added incredulously, "You don't want to go there, do you?"

"Kelhim and I are old friends," Kim said pensively.

"So I saw! He almost ate you."

"I know," Kim sighed. "In spite of that, I . . . I'm sure he . . . he just didn't recognize me. He would never hurt me."

"Ha!" Chunklet scoffed. "He might swallow you whole."

"He just didn't recognize me," Kim insisted. "I'm sure he . . . he'll remember."

"So, you're sure," Chunklet said sardonically. "Sure enough to stake your life on it?"

Kim looked at his little traveling companion. He didn't reply; but after a while, he turned Stardust around and rode off—in the very direction his prickly guide had warned him against. . . .

It took them quite a bit longer than Chunklet had said it would, probably because Stardust couldn't move through the thick underbrush half as quickly as the spiny little creature could. Chunklet continuously whined and complained, trying to dissuade Kim from his plan. But eventually, he understood that Kim's resolve was unshakable, so he pouted quietly.

When they finally arrived at the bear's lair, the surrounding forest was almost as dark as an underground tunnel. The den was located in a glade deep in the heart of the forest—so well hidden that Kim would have ridden right past it if Chunklet hadn't reluctantly shown him the way there. Far above their heads, the tops of the ancient trees interlaced, forming an impenetrable roof of leaves through which barely any moonlight could pass. Kim saw nothing but black silhouettes all around him.

The den wasn't much brighter. It wasn't a mountain cave like the one Kelhim previously inhabited, but a hole, leading down into the ground at an angle.

"Well?" Chunklet growled. "Satisfied now?"

Kim listened. He heard nothing but the soft rustling of the forest and the hammering of his own heart. It was eerie and still.

"He doesn't seem to be here," Kim murmured.

"Oh, that will soon change," Chunklet said spitefully. "Sooner than you'd like."

Kim dismounted, ignoring Chunklet's loud and insistent protests, and cautiously approached the large den. As he walked, he caught a slight whiff of decomposing flesh, which grew stronger the closer Kim got to the cave. It smelled like a carnivore's den. What if Kelhim didn't recognize him this time, either? Kim chose not to think about that. After glancing in all directions just to be sure, he cautiously began his descent.

He left the last gleam of light behind him as he crawled on all fours, yard after yard, until the steeply slanting shaft leveled off again. Now completely dark, the cave's stench truly was overwhelming.

With outstretched arms, Kim blindly walked forward, groping his way—before promptly stumbling and falling flat on his face. As he straightened up again, cursing and muttering, he touched a piece of wood. Surprised, he immediately jerked his hand back. When he reached out again, however, he could feel that the object actually was a torch. Surprised—and also relieved that he wouldn't have to grope around helplessly anymore—he checked the pockets of the jacket that Brobing had given him and found what he was looking for: two flints, which people in this land always carried with them.

Before long, the flickering reddish light of the flames banished the foul-smelling den's darkness. Soon, Kim also found an explanation for his discovery: The owner of the torch—or, rather, what was left of him—was lying not far away. It was skeleton, and not the only one. Kim shuddered as he lifted the torch high over his head and slowly turned in a circle. Countless bones, skulls, and skeletons were scattered around, and not all of them belonged to animals. Judging by appearances, it seemed Brobing had been right when he'd stated that Kelhim had become a murderous predator. It was insane to come here.

It was too late for such regrets, though. No sooner had Kim thought this than he heard a scuttling sound. Chunklet suddenly appeared in the area illuminated by the torch.

"He's coming!" he cried. "The bear! Run! Hide somewhere, you fool!"

Hide? Kim desperately considered his options. *Where?* While the cave was large, it was empty except for gnawed bones. For a moment, he seriously considered hiding under one of the bone piles; but then, he immediately changed his mind. Kelhim would catch his scent in an instant, Kim was sure of that.

Besides, he hadn't come here to hide. He wanted to talk with Kelhim.

Kim bravely turned and raised the torch a little higher, keeping an eye on the cave entrance.

He didn't wait long. Despite Kelhim's enormous size, the bear moved silently, like a cat. His shadow filled the bright circle of the entrance long before he actually appeared there. Kim could smell him.

He shuddered again. He'd never noticed before that Kelhim had an unpleasant odor—but the scruffy, giant creature that suddenly appeared in the cave entrance stank like a savage beast,like death.

For several seconds, which felt like eternity to Kim, the bear simply stood there and stared at him. His one eye flashing angrily, he looked wary—perhaps even puzzled by this tiny human who had dared to invade his realm. Kim also stood still and stared at Kelhim. A terrible realization grew within him:

He had made a fatal mistake. He was so afraid that he couldn't think straight, but he didn't move—not even when Kelhim finally woke up from his trance and slowly started to move toward Kim. Kelhim warily scanned the cave and sniffed like a hound homing in on a scent. Perhaps he feared an ambush. The bear could have reached Kim in one leap, killing him on the spot with a single swipe of his paw. Instead, he approached with small, cautious movements.

Kim raised the torch a little higher, so that its light illuminated almost the entire cave. The hand that held the torch shook so bad that the shadows on the cave wall danced chaotically. Nevertheless, he didn't retreat a single step as Kelhim padded toward him.

In the end, it was the bear who stopped. Although Kim knew better, he thought he discerned a puzzled expression on Kelhim's face as the bear assessed the trembling human. His sensitive bear nose probably smelled something akin to the scent given off by a frightened flock of sheep that caught sight of a wolf but made no attempt to flee.

"Hel-lo, Kelhim," Kim stammered. His voice sounded strange to his own ears. "Are y-y-you h-h-happy to s-s-see me again?"

Kelhim stared at him for a while longer before letting out a growl that shook the entire cave. Dirt and little rocks rained down from the walls.

"It's me, Kelhim!" Kim shouted desperately. "Think! You know me! We're friends!"

Kelhim stood up on his hind legs, bared his fearsome teeth, and spread his claws, each one the size of a small dagger. He lumbered a step closer.

Everything inside Kim screamed at him to back away, but he kept his fear under control and bravely looked Kelhim in the eye.

The bear actually hesitated again. His gaze started to reflect something like confusion, and then his face took on a peculiar expression: sadness, pain, and a spark of memory—but also unbridled fury.

"Kelhim!" Kim pleaded. "Come to your senses! We're friends! Remember the battle for Gorywynn? Our journey on Rangarig's back?"

Kelhim's growl deepened, becoming throatier. The bear couldn't make up his mind. It looked as if he were suffering unspeakable pain.

In truth, he was. Kim saw the animal stubbornly fighting a battle inside himself—struggling with something there the whole time but forgotten . . . buried deep, deep beneath the predatory instincts.

"Please, Kelhim!" he begged. "Remember, we—"

The predator won out. Before Kim even had time to register the movement, Kelhim's paw swung at him. He was flung across the cave into the back wall, where he lay gasping for breath. The torch flew out of Kim's hand and sailed off in a high arc. It didn't go out, though.

"K-Kelhim!" Kim stammered. "Please don't! We're friends!"

Kelhim growled, returned to all fours, and sauntered closer, his teeth bared.

"No!" Kim screamed, raising his hands protectively over his head. "Kelhim! *Please!*"

Suddenly, the monster halted.

Two other shadows—one tiny and one huge—had appeared outside the entrance to the cave.

A jeering voice sneered, "P-p-please d-d-d-don't, Kelhim. We are f-f-friends!"

Kelhim turned his head with an angry growl.

Someone outside approached with a light, tripping gait, continuing his mocking imitation of Kim's voice: "Your f-f-f-friend, he's going to eat you up, you fool. I came just in time to see the best part, didn't I?" The dwarf giggled like a madman and started hopping about, slapping his thigh in pure pleasure.

Jarrn!

Kelhim's gaze wandered uncertainly back and forth between Kim and the drooling dwarf, and Kim could see something going on inside the bear's scruffy head. Then, Kelhim slowly turned toward Jarrn, rising up on his hind legs.

Jarrn stopped behaving like Rumpelstiltskin. He made a brief hand movement. From behind him, Chonk stepped into the cave, his menacing iron claw open.

"Stay where you are, you overgrown teddy bear!" the dwarf said angrily. "Get that one over there." He pointed at Kim. "That should be enough to satisfy your hunger. Or leave him to me: I have a score to settle with him."

"Kelhim," Kim whimpered. "Help me!"

Somehow, this whispered cry for help accomplished what Kim's appeals to their old friendship had failed to do. Kelhim stared at him, then whirling around and throwing himself at the iron man with a tremendous roar.

What happened after that was like a nightmare to Kim, when he thought about it later. The two giants collided with indescribable force, causing the whole cave to shake. Kelhim roared and bellowed as his massive paws crashed down on the iron giant's head and shoulders. His blows were so powerful that the iron man tottered.

Chonk fought in silence, but his blows were no less powerful. Time and again, Chonk's terrifying claw struck the bear, and it was evident that Kelhim's strength gradually waned. Unlike the bear, Kelhim's iron opponent knew neither exhaustion nor pain. As great as Kelhim's strength was, it wasn't enough to break apart the iron plates Chonk's body comprised.

It seemed as if the two black giants pounded each other forever. The cave shook. Near the entrance, a whole piece of the ceiling fell down, covering Chonk with dirt and rocks, without harming him.

In the end, the bear began to retreat.

Kelhim was staggering. Several of his claws had broken off. His paws and snout were bleeding, and his growl betrayed his pain. He was shuddering more and more under the onslaught by Chonk's iron claw.

"Kelhim . . ." Kim whispered. Suddenly, he realized that the bear had been beaten, and that the iron man wouldn't stop striking until his adversary lay dead on the ground. Kim's eyes filled with tears.

Jarrn broke into shrill laughter. "Now you see how scared I am of you, teddy bear!" he screamed. "No one gets in my way without paying for it with his life. No one!" Gleefully hopping up and down, he pointed his spindly finger at Kim as if it were a dagger. "And you're next! I'll think up something special for you, you vile oaf!"

"Maybe," said Kim quietly. "If you have enough time, that is." He abruptly lunged forward and grabbed the dwarf.

Jarrn wasn't unprepared this time. Even so, he was sufficiently surprised. He tried to pull out a dagger from under his cloak; however, Kim thwarted this attempt with a kick, which hurled the dwarf backward and knocked the weapon from his hand. Out of the corner of his eye, Kim saw Chonk abruptly move away from his victim and swivel around. But before the iron man had completed this motion, Kim got to the dwarf, yanked him to his feet, and put his own dagger to Jarrn's throat.

"Order Chonk to back off!" Kim said through clenched teeth.

He didn't speak very loudly; perhaps that was what made Jarrn understand how seriously he meant this threat. The dwarf gulped and arched his head back as far as he could, but the point of Kim's knife relentlessly followed this movement. Jarrn's eyes started to cross as he tried to watch the blade.

"Back off!" he snarled. "Chonk! Let him be."

The iron man halted close behind Kim. His murderous claw already was open, prepared to seize Kim.

"Send him away!" Kim demanded. "Tell him to get out of here! Tell Chonk to leave and go back to Brobing's farm!"

"You—"

Kim emphasized his order by increasing the pressure on the dagger, scratching Jarrn's thin neck. Suddenly, the dwarf was in a hurry to comply. "You heard what he said, Chonk!" he croaked. "Go back to the farmer's brood. Wait for me there."

The ground under Kim's feet started to shake as the iron colossus obediently turned around and left the cave. After a few seconds, Kim heard cracking and splitting sounds as Chonk made his way through the underbrush.

He slowly withdrew the knife blade from Jarrn's neck, but he didn't release his grip on the dwarf.

Although Jarrn loudly resisted, Kim held him down, ripped a strip of cloth from his cloak, and bound the dwarf, securely knotting the material. Then, he unceremoniously dropped this gift-wrapped package on the ground next to the cave's entrance and hurried over to Kelhim.

What he saw broke his heart: Kelhim had collapsed on the ground. His chest rose and sank in rapid, shallow breaths, and his entire face was covered with blood. His single eye looked dull; deep, labored rumbling and rattling came from his chest. More than anything else, this sound told Kim how severely wounded the giant bear was.

"Kelhim," he whispered. "Kelhim, wh-what happened to you?"

Kelhim didn't reply, but his eye searched for Kim; despite the pain and bottomless despair reflected in the bear's gaze, Kim saw that he no longer was regarding a wild animal. Kelhim was restored to his senses.

But at what price!

"Kelhim!" Kim whispered once again, close to despair. "How are you?"

"Kim?" murmured the bear in reply. "Is that . . . you?"

"Yes." Kim slowly sank to his knees next to the bear's massive head and reached out to touch the bear's snout. His eyes filled with tears, which he didn't try to hold back. He knew that Kelhim was going to die. Chonk's blows had severely damaged something inside his body. "Yes, Kelhim," Kim said once again, "It's me."

"Kim," the bear said softly. He tried to move but no longer had the strength. "You came. Good."

"Don't talk," Kim said, sobbing. "Save your energy, Kelhim. Everything will be all right." His voice broke; he couldn't say anything more.

"Good," Kelhim repeated. His eyes began to glaze over, and suddenly his breath was very, very slow and laborious. "Go to . . . Gorywynn," the bear whispered. "You must free . . . Themistokles."

"Free Themistokles?" Kim blurted out. "So, he's been captured?"

"Themistokles . . ." Kelhim sighed deeply. "Go and . . . Themistokles . . . dwarves . . . the . . . the children." His voice was getting weaker and weaker; Kim could make out only bits and pieces.

"Wait!" he cried. "Kelhim, please—you can't die!"

"Go," Kelhim murmured with the last of his strength. "The dwarves . . . go to . . . another . . . Go . . . and . . . save Magic Moon . . . little hero. . . . You can do it."

Then, with his massive head cradled in Kim's arms, he died without saying another word.

VIII

Sunrise the next morning found Kim sitting on Stardust's back—far away, it seemed, from that dreadful forest clearing where Kim had rediscovered his friend before losing him forever. It had been worse than anything Kim could have imagined.

He was very tired and more depressed than he'd ever been in his life. For hours, he'd sat in Stardust's saddle, slumped over, simply letting the stallion trot on. His hands had clutched the reins only to keep hold of them, not to guide the horse in any particular direction. Tears had streamed down his face the whole time, until his eyes finally were so dry that they burned.

Kim hardly knew how he'd got here; he had even less idea where "here" might be.

In the first light of morning, he saw softly rolling grassland ahead of him; not too far away, he could make out the shadowy form of a massive cliff, which took up almost half the horizon on the right. The light had a peculiar green hue that Kim couldn't explain—and he didn't worry about it, either. He didn't recall seeing the cliff from afar, although it was big enough that it should have been obvious even at night.

He felt empty and depressed, consumed by pain and grief over the loss of his friend. Only now did he perceive how much Kelhim really had meant to him.

"There's a lake up ahead," chirped a voice ahead of him.

With great effort, Kim pulled himself together, wiped his burning eyes with the back of his hand, and looked down at the red-orange tuft of feathers sitting on Stardust's mane, looking as beautiful as the day.

"Don't worry—you'll get your fish," Kim said in a monotone voice.

Chunklet looked at Kim thoughtfully with his big doe eyes and tried to imitate a human shaking his head. "I'm not talking about the fish for once," he said. "Your horse needs a rest—whether or not you do."

Kim wanted to argue the point, but then he decided it would take too much effort. He just sighed and, for the first time since yesterday evening, pulled on Stardust's reins to change direction. Only then did he notice that the stallion already had left the path on his own and was heading toward a glint of silver water visible through the tall grass. Obviously, Stardust was thirsty.

The lake wasn't particularly large. It was in a natural circular depression, like water that has gathered in the crater of an extinct volcano. However, this wasn't a volcano crater—just the opposite. Kim had never seen anything more magnificent. Wherever he looked, magnificent flowers in every color and shape imaginable blanketed the lakeshore. There were roses, hyacinths, daffodils, chrysanthemums, tulips, and one hundred other varieties that Kim couldn't name and had never seen before—in an array of colors that looked as if a rainbow had fallen from the sky and come to rest right there. The flowers grew in tight, concentric circles around the lake—some so close to the water that they seemed to be bending over to drink. It took a while to find a place where he could lead Stardust to the water without trampling the glorious flowers.

As Stardust thirstily lowered his head toward the water, Kim stiffly dismounted. He could hardly move. He realized he'd been sitting in the saddle for many hours without a break.

He looked around in confusion. Although he still was sad, he couldn't take his eyes away from the beauty of this lake. It was as if someone had gathered together the most beautiful flowers imaginable from everywhere in the world, simply so as to decorate this lake. There was one peculiar thing, however: None of these magnificent flowers had a fragrance. The only thing Kim could smell was the morning dew and the grass.

Kim waited until the horse drank enough water and moved to slake his hunger with the fresh grass. The stallion stepped very cautiously and didn't break a single flower stem as he made his way through the sea of blossoms.

Loud slurping and smacking sounds made Kim look down. A colorful feather duster was squatting right between his feet, doing his best to drink the entire lake dry. Kim patiently waited until Chunklet quenched his thirst. Then, he knelt down, finally taking a drink for himself. The water was ice cold, and it tasted more delicious than any he had ever had before.

How strange!

It took a moment before Kim understood what he was seeing—his own familiar reflection, which his lips touched as he drank. Of course, it was his face . . . and yet, it wasn't. Something about it was . . .

No—words couldn't possibly express it. There didn't seem to be anything evil or dangerous about this curiously altered reflection—quite the opposite. Kim had to exercise self-control to keep from staring at himself. As crazy as it seemed to him, his face was so handsome that he couldn't look away.

He forced himself to sit down cross-legged on the bank. Suddenly, Kim was aware of how tired he was: His back ached, and his arms and legs felt like they weighed hundreds of pounds. He wished he could stretch out on the carpet of flowers, close his eyes, and sleep.

But he couldn't. Actually, he shouldn't have taken this break. He was painfully aware of this. No doubt, Jarrn and his iron companion already were searching for him. When Kim considered how fast they'd tracked him to Kelhim's cave, it seemed that Chonk wasn't nearly as slow as Kim had thought.

Not for the first time since they'd left the forest, Kim wondered why he'd left Jarrn behind in the cave instead of simply taking along the dwarf as he'd done before. Kim was sure he'd have gotten all the information he wanted from the dwarf: Jarrn had a very big mouth, and he was also a very big coward.

Kelhim had tried to tell Kim something—something terribly important. Kim hadn't understood much of it, but at least this was clear: Though the bear had said something about dwarves, Kim had stood up and walked out of the cave, right past the trussed-up gnome. Unfortunately, in his distress over Kelhim's death, he'd forgotten all about Jarrn. . . .

"Are you hungry?" Chunklet asked, suddenly interrupting his thoughts.

Kim shook his head without looking up.

Chunklet flitted over to Kim and nudged him with his soft nose. Almost against his will, Kim had to smile. He lifted his hand and stroked the little animal's velvety soft plumage.

"Can I catch something for you?" Chunklet asked gravely. "A fish? Or a couple of wild pigs?"

"I'm not hungry," Kim said. "Thanks, though."

"All right, I know you're a poor eater," Chunklet persisted, "but still—maybe just *one* wild pig?"

Kim shuddered, and Chunklet's eyes took on a guilty expression. "I'm sorry," he squeaked. "I didn't mean to bother you. . . ." He hesitated a moment before lightly trotting back to the water to look at his own reflection.

Kim's gaze went in the same direction.

That was odd. The face that looked back at him from the water gently smiled, even though Kim knew he was wearing a very serious expression on his face.

"You're deeply grieving, aren't you?" Chunklet asked softly.

Kim nodded. "It was my fault," he said earnestly.

"Your fault? Nonsense! The iron man killed him, not you."

"It was my fault that Chonk went there. See, I led him to the cave. And Kelhim attacked him in order to protect me. Do you understand now?"

"No," Chunklet admitted. "He was a wild animal, after all."

"No, he wasn't," Kim vehemently protested. "Something . . . just turned him into one. He wasn't always like that."

"You mean, he didn't use to be so bad?"

Kim felt tears well up in his eyes again; this time, he held them back.

"I was here in Magic Moon once before, you know," he said. "Back then, Kelhim was . . . " Kim searched for the right word. "He was a friend," he said finally.

"The bear?" Chunklet asked skeptically.

"Back then, everything was different," Kim murmured. "Everything here—this whole land—it was . . ."

"Yes, what?" Chunklet asked encouragingly when Kim's voice trailed off.

Kim shrugged his shoulders, at a loss for words. "I don't know," he admitted. "It was just different."

"It's not bad for things to change."

"I know, but that's not what I mean." Kim suddenly recalled Brobing's words: *"It's as if we're losing something. And we don't even know what it is."*

"This used to be a happy place," he said. "With happy people, and many animals who could speak, and forests that were full of flowers and magical creatures."

"Well, I talk," Chunklet reminded him.

"True." Kim shrugged. His reflection still smiled at him; he was struck by how much his face had changed in the past few days. Exhaustion and fatigue had left their mark on his face, yet he didn't look bad. *Quite the contrary: I look more grown-up because of it,* Kim thought. It was getting harder and harder to look away from his reflection. Chunklet seemed to be affected in the same way, for as they talked, they looked at their own reflections in the water.

Suddenly, Kim heard steps behind him; before he could turn around, a voice said, "If I were you, I wouldn't stare at the lake for so long. It might be bad for you."

Kim whirled around. He had realized immediately from the sound of the voice that the new arrival wasn't Jarrn. However, he still was cautious: The person behind them was a stranger.

The man was very large, very powerful, and looked somehow . . . gnarled. That was the only way Kim could describe him. His skin was dark—much darker than Kim's—and resembled tree bark. Fittingly, he wore a cap of woven leaves. His clothing was green and also consisted of leaves so skillfully fashioned that they looked as if they were a part of him. Although his face was large and rough, the smile dancing in his eyes seemed genuine.

"Listen to what I say," said the man, after he'd given Kim time to take his measure. "Don't look in there too long. It's not good for you."

"Why not?" Kim blurted out.

The stranger laughed—a pleasant, warm sound that immediately won Kim over. Someone who laughed like that couldn't be a threat.

"You're not from around here, are you?" he asked.

Kim shook his head.

The strange-looking man gestured at the water. "That lake is dangerous."

Kim was alarmed.

"We drank water from it!" Chunklet cried excitedly, but the stranger immediately made a reassuring gesture.

"That's all right," the man said. "There's no danger at all from that. You could even bathe in it, if you wanted. The main thing is: Don't look in it too long."

"Why not?" Kim asked once again.

"I'll explain it to you," said the man, "but first, step away from the water—before I end up plucking you and taking you home in a vase."

Kim now was confused completely, but he sensed that the stranger's serious words were meant well. He and Chunklet quickly followed the man outside the circle of flowers.

"Your home must be very far away if you've never heard of the Lake of Vanity," the stranger said.

"Lake of Vanity?"

The man pointed at the water. "It's enchanted," he said. "Its water heals wounds and restores strength, but it's also dangerous: When people look into it, it shows them the image they desire instead of their actual image. Do you understand what I'm saying?"

Kim thought about how pleased he'd been with his own reflection. He nodded hesitantly.

"That's not all," continued the gnarled stranger. "If people look in it too long, they can't break free from their reflected image; eventually, they turn into flowers. Do you see them over there?"

Kim looked at the colorful sea of flowers surrounding the lake. He shuddered. "Are those all . . . ?" he started to say.

The man nodded. "Who are you two?" he asked.

It was a bit hard for Kim to understand the logic behind this abrupt change of subject. Hesitantly, he said, "My name is . . . Kim. I really do come from far away. And this is Chunklet, a . . . a friend."

"Chunklet? Strange name."

"He gave it to me," Chunklet piped up. "Do you want to know why?"

"I don't think that's important," Kim said hastily. In a different tone of voice, he added, "Thank you for the warning, but we have to be on our way now."

"Hey there, not so fast," the man said, extending his hand.

Kim noticed with a mixture of fear and astonishment that the man's skin actually was made of wood. His fingernails were little pieces of darker bark. His cap wasn't a cap at all: Leaves actually were growing from his head!

"I've been watching you two for quite a while. You seem pretty tired. Maybe you'd like to rest a little. You can come with me. I live very close by."

"We can't do that," Kim replied—a little too hastily it seemed, because the stranger's tree-bark eyebrows came together in a puzzled frown. "We have a long road ahead of us," Kim added with an embarrassed smile. "Quite a long road, in fact."

"Where are you going?"

"To Gorywynn," Kim answered after a moment's hesitation.

"The Crystal Fortress of Gorywynn?" the man exclaimed.

"You're familiar with it?"

"Well, I've never been there, if that's what you mean, my boy. None of us ever have been there. Naturally, we've heard of it. If you really intend to go there, that's all the more reason to come with me."

"What do you mean by that?" asked Kim, who now felt trace of suspicion.

"As you say, you have a long road ahead of you," the leaf man answered. He pointed at Stardust. "Even with the horse, it will take you weeks—perhaps even months—to reach the Crystal Fortress. It would be best to build up some strength before you ride any farther."

Kim gave him an uncertain look.

"What's the matter?" the man pressed. "Don't you trust me?"

"Yes, of course I do," Kim hastened to reassure him.

"You're fleeing from something, aren't you?" the stranger asked abruptly.

"How did you know?" Kim blurted out, immediately wishing he'd held his tongue.

The stranger just laughed. "Do you think I'm blind?" he asked. "I said I've been watching you—you and your pretty little friend. What's after you? Trolls?"

Until now, Kim hadn't even known that there were such things as trolls here. He shook his head. "A dwarf," he said.

"A dwarf from the eastern mountains?" His dark face grew somber. "If that's how things stand, that's one more reason for you to stay here with us for a while. No dwarf ever has dared to come to our home up in the tree—no dwarf ever will."

"What do you mean?"

"We're not exactly friends," the man explained. "The dwarves are creatures of the night. They live under the earth and hate the sun and everything that grows and thrives. They fear heights like the plague, and our tree is very high."

Our tree? Kim understood about half of what the leafy man had said, but somehow he trusted the stranger. The grave look he'd seen in the leaf man's eyes when he'd mentioned the dwarf was genuine.

"We're having a festival tonight. You're most welcome to come," the man said, still sensing hesitation in Kim.

"I'm not in a festive mood," Kim replied sadly.

"He just lost a good friend," Chunklet quietly added.

The leaf man nodded sympathetically. "That's painful," he said. "But perhaps this will distract you a little. And if it doesn't, we still have a bed for you where you can get a good night's sleep. Come."

After a final moment of hesitation, Kim consented.

Oak—their new friend's name, as it turned out upon proper introductions—offered to take Stardust to a safe location where the stallion could stay and be well cared for until their return. The Lake of Vanity was dangerous for horses, too. Unfortunately, Oak explained, it wasn't possible for Stardust to ascend his tree. Kim agreed to this arrangement, and Oak took the stallion's reins and led him away.

Stardust obediently followed the man: another indication to Kim that they could trust the leafy man. After all, the horse's response to the dwarf had been just as agitated as Kim's and Chunklet's—that was all the proof Kim needed that Stardust was a good judge of character.

They didn't have to wait long. Oak returned after only a few moments and stated that he would take them to the tree. By now, Kim's curiosity was piqued—especially as he'd looked far and wide and hadn't seen a single tree. There were bushes and shrubs and gorgeous wild flowers as far as the eye could see, but nothing that in any way resembled a tree—even though Oak kept talking about one.

When Kim voiced these thoughts, Oak just smiled knowingly and gestured for them to follow him. Chunklet leaped onto Kim's shoulder, and they marched behind Oak through the waist-high grass. Kim couldn't spot any trees in the direction that Oak led them, no matter how far ahead he looked. Meanwhile, they marched straight toward the cliff that Kim had seen early in the morning.

After a while, Kim realized that the cliff wasn't nearly as smooth as it seemed from afar. The rock was split and cracked everywhere, riddled with caves that apparently extended deep into the mountain. It felt as if the cave openings were jet-black eyes staring at the new arrivals. As they got closer, Kim saw the steps of an enormous staircase hewn in the rock face. The steps ascended in a winding, dizzying, zigzagging course.

When they were finally right beside it, he realized that the mountain wasn't a mountain at all; the steps weren't chiseled rocks, either—instead, they were carved. The mountain was made of wood, not stone. It wasn't a mountain: It was a tree.

This realization hit Kim so suddenly that he stood frozen in place, his head tipped all the way back. He was at a complete loss for words. Once again, he was struck by the peculiar green-tinged light, and only now did he see what caused it; even the sky above them wasn't what Kim had thought it was. An enormous roof of leaves extended above their heads as far as the eye could see, as if gargantuan bushes and mighty branches had grown over the entire firmament. It felt as if they stood on the floor of a forest that spanned the entire world—with adequate light, true enough, but without a direct view of the sky. Except the living roof over their heads wasn't the canopy of a forest, but the top of a single, infinitely large tree!

"Is something the matter?" Oak inquired. The tone of his voice was casual, but he couldn't suppress the amused twinkle in his eyes. Obviously, he was well aware of the effect that this view had on people the first time they saw it, and it had probably been fun for him to keep Kim in the dark about it up until now.

"Is that . . . your tree?" Kim managed to get out.

Oak shook his head. "It's not *my* tree," he said emphatically, "but it is *the* tree, if that's what you mean. Do you know of any other?"

"Of course," Kim replied, bewildered. "There are trees everywhere—just not ones like this."

"Oh, those trees." Oak suddenly grinned like a schoolboy who had just played a trick. "Those aren't trees. They might become trees at some point, but they still need a lot of time for that." He suddenly laughed aloud. "Excuse me for teasing you. Yes, you're right. That's the tree. And there really is just this one."

“I’m sure that’s true,” Kim whispered. He couldn’t tear his gaze away from the enormous tree trunk. Oak’s words and Kim’s own intellect told him that this was indeed a tree, but his eyes insisted it was a mountain. The diameter of the trunk was tremendous, and Kim didn’t dare to imagine how high it was—the thought alone would make him dizzy.

Oak impatiently gestured for Kim to follow. Dizziness soon set in as Kim started following his guide up the enormous wooden staircase, which wound its way up the trunk of the giant tree. Although wide, the staircase was very, very steep, and it lacked a banister. Kim kept his eyes glued on Oak’s back and hoped that no one else would notice his fear.

He stopped counting the steps when he got to four hundred. The lowest of the unbelievably thick branches wasn’t any closer, as far as he could see. They climbed the winding, zigzagging stairs at a quick pace for at least a half hour before finally reaching the tree’s first branch—or what Oak probably called a branch. To Kim, it was more like a road of living wood. Even if it hadn’t disappeared in a leafy green jungle, it was so long that its tip wasn’t visible.

On the other hand, he could see something else: Far in the distance, there were outlines of small white and green houses rising out of the branch. Kim stared at the little spots of color, his eyes wide in astonishment. No doubt about it: A town had been built on this gigantic tree!

“You’re surprised?” Oak asked. He hadn’t failed to notice the confused expression on Kim’s face.

“Those . . . those are houses!” Kim exclaimed.

“Of course they’re houses,” Oak said. “Don’t you live in houses where you come from?”

“Well, yes, of course,” came Kim’s bewildered reply. “But I thought . . . I mean, I believed—”

Oak grinned. “I’d be happy to show you the town now, if you’d like—and the other towns, too.”

“Other towns?” Kim was stunned. “Does that mean . . . there are more of them?”

“Seven or eight,” Oak replied casually, “not counting the hamlets up in the treetop.”

“Uh-huh,” Kim ventured. He couldn’t get over it: a tree as big as an entire country, with towns on its branches!

The closer they came, the more Kim saw of the tree town. Some of the buildings had six or seven stories, and one was as large as any fortress on the ground below.

The people here wore green, red, and yellow clothes—well, they weren’t clothes, exactly, but a natural outgrowth of leaves. They walked on real streets notched out of the branch’s bark, polished smooth by countless feet over thousands of years. The streets looked like glittering asphalt. Here and there, plants peeped out between the buildings. When Kim looked more closely, he saw that these were offshoots of the giant branch. However, they were as large as fully grown trees back home. Of course, Oak would have disputed this—but to Kim, they were trees—rather imposing ones, at that.

"This is unbelievable," Kim muttered, following Oak down the wide streets of the tree city. Continually, Kim discovered new wonders. "And you—you all really live up here? You never go down below?"

"Oh, now and then we do," Oak replied in a gently teasing voice. "Otherwise, I hardly could have met you by the lake, could I? But you're right, of course—we live here and rarely leave the tree. It's our home."

He pointed at a small, very ornate little house on the right. "We're there. My wife isn't home. She's helping with the preparations for tonight's festival. She'll be happy to see you two. We enjoy having guests."

He ducked his head a little as he went through the entry door, which was a bit too short for him, and he made a beckoning gesture. "Come on in."

Kim hesitated—not from fear, but because this building astonished him, too. Contrary to first impression, it wasn't situated *on* the giant branch but was an organic *part of* the tree. Its walls grew directly out of the ground, and living green leaves comprised its roof. Doors and windows never were carved from the wood: The semicircular openings bordered by thick bulges were simply places where the wood had stopped growing.

The inside of the house was like the outside. It had furniture similar to every other house Kim knew—tables, chairs, cupboards, and beds. However, these items weren't simply placed there, they sprouted out of the floor and walls, as if the tree had gone to great effort to offer its inhabitants a home that was as comfortable as possible. There was even a hearth: a rectangular block of wood with a black surface as hard as stone. Obviously, the hearths controlled the fire in a way that didn't seem to hurt the wood in the least.

Oak gave his visitors time to look around while he prepared a meal: A green, sweet-smelling porridge, which he sprinkled with herbs, aromatic dried leaves, and something else that smelled like honey but was thinner in consistency. He put a little bowl on the table for Chunklet and brought the food out. He was more than a little surprised to see the feather duster looking at him with hungry eyes after instantly devouring not only his own portion but also the one meant for Kim. Only after Chunklet had received a huge second helping did the friendly man fill up Kim's dish again.

"So, you're fleeing from a dwarf," Oak said, starting up the conversation after Kim had finished eating. Chunklet still was busy with his third helping.

Kim hesitated before answering. It wasn't that he distrusted Oak—far from it. But these words suddenly reminded him of his friend. No matter how he looked at it, he felt guilty—because he'd forced Kelhim to get involved in his dispute with Jarrn, and Kelhim had died because of it.

"Yes," he said. "He killed a . . . a friend of mine."

"Killed?" Oak looked up, but there was no way to tell whether his frown applied to the word "killed" or to Kim's imperceptible hesitation before the word "friend."

"He didn't do it personally," Kim said, qualifying his statement. "Someone else did who was . . . was with him."

Oak looked at him intently for a long while. "You don't want to talk about it," he observed.

"No." Kim shook his head.

"All right," said Oak. "We don't concern ourselves too much with the affairs of the people down below. If you change your mind and want to talk about it after all, I'll always be available. If you don't, then you don't." He politely changed the subject: "By the way, there's a race tonight. Do you want to take part? You look as if you might be a good runner—that is, if you get a few hours of sleep."

At these words, Kim hardly could keep from yawning. Oak smiled, stood up, and went into a neighboring room. When he beckoned, Kim followed him.

"Sleep for a few hours," Oak said. He pointed to a low bed growing out of the floor next to the door. It was covered with leaves and foliage. "You'll have to put up with my bed," he said apologetically. "I'm building a new house right now, you know. I'll have a guest room there, but it's not finished yet."

Kim no longer listened. The mere sight of the bed made his eyelids feel as heavy as lead. Without another word, he lay down. He fell asleep just as he was thinking how strange it was to lie in a bed with a cover that, of its own volition, crept over his body to keep him warm.

* * *

He woke up screaming.

Kim's whole body was bathed in sweat, and he'd sat up so abruptly that some of the slender twigs covering him were torn apart. The broken ends hastily retracted, and the whole blanket slid off him with a rustling sound.

Kim looked around, his heart pounding wildly. He was alone. The light in the room had changed in some way, he couldn't say exactly how. No one was there except Chunklet, who had leaped up in alarm and now was looking at Kim with a bewildered expression in his eyes. Yet, Kim was sure he'd seen a giant, angular figure just for a moment, staring at him with an eerie green eye.

The events of the previous night probably still were haunting him. Yes, of course. That explained it. He had fallen asleep and was dreaming. But now, he heard something else: Quick, heavy footsteps approached the door. Shortly thereafter, Oak's gnarled figure appeared in the doorway.

"Did something happen?" he asked in alarm. "You cried out."

Kim shook his head and wiped the sweat off his forehead with the back of his hand. "I . . . slept badly," he said. "Everything's all right." Slightly embarrassed, he added, "I think I broke something. A few branches—"

Oak waved that off. "Don't worry about it. As I said, we'll be moving soon. It doesn't matter." He cocked his head to the side and studied Kim with a concerned look. "Did you get enough sleep?"

Get enough sleep? No, absolutely not. But Kim shuddered at the thought of closing his eyes again and resuming that nightmare.

"My wife is back and has made dinner," Oak said. "The festival starts after that."

Kim didn't say anything in response, but he stood up. His stomach was growling again. Chunklet sniffed greedily as they followed Oak to the main room.

Oak's wife stood at the hearth. Her coat of leaves was somewhat lighter than her husband's, but she had the same gnarled face. Her curly, leafy hair hung down to her shoulders. It seemed that Oak had told her about the two visitors because she smiled at them in a friendly way, as if they were acquainted already. Then, she pointed at the table where three dishes of sweet green porridge waited—along with a big trough. With a delighted shriek, Chunklet promptly jumped in the trough, emptying it with breathtaking speed. Oak smiled in amusement; his wife's eyes widened in astonishment.

After they finished eating, Oak filled his pipe and chatted with Kim. Eventually, Oak's wife sat down with them. It took quite a while before Kim noticed that they were avoiding any topics that might make Kim feel awkward. It truly did seem to be as Oak had said: Tree People were not particularly interested in what happened outside their leafy world.

Finally, Oak stood up, stretched so that his arms creaked like wood—which of course, they were—and pointed to the door. "It's about time," he said. "We have to get going if we want to see the beginning of the festival. You're welcome to come along."

Kim declined with a shake of his head. He appreciated the offer but wasn't in the mood to celebrate. He'd have felt despicable, joining in on the merriment after everything that had happened with Kelhim.

"No," he said. "Thank you, but—" Breaking off in mid-sentence, he stared out the opened door, his eyes wide with horror.

On the road in front of the house, he saw a crowd of multicolored Tree People. That wasn't all: Stomping along in their midst was a huge, angular figure—a rust-colored iron man with a single glowing green eye!

"What's the matter?" Oak asked in alarm.

"Chonk," Kim whispered. His whole body began to shake. "That's . . . that's Chonk! He's here!"

Oak's gaze followed Kim's, and his eyes expressed deep confusion when he turned back to Kim. "That's just an iron man!"

"I shouldn't have come here," Kim stammered. "He'll go after you, too—" Then, he registered what Oak had said. He stared at the leafy man, dumbfounded. "Does that mean there are more of them here?"

"Iron men?" Oak laughed uneasily. "Of course. Dozens. They're helping us build the new town where we're going to be living soon. We'd never get the work done without them."

As if hypnotized, Kim continued to stare at the iron man, who plodded among the Tree People with heavy, thunderous footsteps. A corner of Kim's mind noticed that the huge iron feet were tearing little splinters of wood from the branch.

"They're here, too?" he said in dismay. "Don't you know where they come from?"

Oak's confusion visibly increased. "Of course we do," he replied. "The dwarves build them in their caves."

"But you told me that . . . that you and the dwarves were . . . enemies."

"I didn't say enemies," Oak said, correcting him. "They're not our friends—but that doesn't mean they're our enemies. We don't have any enemies." He stood up, went to the door, and closed it, sparing Kim the sight of the iron man. "What's so bad about that?" he asked, when he came back.

Kim didn't answer, but Chunklet replied in a low voice, "It was an iron man who killed his friend."

Kim swallowed. Tears welled up in his eyes at the memory.

"I can imagine how you feel," Oak said gently. "I'm sorry. If I had known, I would have made sure that you didn't have to see him."

"You need to send them away," Kim whispered. "They're dangerous!"

"No, they're not," Oak retorted, smiling. He sat down at the table again, stretched out his fingers, and touched Kim's hand. Although his skin looked hard and gnarled like old tree bark, it felt soft and warm.

"I think I'm in a better position to know," Kim murmured, still fighting back the tears. "I was there when he killed Kelhim."

"They're just tools," Oak replied. He pulled a knife from his belt and laid it on the table in front of Kim. "This comes from the dwarves, too. This and all the other tools we use. We can't smelt iron here any more than the crops that we sell to the dwarves can be grown in their caves. We're not friends, but we do trade with each other because we each have something that the other lacks. What's wrong with that?" When Kim started to object, he lifted his gnarled hand and continued speaking with his voice slightly raised. "You can kill someone with this knife, too, Kim. You're not afraid of it, though, just because it's lying here. The iron men are just like this knife. They're tools. You don't need to be afraid of them. You just need to fear those who misuse them."

"I don't believe that," said Kim. "They're . . . they're more than tools. I know it. I feel it. They scare me."

"They don't have to scare you," Oak sighed. "Even among us, there are a few who think the same way you do, but they're wrong. The iron men are very useful."

Kim laughed at that, briefly and bitterly.

"Tomorrow," Oak said, continuing, "when the festival is over, I'll show you our new town. It's ten times larger and more beautiful that this one. If we didn't have the iron men, well . . . You'll see. There's no reason to be afraid of them. Let's go now."

"Where to?" Kim asked warily.

"Up," Oak replied. "I'd like you to attend this festival. You need something to distract you, Kim. If you stay here alone, you'll end up running headlong into the night at the mere sight of an iron man." He let go of Kim's hand, stood up, and smiled encouragingly.

Kim did indeed follow him—although for a very, very different reason than Oak could ever imagine.

IX

As it turned out, there was an even bigger surprise in store for Kim later on that day, when the festival was well under way and the Tree People had started their contests. First, though, Kim had to practice a sport that definitely wouldn't show up in the Olympics back home but was very popular with the Tree People: stair climbing.

Oak led Kim and Chunklet back to the tree trunk, where they stepped onto the winding staircase and trudged upward for what seemed like eternity. Soon, it was too much for Chunklet, so he followed his usual practice of springing onto Kim's shoulders. Unfortunately, Kim had to rely on his own legs. After a while, his feet started dragging, and he fell behind Oak, who was moving up the stairs with astounding ease. Although the few hours of sleep had refreshed Kim, he still was not back to his old strength.

"It's not much farther," Oak said, pointing up, as if that would ease Kim's mind. "Just four more branches."

Kim groaned. Four branches! They weren't even halfway to the first one. He would never make it up there!

Oak grinned broadly. "Don't worry," he said, as if he'd guessed Kim's thoughts. "We won't need to walk the last part of the way."

Kim tried to figure out what that meant—but he couldn't come up with an answer, so he resigned himself to his fate. He followed Oak, dragging himself up the never-ending staircase. After a while, his legs felt shorter, as if they were attached just beneath his shoulder joints.

They reached the next branch up, and Kim caught a quick glimpse of another tree town, apparently even larger. They climbed countless steps after that, and then Oak suddenly came to a halt. From time to time, they'd passed by large openings that led to the gigantic tree's interior. Now, they stood before another one of these entrances. Oak made a welcoming gesture, and Kim followed him in.

Inside, the space was smaller than Kim had expected: It was a box-shaped room, exactly five square paces wide, with a floor curiously bordered by a waist-high railing. Oak briefly instructed them not to touch the walls. Then, he reached out and tugged on a rope of woven plant fibers that hung down in the middle of the room—or, more precisely, it was suspended from somewhere in the infinite blackness above them. (The space had a floor, but not a visible ceiling.)

One moment later, Kim cried out in surprise when the floor jerked suddenly. The entrance abruptly disappeared, and the walls raced down past them into the depths.

The cavity was an elevator shaft!

"Nice, isn't it?" Oak grinned, clearly enjoying Kim's surprise. "Soon, we'll have the shaft bored through the entire tree, and then we'll progress much faster. We're planning an even bigger elevator, in fact."

"That's . . . fantastic," Kim said hesitantly, but he didn't think it was—just the opposite. Why did this elevator make him feel uneasy? "How does it work?"

"It's very simple," Oak explained with obvious pride. "The platform hangs on ropes. If it's supposed to go up, then we drop a counterweight from above."

"Ah." Something about this explanation worried Kim.

"It's really convenient," Oak continued, suddenly very talkative. "The iron men built it."

Kim looked at him inquiringly. His anxiety increased.

"This would have been impossible without them," Oak said. "Can you imagine how much work it is to cut a shaft in the tree?"

Kim couldn't imagine it, and he didn't want to, either. Apprehensively, he asked, "The tree doesn't mind?"

"What?"

"When you cut holes in it?"

Oak laughed. "What are you thinking of! The tree's so big, it wouldn't even feel it if we cut one hundred shafts in its trunk. This is not a tiny little sapling like the ones you know, Kim. No, no. No need to worry."

But Kim did worry, even though he saw no reason to doubt Oak's statements. Something wasn't quite right.

They were silent for the rest of the trip. Now and again, an entrance whisked past them as the elevator steadily continued its long way up. Eventually, it slowed down, finally coming to a stop.

When he stepped out of the elevator, Kim squinted his eyes against the bright light. For the first time since coming to the tree, he saw the sun. Here, too, a roof of green leaves spanned the sky, but it wasn't as dense as down below. He could see spots of bright blue.

Lively activity reigned on this branch; the sound of laughter and happy voices met them. Thousands of Tree People were there. Fruits roasted over fires that burned at small, specially prepared sites; mugs were passed around. A short distance away, Kim saw a tent decorated with colorful flags and pennants where many multi-colored Tree People crowded around.

"Come on," Oak called out in high spirits. "I'll introduce you to a few friends."

Kim and Chunklet reluctantly followed him. Their host plunged into the crowd and, after a while, Kim found himself the center of everyone's attention, to his great discomfort. Oak seemed to have countless friends: He spoke to almost everyone. All of them greeted Kim and his colorful companion. After a while, Kim found the happy, relaxed mood contagious. To his great surprise, before even half an hour had passed, he heard himself laughing with his new acquaintances. Chunklet, who quickly had discovered that the roasted fruits were meant for everyone, flitted from fire to fire, doing his best to eat the entire harvest in one evening. When Kim saw the dedication that his colorful friend brought to the task, he figured Chunklet's chances of accomplishing this feat weren't half bad.

Kim might have forgotten the terrible events of the previous night if a minor incident hadn't disturbed his relaxed mood. He had no premonition of anything bad. Yet, as he was standing with Oak and a few new friends, eating a piece of absolutely delicious roasted fruit, he began to choke.

"What's the matter?" Oak asked in alarm.

Kim didn't answer, but when Oak looked around, he understood: Not far from them, the angular shoulders of eight or ten iron men jutted out over the heads of the crowd.

"Don't worry," Oak said in an impatient tone of voice. "I told you, they're our helpers."

"Wh-what are they doing here?" Kim stammered.

"I've been asking myself the same question," said one of the Tree People—a very young man whose leaves were a pale yellow color.

Oak gave him a dirty look but didn't say anything in reply. Instead, he turned back to Kim. "They're going to compete in the race tonight."

"The iron men?" Kim asked, surprised.

"That's ridiculous," the yellow leaf man said. "And it's an insult to us all."

"Be quiet, you," Oak rebuked him.

Another man, clothed in green leaves like Oak, took Oak's side. "Don't get excited. He's yellow—what do you expect?"

"At least I'm not contributing to the destruction of our tree," the gold man retorted.

The dispute grew heated. Kim followed it with mounting confusion. He didn't realized it was possible for Tree People to argue.

"Please!" Oak now intervened, his voice urgent. "We're here to celebrate, not quarrel. So, restrain yourself, Tarrn. And you, Limb," he said, turning to the yellow man, "If you have such a low opinion of the iron men, why don't you run against them and beat them?"

Limb's lips curled in scorn. "I'm not going to compete against a . . . a thing that doesn't even have a soul."

Tarrn let out a deep sigh. "That's just typical," he said, a touch of spite entering his voice. "If it were up to you yellows, we'd have to tear down our houses, wouldn't we? And we'd live naked on the branches again, like our ancestors."

"What was so bad about that?" Limb asked defiantly. He glared at the man across from him before turning to Kim. "You tell us, kid: Is it right for us to destroy our own world?"

"But we're not doing that," Tarrn protested.

"That's enough!" Oak gave the yellow man a stern look. "I won't tolerate my guests being dragged into your ridiculous quarrel."

Limb's eyes flashed angrily, but he restrained himself and said nothing more. A moment later, he turned and strode off, quickly disappearing into the crowd.

Tarrn followed Limb with his eyes, shaking his head. "Yellows!" he said in disgust. "Complete idiots."

"That's enough now," Oak warned.

"Bah!" Tarrn snorted. "As if a few iron men were endangering our world! What's wrong with not having to climb stairs or living in larger houses?"

"I said, that's enough," Oak repeated sternly. Then, he forced a smile. "Let's go and watch the preparations for the race. It's about to start."

Kim had lost all interest in the competition. He would've preferred to speak with Limb. He had a feeling he'd found an ally here. Nevertheless, he politely followed Oak toward the middle of the branch, where the large tent with the pennants was located.

As they hurriedly made their way through the jostling crowd, Kim suddenly noticed that the throng of spectators also included people like him, humans who wore clothes and didn't have hair consisting of foliage. Obviously, the festival attracted visitors from all around, not just the Tree World. Additionally, the Tree People didn't seem to be as indiscriminately mixed as it had seemed at first glance. There were yellow, green, red, blue, violet, and white Tree People; on closer observation, it was obvious that individual colors had gathered in groups. Only a few Tree People stood among individuals with a color different than their own.

When Kim asked about this, Oak was happy to explain: "There are different tribes," he said, "but the color is not significant—at least not very. Except for maybe the blues—you should keep away from them. Those folks who live high up in the treetop are a pretentious lot. They think they're better because they're closer to the sky."

That left a bad taste in Kim's mouth. He was beginning to understand, and it frightened him to the core.

For the time being, however, he wasn't able to ask Oak any more questions, for they had reached the festival tent. It was a giant tent that had room for two or three hundred people. Its ropes had been secured with large steel stakes driven deep into the wood of the branch.

Kim noticed that the back third of the tent had been roped off; only a handful of individuals were there, although the rest of the tent was almost bursting at the seams with visitors.

"What's going on over there?" Kim inquired.

"Those are the competitors in the race," Oak replied. "It's going to start soon. Wait—I'll lift you up so you can see better."

Before Kim could protest, Oak had lifted him up on his huge shoulders as if Kim were a little child.

Of course, from this height, Kim had a much better view. He now saw that, in addition to the eight iron men he'd glimpsed earlier, five or six Tree People of each color had gathered in the roped-off area, along with a number of runners from elsewhere. And why not? After all, Oak had invited Kim to take part in the race.

Then, he saw . . . a black knight! At first, the knight barely was noticeable: just a dark figure among the riotous colors of leaf clothes. When he moved, though, Kim saw that the man—slender and not much bigger than Kim—was wearing armor. And it wasn't just any armor: He wore a battered, stained breastplate, a bashed-in helmet, and arm and leg armor that evidently once had been black but now looked as if it were absorbing all the light and color that touched the metal.

It was the same kind of armor that Kim himself had once worn, back when the black knights of Morgon almost had succeeded in destroying all the inhabitants of Magic Moon. But the black knights had been annihilated! How could one show up now, to . . .

"Oak! Let me down!" he cried, impatiently wiggling. "Fast!"

Oak complied with a puzzled look. As soon as Kim's feet touched the ground, he took off, trying to fight his way through the crowd to the front. He had to get a closer look at this stranger. He had to convince himself that his eyes hadn't played tricks on him because of the distance. If the horrors of Morgon had been resurrected, then Magic Moon was in even greater danger than Kim had imagined!

He didn't make it in time. The bystanders were packed together closely, and Kim hadn't quite reached the rope when a loud bang rang out and the whole back wall of the tent opened up. The crowd gave a mighty roar as the runners shot out.

Kim stumbled forward, ducked under the rope—and took off after them! A man with white leaves tried to stop him, repeatedly shouting something like "registration," but Kim nimbly dodged him. He increased his speed in order to catch up with the runners. The dull, black color he sought moved somewhere among the other participants. Despite the hundred-pound weight of the black armor, the man maintained a surprisingly fast pace.

Kim soon realized that he'd overestimated his own ability. It was all he could do not to fall too far behind the other runners. Catching up with them was out of the question. Even the iron men were running almost as fast as Kim, although they gradually started to fall behind.

That meant nothing; Kim knew all too well that the rust-colored giants didn't experience exhaustion.

"Hey there!" a little voice behind Kim suddenly chirped. "Where are you going?"

Glancing back over his shoulder as he ran, Kim spotted Chunklet, who was scampering behind him, as nimble as a weasel.

"You can't leave me behind all alone!"

"No time!" Kim breathlessly shouted. "Wait for me here."

Chunklet very clearly didn't like that answer. He sped up, crouched down, and then landed back on his customary perch: Kim's shoulder.

The front-runners gradually approached the massive tree trunk, where they began to sprint up the stairs. Not half so light on his feet, Kim followed them at an ever-increasing distance—coughing, wheezing, and profusely sweating. Before the first flights were behind him, he was so exhausted that he wished he could lie down on the spot. But that wasn't an option. A black rider from Morgon? Unimaginable! Kim had to catch up with him.

Gasping for breath, he reached the next tree branch up. Some of the runners were already out of sight. There was no town here. This branch had exuberant growth, with undisturbed, tree-sized sprouts, as well as side branches that created a kind of forest. Some runners already had disappeared into it. The iron men—and the black knight, as well—now were significantly behind: Except for Kim, they made up tail end of the field. Perhaps the black knight gradually began to feel the weight of his armor.

But the longer Kim ran behind him, the less likely it seemed. The black knight's steps didn't look any less smooth or surefooted. He was slowing down steadily, almost as if he intentionally were falling behind the others. Finally, even the iron men were a good distance ahead of the black knight—and the distance between the knight and Kim dwindled in the same measure.

Then, the knight stopped suddenly. Kim stopped, as well, diving behind a short bush. Kim moved just in time, because the stranger quickly and furtively looked in all directions before heading off at a right angle.

"Hey!" Chunklet squeaked in surprise. "What's he doing?"

"No idea," Kim admitted, "but we're going to find out." As quickly and quietly as he could, he entered the underbrush and set out after the knight.

The forest was so dense that Kim would have made little progress if he hadn't been able to follow the trail that the black knight had forged. Suddenly, he stood at the edge of a yawning precipice: Kim had reached the edge of the branch.

Beneath him, there was nothing but empty space until the surface of the next branch down, which looked a good two or three minutes' vertical free fall away. Half a step farther, and Kim would've plunged downward. He hastily backed up and scanned his surroundings, his heart beating wildly. Where was the stranger?

Only after a thorough search—in a direction he least expected—did Kim find the knight: directly beneath him. The steel figure was slowly but skillfully descending a knotted rope anchored to the branch.

"That fellow is cheating!" Chunklet huffed. "He's taking a shortcut!"

That seemed a little off-track to Kim. This kind of cheating was much too crude—and completely pointless. After all, Oak had said that the sole object of this race was to win. The victor's only prize was the victory itself. Maybe the black knight hadn't separated from the others for victory . . .

Kim cautiously knelt down, leaning forward so that he could keep the knight in view without himself being seen. He waited until the tiny figure below reached the next branch down. Then, summoning all his courage, Kim turned around and climbed down the knotted rope, using a hand-over-hand technique. Chunklet yelled at Kim in increasingly offensive terms, but Kim steadily continued his descent.

Climbing down the rope was tiring, but it was easier than Kim had anticipated. By the time his feet were on solid ground again, his arms and legs felt like overstretched rubber bands, and he had to stand still for a moment to regain his strength. Nevertheless, he didn't feel half as exhausted as he ought to after such tremendous effort.

He looked around. There was no trace of the black knight. No wonder: The surface of this branch was even wilder than the one above. The "trees" were so dense that, in many places, there wasn't a way through them. A thick layer of dead leaves and humus covered the ground. Kim found it difficult to remember that he was on the branch of a giant tree, stuck midway between earth and sky—not on firm ground.

After a while, though, he found what he'd been looking for: tracks left in the soft ground by heavy, metal boots. He followed them.

Although he'd lost a lot of time climbing down the rope, Kim soon caught up with the stranger. The knight had halted not too far away and now crouched behind a bush only a few hundred feet from Kim, gazing intently at the narrow path that wound through the thicket. Surprised, Kim stood still. It took a while before it occurred to him that he needed to hide quickly. He felt a rush of fear. If the black knight hadn't been concentrating so completely on the path ahead of him, he certainly would've noticed Kim.

Kim cautiously looked down the path, peering over the top of the bush that hid him. He squinted his eyes, gazing beyond the shoulders of the man in front of him. At first, he didn't notice anything unusual. The only remarkable thing was a particularly large knot on the other side of the branch's path: Its surface was so cracked and weathered that it looked like a huge cliff. The path made a tight loop around the knot and disappeared into the thicket on the other side.

Then, Kim heard a noise—very faint at first but then increasingly louder as it approached. It was the sound of rapid footsteps and labored breathing. The front-runners!

Kim was puzzled. Why had the man gone to so much trouble to take a shortcut, only to let the others pass by him now? It made no sense. In fact, the black knight actually crouched even lower behind his bush instead of inconspicuously joining the front-runners—which he undoubtedly could have done, for the closely bunched group had stretched into a long chain with wide gaps in between each racer. Instead, though, the knight patiently waited until the last runners had passed his hiding place.

Well, almost the last runners . . .

A good distance behind the field of competitors, the iron men now stomped forward—not any faster than before, nor any slower, either. Kim saw the knight tense. Was he in league with the iron men and therefore with the dwarves, as well? That was conceivable for a creature from Morgon: an empire of shadows and evil.

However, the knight also let the angular giants stomp past his hiding place without moving—except for his hand, which crept to his belt and curled around the hilt of a powerful sword sheathed there.

Just as the first iron man was about to pass around the knot on the other side of the path, something astounding happened: Around the corner of the massive woody outcrop, a second tree suddenly sprouted up, in a manner that Kim found extremely odd. The tree grew with astounding speed. Actually, it popped up horizontally from behind the cliff—but it "grew" backward, its dead roots appearing first.

Carried by forward momentum, the first iron man crashed into this unexpected obstacle. A loud boom shattered the stillness of the forest, as the robot's iron head flew off in a high arc, while its torso continued to writhe for a short time before crashing to the ground.

Kim stared at this unbelievable sight with his eyes wide open and jaw dropped. The strange tree swung upward, now crashing down on the head of a second iron man with terrible force, squashing him like an empty tin can. Three of the four remaining iron men abruptly stopped in mid-step, standing still in apparent indecision before advancing in unison, disappearing behind the corner of the cliff.

Kim heard an angry roar, and then loud crashing sounds ensued, as if someone had tipped over a whole truckload of appliances.

The sixth and last iron man was about to follow his comrades—but at that very moment, in one fluid motion, the black knight rose from his hiding place and stepped out onto the path. Although he had moved very quietly, the iron man had heard him somehow, because he turned around and raised his arms high.

The knight drew his sword, thrust, and then struck hard. Kim watched, dumbfounded, as the blade struck the iron man's slender right hand, slicing through the metal as if it were paper.

The iron man recoiled, lifted the stump of his arm, and studied it for a second with his eerie green eye, as if he couldn't comprehend what he saw. Then, he turned back toward his adversary—who looked pint-sized in comparison to him—and he abruptly lashed out with his powerful left hand.

Moving with incredible speed, the black knight dodged, ducked under the claw, and thrust his sword so deeply into the iron man's chest that more than half of the blade disappeared from view. The iron man didn't seem to be affected by it, however, because his claw snapped shut at that same moment, grazing the knight's shoulder; even this brief contact was enough to knock the sword out of the black knight's hand. The weapon whizzed through the air and bored into the ground so close to Kim's feet that it seemed planned.

The knight staggered. He managed to dodge another blow, but in doing so, he lost his balance and fell flat on his back. The iron man caught up to him with a single step and bent down over him.

Kim finally woke from his trance. Moving of its own volition, his hand grabbed the hilt of the sword and pulled the blade out of the ground. At the same moment he touched the sword, something strange happened: an invisible power flowed from the black metal of the blade into Kim's body. The sword was heavy, weighing fifty pounds at least; normally, Kim would have needed two hands just to lift it. Now, he hardly noticed the weight.

That wasn't all. The sword fit in his hand so well that it didn't feel like a weapon; rather, it was a natural extension of his arm. When Kim raised the sword high and charged toward the iron man with a loud cry, he wasn't acting on his own—instead, he was willed forward by the weapon.

The iron man noticed this new threat only at the last moment, and his reaction came too late. He stared at Kim with his angry green eye; in the same fraction of a second, the blade hit his angular head, severing it from his shoulders. Kim felt no resistance at all as the steel sliced through the thick iron plates.

The metallic colossus froze. At first, it stood motionless in a grotesquely bent posture; then, it began to totter; finally, it fell forward with a crash. The knight flung himself to the side just in time to avoid being crushed to death.

Kim lowered the sword and bent over to see how the stranger was. The knight struggled to a sitting position, his armor clanking; then, he snatched the sword out of Kim's hand. Before Kim even had time to cry out, the knight jumped up and raced off in the direction of the melee.

Kim followed him.

When he rounded the corner, an astonishing sight met his eyes: The remains of four iron men lay on the ground, broken to pieces; just as the black knight was about to enter the fray, the massive tree root, which had sprouted up so quickly before, struck and crushed the fifth robot.

Kim realized someone was using the roots of the ripped-out tree as a cudgel—and this someone, as it turned out, was just the right size for the job. Before them stood a giant! Drenched in sweat and aggressively swinging his unusual bludgeon back and forth, the giant was more than twice the height of the knight. He had black hair, muscles that bulged like knotted ropes beneath his suntanned skin, and a face that—

"Gorg!" Kim whispered, thunderstruck.

The giant's head jerked around. His eyebrows drew together in an angry frown. Then, a completely astonished expression appeared on his face.

"Kim?" he asked softly. "You? . . . Is it . . . is it really you?"

Suddenly, he dropped the cudgel and was beside Kim in one leap, lifting the boy into the air. It actually was Gorg—Gorg the good-humored giant, who so enjoyed playing the coward and the fool (but was, in fact, neither) and who had once accompanied Kim on a dangerous trip through the land of Magic Moon.

Kim was jubilant. He laughed with joy.

Gorg swung Kim around and around, roaring his name over and over.

Finally, Kim calmed down and tried to free himself from Gorg's huge paws, but he met with little success. "Let me go, you big lug," he laughed. "You're squeezing me to death!"

Gorg gently set him down, but his excitement remained.

"It's you," he kept repeating. He simply could not believe it. "We were all hoping you would come, but no one dared believe it! Now, you're here, and everything will be all right." He waved his hand, excitedly beckoning the black knight. "Look who's here!" he said. "Take a look!"

The black knight slowly walked toward them. He'd put his sword back in its sheath and now stood unmoving while Gorg and Kim got carried away with their reunion. Although the helmet's black visor was down still, Kim sensed that it hid another surprise.

"I know," the knight murmured. "I . . . I already recognized him."

That voice! Kim thought. It sounded distorted, but Kim recognized it!

"Is it you?" he whispered.

"Yes," replied Prince Priwinn of Caivallon, removing his helmet.

They hugged and clapped each other on the back, laughing until they couldn't catch their breath.

"Where did you two come from?" Kim asked breathlessly. "What are you doing here, and—"

"One thing at a time," Priwinn said, interrupting him. His eyes shone as he looked at Kim. The young prince hardly had changed. Still slender and dark-haired, he had a noble face that almost resembled a man's but probably would never lose its youthful merriment. However, Kim saw something that hadn't been in Priwinn's eyes before: a certain bitterness, which was at odds with the prince's youthful appearance.

They didn't have a chance to talk; footsteps proceeded a figure covered in light-yellow leaves, stepping out of the underbrush.

"Have you taken leave of your senses?" Limb hissed. "You're making such a racket. They can hear you two branches away. You—"

He stopped in mid-sentence when he caught sight of Kim. His eyes narrowed. "What is he doing here?" he asked suspiciously. "I saw him with Oak earlier."

Gorg raised his hand in a calming gesture. "It's all right," he said. "He's a friend of ours."

"You can trust him," Priwinn added, "just as much as you trust Gorg and me."

Limb hesitated. The mistrust in his eyes didn't disappear entirely. Then, he saw the smashed iron men, and a satisfied look spread over his features.

"You got them," he said. "Good."

"Was there ever any doubt?" Gorg asked, slightly insulted.

"There are only five," Limb noted without answering the giant's question.

"Another lies on the path over there," Priwinn stated. He pointed at Kim. "Our friend took care of him."

"Good. Now, we should get away from here. If anyone sees us, it's all over. Oak already was worried when this young fool took off after you." He started to leave, but then he stopped again at the edge of the forest. "We'll meet up in the new town—hurry." With that, he disappeared.

"What does he mean by that?" Kim asked.

Priwinn dismissed the question with a brief gesture. "Limb's right. We can't stay here. It's too dangerous." He turned to Kim. "You're coming with us?" It was more of a statement than a question.

Kim nodded almost automatically—but then, he looked around, searching. Where was Chunklet? Kim remembered Chunklet jumping off his shoulder when he'd charged the iron man, but he hadn't seen the feather duster since.

"What are you looking for?" Gorg asked.

"I'm missing someone," Kim replied. "A friend."

"A friend? What does he look like?"

"Oh, you'll know him when you see him," Kim replied. "Wait a moment. It won't take long." Without waiting for Gorg's reply, he stepped back onto the path and called Chunklet's name a few times.

The feathery, reddish-orange creature tripped out from behind a bush after a few moments. "Is it all over?" he asked in a small voice.

Kim smiled. "Yes. Come here, you little coward."

"What's going on?" Chunklet asked as he obediently sprang up onto Kim's shoulder. "Who are these two?"

"I'll explain later," Kim replied. "We have to leave."

But first, he knelt down next to a destroyed iron man. With a thoughtful look, he reached for the robot's severed head and turned it over.

The head was completely empty—so was the rest of the rust-colored titan. It was nothing but an iron shell. Kim was confused. He didn't know what he'd expected . . . maybe a complicated system of gears and levers, an intricate mechanism—*something.* But *nothing?* What made the iron men move and work?

"Weird, isn't it?" asked a voice above him.

Startled, Kim looked into Priwinn's eyes.

The prince had approached silently and, like Kim, gazed down at the iron man; his face didn't show confusion so much as anger—or hate.

"I don't get it," Kim murmured. "What keeps them alive?"

"Magic," Priwinn replied; now, his voice truly did sound full of hate. "Magic from the dwarf folk of the eastern mountains. We have to get out of here. I'll explain everything to you as soon as we're safe."

* * *

For at least the next hour, Kim had no opportunity to whisper even one of the countless questions he was dying to ask. They set an astonishing pace, traversing the branch jungle and later hurrying up the stairs. Kim's legs soon felt as weak as a wet noodle, and even Priwinn's strength was waning noticeably.

Eventually, this was too much for Gorg to bear. Without further ado, he put the two humans on his shoulders and continued running up the staircase, taking seven or sometimes even ten steps at a time.

Despite their hurry, they approached the summit of the tree just as dusk began to fall. The sun still shone, but the shadows had lengthened, and the light mixed with a touch of gray.

Down on the ground, which seemed infinitely far away, nighttime must have set in already. Kim was surprised by what awaited them on the high and thin branches: the largest and most magnificent town Kim had seen on the tree thus far. The buildings were taller and more spacious, constructed in a much more expensive—though not necessarily beautiful—style. As they neared, Kim saw that the town didn't occupy just this one branch; it extended out into open space, like a spider web supported by a huge framework of beams. In some places, it extended as far as the neighboring branches.

He also noticed that this town was dead. Nothing moved anywhere. Not a single light shone. Not a sound could be heard.

"It's not finished," Priwinn explained. "Nobody lives here yet—assuming someone might move here someday, that is."

Kim gave him a puzzled look, but Priwinn motioned for him to keep silent.

The prince quickly looked around in all directions. Then, he swiftly walked toward one of the empty buildings. Kim and Chunklet followed, while Gorg stood in the shadows to keep watch—or so he said. In truth, Kim guessed, the house probably was too small for him. Gorg had plenty of experience banging his head on low ceilings and doorjambs.

"Are we going to meet your friend here?" Kim asked after they'd entered the building.

"Limb?" Priwinn shook his head. "He's not my friend," he said. "He's just our ally. Sit down. We have a lot of things to discuss."

Kim obeyed hesitantly, feeling uneasy. He didn't like this house. There was something about the way Priwinn was talking that he didn't like, either. After they sat down at the table, a large shadow appeared in one of the windows, and Gorg's broad face peered in at them. Priwinn gave him a quick nod before turning to Kim.

"I still can't believe you're back," he said. "We all were waiting for you."

"For me?" Kim asked, puzzled.

"Not just Gorg and I," Priwinn affirmed. "All Magic Moon has been begging for your return—at least, the ones who aren't corrupt yet," he said.

"What do you mean by that?"

Before Priwinn could answer, a slender black shadow appeared in the corner of the room and came toward them. Chunklet made a frightened noise and crept as close as he could to Kim's throat. The shadow came closer and turned into a huge, pitch-black cat, which gazed at Kim and his colorful little friend with glowing eyes.

"Hello," Kim said, pleasantly relieved. "Who are you?"

"That's a question I should be asking you," the cat snarled. "After all, you barged into my house, not the other way around."

Kim groaned while Priwinn laughed with his hand over his mouth.

"He understands me!" Kim blurted out.

"Of course," meowed the cat. "What did you expect?"

Priwinn could no longer contain his laughter. "Sheera likes to have a little fun surprising people," he said. "He's a nice guy, even if his manners sometimes leave something to be desired," he added with a reproachful sideways glance at the cat.

"What do you mean, 'manners'?" Sheera said, offended. "Am I the one who walked in without knocking? Did I make myself at home in someone else's house without being invited? Or was it him? He hasn't even introduced himself."

"My name is Kim," Kim said hastily. He tipped his head toward his shoulder. "And this is . . . Chunklet."

"Chunklet, eh?" Sheera snarled. "'Tiny' would fit better. Why he is so brightly colored?"

"Why are you so black, you big lout?" Chunklet retorted angrily. "And what kind of behavior is that, going after guests like this?"

"Guests? Ha!" Sheera lifted a paw and unsheathed five razor-sharp claws. "Better watch your big mouth, or I might show you what I do with tramps who come into my house uninvited."

"Just try it. Come on! Try it!" Chunklet scoffed, aggressively bouncing up and down on Kim's shoulder.

Sheera's eyes narrowed into thin yellow slits. "Feel pretty safe up there, do you?"

"Stop this, both of you," Priwinn said sternly.

Chunklet and the cat couldn't be restrained that easily, though.

"If you think I'm afraid of you, you're wrong, you big black beast!"

"Is that so?" Sheera snarled. "Then, come down from there. Let's step outside and settle it there!"

"Sure . . ." Chunklet murmured. "I'd be happy to . . . in theory."

"And in practice?"

"I don't fight with rabble," came the answer from above.

"Rabble?!" came a screech from below.

"Well, if you insist, then—" Chunklet said bravely.

"All right, let's go," Sheera snarled, unsheathing all his claws.

"Not now," Chunklet replied archly. "I'll expect you right after sunset."

"Whatever you say," Sheera said, bowing low.

"You might want to reconsider that," Kim interjected. "Chunklet is—"

"Stop—it's over," Priwinn said, impatiently interrupting him. "Leave, Sheera. And your little friend there," he added, turning toward Kim, "ought to keep his big mouth under control. This is not a joking matter with Sheera." He made an angry gesture. "I think we have more important things to discuss."

That was an opinion Kim wholeheartedly shared. Nevertheless, he watched the cat as he strolled out of the house with his head proudly raised.

"Where did you get him?" he asked.

"Sheera?" Priwinn smiled, but at the same time looked a little sad. "He came running to me about a year ago—or I ran up to him. However you want to describe it."

Kim followed the cat with his eyes, thinking that over.

"There used to be a lot of talking animals," Priwinn said gloomily. "But that was a long time ago. It's been forever since I've run into any—except for Sheera. Sometimes, I think he's the last of his kind."

"What happened?" Kim asked in a low voice.

Priwinn sighed. "I wish I knew," he said. "Something is . . . happening in Magic Moon, something terrible." He looked expectantly at Kim, just like farmer Brobing had before. "I . . . I was hoping that you could answer that question for me."

But Kim still couldn't, so he began to tell how he'd come there, and what he'd experienced thus far. Priwinn listened without interrupting a single time, and much of what he heard shook him deeply. After Kim finished his report, an oppressive silence reigned for a while.

"Kelhim's dead?" Priwinn finally murmured. "That's . . . that's terrible news."

Kim briefly glanced at the window. Gorg had turned his face away, but his shoulders were shaking as if he were fighting back tears.

"And yet it gives me reason to hope," Priwinn suddenly said.

Kim looked up, surprised.

The prince continued. "From what you've said, he couldn't have turned into a completely wild animal because, in the end, Kelhim was himself again. That means that not all hope is lost."

"Hope for what?" Kim wanted to know.

"That everything . . . might return to how it used to be," Priwinn replied hesitantly. "Magic Moon has changed, Kim. It's still changing—ever faster and for the worse." The Prince of the Steppe earnestly nodded to emphasize his words. "Take the Tree People: They're the most peaceful people in our world. Yet, even they have changed. They used to be a people who took joy in life and liked to laugh and had festivals all the time. Today . . ." He struggled for a moment. "You've met Limb and the others at the festival. This tree used to be one big community that didn't care who people were or what they looked like. Even a few years ago, the people here didn't know the meaning of the word 'quarrel.' Today, the individual clans live in separate towns. The blues despise the greens, the greens make fun of the yellows, the yellows hate the whites, and so on. And they don't even notice what's happening to them."

"Some do, obviously," Kim pointed out.

"Do you mean Limb and the other yellows?" Priwinn sadly shook his head. "Oh no, that's not as it seems. Sure—they're right that the iron men are damaging the tree. But their goals are so extreme—"

"Someone's coming!" Gorg interjected from his position by the window.

"Limb?"

"Yes," the giant replied after a few moments. "He seems to be in somewhat of a hurry."

Priwinn and Kim peered at the door, and Limb indeed came storming in not long afterward, completely out of breath and bathed in sweat.

"You have to leave!" he shouted immediately. "You've been betrayed. We all have. They've found the remains of the iron men and know what happened."

"Heavens!" Priwinn cried, jumping up. "How can that be?"

"I don't know," Limb replied, still gasping for breath. He probably had run the whole way up there. "And it gets worse: They know we're hiding in the new town and are on their way here. We don't have much more time. I have to be off. I have to warn the others." Suddenly, he clenched his fists. "I wish I could set this whole cursed town on fire."

"Why?" Kim asked, puzzled.

Limb glared at him. "You're asking 'why'? Because the cost is much too high. Look around!"

Kim did just that. Nothing caught his attention in particular—except, perhaps, that the building was larger and constructed more carefully than Oak's house on the first branch.

"You don't see anything?" Limb cried, outraged. "Then, look here!" With that, he grabbed the chair that Priwinn had been sitting on, swung it up in the air, and smashed it against the table with all his might.

The table and chair both broke into pieces, and then Kim understood what the yellow leaf man meant.

These furnishings were not natural outgrowths of the tree, like in Oak's house. Instead, they were made of separate pieces of wood: each planed and skillfully finished, the same way everything else in this room and house—indeed, in this entire town—had been.

"They're cutting this wood from the heart of the tree!" Limb said. "What took centuries to grow is now being carved up and destroyed in no time at all—and only because what we used to have is no longer enough."

"It's just a few boards," Kim cautiously interjected.

"No!" Limb objected. "It's not a few boards—it's the beginning of the end. Who's going to live here when there's nothing left from the heart of this tree?"

"Won't it grow back?"

"Well, if it does, it will happen so slowly that it will be meaningless for us. This tree is old, Kim, nearly ageless. And there's just this one tree. Our people can't live anywhere else once it's used up."

He broke off, and Kim didn't say anything else, although much dangled on the tip of his tongue.

"We should go now," Priwinn warned, breaking the uncomfortable silence. "If they find you, Limb, you'll have to answer a lot of unpleasant questions."

"They won't find me," Limb said defiantly. "But you three should go to Gorywynn and speak with the wizard, Themistokles. Maybe that will help the fools here see the light. Get going!"

Priwinn and Kim left the house and Gorg joined them outside. Kim was about to turn toward the staircase, but Prince Priwinn shook his head.

"That's not a good idea," he said. "We would run right into them. We'd better take a different route." Suddenly, Priwinn smiled again.

"Watch out!"

He leaned his head all the way back, put his hands in front of this mouth like a megaphone, and made a high trilling sound.

For a few moments, it was quiet; then, Kim heard a loud rustling sound. When he looked up, he saw a huge golden shape heading down toward the tree, almost as if it came from the setting sun.

All at once, a giant golden dragon landed on the branch right next to them. Priwinn and Gorg quickly climbed onto the back of his neck. Before Kim had time to express his joyous surprise, Gorg lifted him and his little friend to sit in front of him. The next moment, Rangarig the dragon swung up into the air with a mighty stroke of his wings, turning south.

X

As Rangarig's shimmering gold wings carried them over the countryside, something happened that Kim had heard of before but had never experienced for himself: They overtook the day. The dragon flew faster than the sun moved; so, for the first time, Kim enjoyed the rare spectacle of watching the blazing red fireball climb back up the horizon before it had set fully. Of course, it didn't go up very high. Even though Rangarig was a powerful creature with almost inexhaustible strength, he had flown so fast that he now began to lose altitude. He started looking for a place to alight.

They found a spot that looked safe to them: a bare mesa with a few scrawny bushes and moss. Vertical cliffs with a thousand foot drops were on all sides. Nothing could reach them up there unless it had wings or could climb like a spider.

On this natural fortress, the dragon gently landed like a falling leaf; one after another, the passengers climbed off his back. Kim's legs were shaking. Although Gorg had kept a tight hold on him, the dragon's flight had been so tremendously fast that Kim had clung with all his might to the hornlike protrusions that grew on the back of Rangarig's head. Kim's face was windburned, and his aching eyes teared up.

Despite all this, as soon as Kim's feet touched the ground, he hurried around the dragon; jumped over the long, scaly tail; and ran forward so he could look in Rangarig's eyes. The dragon seemed much larger to him than before; and in the light of the sun—which was now setting for the second time this evening—Rangarig's palm-sized scales shone more like burnished copper than gold. His eyes, each bigger than Kim's whole head, looked down on Kim without expression. His breath was raspy. The headlong flight clearly had exhausted the dragon.

Kim stood there with his head tilted back, looking up at the dragon's gigantic face. He couldn't think of what to say. His joy at seeing Rangarig again was just as great as it had been when he'd encountered Prince Priwinn and Gorg. But some time had passed since Rangarig had landed on the tree, and Kim sensed that something wasn't quite right with the dragon.

"Rangarig," he said, finally addressing him. "How are you?" He felt a little silly, but it was all he could think to say. For the first time since he'd met this powerful creature, he experienced real terror.

"Fine," Rangarig growled—truly an unusual answer for the dragon, whose penchant for talking was legendary in these parts.

What's the matter with Rangarig? Kim hadn't necessarily expected the dragon to jump up and down with joy . . . but for him to show no sign of recognition at all?

"We haven't seen each other for a . . . a long time," Kim said hesitantly.

"A long time for you, maybe," Rangarig rumbled. "We dragons measure time differently." In a tone of bored politeness, he added, "How have you been, meanwhile?"

"Fine, also," Kim murmured, embarrassed. He saw Priwinn giving him a look and realized that the young prince wanted to tell him something. "We'll talk again later, all right?"

Rangarig indifferently turned away his huge head and laid his snout on his forefeet, which were folded in front of him. "Sure."

Kim felt relieved when he moved away from the dragon. Bewildered, he turned to Priwinn. "What's going on with him?" he asked.

Priwinn hastily put his forefinger to his lips, nodding to indicate that Kim should follow him. They went almost to the other end of the mesa to ensure they were out of the dragon's hearing range.

"What's going on?" Kim asked again. "Why is he so distant? Did I offend him in some way?"

"No," Prince Priwinn hastily replied—again wearing a strangely pained smile. "It has nothing to do with you. He has . . . changed. He's not always this way, though. Don't worry. Probably, by tomorrow morning, you'll have your hands full trying to keep him from smothering you with kisses of pure joy."

Kim stayed serious. "What happened?"

"The same thing that's happening everywhere in Magic Moon," Priwinn replied bitterly. "Remember Kelhim? Rangarig has become moody.

Sometimes, he's as grumpy as an old man. Sometimes, I'm almost afraid of him. That's what I'm talking about, Kim: Our world is dying."

"Nonsense!" Kim objected, but he said it too quickly and too vehemently to convince even himself.

"Of course it will continue to exist," Priwinn said. "But it will no longer be the world that you once knew. Its people are becoming angry and hard. No one gives freely to others, anymore. Friends are becoming enemies, and neighbors are becoming strangers."

"Like the Tarn King and your father, Harkvan?" Kim asked.

Priwinn winced as if he'd been struck. His lips tightened, and Kim immediately regretted his clumsy words. "I'm sorry."

Priwinn waved it off. "No, you're right," he said despondently. "So, you've heard."

"Yes, but I couldn't believe it," Kim replied.

"Well, it's true," said the Prince of the Steppe. A lot of other things are just as bad."

"What in the world happened?" Kim asked in anguish. "Has Morgon been resurrected?"

"No, it's not that simple. There's no enemy threatening us from without, Kim. It's much worse." He gave a deep sigh and fell silent for a while. Finally, he said, "It's as if . . . as if we are becoming our own enemies."

An uncomfortable silence ensued and probably would have lasted for a good while longer if a black shadow hadn't appeared suddenly out of the dusk, arching its back and looking up at Kim with shining yellow eyes—or, to be more precise, looking up at the reddish-orange tuft of feathers still perched on Kim's shoulder.

"Hey, charlatan!" Sheera snarled. "Thought you could just disappear, did you?"

Chunklet looked at the black cat, flabbergasted. Kim, too, shook his head in surprise. It had escaped his notice that Sheera also had jumped onto Rangarig's back.

"Well—" Chunklet started to say, but he immediately was interrupted by Sheera.

"You're not getting away that easily. We have an appointment—remember?"

"I didn't know you cared!" Chunklet now had returned to his usual impertinent manner.

Sheera gasped and arched his back. "You there!" he growled. "Come down from there! I've had enough of this!"

"Hold on," Chunklet casually replied. "The agreement was for after sunset." He bounded off Kim's shoulder, looked around quickly, and then pointed with his paw at one of the few bushes growing on the bare plateau. "I'll being waiting for you over there, as soon as it's dark. If you need reinforcements, ask the dragon if he can help you."

Sheera's jaw dropped at this latest impudence, and it was only with great effort that he kept himself under control.

Chunklet scampered off without a word.

His back arched, Sheera impatiently waited for the sun to sink below the horizon.

Kim sat down on the ground cross-legged; after a few moments, Priwinn did the same. Shortly thereafter, Gorg joined them. Up until that point, he'd been waiting by the dragon. Priwinn gave him a questioning look.

"He's sleeping," the giant replied. "I believe it's not so bad today."

The last red streaks of sunlight disappeared; at the same moment, Sheera shot out like a bolt of black lighting and charged into the bush where Chunklet had disappeared. Branches cracked and split, and then a shrill, horrified scream rang out.

Priwinn look up, a question in his eyes. Gorg knitted his brows.

"Sounds like he found Chunklet," Kim said matter-of-factly.

Priwinn was of the opinion that the two bantam roosters didn't need any assistance, so he resumed the conversation as if there had been no interruption: "The boy in the hospital—the one you were telling me about," he began. "Can you describe him to me? What did he look like?"

Kim thought hard. He could picture the boy's face, but how should he describe the kid? "Like a boy," he said, at a loss for words.

Furious screaming and screeching erupted from behind the bush, and the branches began to shake.

"He was bigger than you . . . but younger, I think. He was very pale and had dark hair."

Priwinn was disappointed visibly. The screeching behind the bush became louder, and he cast a worried glance in that direction before he replied, "That doesn't help much, Kim. Most Steppe riders have dark hair."

"Are you thinking of someone in particular?" Kim asked. Priwinn nodded and Kim added sympathetically, "A friend?"

"Yes," Priwinn replied after a short pause. "A friend."

Kim thought of Jara and Brobing; they, too, had to deal with a painful loss.

Suddenly, something occurred to him that he hadn't thought of before. He looked at Priwinn, thunderstruck. "The last time I was here," he said with a puzzled frown, "Jara's child still was very small. Now, Torum is almost my age. How can that be?"

"You do know, don't you, that time follows different laws here in Magic Moon than it does in your world?" Priwinn reminded him.

"But you, Priwinn—you're not a single day older!"

Priwinn smiled tolerantly. "Of course not," he answered. "Have you forgotten already? I won't get any older as long as my father is alive to rule Caivallon. A prince becomes a man only when the old king dies. At that point, he takes his father's place on the throne."

"And you don't know any more than Brobing and Jara about the children who disappeared?" It was hard for Kim to believe this.

"No," said Gorg, answering for Priwinn. "But in three days, we'll be in Gorywynn. Then, Themistokles can answer all our questions."

The entire time they were talking, the bush had been shaking as if invisible hands were pulling on its roots; sometimes, clumps of black fur flew up in the air. Broken-off quills rained down along with greasy red feathers.

All at once, the noise ended. All eyes anxiously turned toward the thorny bush. A few seconds passed, and then the branches parted and two very disheveled figures stepped out.

Chunklet, now in his nocturnal form, was limping. Many of his spines were bent, and the rest went every which way; he looked as if he'd been hit by cyclone. One of his eyes, which were watery to begin with, was swollen almost shut.

Sheera didn't look much better. The cat was limping, as well. His formerly smooth, shiny fur was disheveled, and his muzzle looked as if he had tried to kiss a cactus.

"What *is* that thing?" Priwinn groaned, pointing at the ugly creature weaving toward them.

"Chunklet," Kim said blithely. "I have to admit, I don't care for his night clothes, either. But as you can see, they came in handy."

"A . . . a werecreature?" Gorg gasped. "He changes shape. Why didn't you say so?"

Chunklet said nothing for a while, clearly enjoying himself. "Because I would have missed out on a magnificent brawl," he finally admitted.

"Me, too," added Sheera, who was having difficulty staying on his feet. "Still, just wait until next time . . ."

The two started laughing heartily while the others just stared at them, bewildered.

Then, they gave each other a big hug—which didn't end up particularly well for Sheera. He drew back with a startled screech and, with his eyes crossed, examined the new spine in his muzzle. However, one more didn't make that much difference. . . .

Chunklet chuckled and yawned extravagantly. "And now for a little nourishment." He looked around, searching. Finally, his gaze rested on

Rangarig, who was curled in a ball. Chunklet licked his pimply lips and started slobbering in greedy anticipation.

"No," Kim said sternly.

Chunklet looked disappointed, but he didn't say anything. Instead, he sauntered off with Sheera until the two of them disappeared in the darkness, chuckling all the while.

"You are too much," Gorg said, shaking his head. "Why didn't you tell us that you were traveling with a werecreature?"

"Until now, I didn't even know what that was," Kim said in his own defense. "I'm sorry."

"You don't need to apologize," Priwinn said. He looked in the direction where Sheera and Chunklet had disappeared. "I'm glad they still exist."

"Well, that won't be the case for much longer," the giant growled.

The next morning, they left before the sun had risen even halfway above the horizon. As for Priwinn's prediction regarding Rangarig's behavior, it turned out to be true: It was as if the golden dragon had no memory of his rude manners the previous day. His joy over the reunion with Kim was so effusive that Kim feared being crushed between the dragon's powerful paws as Rangarig hugged him. When they finally rose up in the air, Rangarig flew in such high spirits that his guests worried they might be thrown off. Cavorting in mid-air, he playfully dived so steeply a couple of times that even Gorg cried out in alarm; and then, he made loop-the-loops several times in succession, until Priwinn sharply told him to behave himself.

As for the morning, it was exactly the opposite of the previous evening: Instead of flying into the day, they chased the night—so, the gray of dawn seemed endless.

Kim was miserably cold. Although Gorg sat in front, his big shoulders shielding the others from the icy stream of air, the night chill still was intense. By the time Rangarig finally began to descend in search of a landing place for their first rest, Kim had lost all feeling in his arms and legs. He felt like a block of ice. His hands and feet were so numb that the giant had to lower him from Rangarig's back—he couldn't manage to dismount by himself.

Chunklet, too, was shivering.

When the long night finally ended, however, the rays of the sun quickly gained strength. As the travelers felt the terrible cold recede, life gradually returned to their bodies. Luckily, they'd landed on a mountain, and there was plenty of dry wood. Moreover, Kim still had Brobing's flints, so he suggested that they make a fire. The Prince of the Steppe, however, dismissed the idea, tersely noting that that it wouldn't be worthwhile. Then, he turned around and was about to walk off, leaving Kim standing there. Kim swiftly reached out, though, and forcibly held the other boy back.

"That doesn't make any sense," he said. "Why are you against making a fire?"

Priwinn gave Kim a puzzling, unfriendly look and tried to break away, but Kim held him with an iron grip.

"And why do we always rest in such isolated places?" Kim continued, gesturing at the rugged landscape.

"Ask Rangarig," Priwinn replied truculently.

"I'm asking *you*," Kim retorted. "Priwinn—you're hiding something from me, aren't you? This mountain is just as impassable as the mesa yesterday. And you don't want to make a fire. What are you hiding from?"

Priwinn didn't answer.

Now that Kim had started up, he finally asked the question that had been gnawing at him ever since he'd met up with the prince again: "What are you doing here, Priwinn? Why aren't you in Caivallon with your father? And why are you wearing this armor?"

"It's very useful," Priwinn replied, adroitly evading the other questions. "You should know that better than I do—you wore it long enough."

Kim looked again, this time more closely. Finally, he understood. His eyes widened in astonishment.

"You're seeing right," Priwinn said. "This is the armor that you wore when you led us in the fight against Boraas' army. We saved it so that we would always remember those terrible days—and also, I believe, in order to honor you a little." Suddenly, he smiled. "If you want, I'll give it back to you. It does belong to you, after all."

For a moment, Kim was tempted to accept Priwinn's offer and once again wrap himself in the black steel of Morgon. The armor was more than just armor, at least for him. He had felt the magical power dwelling in the sword, making him invincible. Yes, for a moment, he imagined what it would be like to don the armor and once again ride to battle at the head of an army.

But in a battle against whom?

"No, thanks," he said after a while. "Go ahead and keep it. But tell me—why are you wearing it all? And who are you running from?"

"No one," Priwinn replied much too hastily to sound convincing. When he noticed Kim's skeptical look, he saved himself with an embarrassed smile and a shrug of his shoulders. "I wouldn't necessarily say we're on the run," he said. "But you're right. It's better for us if we're not seen."

"Why? Tell me the reason," Kim said.

Again, considerable time passed before Priwinn answered. "Remember Limb, the yellow fellow?"

"How could I not?" Kim said. "It wasn't that long ago!"

"Then, you're also aware of how the others on the tree reacted to him. They despise him and those like him. His presence is unwelcome. I'm sure if the others could do so, they would harm him."

"What does that have to do with you and Gorg?"

"We're in the same position," Priwinn replied. "We share Limb's views, and I'm afraid we'll also share his fate."

"I don't understand a word you're saying." Kim was losing his patience.

Priwinn shrugged his shoulders and looked at the ground. "Let's just say . . . word has gotten around that Gorg and I have something against the iron men. People have let us know that we're not all that welcome, if you understand what I mean."

"You?" Kim asked skeptically. "The Prince of Caivallon?"

Priwinn sighed. "I've already said this several times: Some things have changed."

"You could say that," Kim said, heading back toward Rangarig and Gorg. It was about time that he saw Themistokles again, so he could get answers to the questions that he was dying to ask—a great many answers to a great many questions.

XI

It took them a long time to reach Gorywynn: almost six days. They lost another night on the evening of the sixth day, when the crystal fortress appeared on the horizon like a sparkling, rainbow-colored jewel; Priwinn told Rangarig to land before they reached the city. They alighted not on a remote mountain this time, but in the middle of an almost impenetrable forest, where the dragon's huge wings had to clear a path before he could land.

Kim had firmly resolved not to ask the prince any more questions, as the other boy would answer only in vague terms. Although they'd talked a lot during the previous six days, Kim had observed that Priwinn simply turned deaf in response to certain questions.

Now, Kim blew his top: "What do you think you're doing?!" he shouted at Priwinn as soon as they'd climbed down from Rangarig's back. "We could be there in half an hour!"

"We're going to spend the night here," Priwinn replied firmly. "Rangarig is tired, and so am I."

"Nonsense!" Kim protested. He, too, felt tired after the long journey, and he understood that the golden dragon was yet more exhausted. After all, Rangarig had to carry all their weight. Still, for the final stretch to Gorywynn, the dragon would've had to beat his wings only a few more times. Those few wing strokes definitely were not the issue.

"I have to know what's going on before I enter Gorywynn," Priwinn said. "It's been a long time since Gorg and I were last there—several months, to be precise. Who knows what things are like there now?" Priwinn held up his hand, halting Kim from interrupting. "We're going to meet with a friend tonight," he continued. "A man from Gorywynn. He'll tell us what the situation is there. After that, we'll decide what to do next."

"I don't want to wait that long," Kim countered. "I need to talk with Themistokles."

The prince shrugged. "So go," he said, "by all means. I'm not holding you back. Go ahead and start walking. Meanwhile, Gorg and I are going to get a good night's sleep. Once the sun comes up, we'll follow after you and pick you up on the way."

Kim had to stop himself from clenching his fists and charging at Priwinn. He might have done so, if it hadn't occurred to him that this, too, was part of the terrible changes happening in Magic Moon. Kim was changing, as well. He'd become irritable and impatient—and not just because of the exertion this journey entailed.

So, he stared at Priwinn with barely contained anger, and he turned around and headed across the clearing toward Rangarig, who was curled up at the edge of the forest. Although Kim had conversed often with Priwinn and Gorg, he'd talked only briefly with Rangarig in the past few days. Rangarig had raced through the air for long periods of time, and the journey had taken him more effort than anyone else. In the evenings, he'd curled up and fallen asleep almost as soon as they found firm ground under their feet. His eyes were closed this time, as well, so Kim feared he might be asleep already. But as Kim approached, the golden dragon's big eyelids opened, and a faint smile appeared in his eyes.

"Hello, little hero," he said. "We're almost home now."

"We could be there already," Kim hesitantly began.

One of Rangarig's eyes veered away, taking in the view across the clearing, and Kim realized that Rangarig had understood every word he and Priwinn had said, though they'd been very far away. "True," Rangarig noted, sighing. "But he's right, you know. It's better to find out what things are like in Gorywynn first—and better yet, to get some rest and recover our strength. We might need it."

"What for?"

"For example, if we have to get out of there in a hurry."

"Flee? Is that what you mean?" Kim asked skeptically. "Gorywynn is your home."

Rangarig's gaze grew sad. "That may well be," he murmured. "I used to live there . . ." He hesitated for a moment; then, he said, "I'm not sure if I still belong there."

"How can you say that?!" Kim exclaimed.

Rangarig shook his head. "Why don't you believe Priwinn?" he asked. "The Crystal Fortress isn't what it used to be. And *I'm* not, either." He sighed again, this time very deeply. To Kim's ears, it sounded almost like a sob. "You see, little hero, sometimes I long for a place I don't even know."

Kim said nothing. After a while, Rangarig continued in a lower tone of voice: "Sometimes, I sense something inside of me that scares me. At those times, I long for wilderness, solitude, and the rugged mountains, where my relatives live. Maybe that's where I belong. . . ."

"I don't know your relatives," Kim replied earnestly, "but from what I've heard, other dragons are wild monsters that frighten people."

"Exactly," Rangarig murmured.

Kim wanted to respond, but it seemed as if he were looking at Kelhim's face: the face of the bloodthirsty beast that the bear had become.

Kim shuddered. Kelhim had been a creature that could talk—just like Chunklet, Sheera, and Rangarig, too. *Is that what it is?* he thought, horrified. *Is that what Priwinn means—what all of us sense? That the magic is dying?*

"That's possible," Rangarig replied, and Kim realized with a shock that he'd spoken that thought out loud. "Sometimes, I think that's what's going on. Maybe the magic of Magic Moon is dying out. If that's the case though, little hero, then promise me one thing."

"What?"

"Don't be anywhere near me when it happens," Rangarig said. "Don't try to help me, because you won't be able."

Suddenly, Kim had to fight with all his might to hold back the tears that welled up in his eyes. "I promise," he replied, but it was hard for him to utter those words. When he finally had himself under control again, and the dragon was no longer a blurry figure dissolving before his eyes, Rangarig already had fallen sleep. Kim didn't know if Rangarig had heard his promise.

Dejected, Kim returned to Priwinn and the giant. They ate in silence. Not even Chunklet's and Sheera's ribald humor could cheer Kim up. For a few moments, he seriously considered taking up Priwinn's offer to set off for Gorywynn by himself—not because he believed he could get there faster than he could the next morning on Rangarig's back—simply so he could be alone.

Of course, he didn't do that. Shortly after night set in, Kim managed to stretch out on the soft moss of the forest floor and fall asleep—not for long, though.

Kim woke up with a start. From the position of the moon in the sky, he could tell that it still was relatively early. He hadn't awakened on his own but had been roused by Gorg's and Priwinn's voices. Groggy with sleep, Kim sat up all the way, blinking a few times. In an instant, he was wide awake. His friends were not alone.

Prince Priwinn and Gorg the giant had moved away from Kim about a dozen paces and were conversing in hushed tones with two very tall men. One of them continually gestured as he spoke. The other stood there, not saying anything, alternately looking at the toes of his boots and at the sleeping dragon, which resembled a mountain of golden scales on the other side of the clearing. One of those things made him very nervous.

Kim stood up and approached the little group. At this, Priwinn and the stranger broke off their conversation, and the prince introduced Kim as a "friend" without mentioning his name. The man briefly looked him over with unconcealed mistrust. However, the man seemed to accept Priwinn's explanation, for he turned back to the prince and continued.

"Not anymore. Something is happening in the fortress, though, my lord. No one has seen Themistokles for weeks. Meanwhile, the place is teeming with dwarves. Before long, they'll own the whole fortress and the crystal city around it, as well."

"Dwarves?" Gorg made a face, and Kim winced. "And the wizard isn't doing anything to stop it?"

"I already told you—no one has seen him. Besides, what is he supposed to do? They didn't force their way in."

"As they normally do?" Kim asked.

The man gave him another suspicious look and answered only after Priwinn urged him. "They were summoned."

"By whom?"

"By those fools in Gorywynn!" the man shouted vehemently. "Iron men here, iron men there! Dwarves here, dwarves there!" he said hotly. "They're building and digging and overturning everything, everywhere you look. That's not the way I want to live!" He turned to Priwinn. "The time finally has come to start the attack, Your Majesty!"

Priwinn shot him an almost conspiratorial look, but it was too late.

"Start the attack?" Kim asked. "What does he mean by that?"

"Oh, nothing," Priwinn said evasively.

"Hogwash!" Kim said furiously. "I haven't been here long, Priwinn, but I'm not stupid. You smash iron men to pieces wherever you see them. You avoid all living beings, and you're afraid to be seen in Gorywynn. Now, this man is talking about attacking. What's going on?"

Priwinn didn't answer, but the stranger gestured at Kim and asked, "Who is this boy, Your Majesty? Why do you permit him to talk to you that way?"

"My name is Kim."

The man's eyes widened. "Kim?" he repeated. "You're—" Suddenly, he gasped and—to Kim's mortification—fell to his knees. "Of course!" the stranger gasped. "Please, forgive me for not immediately recognizing you! It's you! You've come back! Now, everything will be all right! With you at the forefront, we'll be victorious!" He turned to Prince Priwinn. "Why didn't you tell us that he's back?"

"There was no opportunity," the prince said hastily. "He only just arrived here."

Kim looked at Priwinn in astonishment. Neither Priwinn nor Gorg said anything. Chunklet grumbled testily, "You still don't get it yet, do you, little fool? Unless I'm mistaken, your nice friends have been whetting their knives for quite some time, getting ready to cut off some heads. Am I right?"

Priwinn gave Chunklet a furious look. Then, to Kim's surprise, the prince replied, "No heads—at the most, a few empty iron skulls."

"You want . . . an insurrection?" Kim murmured incredulously.

"No, of course not!" Priwinn said. "We just want to get things back on the right track, that's all. The dwarves and their iron men are dangerous. If people don't understand that, then we'll just have to—"

"Make them do what's good for them," Kim interrupted bitterly.

"If that's how you want to put it." Priwinn clenched his fists angrily. "I for one am not going to stand by and do nothing while Magic Moon goes to ruin."

"And you think I'm going to help you with this?" Kim sputtered.

"Do whatever you want." Priwinn abruptly turned around and stalked off.

Kim watched him go with a growing feeling of helplessness. He wanted to follow Priwinn, but something held him back. For the second time that evening, he fought back tears. This time, they were tears of anger and frustration. It was all so different from his first visit to Magic Moon. The existence of this land had been at stake back then, as well, but at least then they'd known who their enemies were. This time, it really seemed as if . . . as if they all were becoming their own worst nightmare.

"I . . . I don't understand, my lord," said the stranger with whom Priwinn had spoken. The other man still stood there, silently staring at Kim with wide eyes. "Didn't you come back to . . . to help us?"

"Yes, I did," Kim replied. "However, I still don't know enough."

The man was about to reply, but Gorg held up his hand, commanding silence. "Go now. We need to confer. Tomorrow, an hour after sunrise, we'll meet up in Gorywynn. Go!" The last word was almost shouted.

The two men hastily turned around and disappeared in the forest. Rangarig fleetingly opened one eyelid, blinked, and then resumed his snoring.

Grim silence prevailed for a while after the two visitors had disappeared. Gorg let out a deep sigh and looked at Kim. All at once, Kim felt small and petty. The giant was his friend; Prince Priwinn was, too. They may have failed to tell him the whole truth—but not to conspire against him.

Gorg, in the meantime, continued to stare at him. Then, he spun around, grabbed Kim by the arm, and swept him over to the snoring dragon.

"Rangarig!" Gorg bellowed so loudly that the whole forest echoed with his words. "Wake up! We're going on a little ride!"

Gorywynn truly was not very far from the forest when Rangarig's powerful wings took to the air. However, the winged dragon headed down for a landing before they reached the river. A small, fortified town was located at the river bend, so they had to go considerable distance on foot. Kim almost ran into the defensive wall that surrounded the town on three sides. The wall was such a dark color that it barely stood out from the night. In the nick of time, Gorg reached out with one hand and held Kim back, putting the forefinger of his other hand to his lips. "Shh!"

"What's this?" Kim whispered.

High above him, Gorg shrugged his shoulders. "I wish I could have spared you this sight, but I guess this is how it has to be. You're being terribly unfair to Priwinn, you know."

"Well, maybe he should've told me what's actually going on here," Kim whispered, becoming angry once again.

Gorg just smiled. "Don't you think he would do that if he could?" He held up his hand when Kim made to reply. "Quiet now. Come, I'll put you on my shoulders so that you can see over the wall."

Before Kim's head had risen above the top of the wall, he got his first surprise: As his hands glided along the top, searching for something to hold onto, he felt how cold and smooth it was—much too cold for wood and too smooth for stone.

"It's iron!" Kim exclaimed.

"Right," Gorg rumbled. "This entire town is built of iron. But be quiet, please. If they see us, we're done for."

Kim wondered what kind of danger might frighten even a giant, but he obediently kept silent. When Gorg lifted Kim so that he could look on the other side of the iron wall, the sight left him speechless, in any case.

As Gorg had said, the entire town was made of iron. To Kim, it seemed more like a fortress than a town. Red light streamed out of numerous windows, so the irregularly shaped town square looked as if it had been dipped in blood. Shadowy figures moved between the buildings—some of them large and angular. However, there were also small shapes no larger than children that moved nimbly, like weasels. They had shrill, dissonant voices.

"Dwarves!" he whispered.

Gorg's up-stretched arms shook as he nodded his large head. "Yes. They built this town. They give the orders here, too."

Kim took a look around. Reddish light streamed through some of the open doors, and he could hear hammers ringing and clanking. From time to time, sparks flew, and the wind carried the smell of molten iron and burning coal.

"Forges!" Kim noted with surprise. "What are they building here?"

The giant held Kim up high for a few seconds more before gently setting him down. Then, he replied, "Anything people want: wagons, tools, weapons . . ."

"I thought their workshops were in the eastern mountains."

"Yes, most of them are," Gorg confirmed. "Maybe the iron men are made there, too, but that's their secret. In any case, they often work throughout Magic Moon. As the inhabitants of Magic Moon buy more and more iron goods, it's too burdensome for them to transport everything all the way from the eastern mountains. No one had any objections when the dwarves suggested building forges here."

Kim's gaze wandered over the eerie black wall. He shuddered. In the night, the iron didn't look like iron at all, rather like something that swallowed up light and warmth the way a sponge soaks up water.

"You should see it during the day," Gorg murmured. "Anyway, come along. That's not the only thing I wanted to show you. And keep it quiet!"

Dejected, Kim followed the giant. They walked a good distance from the iron town before they headed back toward the river. Before they were halfway there, the giant got down on his hands and knees. Kim stopped and peered into the darkness, curious and alert.

After a while, he saw what Gorg was worried about. It wasn't absolutely dark ahead of them: A dusky red glow seemed to shine up directly from the earth. Muffled voices and regular, sharp pounding could be heard, apparently coming from underground, as well.

They cautiously moved forward. When Kim realized what they approached, he had to exert all his willpower to keep from crying out.

Before them was a huge, pitch-black hole. It was so deep that it resembled the crater of a volcano, and the figures moved about on the floor looked like toys.

Gorg reminded him to keep quiet as Kim got down on his belly, inching forward until his head and shoulders extended past the edge of the pit. It took quite a while for him to figure out what was going on down below.

Men struck the walls and floor of the pit with sledgehammers and pick axes. Others loaded the broken rock onto iron wagons, which then were hoisted up with great effort. A dozen men labored on each of the fully laden carts. Iron men and dwarves moved among these figures, supervising the workers. Sometimes, Kim heard the crack of a whip.

It looked like a pit mine. "If the men down there are working voluntarily, then why are the overseers behaving like slave drivers?" Kim whispered.

"Because that's what they are," Gorg hissed angrily.

"Slaves?" Kim asked incredulously. "I don't believe that. Themistokles would never allow such a thing!"

"Well," Gorg replied softly, "this is how it works. You were talking about Brobing, remember? He bought an iron man, and a dwarf came to collect the money. Do you remember saying the dwarf seemed almost disappointed that Brobing had no difficulty paying?"

Kim nodded.

"He didn't just seem that way," the giant growled, "believe me. Those men down there were once like Brobing. They bought iron men and other dubious things. The dwarves make it easy: If people don't have the money, then they can buy on credit and pay later in installments. Some manage to clear the debt, like our friend. Most of them do, to be quite honest—but not everyone. The ones who don't live up to their obligations . . . well, they have to work for the dwarves until their debts are paid off. They mine more iron ore so that more idiots can become indebted to the dwarf folk."

"That's unbelievable," Kim murmured. "Themistokles isn't doing anything to stop it?"

"No," Gorg rumbled. "And this isn't the only place where this is happening. Soon, all Magic Moon will belong to the dwarves." He cautiously crawled backward and stood up. "Now, I'm going to show you something else," he whispered.

Kim wasn't sure if he wanted to see more, but Gorg kept on walking, so Kim had to follow.

They made a wide detour around the pit, heading toward the river until they came to a broad, perfectly straight road. Kim thought they would continue their way along the road, but the giant stopped at its edge and squatted down. Without saying anything, he pointed down.

Kim's heart jumped from the shock when his fingers touched the ground. The street, too, was made of iron.

"Do you see what they're doing to us?" Gorg said. His voice sounded full of hate. "They're killing the soil! Nothing ever will grow here again, Kim, no matter how much time goes by. This bit of ground is dead; more land will die if we don't stop them. This is what Limb was talking about. They're building iron roads across the land. They're building iron cities. They're beginning to dam up the rivers to get waterpower for their forges. Do you want to see the river? They've built an iron wall across it. Their hammers now work ten times as fast, but the land on the other side of the wall is drying up. Where there used to be fertile farmland, there will be arid wasteland a year from now. Do you want to see it?"

Kim silently shook his head. He believed his friend.

He felt a helpless, almost painful anger. "Let's go back," he said. "I think I understand Priwinn now."

Without saying anything more, they went back the way they'd come.

They were halfway around the pit when Gorg suddenly came to a halt. Kim saw his powerful shoulders straighten. Before the giant even had time to call out a warning, three figures appeared as if conjured by magic: a dwarf and two angular iron men.

Initially, the dwarf seemed as surprised as Kim, but he quickly recovered and immediately began to rant.

"What are you doing here?!" he shouted in a shrill, unpleasant voice. "Why aren't you working, and—" He broke off in mid-sentence when his gaze fell on the giant. Then, he wailed: "You're the ones! You . . . you're the rebels! Seize them!"

The iron men immediately advanced in Gorg's direction. The dwarf pulled a dagger from his belt and lunged at Kim.

Kim dodged a violent but unskilled thrust of the blade. He grabbed the dwarf's collar with his left hand and slapped the little twerp on the cheek so hard that the dwarf dropped his weapon with a squeak, plopped down on the ground, and covered his face with both hands. His shrill voice began to howl.

The giant, in the meantime, had grabbed one of the two iron men and was swinging him around and around. Gorg hadn't brought his cudgel along, so he had to fight the two iron giants with his bare hands—definitely not an easy task even for a giant. He defended himself by repeatedly slamming one iron man against the other. Finally, the strain was too great even for the iron men. With a harsh crack, one of the iron man's arms broke off—and now, Gorg had a cudgel.

He knew how to use it. After several thuds, two motionless iron men with bashed-in heads laid in the dust next to the whimpering dwarf.

Kim grinned happily when he saw the little man's eyes pop out of their sockets. Obviously, up until now, the dwarf had considered his two iron bodyguards invincible.

"So," Kim asked, "does that answer your question about what we're doing here?"

"Dirty rabble!" the dwarf gasped. "Pack of thieves! You've earned what's coming to you!"

"No," Gorg said gravely. "Don't worry. I'm not asking for a single penny."

Kim bent forward, pointing his forefinger at the dwarf. "So, now you are going to answer a few questions of ours," he said. "And I advise you not to lie, or else my friend here will give you a lesson on how to tell the truth."

The giant grunted in agreement and scowled so fiercely that even Kim was afraid for a second.

"All right," Kim began, getting directly to the point, "what do you have to do with the children who have disappeared?"

"Children?" the dwarf murmured. His gaze moved back and forth between Kim's face and the giant's. He gulped; Kim could see the Adam's apple on his spindly neck hop up and down. "We hate children," he said. "We definitely have nothing to do with—Ack!"

The giant had grabbed the dwarf's right foot with two fingers. He lifted the little man about ten feet up in the air, and the giant was pretending that he was going to drop the dwarf.

"That wasn't the answer that I wanted to hear," Kim said. He gave Gorg a look that told him not to do any real harm to the dwarf, and Gorg nodded. He didn't drop the little twerp, but he did shake the little man until his teeth audibly chattered.

"Let me go!" the dwarf cried shrilly.

"Be happy to," Gorg said, letting him go.

The dwarf howled—howling all the louder when Gorg caught him at the last second.

"Well?" Kim prompted.

"The caves!" whimpered the dwarf. "They're in the caves. They—"

Suddenly, the surrounding darkness swarmed with black, iron robots. Gorg gasped in pain and shock when one iron man's shovel hand suddenly struck him in the neck. He reeled, fell to his knees, and let go of the dwarf. A second iron man appeared out of the darkness and knocked the giant all the way to the ground.

Kim, too, found himself under simultaneous attack by two opponents. He managed to dodge the snapping claws, but he paid for it with a shredded shirtsleeve and a bit of skin. Crying out in pain, he fell, touched something hard, and instinctively grabbed it. It was the dagger the dwarf had dropped.

When one of the iron men bent over to deliver a final blow, Kim thrust the blade upward at an angle. The iron man tumbled backward, his arms pulling the second iron man down, as well.

Gasping, Kim got back on his feet.

Likewise, Gorg had rid himself of his assailants and now stood. The fight was by no means over—quite the contrary. More iron men appeared out of the night, and it became harder for Kim to dodge their grasping claws. Gorg struck down four or five; but for every one he destroyed, the night spewed out three more. Step by step, Kim and Gorg were driven back until they were cornered by the pit's entrance.

The dwarf urged his iron men on with shrill cries. "Get them," he shouted over and over. "Strike down the giant! I want the boy unharmed."

"You'll never take me alive, anyway!" Gorg thundered, grabbing one of the iron men with both his hands. In a tremendous show of strength, he quickly lifted the robot and threw him like a live cannon ball. Struck by their comrade, five or six of the robots broke into pieces.

Nevertheless, Kim and Gorg were losing the battle as more and more iron men appeared. Then, the dwarves arrived—three or four little men who had been attracted by the sound of battle now swung their daggers and gave piercing cries.

Abruptly, an enormously loud roar sounded.

Before Kim could grasp what had happened, a giant golden shape sliced through the air. The dwarves whirled around at the blood-curdling roar. Even the iron men hesitated a moment.

Rangarig shot down out of the night like an attacking falcon. His gigantic wings whipped the air, generating storm winds strong enough to blow Gorg off his feet. The iron men were too heavy to be knocked over, but that sealed their fate.

Rangarig's golden wings struck the robots, smashing and scattering them like dry leaves. Any iron men that survived the initial attack fell victim to Rangarig's grasping claws and thrashing tail.

The dragon raged among the iron figures like a golden demon. His strong jaws crushed iron plates; his claws shredded and tore iron limbs; and with a single motion, his tail swept a half-dozen iron men over the edge of the pit. Half a minute after the dragon had appeared, the fight was over. Not a single iron man survived.

Kim laboriously picked himself up. He immediately turned around, intending to grab the dwarf and continue the interrogation. However, Gorg restrained him. "Forget it," the giant said hurriedly. "They'll send reinforcements. Rangarig can't take on hundreds of them! Hurry!"

Kim wasn't so sure about that. After what he had just seen, he thought the dragon could handle anything—but he sensed that wasn't Gorg's only reason for haste. He glared at the dwarf and left it at that. Then, he quickly followed the giant onto the dragon's back.

Rangarig still was frenzied. His claws tore up the ground, and his tail and giant wings whipped the air.

"More!" he thundered. "Where are they?! I'll rip them to pieces!"

Kim shuddered. He couldn't express it in words, but what he heard in Rangarig's voice frightened him to the core. The dragon was like a wild predator that had tasted blood for the first time. Kim was almost afraid of the dragon as he climbed up and grabbed onto Rangarig's scales.

The winged creature rose up and disappeared into the night as swiftly as an arrow.

XII

"That wasn't a particularly good idea," Priwinn remarked when Kim told him what had happened, "but at least you now know what's really going on." That was his only comment.

Indeed, there was barely any time to say much more than that. Rangarig waited on the ground just long enough for the prince, Chunklet, and Sheera to climb upon his back. Then, with a powerful stroke of his wings, he immediately rose up in the air and flew south, toward the crystal fortress' lakeshore. In Priwinn's opinion, there was no point in playing hide-and-seek; they'd be safer in Gorywynn than here in the forest, where dwarves and an army of iron men undoubtedly were tracking them down.

Although it was almost midnight, the city surrounding the fortress was illuminated as bright as day. Rangarig approached from high in the air, and the city gradually emerged from the clouds.

At first, they saw only a faint, colorful glimmer—like a pale northern light. Then, a jewel shining with all the colors of the rainbow gradually transformed into a breathtaking spectacle of pinnacled towers, huge walls, and defensive battlements: a giant, sparkling diamond in a thousand hues, gleaming on the lakeshore like a magic star fallen from heaven. As Rangarig slowly spiraled downward, circling the city with his wings outstretched like a glider, Kim saw that the canyonlike streets still bustled with activity, despite the late hour.

A warm, happy feeling overcame Kim as the dragon flew in ever-tighter circles, looking for a place to land. Although Kim had been to Magic Moon only once before—and he now sensed that new horrors awaited him behind those shimmering walls—he still felt like he was coming home.

He would see Themistokles again; and no matter how ominous the circumstances, he was looking forward to that.

His disappointment was that much greater when, all of a sudden, Priwinn told the dragon not to land directly in front of the gates but, instead, where they couldn't be seen from the city.

"What's going on now?" Kim muttered irritably as he slid off the dragon's back. The giant remained seated on the dragon's neck. Rangarig barely waited until Kim and Priwinn had taken a few steps away before he rose back up in the air again and disappeared into the night.

"Gorg isn't coming along?" Kim asked, confused.

"No," Priwinn replied. "He would attract too much attention. Besides, it's better if one of us stays outside—in case we need help. Who knows what awaits us in the city?"

While Kim looked at him, still disconcerted, the prince dug around in his bag and pulled out a piece of brown material: a tattered cloak. Priwinn unfolded it and threw it over his shoulders. He hid the black helmet and gloves in the bag, also pushing the sword around behind him so that it stayed under the tattered cloak, concealed from curious eyes. Then, he scooped up a handful of dirt and rubbed it on his face. *Now, he looks like a beggar,* Kim thought, *instead of the Prince of Caivallon.* Obviously, he considered it very important not to be recognized.

After Priwinn completed his disguise, he regarded Kim with a critical eye. What he saw seemed to satisfy him—by this point, Kim's clothing was in rags. With a quick sideways tilt of his head, the prince gestured at the dwarf's dagger, which Kim had stuck in his belt.

"Better hide that," he said. "Poor kids don't own valuable weapons."

Kim pulled out the dagger and looked at it, puzzled. To him, the dwarf's dagger looked shabby.

"Keep a close eye on it," Priwinn said earnestly. "It's a blade that was forged in the dwarves' caves." He patted his cloak. "Except for my sword, only the dwarves' weapons can pierce the armor of an iron man."

Kim remembered how easily the slender blade had passed through the thick iron plates and how devastating its effect had been on the iron man. He quickly stuck the little dagger under his shirt and checked to be sure that he wouldn't inadvertently injure himself. Then, they headed toward the gate.

Rangarig had set them down a considerable distance away, so it took a while before they reached the city. Kim's joy at seeing the gate again was mixed with a hint of sadness when he observed that it was locked. As far as he could remember, Gorywynn's gates had been closed on only one single occasion: during the siege by Boraas' black riders.

Kim was shocked when he took a closer look at the gate. Unlike the walls and battlements, it wasn't made of colored glass; it was made of iron!

It was an ugly gate—heavy, bulky, and so massive that it looked as if it could withstand cannon fire. It was dotted with fist-sized rivets, each of which ended in a barbed hook. It resembled a hideously scarred wound on the shining crystal fortress' wall.

Someone must have spotted them because, as they came closer, Kim saw shadowy movement behind the wall's translucent glass. The gate itself didn't move, however. Only after they were within a couple of paces of the gate did a peephole open in its huge black surface. A pair of dark eyes peered out at them suspiciously.

"Who goes there?"

Kim was about to answer, but Priwinn stepped forward, signaling with a quick, furtive gesture for Kim to keep quiet. "Two travelers," he said quickly. "We're tired and hungry and looking for a place to spend the night."

"Somewhere to spend the night? You're too late. Come back when the sun is up. Or better yet, don't come back at all. There's no room for beggars or peddlers here."

"We're not beggars," Priwinn said. He reached under his cloak and pulled out a gold coin. "We can pay for food and lodging. Here, see for yourself."

The dark eyes fixed for a moment on the coin glinting in Priwinn's hand. Then, the peephole cover slammed shut. A little later, a low door opened in the bottom of the iron gate. A hand impatiently beckoned them forward and snatched the coin from Priwinn while the prince bent forward to pass through the door.

Kim followed with a pounding heart. When he straightened up again, a soft, pink-tinged light enveloped him. Once again, he stood on the familiar mosaic glass of Gorywynn's streets.

Yet, as Kim discovered to his dismay, this no longer was the same place he'd known so well. He felt a sudden blast of ice-cold wind, and it took a moment before he realized that the cold didn't come from without.

The man who let them in was a tall, gray-haired soldier of uncertain age; he was bulky and wore a hardened expression. A sword hanging from his belt had notches on the blade, indicating that it wasn't merely for decoration but had been used often. There was something greedy and speculative about the guard. Three other armed men accompanied him. They casually leaned on their spears, keeping an extremely sharp eye on Kim and Priwinn. *Since when have there been armed guards here?*

"What about your friend there?" the gray-haired man asked, looking at Kim for a moment. "Can he pay, too?"

"Since when do you have to pay to enter Gorywynn?" Kim burst out before Priwinn could stop him. He seethed with anger.

The prince shot a distressed, almost frantic look at Kim as he quickly reached into his clothing and produced another piece of gold, which he held out to the guard. "I'm paying for him," Priwinn said. "And please, excuse my friend. He hasn't been here for . . . a long time. He's not familiar with the customs here."

"So it seems," the man growled. The gold coin disappeared beneath his belt just like the first one, but the man's expression still registered suspicion. "Who is this big mouth?"

"Just a dumb kid from the countryside, sir," Priwinn said hastily, trying to calm the gray-haired man while giving Kim another conspiratorial look. Before the soldier could ask any more questions, Priwinn continued: "Could you perhaps recommend an inn, sir? We'd rather not spend the night on the street."

After a third piece of gold found its way into his pockets, the guard muttered, "Go to my brother-in-law, Grodler. Tell him I sent you, and he'll give you a room—if you can pay. Just go down this street. It's called the Golden Calf. You can't miss it."

"Thank you, sir," Priwinn said, grabbing Kim by the arm and almost forcibly dragging him along. Kim resisted the temptation to turn around and look at the guards; but as they crossed the large square behind the gate and entered the lane, he could feel their gazes touching his back like unpleasantly warm hands.

"Are you crazy?" Priwinn whispered once they were out of earshot. He kept on walking, however. "Do you want to get us arrested and thrown in the tower?"

"What?" Kim was outraged. "We haven't done anything wrong!"

"Shh," Priwinn said. "Remember: Getting in here is easier and cheaper than getting back out. Now, hold your tongue before we attract any more attention."

Several people already had turned around to give them curious looks. Although Kim avoided looking into their eyes, he could tell that people were staring at them. It didn't feel good.

He also was shocked to see several dwarves among the passersby. Priwinn whispered for him to calm down, though, and Kim did his best. Fortunately, they didn't encounter any iron men as they continued on their way. However, that didn't mean anything: He already had heard from Priwinn that they were here—although perhaps not in such great numbers as elsewhere.

They reached the Golden Calf Inn but didn't go inside—to Kim's great relief. Through the open door, they could hear loud yelling and laughter. The laughter was unpleasant, making Kim shudder visibly.

"Amusing, isn't it?" Priwinn remarked bitterly. "Too bad we don't have more time. Otherwise, I'd show you all sorts of other fun things. Gorywynn really has changed."

"This is . . . terrible," Kim whispered.

"And that's not all," Priwinn said. "Not by a long shot. Look up."

As Kim's gaze wandered in the direction Priwinn's hand pointed, he didn't see anything particularly unusual at first. Then, he saw it jutting up among the city's crystal citadels: a massive, blunt tower, with walls that absorbed the softly glowing light of the crystal city. Kim knew the tower was made of iron.

"Where are we going?" he asked in a low voice after walking alongside Priwinn for a good while in complete silence.

"To the palace," Priwinn replied. "We have to find out where Themistokles is. Maybe they're holding him prisoner. We have to hurry, though. I wouldn't be surprised if that man from the gate is following us to check if we stopped at the Golden Calf. They're suspicious of all strangers."

They didn't say anything to each other as they approached Gorywynn Castle. With each step, Kim saw something else horrifying: Already, some streets were paved with iron; the doors of many houses were no longer made of glass, but consisted of black, light-absorbing metal. They also encountered dwarves here and there, and it became harder and harder for Kim to restrain himself. The terrible changes that had taken place in Gorywynn made him furious.

Priwinn slowed his pace as they approached the palace. The rambling fortress was still the highest city building, towering over the battlements. Kim noted with relief that the use of iron hadn't advanced this far—yet.

Nevertheless, the soft glow emanating from the crystal walls had paled. The light seemed to have lost some of its warmth. It wasn't any less bright, but it was . . . cold.

"How are we going to get in?" Kim asked.

Priwinn shrugged as he gnawed on his lower lip and thought it over. "It's not going to be easy, that's for sure," he said. "You saw the guards at the city gate. Well, the palace is guarded more closely. City residents aren't even allowed to enter it without permission."

Kim blanched. When he'd been here before, no door had been locked, anywhere. Fortress and city had been as one. Everyone had been welcome. This time, though, Kim was racking his brains to figure out how to sneak into that glass building without being seen.

Then, they got a lucky break. Priwinn suddenly grabbed Kim's arm and hurriedly pulled him into a niche between two buildings. Immediately afterward, a fully laden wagon rumbled past them, pulled by two mules driven by a dwarf cracking a whip. Before Kim knew what was happening, his companion pulled him forward. They dove under the tarp that covered the wagon.

"How do you know that it's heading into the castle?" Kim whispered.

He couldn't see Priwinn's face under the tarp, but he heard the prince emphatically gesture in the dark, urging silence. The prince whispered a soft reply, finally: "I *don't* know that—but there's such a thing as luck, right?"

Well, Kim thought, *maybe so. Maybe we'll be lucky.* Indeed, the wagon continued for only a few seconds before coming to a stop. The two boys could hear a huge gate wrench open. A little later, the wagon rumbled on; after much bumping and swaying, it arrived at its destination.

Afterward, of course, Kim knew the wagon ride lasted only a short time; while they hid in the dark, however—trembling with the fear that the tarp might be pulled back and they'd be discovered—time stretched out forever.

Eventually, the voices beside them grew fainter. After a few deep breaths, Priwinn took a chance and cautiously lifted a corner of the tarp, squinting his eyes as he looked out. "Now!" he ordered. "Hurry!"

Moving quickly, they slipped out from under the tarp and rushed across the inner courtyard of the palace. Here, everything was the same, and Kim had no difficulty following Priwinn's navigation. They entered the main building through a narrow side door that Kim recalled led down to the kitchen and supply rooms. After stopping for a moment to listen, they slipped in.

The large room—with its many stoves, cabinets, and shelves full of pots and pans—was deserted. The unpleasant smell of spoiled food and stale water lingered in the air. Running behind Priwinn, Kim noticed that a thin layer of dust covered the floor and furnishings; nothing had been used for a very long time.

After they crossed the room and reached a narrow stairwell, he asked, "What now?"

Priwinn pondered for a moment; then, he pointed. "I think that's the back stairway for the servants," he said. "It goes directly to the upper floors, so the servants don't have to keep carrying food through the main hall. If we're lucky, we'll find the door to Themistokles' chamber."

That was easier said than done. As it turned out, there wasn't just one set of stairs. Although Priwinn had guessed correctly, it soon turned out that—in addition to the wide staircases and corridors of the palace—there was a whole labyrinth of secret passages meant for servants. They opened a dozen doors to find only dusty, abandoned rooms.

They kept seeing the same conditions they'd observed in the kitchen—everything was abandoned, and the air was stale. Kim felt as if he were wandering through a house abandoned by its residents decades ago. He mentioned this to Priwinn; the prince simply shrugged.

Finally, they found a chamber that didn't seem as "unlived in" as the other rooms. For a moment, Priwinn hesitated to step out from behind the curtain that hid the servants' door. Kim, too, took only a single, hesitant step into the room.

The chamber was very large, very quiet, and almost empty. Directly across from them was a narrow, straight wall, with a second, wider door. Aside from that, the room was circular and had windows facing all directions. Evidently, they were beneath the highest point of the tower. Although they could see precious paintings and tapestries on the walls, there was hardly any furniture—just a narrow bed; a simple table; and a large, sturdy chest made of oak planks. The only other furniture was an enormous chair carved from a single piece of wood. It had been pushed over to the window, so Kim and Priwinn could see only its high back. No one was in the room.

Kim looked around, disappointed.

Priwinn frowned. "I don't understand," he said. "This should be Themistokles' chamber. I've heard that it's at the top of the tower, and I was hoping that the wizard would be here." He sighed.

"You are absolutely right," came a voice.

Kim and Prince Priwinn whirled around in surprise.

The prince's hand flung back his cloak and closed over the handle of his sword. Kim's fingers also automatically reached for the dwarf dagger, which he'd carried under his shirt.

A figure now rose from the chair. Everything about him was white: his thick, shoulder-length hair; his bushy eyebrows and long, flowing beard; even his white robe that reached down to his ankles. An old man—very old—with shoulders stooped from carrying an invisible burden for countless years. Nevertheless, it was obvious that he must have been very tall at one time. His gentle eyes glowed with warmth and wisdom.

Kim trembled with excitement. "Themistokles?" he exclaimed. "You . . . you're alive!"

The old sorcerer smiled. "Why wouldn't I be? I may not be immortal, but I'm nowhere near the end of my days—even though some might consider me a little on the feeble side." His last words, accompanied by a gentle smile, were directed at Prince Priwinn, who stood motionless, staring at the wizard. A distressed look appeared on Themistokles' face when he saw that the young Steppe rider's hand still rested on the hilt of his sword.

"Priwinn, Priwinn," he said, shaking his head. "You haven't learned a thing, apparently. You're as much of a hothead as your father was—and still is, it seems to me. Why are you armed? And why did you come through the servants' door like a thief in the night, instead of knocking on the main door and asking for permission to enter, like a friend?"

The prince ignored his question. "You're . . . free?" he asked uncertainly. He quickly scanned the room as if expecting a trap. "You're not . . . a prisoner?"

"A prisoner?" Themistokles chuckled softly. "Here, Prince Priwinn? In my own fortress? Who would hold me captive in Gorywynn, where I am among friends?"

"Do you know, my lord, that your *friends* are demanding gold just for permission to enter the city?"

Themistokles sighed. "Yes, I've heard about that. Times are hard. Some things have changed." He sighed again, sank back down on his chair, and motioned at the table with a strangely tired gesture. "Sit down, my friends. I would offer you something, but it's nighttime and the servants are already asleep."

Themistokles' statement seemed very odd to Kim, who recalled the abandoned kitchen and all those dusty rooms. He exchanged a concerned look with Priwinn before sitting down, as requested.

"So you've come back," Themistokles said, now addressing Kim. "I'm truly pleased about that. It's been a long time since you've visited us, my young friend. Did you bring your sister along?"

Kim was confused, but he caught a warning look from Priwinn and restrained himself.

"No, unfortunately not," he said.

"That's too bad." Themistokles shut his eyes. For quite a while, he said nothing at all. Kim wondered whether the wizard might have fallen asleep, the way old people sometimes did in the middle of a conversation.

Finally, Themistokles opened his eyes again and asked, "What brought you here, Kim? The road to Magic Moon is long and difficult, especially for a person from your world. Did you come to visit old friends, or is there some other reason? Is something amiss at home?"

"No," Kim replied, disconcerted. "Just the opposite: I thought it was Magic Moon that needed help."

"Us?" Themistokles smiled. "Why would we need help? No, no. Everything here is just fine. Isn't that true, Priwinn?"

Priwinn's face darkened. "No, nothing at all is fine here," he replied angrily. "And you damned well know that, Themistokles! What is this nonsense? Are you trying to make fun of us?"

Themistokles honestly looked taken aback. "I'm afraid I don't understand your point, my friend," he said, a little annoyed.

Priwinn jumped up. "You—"

"Priwinn, please!" Kim interrupted the prince, gave him an almost pleading look, and then turned back to Themistokles. "I'm telling the truth, Themistokles. You summoned me. It was just a few days ago. Don't you remember?"

"You say I summoned you?"

"It was . . . in front of the hospital," Kim said. *What is going on with Themistokles?* His voice took on an urgent, desperate tone. "Try to remember, please! There was this boy from Caivallon who suddenly showed up in our world. And shortly after that, I saw your face reflected in the café window. Don't you remember, anymore? You looked as if you were afraid."

At first, Themistokles just stared at him, looking confused. Then, something frightening happened: His features became slack. All life disappeared from his eyes and, for a moment, he lost control of his face. His lower jaw sagged open, and his cheeks and eyelids drooped the way they do in the elderly, when they no longer have any control over their body. When he started to sway in his chair, Kim tensed, preparing to jump up quickly to catch Themistokles.

There was no need: The terrible change disappeared as quickly as it had come. When Kim's gaze returned to Themistokles' face, he once again saw the powerful, wise guardian and protector of Magic Moon—not a forgetful old man.

"Lords of Eternity," Themistokles whispered, "What's happening to me?" Trembling, he lifted his hands, touched his face and hair, and studied his fingertips for several seconds—as if looking for reassurance that he still was himself.

"Are you all right?" Priwinn asked, full of concern.

Themistokles nodded. "Yes," he said. "I am. What happened?"

Kim looked at him, not knowing how to answer. "You were . . . strange, somehow."

The wizard nodded sadly. "Strange," he repeated. "Yes, that . . . that' s probably on the mark. Sometimes . . . I feel . . . strange." His expression became more serious. "Like a tired old man, right?"

Embarrassed, his guests said nothing—but Themistokles urged them to answer. "That's how it was, wasn't it?"

"Yes," Kim said hesitantly, avoiding Themistokles' eyes. *First, Kelhim,* he thought. *Then, Rangarig. Now, Themistokles, too? No, that can't be!*

"It is," Themistokles said. Kim realized that the wizard had read his thoughts. "It is exactly as you think, Kim. The magic is fading away."

"But not in your case!" Kim cried in despair.

Themistokles smiled painfully. "When magic disappears from a land, the magical beings first sense it in their own bodies."

"What's happening here?" Kim asked wailed.

"We don't know," Themistokles replied. Then, with a resolute gesture, he continued in a changed tone of voice: "But enough of this. Time is short, and we have better things to do than waste it commiserating."

Kim breathed an inner sigh of relief. *Yes! This is the Themistokles I know!* With a few brief words, Kim related what he'd experienced and discovered on the journey there. The wizard listened in silence; however, he didn't seem particularly convinced when Kim finally got to the end, finishing with his suspicions that the dwarf folk from the eastern mountains had something to do with the disappearance of the children.

"I know that's what some people think," Themistokles said with a significant look at Priwinn, "but it's wrong, believe me. If it were that simple, we already would've gotten to the bottom of this mystery."

"The dwarf admitted it!" Priwinn cried.

Themistokles smiled tolerantly. "Let me ask you a question, Prince of Caivallon," he said. "If a giant grabbed you by the legs and shook you like a sack of berries, wouldn't you also confess to anything someone wanted to hear from you?"

"I believe Priwinn is right, though," Kim said in support of his friend. "This land is . . . going to ruin, Themistokles. When I was here last, everything was different. People and animals and plants lived together in harmony—and there were no iron men."

"Do you truly believe that thought never occurred to me?" Themistokles asked sadly. "No, Kim. As much as Priwinn and his hotheaded friends would like to blame the dwarves for everything, it's not their fault."

"They're disgusting folk!" Priwinn cried fervently.

"That may well be—in your eyes," Themistokles observed. "And they probably don't like you, either. But consider this, Prince: this unfortunate turn of events began before the dwarf folk appeared."

"But the mines!" Kim reminded him. "They're destroying the land, Themistokles. The dwarves are building streets of iron and killing the rivers."

"It's not the dwarves, my young friend," Themistokles repeated gently. He sighed deeply, looked past Kim into empty space for a minute, and then pointed at one of the tower room's many windows. "I often stand here and look out, Kim. Oh, I do see what's happening with this land—believe me. I see what you two have seen, and much, much more. The magic is fading away, Kim, that's true. But it's not the dwarves who are stealing it from us. The dwarves are here because the inhabitants of this land have summoned them. They didn't enter by force. The men and women of our world went to them. Maybe they *are* killing our world, but they're doing it because that's what the people here wanted."

"That's not true, Themistokles!" Priwinn protested. "Before very long, the whole land will consist of iron."

"Yes," Themistokles agreed sadly, "Because its inhabitants' hearts have changed, becoming as hard as iron and as cold as stone. Who knows? Maybe all these children didn't disappear—maybe they fled."

"Is that all that you have to say about it?" Kim asked softly.

"What else should I say, little hero?" Themistokles replied earnestly.

Kim sighed. "I . . . I don't know," he admitted. "I thought that we'd fight together against an enemy that's threatening Magic Moon . . . the way we did before."

"Fight?" Themistokles' gaze passed over the black armor that Priwinn wore before zeroing in on the dagger hidden under Kim's shirt. "No, Kim. The enemy threatening us this time does not come from without; it resides within us. The time of magic is over. It's as simple as that. All too soon, Magic Moon may no longer be a land of dreams and a place of fantasy. And if that's what its inhabitants want, I have neither the right nor the power to forbid such development. I've gotten old, Kim. Just as your friend Rangarig is turning into an evil old dragon, I am turning into a tired old man. I can't help you."

"It's not true!" Priwinn burst out, furious. "Not everyone here wants it that way. Not everyone is willing to let the magic vanish."

"I know," Themistokles said. "You and your friends are fighting against that. But your way is wrong: It won't lead you to your goal. I can't protect you forever. Besides—what do you want to do? Force the others to return to their former way of life?"

"If need be—yes," Priwinn said with absolute conviction.

"And if they don't want to? Do you want to start a war? Do you want brothers to fight against brothers, fathers against sons? The sword is not the answer, Prince Priwinn."

"Tell me an alternative!" Priwinn demanded.

"I can't do that," Themistokles retorted.

"What if . . . what if I go back to the Rainbow King?" Kim suggested. Prince Priwinn looked at him in surprise, while Themistokles' expression revealed he'd been waiting precisely for this suggestion.

"That wouldn't do any good," Themistokles said after a while. "He did help us once. That's true. This time, however, even he can't do anything for us."

"Why did you summon our friend, then?!" Priwinn exploded, pointing at Kim.

"He knows the answer," Themistokles said. "He's not aware of it yet, but the solution to all riddles is hidden deep within him. And your task, Prince of Caivallon, is to help him find the answer."

Before Priwinn could reply, there came a loud pounding outside the door, and an imperious voice demanded entry. Kim and the Steppe rider exchanged alarmed looks and made to stand up, but Themistokles gestured that they should be calm. He called out in a loud, calm voice, "Yes, what is it?!"

The door jerked open. Two men stormed in, clad in the same uniform as the guards at the gate. They were not alone. Behind them darted a spindly little figure, no larger than a child, with a dirty, wizened face. When Kim and Priwinn recognized the dwarf that Gorg had interrogated, they both were startled.

With a curse, Priwinn threw back his cloak and drew his sword. Kim also pulled out his weapon from beneath his tunic. The dwarf jumped back with a startled squeak, while his two companions likewise reached for their blades.

"Put down your weapons!" Themistokles' tone cut through the room like a knife, no longer the voice of a tired old man at all. It rang with so much authority that Kim almost was afraid as he sheathed his dagger. Priwinn and the two soldiers lowered their swords, as well.

"What do you think you're doing, drawing weapons in my chamber?!" Themistokles thundered. "Who are you? What do you want?"

"Those two!" the dwarf said hoarsely. He'd seen that Themistokles' anger was directed at his two visitors, as well, and now he pressed his advantage: "It's them! Seize them! I demand that they be locked up immediately!"

"You have no right to demand anything here, dwarf," Themistokles growled. His eyes sparkled, and the dwarf retreated half a step. "These two are my guests! I didn't invite you here, as I recall. Restrain yourself!" Somewhat more calmly, yet still in a sharp tone, he turned to one of the two soldiers. "What is the meaning of this, Captain?"

The captain hastily sheathed his sword and started to shuffle his feet.

"I beg your pardon, my lord," he began uncertainly, "but . . . but this dwarf has made some very serious charges against your two guests."

"Of what kind?" Themistokles asked.

"That one over there," the dwarf said, pointing his dirty forefinger at Kim like a dagger, "ambushed me and my friends. Together with a giant, he attacked us. They destroyed many of our iron men and would have killed the rest of us if we hadn't fled. We were going about our business when they appeared and began to attack us for no reason at all!"

"This boy? Against twelve of your iron men?" Themistokles chuckled. "You're joking, dwarf."

"As I said, he was with a giant!" the dwarf protested. "And a winged dragon was with them, too."

"Of course," Themistokles said calmly. "I know them."

The dwarf glared at him. "I demand my rights. These two must pay for the damage they caused."

"If that's all . . ." Themistokles smiled. He made some signs with his left hand, and a palm-sized golden nugget appeared in the air before the dwarf. "This ought to be more than enough to cover your losses, sir," Themistokles said.

The dwarf quickly bent down, picked up the gold, and stuck it in his pocket. The material tore under such a heavy weight, and the nugget clunked down on the dwarf's toes. He hopped around on one leg, screeching.

Kim suppressed a grin, and the two soldiers' faces also twitched suspiciously.

Themistokles was the only one who remained serious. "Does this settle the matter?" he asked.

"No," the dwarf said sullenly, after he'd calmed down and picked up the gold nugget again. He pointed accusingly at Kim. "So, you admit that this fellow is guilty. I demand that he be turned over to me. And the other one, too—I know he's one of the rebels who lives in the forests and ambushes our blacksmiths."

"Is that true?" Themistokles asked, turning to Prince Priwinn.

"Nonsense," Priwinn replied. "We don't live in the forests."

"So, there you have it," Themistokles said. "Nonsense." He laughed, but it sounded more like a snigger.

Kim gave the wizard an astonished look. That wasn't the way Themistokles normally behaved, making silly jokes like that . . .

The dwarf exhaled angrily. Then, he turned to the two guards and made a rude gesture. "I demand my rights, Captain," he snarled. "Those two treacherously attacked us. Are we dwarves so much less valuable than humans that people can treat us this way and get away with it?"

It was obvious that the captain was growing more uncomfortable with every passing second. He didn't look Themistokles in the eyes when he addressed the wizard. "Forgive me, my lord, but . . . but if the dwarf is telling the truth, then you must turn both your guests over to us. They committed a crime."

"We didn't!" Kim exclaimed. "This dwarf attacked us. We simply defended ourselves!"

"There, you heard it!" the dwarf snarled. "He admits it!"

Themistokles didn't answer immediately. When Kim turned around after a few seconds and looked at his face, he was deeply shocked. Themistokles' eyes flickered. It looked increasingly difficult for him to concentrate on the discussion; with effort, he managed to return to his former self.

"If that is the case, Captain," he said, "then I myself will pass judgment over them—or do you doubt my ability to judge?"

"Of course not, my lord," the captain hastily replied. "I beg your pardon."

"Granted," Themistokles said, trembling. "Now leave. I will hear what these two have to say and will decide what's to be done with them. Go—and take this ugly creature with you, before I turn him into a toad!"

The captain's eyes widened, and the dwarf's mouth gaped open in disbelief.

Before he went, the dwarf turned to Kim and glared at him with hate-filled eyes. "We'll meet again," he said with assurance. "Don't think for a minute that I'm going to drop this."

After the dwarf and the two soldiers left, Kim and Priwinn both hastily turned to face Themistokles. However, they couldn't bring themselves to say anything. The old sorcerer swayed, no longer possessing the strength to stand on his own feet. He dropped down on his chair with an exhausted sigh that sounded like a cry of pain.

"Themistokles!" Kim cried in fright. "What's wrong?"

"Weak . . ." Themistokles gasped, "I . . . I feel so weak. It's as if . . . something were draining my strength."

"The dwarf!" Priwinn cried, full of hate. "I'll show that fellow—"

"You'll do no such thing," Themistokles interrupted in a faint voice. "You must . . . flee. I don't know how long I can continue to protect you. The dwarf will come back. Go—while I am still . . . in control of myself. Go the same way you came. And watch out; they will try to ambush you."

"We can't leave you here alone!" Kim cried.

Themistokles shook his head again. Clearly tired, he extended his trembling hand and briefly touched Kim's cheek. "You are brave," he murmured, "but your courage would be wasted. Don't worry. I still am Lord of Gorywynn, and they wouldn't dare to raise a hand against me." He laughed softly, without the least trace of humor. "It's also completely unnecessary. Before long, I'll be nothing but a forgetful old man who sits in his tower chamber and counts the few stars that his shortsighted eyes can see. Maybe it's best this way. I am so tired. So infinitely tired . . ." With that, he actually fell asleep in mid-sentence.

Kim stared, beside himself. Then, he cried out and started to shake Themistokles' shoulder, not stopping until Priwinn forcibly pulled him away. Kim brushed Priwinn's hand aside. "Leave me alone!" he yelled.

"There's nothing we can do for him," Priwinn said earnestly. "Themistokles is right. We have to save our own lives."

"I'm not going to leave him behind!"

The Steppe rider sadly shook his head. "They won't harm him," he said. "Just look at him: He's no longer any threat. I think this conversation with us used every ounce of strength he had left. Let's go."

For a long while, Kim just stood there, looking at the old man asleep in the chair. Once again, his eyes filled with tears. The sight broke his heart.

Eventually, he realized that Priwinn was right. There was nothing they could do for Themistokles, and they themselves still were in danger.

He wiped away the tears, straightened his shoulders, and headed for the concealed door through which they'd entered the room. Then, he noticed that Priwinn stood at one of the windows, making that trilling sound. In mere seconds, the whoosh of huge wings interrupted the stillness of the night, and Rangarig arrived to pick them up.

XIII

This time, as well, they flew only a short distance on Rangarig's back. However, any pursuers traveling on horseback or foot would have needed a long time to catch up with them—assuming they even knew where to search.

Kim was so impatient that he couldn't sit still. During the flight, he tried to talk with Priwinn and Gorg, but the whistling wind made it impossible to understand speech. As soon as they slid off the dragon's broad back, though, he descended on Priwinn.

Priwinn didn't answer Kim's barrage of questions immediately. Instead, he hastily pulled Kim away from Rangarig. The dragon was restless. His claws tore up the ground, and his twitching tail uprooted bushes and small trees. His head moved back and forth as if he were searching the sky.

When Priwinn finally stopped walking, Kim asked, "What did Themistokles mean when he said he couldn't protect you any longer? And what did the dwarf mean by 'rebels who live in the forests'?"

"It's all nonsense," Priwinn snapped. "I already said so. We don't live in the forests."

Kim had to exercise all his self-control to keep from screaming at the top of his lungs. "You know exactly what I mean," he said tensely. "Well?"

Priwinn appeared hostile as he looked Kim over; again, it was Gorg, the good-humored giant, who intervened.

"It's not all that big a secret," Gorg said. "There are quite a few people like us who don't agree with what's going on here."

"I see," Kim murmured. "And you want to mount an attack to destroy the iron men and break the dwarves' power."

"If necessary." Suddenly, Priwinn's voice became almost pleading. "You saw what's happening in Gorywynn. You saw Themistokles. Haven't you seen enough?"

"Well, yes," Kim replied, "except I also heard what Themistokles said. The dwarves—"

"He doesn't even know what he's saying!" Priwinn interrupted. "Kim, you saw it yourself! He's become a weak old man. Any child could deceive him. The dwarves have something to do with the changes in Magic Moon; you said that yourself, right?"

Kim didn't know what to think. After everything he'd seen, he trusted Priwinn and Gorg—but he also trusted Themistokles. Was it possible that two truths could exist simultaneously—that both sides could be right, each in their own way? It was confusing. Thinking about it gave him a headache.

"So, you're planning a rebellion of some kind?" Kim guessed.

Priwinn was very annoyed by that question.

"As a matter of fact, yes," Gorg said.

The prince gave him a venomous look.

"Yes," Gorg repeated, undeterred. "Now that you're here . . ."

"Me?" Kim asked incredulously.

"Yes, you. Of course!" Priwinn said. He flung back his cloak and pressed his hand flat against the breastplate of his black armor. "The people here haven't forgotten what you did for them, Kim. You saved our world once before. I'm sure they would follow you if you if you asked them. Put on this black armor. Lead us. Together, we'll chase those dwarves back to where they came from."

"Whether or not they're guilty, right?" Kim retorted.

Rangarig moved restlessly. "We shouldn't stay here too long," he rumbled. "I think someone—or something—is coming."

"One more minute, Rangarig," Priwinn called without a glance at the dragon. "This is important." He looked at Kim intently. "So, what is your decision?"

Kim was silent. He felt at a loss. Priwinn's question seemed unfair. He couldn't make a decision like that within mere seconds. So, he said, "I can't decide—not right away."

"When, then?" Priwinn asked furiously. "When it's too late?"

"I know where you're coming from," Kim murmured. "You're . . . you're angry. You're afraid your world is going to ruin, and you're attacking the first ones you find to blame."

"You're starting to sound like Themistokles!" Priwinn spat out.

"Which is not necessarily the worst thing," Gorg commented.

The Prince of the Steppe spun around, about to unload his anger on the giant; but at that very moment, Rangarig rumbled once again, his voice low, "Someone's coming. Hurry up!"

They didn't hesitate any longer. No matter how important their discussion was, if Rangarig was behaving this way, it was best to do what he said.

Rangarig suddenly reared up with a blood-curdling roar, spread his wings, and took off into the air. He shot into the sky like a golden lightning bolt, and the backlash from his thrashing wings knocked everyone off their feet—even the giant tumbled yards away.

Kim tucked in his head as dirt, stones, broken foliage, and branches rained down. A few seconds passed before he dared to remove his hands from his face and look up at the sky.

Rangarig circled over the forest, so high that he was visible only as a glittering fleck of gold. He wasn't alone.

A second shape headed toward him: gigantic, ungainly, and discernible only in outline. Its movements were strangely disjointed, but they merely looked that way. Rangarig and the second shape circled each other like two gigantic birds of prey; neither one seemed noticeably faster than the other.

"What's that?" Kim whispered in horror.

"I don't know," Priwinn replied in the same tone of voice. "If it's something that even Rangarig fears, though . . ."

A tremendous roaring and crashing sound drowned out the rest of his words, as the two shapes collided in the sky. For a few moments, they merged into a single silhouette of thrashing wings, slashing claws, and undulating blackness.

Kim and the others could hear Rangarig's claws encounter resistance; and something struck the dragon, too. There was a shower of sparks. Then, the two shapeless giants separated and circled each other.

"A dragon?" Kim whispered, beside himself. "Is that . . . a dragon?"

"No," Gorg said with conviction. "That must be something else."

Kim strained his eyes. Still, when Rangarig collided with the mysterious silhouette a second and third time—with crashes that made the entire sky vibrate—all Kim could see was an enormous and phantomlike shape. Rangarig's roar expressed his fury and pain; by the fourth time he and his adversary broke apart, Kim clearly saw that the golden dragon had lost much of his power and grace.

His opponent was also hit hard; it wobbled across the sky.

Rangarig swung around and, with a powerful stroke of his wings, managed to get above the attacker. Then, he dove down directly on it, like a falcon striking his prey. There was another shower of sparks. While the two figures were locked momentarily in a deadly, clawing embrace, something abruptly fell away from them. The object plunged downward, trailing sparks like a meteor plummeting from the sky. It impacted a few dozen feet from Kim and the others, landing with such force that the ground shook.

Kim jumped up and ran toward it, while high overhead the two adversaries pulled apart again. The phantom took to flight—but Rangarig gave chase, tearing into him with claws and teeth. The golden dragon had won the battle; for some reason, though, Kim didn't know whether to rejoice.

Kim stopped and his eyes widened in disbelief.

Directly in front of his feet was a newly created crater, which was a good fifteen feet in diameter.

The ground was smoking. A severed claw was stuck in the center of the hole in the forest floor. The claw was bigger than Rangarig's claws, curved, and razor-sharp—and its severed end glowed with a dark, ominous red color.

It was made of *iron!* Kim instantly looked up, tilting his head all the way back. The shadowy shape, still pursued by Rangarig, was almost out of sight.

"Damn," murmured Gorg, who together with Priwinn had appeared at Kim's side. Gorg, too, stared down at the steel claw in complete disbelief. Priwinn didn't say anything; yet even in the darkness, Kim could tell that he'd turned as pale as a ghost.

The giant stepped into the crater, bent down, and carefully picked up the claw. Even though he held its glowing red end far away from him, it was so hot that he winced.

Kim shuddered. The claw was a big as a scythe and ten times as sharp. It was simply beyond his powers of imagination to picture the creature to which it belonged. He didn't want to try.

"Th-throw that thing away," Priwinn said hoarsely.

Gorg immediately obeyed. Almost nauseated at the sight, he dropped the claw and stepped back out of the crater.

"What is that?" Kim whispered, stunned. A dark seed of suspicion started growing in him. The mere thought was so horrible that he simply refused to think it through to its logical conclusion.

Priwinn stared at Kim as if all this was his fault. "The dwarves," said the prince. "We . . . we've suspected for a long time that they were working on something like this."

"So, you think they built an iron dragon?" Kim gasped.

Suddenly, Priwinn yelled at him, "How much more evidence do you need, you idiot?! Ask Rangarig when he comes back!"

Kim said nothing. He wasn't at all offended by the prince's outburst. He knew that Priwinn was nearly insane from worry. Kim was going through the same thing. He, too, would have liked to scream at—or even hit—someone.

That was a sobering thought.

All at once, Kim understood what was happening inside Priwinn and the others. He now was experiencing the same powerlessness: a feeling almost physically painful, which cried out for someone to blame—someone who would pay for everything, whether that person deserved such punishment or not. Kim didn't approve of Priwinn's behavior, but he understood it.

At that moment, Kim knew what he had to do. The solution was so simple that he wondered why he hadn't thought of it immediately: "I am going to help you," he said.

Priwinn's eyes flew open. "You're—"

"I'm not going to put on that armor and lead you into battle against your brothers," Kim said, hurriedly interrupting him. "No way. But I *will* help you. As I said to Themistokles, we have to return to the King of the Rainbows. We have to go on that journey again! He'll support us. He has to help us—I'm sure of it."

"That's crazy!" Priwinn retorted, although not quite as passionately as before. "Go back through the Abyss of Souls, where the Tatzelwurm lives . . . then, traverse the subterranean river? Not to mention the Castle at the End of the World! That will take too long!"

"Possibly," Kim said. "But how long would it take to destroy every single iron man and ferret out all the dwarves in the eastern mountains? Much longer, I bet."

Priwinn was about to object again, but the giant came to Kim's aid. "He's right, Prince," he said. "We did it before, and we'll do it again. As for the Tatzelwurm . . ."

"So, Tatzelwurm is still alive?" Kim asked.

"Well, of course. Don't you remember? After the wizard Boraas was defeated, everyone we thought was dead came back to life. But don't worry. Rangarig got away from him once, and he'll do it again this time. The rest will take care of itself."

Priwinn wasn't convinced, but he didn't contradict Gorg. Instead, he stared back and forth from Gorg to Kim before finally shrugging his shoulders. "Let's hear what Rangarig has to say about it," he said.

The dragon returned a while later. He didn't land immediately, instead circling over the forest a couple of times, furiously lashing out with his claws, snatching and shredding treetops. When he finally did land, he moved in such an agitated manner that the companions didn't dare go near his wings or thrashing tail.

"Rangarig!" Priwinn cried. "What was that? Did you destroy it?"

"Destroy!" roared the dragon. "Yes. Shred—tear—destroy—rip—slice—kill—kill—*kill!* Yessss!" Rangarig had gone mad. His claws grabbed a tree and bent it until it snapped—similar to the way Kim might have broken a dry twig. He was foaming at the mouth. "Rip to pieces!"

It was beyond frightening.

"Rangarig! Please, wake up!" Kim gasped. "It's us—your friends!"

Rangarig's head swiveled around. His huge eyes fixed on Kim; for a second, Kim saw the gaze of a wild, bloodthirsty monster.

"Rip to pieces," Rangarig growled. "Kill. Yessss!"

Kim took a step toward the dragon. Priwinn gasped in horror and lunged to drag him back, but Kim brushed away his hand and continued walking toward Rangarig. Without wavering, he continued to look directly into the dragon's enormous eyes.

"Come back!" Priwinn shouted in desperation. "He'll kill you!"

Kim kept on walking. He wasn't certain that Priwinn was wrong. He was afraid. His heart pounded, and his knees shook so bad that he hardly could put one foot in front of the other—but he knew that he couldn't go back. If he tried to turn around and run away, Rangarig would kill him without hesitation; that much was clear.

"Please, Rangarig," Kim whispered. "Snap out of it! It's me, Kim. We're your friends! Please remember!"

The dragon still was in a frenzy: His claws tore up the ground. "Shred. Kill. Yes, yes, yessss!"

"No," Kim said quietly. "That's wrong. We're not your enemies. You're not an evil dragon, Rangarig. Remember! Wake up! Snap out of it! Please!"

Slowly—very, very slowly—the murderous fire in Rangarig's eyes flickered out. It took a very long time, yet all the while, Kim stood there, his heart pounding and hands and knees trembling. Kim watched as the dragon slowly, with infinite effort, turned back into what he'd once been: Rangarig, the golden dragon of Gorywynn, friend and protector of Magic Moon.

Kim sighed in relief, took a final step forward, and wrapped his arms around Rangarig's huge neck. Trembling, he stood there with his eyes closed, pressed against the dragon's scaly face. "Oh, Rangarig," he sobbed. "I . . . I thought we had lost you."

The dragon didn't answer, but something wet and warm covered Kim's face and hands. When he looked up, he saw a big teardrop roll down from the corner of Rangarig's eye.

The dragon was crying.

"Soon, my little friend," he whispered. "Soon, I'll be your enemy. Go while you still can."

"Never," Kim replied. "I'm staying with you. We're all staying with you. We'll do this together. We'll defeat this iron monster—all of us together. You've already driven it away!"

"It's stronger than I am," Rangarig replied. "They just sent it out too soon. It's not ready. Soon, I won't be able to defeat it. Even if I could, after that victory, I would no longer be myself." He gently nudged Kim with his snout, and Kim reeled back a couple of steps. "I must leave you," he said. "Now."

"No!" Kim cried in despair. "You're wrong, Rangarig. You defeated that flying beast, and you'll defeat it again!"

"Don't you understand? That monster is not what I am fighting," Rangarig rumbled. The tears had stopped; for a brief, terrible moment, the rage that had so frightened Kim again flashed in Rangarig's eyes. "It's not just the steel dragon! I am the one you must fear! As long as I'm with you, the steel dragon will pursue you. He will defeat me, eventually, and kill you afterward. Or I'll defeat him, but then I'll be the one that you'll have to fear. This cannot be changed. I must go."

"Just a moment!" Kim pleaded. "Please, one more minute. I know how to help you!"

The dragon already had spread his wings halfway. Now, he paused.

"I'm going to do it again," Kim burst out. "I'm going to the King of the Rainbows. He'll help us. He already saved Magic Moon once! But I can't get there without you. The way is too far. Please!"

The dragon thought that over. His gaze passed over Kim's face; then, he looked over at his two friends. "You know the dangers lurking along the way," he said finally.

"They're no worse than what we're facing here," Kim replied. "Please, Rangarig! Take us there."

Once again, the dragon hesitated. He looked at Priwinn and Gorg.

Gorg nodded.

"All right," Rangarig finally said. "As far as the Abyss of Souls and the Tatzelwurm's lake. You know the rules of the game."

Suddenly, there was a bitter, prickly lump in Kim's throat. Oh yes, he did know the rules of the game. There was only one way to get past the terrible Tatzelwurm who guarded the entrance to the underground river: an equally equipped adversary had to challenge him to a duel. That's just the way it was.

Hardly anyone survived the fight with the Tatzelwurm.

With a feeling of indescribably deep pain, Kim realized that Rangarig had accepted facing mortal danger.

The way was far, and Rangarig was exhausted and wounded, so it took them over a week to reach the mountains of the Abyss of Souls. Kim found many things on this journey deeply disturbing.

They soared over a land that was no longer recognizable. At first, the changes were minimal: a new street, a town that Kim didn't know, an artificially straightened river course, a field a little larger than before . . . The farther north they went, the more extensive the changes became, until Kim no longer could close his eyes to the truth. The towns were large and dark; some looked as if they were built entirely of iron. Beneath them there were roads so broad that they resembled rivers of black metal. Ten wagons could have driven side by side. The rivers now channeled into iron riverbeds as straight as a ruler. Foaming, rust-colored water coursed down the channels, carrying along anything that tried to establish a foothold on the metal embankments.

Then, there was the fire.

They saw it the first night they set up their camp: a pale, reddish glow far behind them, over the horizon. They also saw it the following night, and the one after that—in fact, every night until they reached the mountains. Sometimes, when the wind blew in the right direction, it carried the sound of hammering to them. While Rangarig licked the wounds he'd suffered during the battle with the steel dragon, someone spent the night forging something.

Sometimes, Kim could see Rangarig cock his head and listen. The expression on Priwinn's face also was marked by deep worry as he looked toward the south every evening. Moreover, the fire was coming closer and closer—every night, just a little closer . . . yet slowly, inexorably closer.

They spent the last night before the Abyss of Souls on a high plateau: a desolate, inaccessible bit of rock that was part of the Shadowy Mountains. No one slept well that night, and when Kim woke well before sunrise, he noticed that everyone else had gotten up already.

Priwinn and Gorg lit a fire. They sat there: two silhouettes completely disproportionate to each other, talking in hushed voices, huddling together for protection against the chill of the night, rubbing their hands over the flames. On the other side of the fire were two smaller, completely different silhouettes: Chunklet and Sheera, who were inseparable, although noticeably quieter and more serious the closer they got to the Abyss of Souls.

Kim suddenly felt very lonely.

Taking his time, he unwrapped his blanket and stood up. The cold bit into his skin like glass teeth would, so he was about to walk to the fire—but his eyes briefly passed over the dragon's face, and he saw that Rangarig was awake, as well. He hesitated.

Priwinn lifted his head and looked over at Kim, but when the prince started to say something, Gorg halted him with a gesture. Kim stood motionless for a while; then, he walked toward Rangarig, even though the cold became ever more intense.

"Good morning, little hero," the dragon said in greeting. After the sullen, surly way he'd behaved in recent days, these words came as quite a surprise.

"Hello," Kim said hesitantly. It seemed as if his head had been swept clean. He couldn't remember a single thing he'd been planning to say. It all seemed so superfluous to him.

"I . . . I wanted to tell you something, Rangarig," Kim ventured hesitantly. He summoned all his willpower, but he couldn't look the dragon in the eye.

"I'm listening."

"You don't have to come with us," Kim said. "I mean, you don't have to go to the Lost Lake. You . . . you brought us here, and maybe . . . maybe you could still take us as far as the Abyss of Souls. After that, though, we can continue on alone."

"You know you can't do that," Rangarig rumbled.

"Why? Because—"

"That's how it is," the dragon said, interrupting him. "The journey across the Tatzelwurm's lake has to be paid in blood. He demands a life in return for unbarring the way. If you try to trick him out of his due, he will kill you all."

"Why does it have to be your life?" Kim asked in despair.

"It doesn't have to be mine," the dragon replied. Kim looked at him in surprise, and Rangarig tipped his head in the direction of the fire. "Which of your friends do you want to sacrifice? Priwinn? Gorg? That funny little fellow always with you? Or the cat?"

"That . . . that's not fair," Kim stammered.

"Fair?" Rangarig made a noise that might have been a laugh. "Whoever said life is fair?" he asked. "So, who do you want to sacrifice? Yourself, maybe?"

"Stop!" Kim cried. "You . . . you know I didn't mean that."

"Of course," Rangarig said. "And *you* know there is only one way past the Tatzelwurm." He rumbled. "I thrashed him once before, remember? I'll tie his dirty neck in a knot. I think that will hold him up long enough for you to get past."

"But you'll die," Kim said softly.

Suddenly, the dragon became very serious. "That may well be. But I would be dying for all of you—and for Magic Moon."

As if that is any consolation! Death is bad, Kim reflected, *and the death of a friend is doubly bad.*

To pay one's life as a price for something . . . that was horrible.

"I'm going to die in any case," Rangarig said abruptly. "Have you forgotten what's happening to me? Soon, little hero, the Rangarig you know will no longer exist—one way or another. I feel it. Something wild is awakening in me, Kim. Maybe in a few days, I won't be myself any longer."

"But you'll be alive!"

"Will I?" Rangarig asked. "Then, tell me something, little hero: What difference does it make whether I die because my body is destroyed or because my memory is destroyed? Am I not as good as dead if I open my eyes every morning and don't know who I am? If I forget you and Priwinn and the giant and everyone I know? My body will be alive and inside it will be . . . a new Rangarig. Tell me: Who will *I* be when I wake up on that morning?"

Kim had no answer—how could he know? Who knows the meaning of life?

Rangarig laughed softly. "Oh, you humans! You are so small and so brave. You have such a short life compared to beings like me; yet, in that time span, you accomplish such amazing feats—at least, sometimes. If it suits your purposes, you even challenge the gods. Then, something as natural as death makes you despair. There is nothing bad about dying. Without death, there is no life."

Kim was silent for a long time. He'd never thought about these issues.

"You're young," Rangarig said. "So, get along now. Go, join your friends by the fire, warm yourself, and eat something. We have a long, hard road ahead of us."

They kept flying farther north, and the land beneath them turned more barren and desolate with every stroke of Rangarig's wings. Kim avoided looking down because every square foot of ground was linked to painful memories. This was where he'd fought his greatest battle. He never had felt greater triumph or greater grief.

"Something's wrong here," Rangarig called out. His powerful dragon voice was the only thing that could be heard over the howling wind—everyone else's words immediately were swept from their lips. "Too many people."

Puzzled, Kim looked down. They were flying so high that he had trouble making anything out—especially individual figures. But Rangarig had proven on more than one occasion that he had much sharper senses than Kim did.

Now, the dragon descended and flew slower.

They saw an occasional hut or farmhouse—and once, a whole village, with a dozen compact, black-iron houses. Streets meandered between the dwellings as if they were metallic snakes; sometimes, one of the tiny figures on a road stopped to look up at them.

Strange. Up until now, Kim always had thought there were no settlements this far north. The Abyss of Souls made everyone fearful. No one came here if it could be avoided. No one *lived* here—at least, that had been the case the last time they'd come.

The dragon glided on, more slowly than before, barely as high as the treetops. They made a wide detour around the houses, although it was inevitable that Rangarig would be spotted. Kim was uncomfortable with the idea that someone might know where they were headed, but pursuit was no longer a factor.

Once they were past the Lost Lake and the Tatzelwurm, their pursuers would have to think of something very clever in order to stay on their tracks.

Finally, the Abyss of Souls came into view. Kim involuntarily shivered when he caught sight of the gaping crack in the ground, which looked like a multiple-branched lighting bolt splitting the land. The canyon was so deep that its floor couldn't be seen, and a darkness that touched the soul like an icy breeze filled the chasm. Hence, the name of this gorge was the Home of Fear. No matter how large or small, strong or weak, courageous or cowardly—no one could escape its dark breath. The first time they were here, even Rangarig had trembled with fear.

This time, he didn't.

It would be a while before Kim understood that this part of Magic Moon had changed, as well. He did feel unease, but that probably was due to the darkness below triggering Kim's memories. However, the terrible fear that neither courage nor rational thinking could allay—that was absent. The gorge beneath them was no more or less threatening than any other deep gorge.

Rangarig stopped flapping his wings and dove directly down into the dark canyon. When his claws touched the ground, Kim shivered, but only because it was icy cold down there. The sun wasn't high enough that its warming rays could reach the bottom of the gorge.

"What's happened here?" Gorg whispered. "It—it's gone. I don't feel a thing."

"Me neither," Priwinn murmured. "It's not here. Whatever used to dwell in this place is no longer here."

"What's so bad about that?" asked Kim, who had vivid memories of the last time they'd crossed the abyss. "You should be glad!"

Priwinn and Gorg looked at him as if he'd said something incredibly stupid. Rangarig said quietly, "Fear also has a place in the world, Kim."

"Well, I do just fine without it," Kim said.

"And how will you ever be brave, if you're unacquainted with fear?"

Kim had no answer for that.

They set out. At least one thing was the same: Afterward, Kim couldn't say how long it took them to walk through the gorge. It might have been an hour; but on the other hand, it could have taken half a day. Finally, they rounded the last bend and saw the cave where the river disappeared into the Lost Lake—at the bottom of which, the Tatzelwurm lived.

To be more precise, they saw the place where those two things *used* to be. The lake still was there, but it was no longer the monster's wild abode, surrounded by rocky pinnacles and crevices. It was a smooth, perfectly circular mirror in a black iron frame. Its water was so clear, one could see down to the bottom, even though that was hundreds of feet below the surface. Nothing moved in the crystal-clear water: no fish, no plants—definitely no Tatzelwurm.

That wasn't the worst of it: where the Lost River once had begun, now there was . . . nothing.

On the opposite shore, where there used to be an unending cliff, there was now a huge, triangular groove. Its sides were made of black iron, and glittering at its base was the same water—devoid of all life—that filled the lake. This artificial gorge extended as far as the eye could see before blurring in the far distance.

"Where . . . where is he?" Kim whispered.

"Could he be dead?" Priwinn murmured.

"No," replied Rangarig, "the Tatzelwurm is alive."

Priwinn looked at him with wide eyes. "How do you know that?"

"Because *I* am alive," Rangarig explained. "If he were dead, I would be, too. He . . . must have fled. The iron men probably drove him away."

"You're saying the Tatzelwurm fled from those creatures?" Priwinn asked. "I don't believe it!"

Kim stared at the dragon. It was too absurd. The Tatzelwurm was the worst of all beasts. Kim had feared him more than any other creature in Magic Moon. Now, all of a sudden, Kim felt something like sympathy for him. Laboriously, as if this movement cost him tremendous effort, he turned around and pointed at the place where the Lost River's entrance once had been located and the river had begun its subterranean course. Kim had the feeling that an invisible, icy hand was touching him. The sight of the perfectly straight groove, which looked as if it had been cut with a knife, filled him with fear. He could still hear Brobing's words: *They can move mountains.*

He hadn't believed that, but now he saw it with his own eyes.

"Why did they do that?" Kim whispered. He knew the answer, though; Brobing had provided it long before Kim had even known to ask: Humans needed new land.

In the end, Priwinn was the first to wake from the trance of that terrible sight. With a forced smile, he turned to Rangarig and said, "I'm afraid you can't slip away so easily, old friend. We still desperately need your services."

XIV

Hour after hour, Rangarig's wing strokes carried them farther north. The view beneath them didn't change. Where the Shadowy Mountains once had marked the border of Magic Moon, there was now an iron-lined river channel, flowing in a perfectly straight line, its water crystal clear but devoid of life. At one point, they soared over a black ship with domed bulges. The ship moved upriver—against the current and without a sail—all the while spewing foul-smelling fumes.

"What's that?!" Kim shouted over the howling wind and the beating of Rangarig's huge wings.

"Riverfolk!" Priwinn yelled back.

Strange—Kim had never heard of them. Priwinn sensed his puzzlement; after a short pause, he shouted in a distinctly angry tone, "It's best to keep out of their way! They're thieves—pirates! Nobody knows exactly where they come from, but people say the river is what changes them."

"You mean they became bad when they—"

"Got to this river—that's right!" Priwinn shouted, finishing Kim's sentence. Then, they gave up trying to make themselves heard over the din.

From time to time, they saw an isolated house or a tiny farm on the banks of the iron river. Once, they spied a fortified city with gray houses hidden behind walls of iron—although there was nothing in this barren land that the city dwellers would have to fear.

Kim estimated that they had been under way for about three or four hours. He felt sure that they already had gone beyond the underground section that previously had taken Gorg, Priwinn, and Kim days to cover. Nevertheless, he still could see no end to the absolutely straight course of the river. To the right and left, as far as Kim could see, there was nothing but gray mountains and jagged black lava. The thought of settling here seemed absurd to him. This part of creation was never meant for homesteads; this was the quiet realm of silence and loneliness, where all life perished one way or the other.

Eventually, the mountains became less steep. The water still flowed in an iron bed, but the lava pinnacles jutting up into the sky on both sides gradually gave way to lower, rounded mountains. Finally, only gently undulating, brown-colored hills and rolling plains remained. Kim's heart started to beat faster. He was excited. They were approaching the land of the ice giants, and the Castle at the End of the World surely would come into view soon. Then, everything could be decided. The ice giants would know what to do; if they didn't, then the King of the Rainbows, who lived beyond the Great Void, would tell him. Kim had been there once before; if necessary, he would go that route again, despite the difficulty.

"It's too warm," Rangarig abruptly called out.

Startled out of his train of thought, Kim looked up, puzzled. *Too warm?* He was freezing miserably, even though he'd wrapped himself in a blanket. Chunklet, who had crept under his shirt, trembled like an aspen leaf. The wind was so icy that it not only made Kim's eyes tear up but also immediately froze the tears on his eyelashes. "Well, it's cold enough for me!" he shouted back. "I'm turning into an icicle!"

"Maybe you are," Gorg rumbled behind him, "but look down. Where is the ice?"

Kim leaned to the side slightly so he could look past Rangarig's scaly neck to see below: an endless wasteland of brown muck, interspersed with mirroring pools of half-frozen water. No ice for as far as the eye could see.

"It's too warm!" Rangarig shouted once again. "I'm going down to take a look."

Kim easily could have imagined about a million things he would rather do than wade around in that endless bog, but Rangarig already had swept back his wings and was heading downward in a steep dive. When he landed, the muck splashed so high that it splattered everyone. Kim cursed, wiped his face with the back of his hand, and spit out dirty water. Chunklet, too, unleashed a stream of invective.

Shivering, Kim looked around: nothing but brown muck and mud. It was cold enough to make everyone's teeth chatter but not half as cold as it should have been. Where was the river? Where were the ice giants? Above all, where was the Castle at the End of the World—the mighty ice palace of the Guardians of the World?

"Are we really going to climb down into this?" Kim asked.

Frowning, Priwinn looked at the muddy ground. Rangarig had sunk up to his belly in the brown muck because of his enormous weight. It would be hard for the rest of them to move around in this, as well.

To Kim's relief, Gorg said, "Why should we? There's nothing here worth seeing. Can you find the Castle at the End of the World, Rangarig?"

Rangarig thought it over. "Maybe if I fly high enough. That would be a bit uncomfortable for you, though."

"We'll wait here," Priwinn said. "Come on."

Without waiting for an answer, he jumped off Rangarig's back and immediately sank up to his knees in the soft mud. Disgusted, Kim made a face, but he accepted his fate and followed Priwinn. A second later, they both hopped to the side, startled, when Gorg jumped into the muck and splattered them anew with brown, sticky sludge. Rangarig waited until they moved a few feet to the side, and then he pushed off and bounded up into the sky.

Kim kept his eyes on Rangarig until the huge dragon turned into a tiny golden speck and disappeared entirely. Kim was shivering, and not just from the cold. Something in this desolate moonscape of mud and half-frozen puddles made him afraid.

"What could have happened here?" he whispered, shuddering.

Priwinn just looked at him, perplexed; Gorg, too, was silent. Part of a little reddish-orange face poked out from under Kim's shirt. Chunklet said in revulsion, "It was them!"

"Them?"

"Bipeds."

"Do you mean—" Priwinn began.

"Who else?" The one interrupting him wasn't Chunklet, but Sheera. The cat, who had traveled under Gorg's shirt, now climbed onto the giant's shoulder, ruthlessly using his claws to help him up. Gorg didn't even seem to feel it. "They were here—not long ago. I can still smell them."

"I . . . I don't believe that," said Kim. "Who would want to live in a place like this?"

"No one," Chunklet said, speaking up again. "And so what do they do? They just change it. All this here used to be ice. Now, it's mud. Soon it will be dry and warm, and they will spread out on it like a disease, until they've destroyed this part of the world, too."

The anger that Kim heard in Chunklet's voice astonished him. He hadn't heard anything like it from Chunklet before. "Maybe . . . there's another explanation," Kim said hesitantly. He hoped so, at least.

"The farmers need land in order to live," Gorg said, supporting him. This explanation didn't sound very convincing, though.

"They have no right to do that!" Sheera said passionately.

"Why are you two so upset?" Priwinn wanted to know. "I mean, who is harmed when a few mountains are turned into productive land? Maybe soon there will be flowers and trees growing here—"

"Because you like it that way?" the cat asked, interrupting him. Sheera's eyes narrowed into thin yellow slits. "Oh, fool that I was, I thought you were different from the rest. You're just as blind. Why does the whole world have to look the way you like? Do you think this place had no rhyme or reason? Do you think the only things that should be allowed to exist are what seem useful to you? You're wrong about that, Prince. Deserts and oceans, barren mountains and tundra—they all were created for a purpose. What if, one day, a group showed up that felt comfortable only in desert conditions? What would you say to them if they started to chop down your forests?"

"That's different," Priwinn objected. "After all, there was no one living here."

"And?" Sheera snapped. "Do you think that *life* is the only thing that counts? Does the word *creation* mean anything to you, biped? And maybe something like *respect* for it?"

"Stop," Gorg rumbled. "Rangarig is coming back." He pointed up at the sky, where a tiny, glittering object had appeared.

Priwinn frowned. "That was fast. I didn't think he would come back so soon."

"Me neither," Kim added in the same thoughtful tone. "He's coming from the wrong direction, too," he noted in astonishment.

"That's not surprising," Chunklet remarked ironically, "because it's not Rangarig! *Run!*"

He shouted the last word so loudly that Kim's ears rang. In one continuous movement, Chunklet popped out of Kim's shirt, leaped into the muck, and immediately sank down into the brown brew. Sheera gave a frightened hiss and jumped right behind Chunklet.

The small glittering object in the sky turned into a giant, silvery-gray shape that rapidly approached them.

No, it wasn't Rangarig, but it was a dragon!

It was enormous—much larger than Rangarig—and in a way that was hard to describe, it looked angrier. A mechanical monster with steel wings and flashing chrome teeth, it moved in a jerky manner, like a marionette whose puppeteer has not yet fully mastered the controls. Whereas the loud whooshing sound of beating wings accompanied Rangarig's flight, this contraption had a continuous clanking and whining—like something akin to the rhythmic beating of a huge iron heart. Gray steam billowed out of the steel dragon's nostrils—and its eyes, which were made of glass and ten times as cold and immobile as a snake's, glowed with an ominous green light. Four or five figures clad in shabby black cloaks crouched on the monster's metallic neck. Even from this great distance, Kim heard the dwarves' triumphant cries as they caught sight of their defenseless prey.

Finally, Kim and the others woke from their stupor.

Gorg was the first to run off with giant strides. He yelled at the top of his lungs, "Scatter! Everyone in a different direction, so it can't catch us all at once!"

Kim automatically had started to follow the giant but now spun around and ran in the opposite direction. Priwinn took off, too, as did Chunklet and the cat. Barely a second later, a huge shadow darkened the sky. Kim was hit by a gale created by the thrashing steel wings.

Their maneuver upset the attacker's plan. Instead of three tiny, closely bunched victims, which it probably could have finished off with a single sweep of its claws, three figures zigzagged in different directions

Kim heard a harsh, angry cry as the monster's steel claws grabbed nothing but muck. Then, the flying machine passed over Kim so closely that the backdraft blew him off his feet, sending him tumbling in the mud over and over for yards.

The soft marshy ground cushioned the impact, but Kim got the wind knocked out of him, and he was blinded for a few seconds. By the time he sat up—coughing and rubbing the dirt out of his eyes—the metal dragon already had regained altitude and was peeling around for its next attack.

Kim plotted the steel beast's trajectory in his mind and wasn't surprised at the result: The next attack was aimed at him. Hastily jumping to his feet, he ran a few steps, darted off to the right, switched to the left, and finally turned on his heels and took off in the same direction he'd come.

Once again, he was lucky: In that pass, the dragon's grasping claws missed him by less than three feet. But any miss was as good as a mile, and this time Kim was prepared for the blast of wind, so he managed to stay on his feet as the dragon passed over him.

He wasn't prepared, however, for the three-foot-tall body that suddenly jumped onto his neck, flattening his face in the mud.

Instinctively, Kim rolled over, using his weight to squish his unwanted passenger into the muck. Picking himself up, he hastily wiped his eyes with his hands so that he could see.

A spindly hand grabbed his ankle and yanked. Kim broke loose. Two more burrs clung to him now. While he simultaneously tried to fend them off and keep his balance on the slippery ground, two or three more spindly figures popped out of the mud on either side of him. The dwarves had jumped off their dragon's back.

A half-dozen dwarves was more than Kim could handle. He grabbed two little men and hurled them away, but they got back on their feet with amazing speed and fought like demons.

Kim tucked in against a hail of punches and kicks, and blood soon sprinkled his face. It was hard for Kim to evade the furious blows; he felt his strength wane.

His second attempt to save this land where fantasy became reality probably would have come to an inglorious end at that very moment if a giant figure hadn't appeared over him and plucked the dwarves off Kim like they were fruit on a vine.

Gorg hurled the dwarves dozens of feet away. When a particularly treacherous dwarf suddenly pulled out a knife and tried to stab Kim with it, Gorg grabbed the weapon and broke it in two—at which point the dwarf fled, screeching in terror. Then, the giant pulled Kim to his feet.

"Let's go!" he bellowed. "Anywhere but here!"

Unfortunately, they got only a few steps away. With a mechanical roar, the steel dragon dropped from the sky and landed in the muck with its claws outstretched and wings spread, suddenly towering over the two companions like an insurmountable iron wall—if that wall had menacing claws and bared teeth.

With a cry of alarm, Gorg swerved to the left, dragging Kim with him—and then, he leaped back when a thin, multi-branched stream of electricity streaked from the dragon's mouth, exploding in the mud near Gorg's feet. A wave of boiling mud and piping hot steam swept over them both, causing them to scream in pain.

In spite of that, Gorg changed directions with lightning speed and tried to escape. This time, the dragon's stream of blue fire missed him by a hair, and Kim heard the giant groan in pain when the heat singed his skin.

"That's enough, you fools!" yelled an unpleasant voice behind them. "Do you really want to die here?"

Kim recognized the speaker's voice before he turned around to see his face. The dwarf had sunk almost up to his hips into the mire, and his face was covered with mud. Nevertheless, there was no doubt about it: It was Jarrn.

"You have a choice," he said angrily. "You either can give up or be killed on the spot. It's all the same to me."

Gorg flashed an angry look at him. "I'm not afraid of death!"

Jarrn gave him a contemptuous snort. "You're dumb enough. But I don't want anything from you." He pointed at Kim and tried to draw himself up a little farther, but the sticky muck held him back. "We want the boy. Turn him over to us and nothing will happen to the rest of you!"

"Only a dwarf could propose something like that." That was Priwinn, who suddenly popped up behind Jarrn—close enough to grab the little man. But three other dwarves had come between the prince and Jarrn, and they brandished their weapons in a threatening manner.

The prince sneered. "You think we'll sacrifice one of our own so the others can get away? Surely, you don't believe that."

Jarrn didn't even dignify the prince's question with an answer. His cunning little eyes bored into Kim's.

Kim's mind raced. Behind them, the dragon hovered like a mountain of steel, ready to destroy them at the wave of Jarrn's hand. He saw in Jarrn's eyes that the dwarf absolutely was determined to give this signal if need be.

"It's all right, Priwinn," Kim said in a low voice. "I'll do what he asks."

Priwinn gasped. "You're crazy! They'll kill you!"

They could have done that long before, if they'd wanted to, Kim thought. *For some reason, they want me alive.* He didn't say anything about that, however. Instead, he looked at the dwarf intently and asked, "Do you give me your word that you will leave the others alone if I go with you?"

"Certainly," Jarrn agreed. "They are of no concern to me."

"Don't do it!" Priwinn headed toward Kim, his eyes desperate and pleading; the dwarves immediately barred the way, raising their weapons.

"I'll come with you," said Kim again. "I . . . will not resist. I promise." He held up his empty hands and took a step toward Jarrn. Without warning, the steel dragon rose up into the air, unleashing a storm wind that knocked everyone off their feet—including Kim, who ended up facedown in the mud.

A golden shape flashed in the sky, plunging toward the steel dragon with a shrill cry. The mechanical monster tried to gain altitude, meanwhile peeling around to face its adversary. Although the golden dragon was smaller, he was faster. His powerful wings struck the other dragon's metallic body, spinning the machine around like a dry leaf. Seconds later, Rangarig's golden claws dug into the steel monster's back, causing sparks to fly.

"Rangarig!" Priwinn shouted. He whirled around and took a menacing step in Jarrn's direction. "So, little man—I think matters look a little different now."

Jarrn gulped a couple of times. Beneath the crust of half-frozen mud, his face lost a little color. "Well now," he began in an uncertain voice, "maybe we can discuss this calmly and—"

He got no farther. Priwinn lunged at him with outstretched arms; at the same moment, Kim grabbed one of the dwarves by the collar, using his other hand to wrest away the little man's weapon. In an almost casual manner, Gorg reached out and grabbed two of the ugly dwarves.

The two remaining dwarves tried to save themselves by running away.

They didn't get very far.

Two nimble, mud-caked bodies shot out of the muck. The dwarves fell to the ground screeching as Sheera and Chunklet set upon them with teeth and claws. The fight—if wrestling and shoving could be called such—lasted a short time. Then, all the dwarves were disarmed and in safe custody.

Kim looked at the dwarf he'd seized, wrapped the little man's cloak around him, and carried his bundle to where Priwinn and Gorg had set down their captives. Chunklet drove a very chastened dwarf before him; while the cat, hissing with bared teeth, crouched on the chest of his captive dwarf.

"It's all right, Sheera," Gorg said. "The fight is over."

"They don't taste very good, anyway," Chunklet complained.

Kim's gaze wandered up to the sky. The two titans still circled overhead, constantly striking at each other with teeth, claws, tails, and wings. They'd moved a good distance away, but the tremendous noise of their furious combat meant that Kim and the others had to shout to make themselves heard.

"He's doing it!" Priwinn shouted. "Rangarig is beating him! Look!"

"I wouldn't be so sure about that," Jarrn snarled; then he abruptly fell silent when Priwinn shot him a menacing look.

For his part, Kim wasn't as confident as the prince in regards to the battle's outcome. The two raging giants kept circling each other like birds of prey. Time and again, Rangarig's claws struck the steel dragon, sending sparks showering from its body. Once, Kim thought he saw something mechanical break off and fall to the ground far away. Eventually, Rangarig's claws pulled off a huge piece of the metal wing.

Priwinn cheered excitedly.

For all that, however, the golden dragon also was hit many times. His movements had become slower, and he lumbered almost as much as his adversary. Kim saw that it took great effort for Rangarig to stay aloft.

Suddenly, the steel dragon emitted a thin, bluish-white flame that hit Rangarig directly in the chest. It struck like a needle. Even from such a great distance, Kim could see the dragon's golden scales glow red. Rangarig bellowed in pain, spread out his wings, and tried to shoot upward—but he didn't have the strength. For a moment, he hung in the air like a huge paper kite attached to an invisible string. Then, he tipped over backward and spun helplessly toward the ground.

Aghast, Gorg inhaled through gritted teeth.

Kim cried out when he saw the dragon fall like a stone. "No!" he yelled. "Rangarig—*no!*"

Then, a miracle occurred: At the last moment—when they all believed that the dragon would smash into ground—Rangarig spread out his wings, flipped over, and halted with enormous effort. Barely three feet off the ground, he glided away. Then, he blasted back up in the air, spiraling past his opponent in an unbelievably adroit move. When the mechanical dragon attempted to follow the movement, he was engulfed by a huge blast of fire that shot out of Rangarig's mouth.

The monster exploded in a brilliant, orange flash. Ashes and glowing white debris fell to the ground in a wide arc. Kim closed his eyes, temporarily blinded.

"He did it!" Priwinn joyously shouted. "He destroyed it! Kim, Gorg, we're saved!" Jumping around joyfully, he embraced Kim and almost hugged one of the dwarves before he realized who was in front of him. Disgusted, he pushed the dwarf back into the mud.

Kim wasn't as elated as the prince. He watched Rangarig, concerned.

The golden dragon wobbled. His movements were unsteady. He lost altitude, once again in danger of plunging to the ground, but he sluggishly beat his wings and came back up again. He couldn't stay on course, crazily zigzagging across the sky. Kim could see that large pieces of his wings had been torn. Between his golden scales, there were bloody wounds.

Serious again, Priwinn turned to Jarrn. "And now—what was it you were saying? Maybe we could just talk everything over once again?"

Jarrn stared at him, his eyes full of hate. "What do you want?" he snarled. "I have no quarrel with you."

"I have one with *you,*" Priwinn replied. "And I advise you not to cause any trouble. Otherwise, you'll find out what it was like for your tin friend up there."

"We're all going to find out!" Chunklet cried.

Priwinn looked at the little creature for a second, frowning. Then, realization dawned and he looked up, tipping his head as far back as he could.

Rangarig had stopped weaving around in the air. He now headed toward them like an arrow, his wings folded back close to his body, his mouth wide open, and his claws spread wide! "Rip!" he bellowed. "Kill! Yes! Yessss!"

The fact that the dragon was exhausted and out of his mind with pain and anger was the only thing that spared their lives. The friends scattered in different directions, and the screeching dwarves also tried to get away—as best they could in their trussed-up state. But Rangarig was too quick. Before Kim realized what was happening, the dragon overshadowed them.

Terrified, Kim threw himself into the mud, sheltering his head with his arms. A blinding white fire flashed over him, vaporizing a section of the bog as big as a football field. A mixture of water and dirt exploded with a roar, coating the dragon. "Yessss!" Rangarig roared. "Kill!"

Coughing, Kim got up on his hands and knees. Through tearing eyes, he saw something move next to him. Kim crawled in that direction.

It was one of the dwarves. He had tripped and fallen on his face; because his hands and feet were tied, the mud covering his mouth and nose put him in danger of suffocating. Kim pulled him up, hastily wiped off his face, and shook him until the little man started breathing again—only then did Kim see that it was Jarrn.

Jarrn probably recognized Kim, too, because he expressed his gratitude by trying to bite Kim's fingers. Kim shoved him back in the mud (taking care that Jarrn didn't fall face down again) and hastily looked around for Rangarig.

The dragon had flown off, still wobbling. He simultaneously tried to maintain his altitude and turn around, but his strength was depleted. He wavered, tipped sideways, and crashed to the ground.

Without thinking, Kim jumped to his feet and waded through the knee-deep muck to get to Rangarig as fast as he could. He heard Priwinn and the giant yell at him to come back, but Kim ignored them, continuing to run as quickly as his legs could carry him. By the time he finally reached the dragon, Kim's heart was ready to explode, and his throat burned as if he'd tried to inhale powdered glass.

Rangarig lay on his side. One of his huge wings was broken; he wasn't able to unfold it. Rattling, labored breaths came from his chest. Kim groaned when he saw the terrible wounds that the steel enemy had inflicted on Rangarig.

Then, his gaze rested on the dragon's scaly face and he froze.

It wasn't Rangarig anymore. His face was as bloody and battered as the rest of his body—Rangarig was a powerful creature, who could survive such wounds. The worst part was that his eyes were no longer the eyes of the golden dragon they knew and loved; they were the eyes of a monster.

The dragon's gaze fixed on Kim with hatred and bloodlust: indiscriminate, unbridled hatred toward everything that lived and moved—the frenzy of a monster who existed only for destruction.

His battered jaws opened. Blood and foam dripped into the muck. Deep, deep inside Rangarig's throat, Kim saw an eerie fire. A faint odor of hell floated on the dragon's breath.

"Please, Rangarig," Kim whispered. "Please, return to the way you were!"

The dragon growled. Laboriously, he lifted a paw and tried to hit Kim with it, but he wasn't up it. His huge chest rose and fell in heavy, irregular breaths, and the muddy ground turned pink as blood flowed from his countless wounds.

"Ripped him," he growled "Ripped him . . . to pieces. Yessss."

"Yes, you did that," Kim said. "You beat him. No one is your equal, Rangarig. You saved all our lives."

"Ripped him," Rangarig repeated. There was a flicker in his eyes. For a moment, Kim thought he saw something like recognition; however, all cogent thought disappeared immediately. Rangarig's eyes were once again those of a killer who refrained from committing murder solely because he lacked the strength to strike. All of a sudden, Kim realized that he had mere seconds to run away.

Instead of fleeing, however, he took another step toward the dragon. "Come back to your senses, Rangarig—I'm begging you! Surely, you recognize me!"

"Go," Rangarig whispered hoarsely. "Save yourself!"

"You do recognize me?!" Inside, Kim rejoiced. He had brought Rangarig to his senses before—he was sure he could do it again. "You recognize me!" he repeated "Everything will be all right now."

"Recognize, yessss," Rangarig groaned. "Human. Hate them . . . all. Go, before I . . . tear you to pieces. Rip to pieces, yessss. Kill. Kill everything. Yessss."

Gorg put his big hand on Kim's shoulder and said quietly, "It's time to go. There's nothing more you can do for him."

"No!" Kim yelled. He tried to brush off Gorg's hand, but the giant kept a firm grip on him.

"We have to get away from here," Gorg said. "We have to disappear before he regains his strength. He'll kill us all!"

"Kill, yessss," Rangarig rumbled.

"Rangarig is my friend!" Kim protested. "He would never do anything to me."

The giant shook his head with sadness. "No, Kim," he said. "He was your friend, once. He's not the old Rangarig: This dragon is our enemy."

Kim knew that Gorg spoke the truth.

Rangarig had predicted this.

They'd all erred regarding the outcome of the battle: Rangarig had destroyed his enemy. But in the end, it appeared the dragon of steel and fire had defeated the dragon of flesh and blood.

* * *

Using a few strips of material ripped from the dwarves' little cloaks, they tied the diminutive men together so that they could walk but had no hope of escape. Then, the travelers all ran in great haste—not in any particular direction, simply intent on putting as much distance as they could between themselves and Rangarig. In that monotonous wasteland of muck and puddles, it was hard to judge distance and even harder to sense the passing of time.

The muddy water was as sticky as syrup; sometimes, it was so deep that Kim sank up to his hips before his feet met with solid resistance. Every step required twice as much strength as the one before.

When they finally paused, Kim wasn't the only one at the end of his strength. The dwarves found it very difficult to go on; more than once, their captors had to grab hold of the little figures' hair or arms to pull them out of the muck, where they were in danger of drowning.

Priwinn was wobbling more than walking, and even Gorg's breath was labored. Finally, they reached an island in the middle of the muddy ocean that had once been the Icy Wasteland. The spot where they rested for a while was a small piece of half-dry ground—almost perfectly circular. They knew they could rest only for a moment; however, that moment turned into half an hour, and all of them laid there, completely exhausted—except Gorg, who kept watch.

After a while, Kim opened his tired eyes and focused. The first thing he saw was Jarrn's face. The dwarf squatted next to him, looking down at Kim with a mixture of anger and scorn. For his part, Kim took a careful, very intent look at Jarrn—perhaps for the first time.

The dirty little face was ugly, to say the least. Kim tried to discern something in the dwarf's expression that he could relate to—even a trace of friendliness. He failed. Although he knew that this actually was impossible, he had the feeling that Jarrn's features were malicious. The tiny man's dark eyes didn't have the least warmth in them—just greed and hate directed at one and all.

"Well," Jarrn snapped after they'd stared at each other for a considerable time. "Are you satisfied?"

"With what?" Kim was irritated.

Prince Priwinn, who had curled up on the ground with his head resting on his right arm, opened one eye and looked at Kim inquisitively, but he said nothing.

"With this mess you've gotten us into, you damned fool!" Jarrn scolded. "We're all going to die—and because of your boundless stupidity."

"What?" Kim murmured.

Priwinn raised his head and stared at the dwarf.

"None of us would be here if you had surrendered right away!" Jarrn continued.

The unmitigated gall of this statement took Kim's breath away, but he sensed that Jarrn meant these words seriously. The dwarf actually blamed Kim for their awkward situation.

"That stupid Rangarig is going to kill us all," Jarrn went on. "I don't even know why we're running. We may as well stay here and wait for him to get us."

"It's not likely to get that bad," Gorg said in a surprisingly calm tone of voice.

The dwarf tipped his head back and looked up at the giant. "Oh? And why not?"

"Rangarig is seriously wounded. It will take quite a while before he regains his strength—enough time for us to think of something." Gorg nodded toward the cat, who had made himself comfortable in Gorg's lap and was alternating closing his right and left eyes. He suspiciously trained whichever eye was open on the half-dozen dwarves tied together. "Sheera caught the scent of settlers shortly before you attacked us; with a little luck, we'll find them."

"With a little bad luck, you mean," the dwarf corrected. He made a vulgar sound. "Oh yes, they're very close. That beast of a cat is right about that. But I wouldn't advise you to cross paths with them."

"Why not?" Priwinn asked.

"They're Riverfolk," Jarrn replied. "A pack of thieves. No one is safe from them, not even you lot. Believe me!"

"Riverfolk?" Kim recalled the eerie vessel topped with bulges. "Just because they have something against dwarves doesn't mean they have something against us, twerp."

"My word on it: They do," Jarrn retorted.

"He's right," Priwinn said. "It would be best if we detoured around the Riverfolk."

"Is that so?" Jarrn grimaced. "And where do you plan to go, grass-eater?"

Priwinn's expression said they were going to have a more thorough discussion about the term "grass-eater" later. For now, he let the insult go without comment and pointed toward the north. "There—where we were planning to go the whole time," he said. "We have to find the Castle at the End of the World."

Kim wasn't certain, but he thought he saw immense fear in the dwarf's eyes. "Castle . . . at the End of the World?" Jarrn gasped. "The fortress that belongs to the Guardians of the World?"

"Exactly," Priwinn said.

Jarrn scornfully shook his head. His eyes flashed maliciously, and then he finally shrugged his shoulders. Taking his time, he stood up and looked at each person in turn with narrowed eyes. "Let's go," he said. "It's a long way."

Indeed, it was. They spent the whole day slogging through the sticky mud, rarely coming across a dry island where they could rest.

Hardly anyone spoke, for they needed every ounce of strength to manage the increasingly difficult task of pulling one foot out of the sticky bog and placing it in front of the other.

Toward evening, one of the dwarves broke loose and tried to escape. Gorg didn't even bother to chase him but just signaled to Sheera. The dwarf was brought back soon and, for his effort, had to bind countless bleeding scratches and nicks with additional strips torn from his cape. There were no more escape attempts.

In the last light of day, Chunklet's sharp eyes caught sight of a slight hummock in the southward bog. They reached it just as the sun turned into a barely visible, red stripe on the horizon. What they saw in that last, reddish-gray light was . . . very unusual—eerily strange, in fact.

Before them stood an island of dirt in the middle of a sea of muddy water. It was larger than the dirt islands they'd encountered previously, and in its center was a rusty iron dome—ten feet high—with countless tiny holes on its surface. The air smelled strange. When they listened, they could hear a low humming and buzzing coming from the interior of the dome.

"What's that?" Priwinn asked in astonishment. Cautiously moving toward the strange iron thing, he stuck out his hand. He touched it very briefly before quickly retracting his fingers. A puzzled expression came over his face. "It's warm!"

Curious, Kim followed his lead and put his hand on the side of the iron dome. The metal felt ancient. It actually was warm—in fact, it felt almost hot, like a hearth where a fire recently had extinguished. Confused, he first looked at Priwinn, and then he glanced at the giant. Finally, his gaze happened to pass over the dwarves.

Jarrn and the others had retreated a short distance. None of the captives were looking in their direction except for Jarrn, and he didn't seem happy—anxious might be a better description.

Why?

Suddenly, the prince inhaled so sharply that Kim turned toward him in alarm. Priwinn still stared at the iron dome, his eyes incredibly wide. He whirled around, stalked over to Jarrn, and grabbed him by the collar, lifting the little man up in the air.

"You damned dwarves!" the Prince of the Steppe yelled, shaking Jarrn so wildly that the dwarf started to screech and flail. "That's *your* work! You all built that, didn't you? That's what happened here!"

Kim had no idea what was going on. Confused, he looked at the iron dome, which radiated an increasingly palpable warmth. Once again, the comparison with a hearth came to mind. Finally, he understood. "The ice!" he whispered. "These . . . these things . . . are melting the ice!"

Priwinn shook the dwarf harder. "And you built them! Right? That has to be it! Answer, dwarf!"

"Let me go, you oaf!" Jarrn screamed. Priwinn actually did let him go—so abruptly that the little man sank deep into the muck.

"How many of these things are there?!" Priwinn shouted, outraged.

"Quite a few," Jarrn replied in a subdued voice, "as you can imagine. I don't know how many—maybe a thousand. It took us a long time. Believe me, it wasn't easy."

"Why?" Kim said softly. "Why—why do this, Jarrn?"

"Why, why, why!" Jarrn said, imitating Kim's voice. "That's what they wanted."

"They—who?" Priwinn asked sharply.

"The Riverfolk," Jarrn replied. "They came to us, and we eventually signed a contract with them."

"A contract to destroy this land?"

Kim looked at Priwinn and held up his hand in a soothing gesture. Then, in a tone of voice so cool and calm that he himself was a little astonished, he addressed Jarrn: "Tell us."

"There's not much to tell," Jarrn said evasively. His gaze quickly passed over Priwinn's hands as if he were afraid the prince would beat him. "They wanted us to drive away the monster, and that's what we did."

"The Tatzelwurm," Gorg guessed.

Jarrn nodded. "Yes. Then, they wanted a canal through the mountains, and they got that, too. Finally, they wanted this: warmth to create fertile land for fields. We did what they wanted. We fulfilled our part of the contract down to the last detail. They swindled us, though. When we tried to collect, they chased us away. They captured the ones not fast enough and put them in chains. Those unlucky dwarves still have to work for them."

"They cheated you," said Priwinn, not entirely without malice. "So, you swindlers have been swindled."

"We don't swindle!" Jarrn protested. "We've never swindled anyone!"

"That's true," Gorg said.

Priwinn gave him a venomous look before addressing the dwarf again. "And exactly where are all these ovens located?" he wanted to know. "How far into this land did you take them?"

"I don't know," Jarrn replied. "We only built them; the Riverfolk installed them."

"Then . . . then, it's possible that everything here has been destroyed irreversibly?"

Jarrn was silent.

Despite the warmth radiating from the iron dome, an icy chill ran down Kim's back.

XV

The farther north they went, the warmer it became. The air was no longer so cold that it hurt to breathe, and more and more often, they came across dry islands in the middle of the muddy wasteland that once had belonged to ice giants. It seemed that what the Riverfolk had done with the dwarves' machines hadn't wreaked mere havoc in this part of the world, but it had also overturned the laws of nature. By the time the sun reached its zenith, the travelers already were walking on dry ground where only a few small puddles and an occasional mud hole remained. As the second day of their journey drew to a close, their destination—the End of the World, a fortress on the edge of time, the residence of the mighty Guardians of the World—was almost within reach.

Sheera's sharp feline eyes had spotted the ice towers early in the afternoon; not too long afterward, Kim saw something white glittering and shimmering on the horizon. This sight—coupled with the great relief that the Castle at the End of the World had survived the destruction of the Icy Wasteland—revived their strength. Although they had eaten their last provisions the previous evening and everyone was exhausted from the forced two-day march, they again quickened their pace.

Even so, many hours passed before they got noticeably closer to the fortress of ice and snow. The nearer they came to the shimmering ice towers, though, the more uneasy Kim felt.

He wasn't the only one: The hope on Gorg's face gradually gave way to disquiet and anxiety. Priwinn stopped speaking altogether.

It wasn't just the fact that no one came to greet them. The ice giants lived an isolated existence in their fortress on the edge of infinity and didn't concern themselves with the rest of the world. But as Kim and his friends approached the ice palace, the feeling that something was wrong intensified with each step. Eventually, with considerable pain, they had to acknowledge reality: The huge ice gate with its engraved symbol of infinity was unchanged. This gate, with its expanse of reflective, smooth, milky-white ice, was larger than many entire fortresses Kim had seen in Magic Moon. But the outline of the ice battlements over the gate was too short and too round. The towers of the fortress looked like giant candles sagging under the warmth of the sun. The ice walls leaned toward one another, collapsing under their own weight. The Castle at the End of the World was melting!

A dozen steps short of the gate, Kim stopped and stared at the huge creation of crystalline ice. He simply refused to accept what his eyes told him. He felt frosty air emanating from the enormous ice walls, and now everyone was shivering again from the cold.

Even so, the catastrophe that had befallen this part of the world also had touched this fortress. True, the huge mass of ice wasn't melting as fast as the drifts, and perhaps the Castle at the End of the World would survive a few more years—a last reminder of what this part of Magic Moon had been once. Regardless, in the end, it simply would disappear, too. Kim felt physically painful grief. They'd risked everything to come here. One of their friends had sacrificed his life so they could reach this destination, and maybe they, too, would die before they found the King of the Rainbows. All because of this last, desperate hope that the Guardians of Infinity might once again intervene in Magic Moon's fate so that everything would turn out well.

It was all in vain.

"Where are the . . . ice giants?" Priwinn whispered.

"Gone," Gorg murmured. The giant's voice trembled, and when Kim looked up at him, he saw deep horror, the like of which never had crossed his friend's face. "They're all . . . gone. They can't live here anymore. They . . . they need the cold and ice in the same way that we need the sun and warmth. Maybe . . . maybe they're dead."

Suddenly, he spun around, grabbed the nearest dwarf, and jerked him up in the air. "Maybe they're dead!" he shouted once more. "You killed them with your damned machines!"

The dwarf screeched, flailed his legs, and then froze when Gorg clenched a fist in front of his face. Gorg's fist was larger than the dwarf's entire head.

"You killed them!" Gorg thundered, his voice violently trembling.

"Gorg!" Priwinn's voice rang out, firm but calming. Quickly walking over to the giant, he raised his arms and tried to pull Gorg's clenched fist downward. Priwinn wasn't strong enough, but Gorg lowered his hand and gently set the dwarf on the ground, anyway.

"There's no proof that they're dead," Priwinn said in a soothing voice. "Maybe they just went away. You yourself said that before." He smiled sadly and extended his hand to give the giant a comforting pat on the cheek, but he couldn't reach that far. Gorg stared past him with dark, vacant eyes. Then, he abruptly turned and stomped away about fifteen feet. Kim started to follow him, but the prince grabbed him by the arm and silently shook his head. Then, Kim understood that his large friend wanted to be alone to mourn.

Kim, too, fought to contain his weeping. It wasn't fair: They had survived all those dangers and gone to such effort—and despite their pursuers and all the obstacles that nature and bad fortune had put in their way, they'd come so far—only to find that everything had been in vain. Kim thought he heard Rangarig's voice uttering the words he'd spoke on their last morning together: *"Whoever said life is fair?"*

"Come," said Priwinn after a while. "Let's look around a little. Maybe all is not yet lost."

Gorg and Kim knew this was wishful thinking. The companions didn't contradict Priwinn, though. Instead, after a brief hesitation, they followed the prince into the ice fortress' interior.

To Kim, the path through the wall of radiant, white coldness seemed like stepping into the past. Seen from the outside, the Castle at the End of the World was dying; but inside, it was completely intact. As they walked across the huge inner courtyard and approached the throne room, a wave of frigid air surged toward them, fogging their breath.

Everything was the same. Here, time itself had frozen; for a moment, it seemed completely absurd to Kim that anyone might be able to harm this bulwark of frozen eternity. Any second, he expected to see a door open, and one of the huge white Guardians of the World stepping out to ask them what they sought.

Unfortunately, nothing of the sort happened. The ice fortress was abandoned. They passed through rooms and halls and corridors, climbed enormous staircases of shimmering ice, and ran across balustrades of glittering white snow. Eventually, they arrived at the throne room—but it, too, was empty. The long table where the ice giants once had sat still was intact, and Kim remembered exactly where he'd stood back then: directly in front of the giant throne and beside Baron Kart, the leader of the black knights, who had pursued him to the end of the world.

Kim's gaze fixed on the narrow door behind the throne, and his heart beat faster as he stepped up to it. Once again, the door opened before he reached it, as if it were moved by an invisible hand. This time, however, when he walked through the doorway, what lay beyond wasn't the smooth, infinite plane where Kim and the black baron had fought their last battle. Instead, there was only a small, empty room. Although Kim probably should have guessed what awaited him, he shut his eyes with a deep, disappointed sigh, and he leaned against the cold wall.

There was no way it could have been there. The ice giants were guardians of entire worlds. They alone decided who was permitted to cross the Void. If they no longer existed . . . the road to eternity didn't exist, either. Kim had known that; but deep in his heart and against all reason, there had still been a tiny glimmer of hope. Now that this hope was extinguished, Kim felt like a part of him had died, as well. He stood with his eyes closed, leaning against the wall until the icy cold crept into his clothes and his back began to ache.

When he opened his eyes again, he saw Gorg across from him. The giant stood there, stooped over because the room was too small for him to stretch out. His breath created a curtain of gray steam in front of his broad face. Nevertheless, Kim could see traces of dried tears on Gorg's cheeks; all at once, his own pain felt petty and ridiculous compared to what his friend endured.

"You knew them? This is very hard for you, isn't it?" Kim asked.

Gorg nodded. He wasn't crying. His face was stony, but the expression in his eyes wasn't as good-natured as before; he looked a tiny bit like Rangarig shortly before the dragon turned into a beast.

That made Kim afraid.

"They belonged . . . to the same people as me," Gorg whispered haltingly. He smiled painfully. "But you don't know anything about that."

"I'm sure they're still alive," Kim said, although he knew better. "They've probably fled."

Gorg shook his huge head. "They're dead," the giant said quietly. "I feel it."

Kim wanted to say something comforting to Gorg, but he couldn't find the words. So, he silently walked past the giant and headed back into the throne room.

There, a stoic Prince of the Steppe stood by the door, staring into space. The dwarves, in their typical, disrespectful way, slouched in the carved ice chairs and loudly debated with each other in a language Kim didn't understand. Chunklet and Sheera crouched next to each other on the table, eying the noisy dwarf folk with mistrust.

"I'm sorry," Kim whispered.

"For what?" Priwinn asked. His voice was flat and expressionless.

"It was all for nothing," Kim said. "Themistokles was right: We shouldn't have come here."

"But the fact is, we *are* here," Priwinn replied. "It was the right thing to do. We had to at least try." He smiled sadly. "I almost led my people to their destruction once because I didn't listen to you, Kim."

"This time," Kim said in a troubled voice, "I was wrong."

However, as he spoke those words, he sensed that it wasn't quite the case. The path that Priwinn and Gorg had chosen was wrong. They once had saved Magic Moon by taking up their swords and confronting an enemy who had come with sword in hand. This time, there was no such enemy—possibly, there was no enemy at all. Maybe what they were trying to fight was just the passage of time. Where was it written that the future had to please those who lived in the past?

"If you two are finished commiserating with each other," Chunklet called from the table, "then I'd appreciate some ideas about what to do now. It's damned cold here."

"And I don't care for the company," Sheera added with a sideways glance at the dwarves.

Kim had to admit that they were right. Their situation was anything but favorable. They hadn't a thing left to eat; they were exhausted; and then there was Rangarig, who might be searching for them at that very moment.

"Those two are right," Priwinn agreed, shivering and rubbing his hands together. "We can't stay here. It's terribly cold. We'd freeze to death tonight."

"Retrace our steps?" Kim asked. "We'll never make it!"

"Do you have a better idea?" Priwinn retorted, shrugging his shoulders.

Kim stared at him. He had no idea what to do. Up until now, not one of them had given any thought at all to how they would return. Why should they have? For one thing, they'd assumed they could cover the distance on Rangarig's back. Then, too, none of them had thought past the King of the Rainbows, who they believed would help them. Now, they would never get to him.

"Real geniuses, aren't you?" Jarrn sneered.

Kim's answer consisted of a warning look. As if by chance, Sheera swiped his razor-sharp claws through the air, just missing the dwarf's face.

Jarrn reflexively jumped back a step before continuing in the same mocking tone. "I bet none of you master strategists has considered the possibility that you, too, might have to find some way to get back. Right?"

"We'll manage," Kim replied curtly.

Jarrn vigorously shook his head. "Oh, I'm sure you will!" he replied sarcastically. "You'll probably drown somewhere out there in the bog or be killed by the dragon. And we will, too. Even if you make it as far as the river—which is rather unlikely—the Riverfolk will get you."

"That remains to be seen."

Kim stepped aside, surprised, when the giant ducked through the door and straightened up to his full height. Gorg was in control of himself again. His voice sounded as deep and calm as ever, and there was a hint of a smile on his lips. At least outwardly, he was the good-natured, fun-loving giant that everyone knew. The deep, suppressed pain in his eyes was apparent only upon close examination.

"I might have a little word to say about that," he rumbled. "I'm definitely not scared of a few worthless villains."

Jarrn's expression was contemptuous as he looked the giant over. "This time, you're overestimating yourself," he said. "Size and strength alone are not everything. They'll catch us all and put us in chains."

Gorg shrugged, unperturbed. "If that's what has to happen, then so be it," he said. "Unless you have a better idea how we can get out of here, dwarf."

Jarrn hesitated for a moment. Then, he said, "Maybe I do."

Kim and the prince exchanged astonished looks. "What do you mean by that?" Kim asked.

Jarrn took another step backward and pointed at his five companions. "We've talked this over," he said. "Believe it or not, we also were surprised at what's happened here. Incidentally, we want to stay alive as much as you do."

"Stop beating around the bush and tell us what you want," Priwinn broke in.

The dwarf gave him a dirty look and muttered something that sounded to Kim's ears like "stupid grass-eater." Audibly, he said, "There's a way out of here."

"What?" Kim and Priwinn asked in unison.

The dwarf grinned spitefully and slowly shook his head. "Oh, no," he said. "It's not that easy, you geniuses. First, I want your word that you will release us."

Priwinn tried to laugh scornfully but didn't quite succeed.

"There's a way back," Jarrn repeated, ignoring Priwinn. "We know what it is. But we'll need to have you with us."

"What sort of way?" Gorg looked at the dwarf suspiciously.

Jarrn hesitated. Quite obviously, he didn't wish to betray too much, but he did seem to understand that their only chance to escape was together. "You know that we live in caves," he explained finally. "And we know many underground passageways through the mountains. One of them is not very far from here. I can show you where the entrance is. And there's a tunnel that leads directly to the big tree."

"That's almost two weeks' journey on foot," Priwinn noted skeptically.

"Not through a dwarf's cave," replied Jarrn, as if this explanation were enough. "So, how about it? Will you release us?"

"As soon as we get to the tree," Priwinn said, but Jarrn stubbornly shook his head.

"No," he insisted. "Now, on the spot."

"So that we can take you to this cave, and you can abandon us in some labyrinth where we'll get lost and die of hunger or thirst?" Priwinn vehemently shook his head. "How stupid do you think I am, little man?"

"I'm not sure you want an answer to that." Jarrn grinned, but he immediately turned serious again before Priwinn had a chance to explode. "I already told you: We can't do it alone," Jarrn said petulantly. "It's dangerous down there. We dug those tunnels, but they don't belong to us these days. The Riverfolk control them now. Together, we might make it through. Well, what's your answer?"

Priwinn didn't look convinced, and Gorg's face had no expression at all. Eventually, Kim nodded and said, "All right, you're free—under one condition."

Jarrn cocked his head to the side and squinted up at him suspiciously.

"What's a dwarf's word of honor worth?" Kim continued after a short pause.

Jarrn puffed up his cheeks and made a rude sound. "As much or as little as yours, kid."

"Then, give me word of honor that you'll escort us safely to the tree," Kim said earnestly. "We don't want to clear the way for you through the Riverfolk's territory, only to have you thank us by leaving us behind halfway."

To his surprise, Jarrn suddenly smiled. "I'm starting to like you, kid," he said, giggling. "All right. You have my word. The truce lasts until we reach the big tree. Then, we go our own ways."

The cave Jarrn had mentioned was close to the Castle at the End of the World. Initially, they retraced the path by which they'd come. Then, they turned west and took what seemed like a completely arbitrary course. Kim suspected it was a cruel trick or the dwarves purposely were leading them astray to plan an escape. But soon, Jarrn stopped and pointed at a circular hole in the ground.

Kim stepped closer and took a look at the shaft, which was a good six feet in diameter. He could have sworn that it hadn't been there a minute before. Shuddering, he leaned forward as far as he dared and surveyed the depths. The sun was low in the sky, so its light reached only a short distance. Anything more than ten or twelve feet below the surface was hidden behind an impenetrable black wall. Everyone sensed that this shaft was very deep.

Kim quickly stood up again, stepped back from the rim, and looked at his companions with doubt. He wasn't so sure that he'd been right to accept the dwarves' proposal.

"What are you waiting for?" Jarrn asked impatiently. "The first section is not dangerous."

Priwinn visibly gathered his courage and was about to start down, but Gorg held him back. "Let me go first," he said. "Who knows what we'll run into down there. Besides, if one of you falls, I'll be able to catch you. The other way around—I would drag you down with me into the depths."

No one objected, so Gorg cautiously lowered himself over the rim of the black shaft, stretching out his arms to find something to hold onto before slowly descending into the depths.

Kim watched him with mounting anxiety. After the giant left the sunlit area, something eerie happened: Gorg's legs and body didn't disappear slowly in the shadows. Instead, it was like he dipped beneath the surface of a pitch-black, motionless lake. After a few seconds, only the giant's head and shoulders were visible—then, just his hands. Finally, he disappeared entirely.

"Now me," Jarrn said, pushing ahead of Kim, who had intended to go second. "That moron will manage to get himself lost down there."

Kim suppressed the furious retort on the tip of his tongue; a quick glance at Priwinn told him that the prince was doing the same. Although they had made a truce with the dwarves, they didn't agree to tolerate everything—not by any means.

One after another, they descended into the depths, and what Kim had observed earlier, he now experienced himself: As he slowly climbed down the shaft, leaving the sunlight behind, he actually couldn't grasp the concept of a dwarf's cave. It wasn't just the absence of light down there; something eerie, dark, and ice cold dwelled in the darkness, which made not only his body but also his soul shudder.

The descent took a very long time. Kim was a good climber, but he estimated that more than fifteen minutes passed before he again heard the others' voices and saw shadowy movements beneath him. More than once, his strength nearly gave out. When he had firm ground finally beneath his feet again, his hands and knees trembled so violently that he had to lean against the wall and rest.

He looked around, his heart pounding. The shaft ended in a round gallery as tall as a man. The walls were as smooth as glass, as if they'd been melted instead of chiseled out of the rock. It wasn't as dark as it had appeared from above: A dim, gray shimmer hung in the air like radiant fog, casting ghostly silhouettes.

Gorg had gotten down on his hands and knees because the corridor was too low for him, even if he stooped over. Priwinn stood next to him, while Jarrn and the other dwarves bunched together on the other side of the gallery. In the foggy gray light, they looked less approachable than usual.

"Where do we go now?" Kim asked after he regained his breath. His voice echoed off the mirror-smooth walls in an eerie, distorted manner.

Jarrn recoiled in fright and frantically waved his hand from side to side. "Not so loud!" he hissed. "Do you want them to hear us?"

"Didn't you say this part of the tunnel was safe?" Priwinn wanted to know.

Jarrn made a movement that couldn't be made out precisely in the dark. "It is—usually," he whispered hastily. "But you never know, do you?" He pointed behind him. "In any case, we need to go that way. I had better go first."

No one objected, and so the dwarves assumed the lead. The farther into the underground tunnel they went, the more Kim's eyes got used to the pale light. He could see no more than five or six paces ahead of him, but at least he could make out more of his immediate surroundings.

The gallery hadn't been created naturally—he clearly saw that now. *What if the dwarves were telling the truth, and this passage way actually does lead to the big tree . . . ?* Kim's imagination simply couldn't conceive how someone artificially could create such a cave system. As it turned out, the dwarves hadn't done that—at least, not entirely.

Kim's sense of time totally became confused as they followed the dwarves through the eerie grayness. They must have spent hours walking through round, melted tunnels and enormous natural caves, trudging over huge heaps of fallen rock and bottomless pits.

Sometimes, they had to climb up rock faces that almost were too challenging even for Kim's skill. On a number of occasions, they wouldn't have managed the passage at all without the giant's assistance. His enormous strength enabled him to climb up vertical walls as if he were an oversized housefly—and he could do so while carrying two or three of them on his shoulders. It was clear to Kim why the dwarves had made this deal: Although they had created a large part of this labyrinth excavated deep in the earth, the path still was impassible for them sometimes. In various places, gaping holes and chasms littered the cave floor, which forced them to undertake perilous climbing expeditions. On one occasion, they passed a particularly treacherous gorge only because Gorg unceremoniously grabbed the dwarves and tossed them in a high arc to the other side.

Above them, the sun must have set hours ago, but they still were walking. The dwarves rejected all suggestions to stop for a rest, nervously urging them onward. All the other travelers were certain it was best to listen to them. Although no one made a remark along those lines, Kim had a feeling that the maze of gorges and tunnels weren't the real danger.

It turned out, he was right.

XVI

The sun had set hours ago, and Kim felt he could collapse any moment. His back ached unbearably, and the unnatural gray light made his eyes—in fact, his whole body—miserable. He didn't even notice when Jarrn, who still led the group, suddenly halted and raised his hand. Kim collided with the dwarf, almost knocking both of them to the ground. Startled, he suppressed a cry of surprise just in time. The dwarf put his forefinger to his lips and wildly gesticulated with his other hand.

"What's going on?" Priwinn whispered behind Kim.

Jarrn's gesturing became more frantic. Without saying a word, he pointed at the sharp turn in the passageway ahead and motioned for them to very quietly walk in that direction.

They obeyed. As they cautiously peered around the corner, it became clear why the dwarf was so afraid.

The tunnel ended in a narrow stone gallery, high upon the wall of an enormous cavern. The gallery issued into another round hole, which led deeper into the earth. That gallery had to be close to one-third of a mile long—and that was just the narrow side of the huge dome. The cavern was illuminated by the same eerie gray light that filled the tunnel world; in addition, countless yellow and red flames burned on the cavern floor. Some distance away, their flickering light reflected on the surface of an underground lake not much smaller than the Tatzelwurm's lair.

A number of little rafts moved on the still water, and far in the distance—barely recognizable as a blurry silhouette—Kim thought he saw the outline of a black ship with a rounded top, like the ones they'd seen on the Lost River.

But the surface of the lake wasn't the only place where there was movement. Among the fire sites below, people were everywhere: Men gathered around in small groups, performing tasks that Kim couldn't identify from such a great distance—perhaps carrying loads or simply lying on the bare ground, sleeping. Intense work went on around some of the larger fires. Sparks flew up, and the travelers could hear the muffled banging of heavy hammers.

"What is that?" Kim whispered anxiously once he and Priwinn had retreated to the safety of the tunnel.

"Riverfolk!" Jarrn replied in hushed tones. "I knew there was an underground town somewhere—but until now, I didn't know where."

"A town?" Kim repeated skeptically. The gloomy cavern didn't resemble a town.

"I bet they live in the caves," Jarrn guessed. "Somewhere nearby."

"So, how do we continue without being seen?" Priwinn asked sullenly.

Jarrn shrugged. His gaze passed over the prince's figure, over Kim's, and finally—very thoughtfully—over the broad shoulders of the giant. "My men and I could slip past without attracting notice," he said, "but you two—and especially that big lug . . ." He emphatically shook his head. "No, we have to find another way."

He mulled over things for a moment before turning around and pointing down the tunnel through which they'd come. "There are a few side branches back there. Maybe we'll find another corridor."

They went back as far as the side tunnel and hurried into it. The road was straight for a good distance, and then it changed into a dangerously steep ramp, which they stumbled down. Finally, they arrived in another cavern—tiny in comparison with the one they'd seen before; still, it was big enough to hold a small village—which was precisely what they found.

Astonished, Kim and the others gazed down at the collection of tiny huts built of unfinished rock: Most of them lacked a roof and consisted of four windowless walls; however, there were also large two- and even three-story buildings. The reddish glow of firelight spilled out of some of the enclosures, and the Riverfolk walked in between the buildings—although there weren't as many people here as in the large cavern. Here, too, the pathway led along the wall—although it was not devoid of hiding places entirely. After a brief survey, Jarrn pointed to a semicircular tunnel entrance across from them. With a little luck, they'd make it. A wild assortment of rubble and sharp-edged ridges were strewn on the ground, so even Gorg could hide easily.

Kim would have liked to get nearer to the cavern village to take a closer look; of course, the danger of being detected was too great. Still, he was the last to leave as, one by one, they hunched over and slipped into the maze of rocks. He lagged behind because he kept stopping to peer over the rocks at the houses. Occasionally, a figure stepped out of one of the doors, and Kim studied it very carefully. He could make out men and women covered in simple, crude fur or leather clothing, which was practical due to the cold down here. Kim even saw a few children noisily playing in the center of the three concentric circles of houses. If this village had been located on the surface of the earth instead of beneath it, there would have nothing at all remarkable about it.

What is it about the Riverfolk that makes the dwarves so afraid of them?

The others were waiting impatiently for Kim to reach the tunnel entrance. Jarrn in particular was agitated, shifting his weight from side to side. Priwinn gestured and frowned in annoyance, letting Kim know that he needed to hurry. Kim stepped quickly; but as he walked, he turned his head to look at the village—and froze in mid-stride.

The tunnel where Priwinn and the dwarves waited for him wasn't the only one. The cavern walls had a great number of different entrances and exits. At that very moment, two Riverfolk stepped out of one of these dark holes, dragging between them a third, smaller figure, who violently flailed and screamed. Kim stood motionless for a second; then, he spun around on the spot, ran a few steps back into the cavern, and ducked behind a rock. He heard Priwinn gasping, but he didn't turn toward the Steppe rider. Instead, he peered at the Riverfolk over the rim of his hiding place, fascinated.

The little group was too far away for him to make out any details, but he did see that the prisoner definitely was a very slender, short man—or a child! Kim didn't hesitate any longer. Hastily turning to Priwinn, he pointed to a place farther back in the passageway where Priwinn and the others crouched.

"Wait for me back there!" he whispered. Then, he cautiously stood up and furtively scrambled from rock to rock, quickly moving toward the village, the two Riverfolk, and their prisoner.

Approaching them was easier than Kim had dared to hope. The village was built on a circular spot in the cavern's center. The ground had been leveled, but no one had bothered to clear the surrounding area of rocks and rubble, so there were plenty of hiding places until he reached the first house. Gasping for breath, Kim looked right and left to make sure it was safe, and then he pressed up close to the wall and crept along the back of the building.

When he reached the corner, he was a few feet away from the two Riverfolk. They already had passed by Kim's location, so they and the squirming figure could be viewed only from behind. But Kim hadn't been mistaken—they were dragging between them a teenage boy.

Kim's heart leaped into his throat when he saw that the writhing figure had dark blue foliage instead of hair on his head. *One of the Tree People!*

The thought that such peaceful people might have any dealings with the scurrilous Riverfolk was so absurd that Kim didn't even consider the possibility.

The boy resisted fiercely. Suddenly, he succeeded in freeing one of his hands, but the second captor continued to hold the boy's other hand in an iron grip. The first man instantly reached out, grabbed the boy's arm, and slapped him so hard that he collapsed, semiconscious.

"Stop writhing around!" the man said furiously. "It won't do you any good."

"Why are you resisting?" asked the other. "You'll have it good where you're going—probably better than with your own people."

The boy with the blue-leaf hair didn't respond to these words, but he twisted and turned more violently. Then, he started kicking with his legs. The first man growled angrily and smacked the boy harder, which robbed the prisoner of consciousness.

"Be careful!" the Riverman's companion warned. "He won't be any use to us if he's dead. No one will pay anything for dead children."

Kim watched them until they disappeared into a large building. Then, with a pounding heart, he went back behind the corner of the house. Every fiber in Kim's being cried out that he should free the boy—but such an attempt bordered on suicide. The two men were too strong for him, and he wouldn't help the boy by getting himself captured.

His hands trembled from excitement. He'd heard the Rivermen's words very clearly, and it didn't take much imagination to figure out what they'd meant.

He quickly spun around—and found himself looking into the prince's face, which had darkened in anger. "Have you completely lost your mind?!" Priwinn whispered furiously. "Are you trying to get us all killed?!"

Kim pointed behind him, gesturing excitedly. "The children!" he burst out. "They're here, Priwinn! The Riverfolk have them—"

Shocked, Priwinn lunged forward and pressed his hand over Kim's mouth; in his excitement, Kim had spoken loudly.

"Quiet!" the prince hissed. "If they hear us, it's all over." He looked at his friend intently for a moment and before slowly pulling away his hand; he kept his arm raised, though, so he could silence Kim instantly if need be.

Kim had himself halfway under control again, though. Speaking very softly now—yet still spewing out words so rapidly that Priwinn had a hard time understanding them—Kim related what he'd observed.

Priwinn listened attentively, his expression clouding with every word. "The Riverfolk?" he asked skeptically. "That's impossible. All those children! They couldn't have—"

"I heard it," Kim interrupted. "He clearly said, 'he won't be any use to us if he's dead.'"

Priwinn was silent for a few seconds. A very thoughtful, determined expression spread across his face, and he nodded. "All right. Let's try to find out what's going on here." He gestured with his head to the rock wall. "Wait for me here. I'll get Gorg and the others." Before Kim could restrain him, the prince had spun around and disappeared among the rocks.

He came back with the others in surprisingly little time. Kim was doubly surprised when he saw not just the giant, Sheera, and Chunklet, but also the dwarves.

Jarrn immediately started in: "Have you completely lost your wits? Do you want them to—"

Sheera whirled around and glared at the dwarf with his yellow eyes. Jarrn broke off in mid-tirade.

Glancing at the cat, Kim had a general idea of how Priwinn had managed to persuade the dwarves to come along.

"Where did they go?" Priwinn asked.

Kim hadn't let the Riverfolk and their prisoner out his sight for a single second. He pointed at a sturdy building on the left side of the square. It was one of the few real houses—complete with roof, windows, and door. Luck truly was on their side, for this door was on the side of the building; wth a little skill, they could get inside undetected. Cautiously approaching, they paused behind the last rock. Only five or six more steps— but Kim realized that his assessment of their situation had been a little too optimistic. The large open area in the midst of the houses teemed with men, women, and children; if one of them happened to turn while the travelers were crossing the last stretch out in the open, all hope was lost.

"I don't like the look of this," Gorg growled. "Who knows what's waiting for us inside!"

"Oh, so the big giant's afraid?" Jarrn viciously goaded him.

Gorg didn't deign to answer, but Priwinn looked at the dwarf and suddenly smiled. "Gorg's right, you know," he said in a deceptively friendly tone. Jarrn looked up at him, irritated; Priwinn continued in the same syrupy tone of voice: "One of us should go first and see what it looks like inside—preferably, someone who is small and can move quickly."

Jarrn turned pale. "You're not expecting me to—"

"I am," Priwinn said, calmly interrupting him. "That's exactly what I'm expecting."

The dwarf was furious. Before he could object, though, a small, slender shape darted out from the rock and rushed right for the door.

Sheera reached the building unseen, disappeared in the shadows behind the door, and reappeared a few seconds later. "It's all right," said the cat. "No one's upstairs in the house, but there's a staircase that leads down."

"Oh yes," Jarrn snarled irritably, "probably straight down into a dungeon, you fools."

"That's what we're hoping for," Kim said, correcting him. He looked at Priwinn and the giant. "What do you two think?"

"It probably would be smarter to come back with an army," Priwinn said, sighing. "But by that time, it might be too late."

Gorg didn't say anything. He gazed at the Riverfolk for a moment, spellbound, and then he silently stood up behind the rock and covered the distance to the house in two giant steps. Kim and the others held their breath;0 miraculously, no one noticed the giant.

"All right, let's go," said Priwinn, addressing the dwarves. "You first."

"Why do we have to go before you?" Jarrn complained.

"So you don't 'forget' to keep up with us," Priwinn replied scornfully. "That could happen, couldn't it?"

Jarrn gave him a look that could have melted an iceberg, but he didn't object. Instead, he signaled his companions and followed the giant.

Although Kim tried to keep a careful eye on the dwarves, he hardly saw them. The tiny figures became gray shadows as they crossed the open space next to the house. Within a few seconds, they reached the door and disappeared inside.

Kim, Priwinn, and the two animals formed the rear. Kim's heart was pounding hard enough to burst as he rushed through the door and came to a stop. For half a minute, he fully expected to hear an angry outcry or trampling feet, but nothing happened. They had made it.

He looked around with a mixture of relief and fear. The interior of the building consisted of single large room, empty except for a number of iron rings fastened to the wall—from which short chains hung. Kim preferred not to think about the use of the chains.

Gorg, in the meantime, knelt down in front of a heavy wooden trap door in the middle of the room. He lifted it with one hand. Red light flickered below. When Kim walked over behind the giant, he saw the top steps of a narrow spiral staircase hewn in the rock. It wound down deeper into the earth.

Gorg opened the trap door all the way and silently lowered it to the floor. Then, creeping on his tiptoes, he led the way down the stairs, followed by the dwarves. Priwinn and Kim again brought up the rear.

The staircase led deep, deep into the ground, ending in a circular room with a half-dozen doors. Gorg put his ear to one of these doors, listened for a moment, and then tried to open it. It was locked. The giant looked at Priwinn, silently inquiring if he should break it open, but the prince shook his head and pointed at another door. Gorg went there and again listened. This time, he was lucky: When he pressed down the wrought iron handle, the door swung open to reveal a long, seemingly endless corridor filled with flickering, dark-red lights.

There were numerous chambers hewn into the walls of this passageway. Measuring perhaps five paces by five paces, they were sectioned off with bars of heavy iron rods. Straw rotted on the floor and a foul odor filled the air. The stench stole Kim's breath. His heart pounding, he followed Gorg into the corridor. They went all the way to the end and looked in every single one of five dozen cages, but every cell was empty. Still, the purpose of this place was clear: This was a dungeon. The dwarf had been right.

Where were the prisoners?

"Are you sure you didn't hear wrong?" Priwinn asked when they searched a second corridor and still hadn't found anyone.

"Yes," Kim replied. "And I saw them bring the boy into this house. He has to be here somewhere."

They checked the three remaining corridors that had unlocked doors; each time, they found nothing but empty cells. They were about to leave the last of these tunnels when Gorg suddenly stopped, motioned quickly with one hand, and closed the door with the other—leaving it slightly ajar.

Not a second too soon! From outside came the sound of a key turning in a lock. Then, a door opened; immediately thereafter, two tall figures dressed in brown leather and fur stepped out. As one of them walked past the partially open door, Kim recognized his face. It was one of the two men who had brought the leafy boy there.

The travelers waited until the two men's steps faded away up the stairs before they dared to leave their hiding place.

"That was close," Priwinn said. "One moment later and—"

"You're all absolutely insane," Jarrn said petulantly. "The only thing we should think about is getting out of here before they discover us. I have no desire to find out what these cages are like from the inside."

Kim shook his head and pointed at the last locked door. "First, let's see what's behind that," he said. "Those two came from there—alone."

The dwarf puffed himself up, preparing to object. However, Gorg already had stepped over to the door, and he didn't hesitate. In a single, continuous movement, he ripped the door off its hinges and placed it against the wall.

Behind the door was another corridor illuminated by gloomy torchlight. Here, too, dozens of cells had been hewn in the walls—but these were not empty! In the very first cell, Kim recognized the leafy boy; and in the chamber on the opposite side was a girl about twelve years old, crouching on the damp straw, staring at them with fear-filled eyes.

These two were not the only captives. Kim saw eight or nine additional prisoners—all children! The oldest one looked about Kim's age, but most of the kids were younger, some no more than ten years old. Unable to stop himself, he ran from cell to cell, rattling the locked bars. Finally, he came back to the pale girl. At a signal from Priwinn, Gorg grasped the rusty iron bars with his powerful hands and bent them apart, allowing Kim and the prince to squeeze through.

The girl looked at them with dark eyes, and when Priwinn held out his hand to her, she backed up, cowering in the farthest corner of the little chamber.

"Don't be afraid," Priwinn said. "We're here to help you."

The child's gaze wandered back and forth between them uncertainly, and then she stared at the giant. The fear in her eyes remained.

"We're not Riverfolk," Kim said urgently. "We're going to set you free."

The little girl still didn't answer. Instead, she kept on staring at them. She had heard Kim's words but probably didn't believe him.

Priwinn turned to Gorg. "Get the others out," he said. "Hurry!" Then, he turned back to the girl and repeated, "You don't need to be afraid. We're friends."

"You're . . . not pirates?" the girl asked doubtfully.

"Definitely not," Kim reassured her, answering for Priwinn. "We're here to help you. Where are the others?"

The girl looked at him, confused. "Others? What others?"

Gorg broke open all the cells, and the corridor filled with children: a good two dozen boys and girls of all different populations of Magic Moon. Some of them were in miserable condition. Their faces were dirty and haggard, their clothes hung in rags, and terror had left deep traces in their eyes. Kim felt a painful twinge at the sight.

"Why are they doing this?" Kim whispered.

Priwinn laughed bitterly. "Remember what you were telling me about earlier? No one pays anything for dead kids. The Riverfolk are selling them—probably to families who lost children and can't get over it, people like Brobing and his wife. You've experienced that yourself."

Kim shuddered at the memory of the pain he'd seen in Jara's eyes. Then, he emphatically shook his head. "That's impossible," he said. "She would never—"

"Steal another mother's child in order to replace her own?" Priwinn sighed sadly. "Yes, she would," he said. "People do terrible things when they can't stand the pain. Those damned river pirates take advantage of pain to enrich themselves. They're selling kids everywhere in the land."

"How do you know that?" Kim asked.

"Jarrn told me. In this case, I believe him." Priwinn turned on his heels and left the cell.

They tried to calm the children with a few brief words. To Kim's relief, most of them understood immediately what they needed to do now: keep as inconspicuous as possible and do exactly what their rescuers asked of them.

Seconds later, they headed up the spiral staircase. Soon after that, they gathered in the empty house on the edge of that cavern's town. Kim went to the door and looked out: Nothing had changed. The open area amid the buildings still was filled with people—not very many, but definitely too many for them to leave the house unseen. They had grown into a large group now.

"Someone has to distract them," Gorg said.

"And how do you propose to do that, genius?" Jarrn wanted to know. He glared at them. "What a crazy idea! We'll never get out of here!"

"Actually, we might," Gorg said. "I . . ." He broke off, pensively gnawed on his lower lip, and looked down at Jarrn and his companions. Then, with a lightning-fast movement, he stuck out his arm, grabbed one of the dwarves, and quickly stuffed him under his shirt.

The dwarf started to gasp and flail about, but he fell silent when the giant menacingly shook his large fist. "I won't hurt you," Gorg directed him roughly, "but I do need you."

He pointed to the square outside. "I'm going to go outside and stir things up a little," he said. "That should give you all a chance to get away. But I can't find the way out of here alone."

Before anyone could stop him, he turned around and stepped out the door. With the dwarf under his shirt, he stooped and crept over to the next house. Then, he stood up to his full height. He roared so loudly that the ground shook. Then, with hands lifted up high, the giant charged into the square.

The effect hardly could have been greater if a bomb had dropped. The Riverfolk froze in fear when they saw a bellowing giant run toward them. An indescribable panic broke out in the underground town. Men, women, and children ran screaming in all directions, scared out of their wits. A few tried to get in the giant's way to hold him up, but Gorg simply plowed through them. One man drew a sword. Gorg wrested it from him, tossed it away it in a high arc, and then grabbed its owner and hurled him after it.

"Now! Hurry!" Priwinn shouted. "Go!"

They left the house, one after another. The dwarves took the lead and guided the children through the maze of rocks and rubble and back to the tunnel that led out of the cave. Kim brought up the rear; once again, he briefly stopped and looked at the village.

Chaos had broken out in the center of the square. More and more Rivermen opposed the giant; Gorg fell to the ground after clashing with so many attackers. Kim could no longer see him among the undulating mass of bodies. Concerned, he asked himself whether the giant might have overestimated his strength.

Then, the prince grabbed Kim by the shoulder and roughly dragged him along. "Come on," he called. "Nothing's going to happen to Gorg! He can take care of himself."

Kim wasn't so sure about that, but Priwinn herded him along until they reached the tunnel where the others waited. The children had crowded together behind the tunnel entrance, and the dwarves stood a little off to the side, worrying about their companion with Gorg. The only one talking was Jarrn, who spoke to the pale girl in a soft, unpleasant tone of voice.

"Leave her alone, dwarf!" Priwinn said.

Jarrn didn't back down. "She has to tell me where our brothers are! They're prisoners of the Riverfolk, too!"

"What good would that do?" Priwinn replied. "We couldn't help them even if we wanted to."

The dwarf's eyes flashed in anger. He pointed an accusing finger at the children who'd just been freed.

"It's not possible, dwarf!" Priwinn insisted, pointing behind him. "Gorg won't be able to distract them for very long. When they notice that their prisoners are no longer there, they'll search for us everywhere."

At that point, Kim quickly stepped between them. "Jarrn's right," he said.

The Prince of the Steppe looked at him in disbelief. "What? You want to help him? Have you forgotten that two days ago he was threatening all our lives?"

"No," Kim replied, "but Jarrn is still right. He showed us the way back. For that reason, we have to help him."

Priwinn shook his head. It was beyond comprehension.

"I'm going with them," Kim insisted. "Alone. You don't have to come along. Lead the others out, and then wait for me."

He turned to Jarrn and looked at him intently. "Just you and me," he said. "The others can go. Agreed?"

Jarrn studied him for a while. Then, he nodded. "All right," he said. "My brothers will escort the others safely to the surface."

Kim was wrong on at least one point: Gorg succeeded in distracting the Riverfolk longer than anyone expected. After Priwinn, the children, and the five other dwarves had disappeared down the tunnel, Jarrn and Kim crept back. They soon reached the stone gallery high above the cave, but the view had changed in the meantime. There was nothing left of the relaxed atmosphere that had previously reigned on the shore of the underground lake. Dozens of men wildly rushed back and forth, many of then headed toward the tunnel entrances along the cave wall. Kim heard excited shouts and yelling. A whole detachment of armed Riverfolk approached from the far side of the cave, marching on the double.

"There are so many of them!" he whispered. "I hope Gorg was lucky."

Jarrn muttered something to himself. Moving cautiously, he got down on his hands and knees, crawled out a short distance onto the stone gallery, and peered down. Kim hesitated briefly before following Jarrn's lead. With all the commotion in the large cavern beneath them, there was little danger that they'd be noticed.

"Down there!" Jarrn's spindly finger pointed at a hole as big as a city gate. Gloomy red firelight flickered from within. "The little girl said that's where my brothers were."

Kim thoughtfully surveyed the domed cavern. He corrected his estimate regarding the number of Riverfolk: There had to be more than one hundred men among them. "How do we get there?" he whispered.

Jarrn pointed at a spot on the wall several hundred yards away from them. "It looks as if someone could climb down there," he said, "but I won't make it by myself. You'll have to carry me."

Kim sighed. That's what he had feared. Jarrn was right, though: Although the dwarves were cave dwellers and their experience with rock and ore benefited everyone, the walls here were too high for them. It was a miracle that they already hadn't broken their necks—or at least a few bones.

Crawling on hands and knees, they covered the distance to a rock face a little less steep; it was riddled with countless cracks and fissures. *Not too difficult to descend—at least, for the first stretch,* Kim thought worriedly. There were more than one hundred reasons why this was a bad idea: tall, broad-shouldered reasons with swords in hand and grim expressions on their faces.

Kim surveyed the cavern a final time, summoned all his courage, and signaled to Jarrn that he should hold on tight. The dwarf clutched Kim's shirt and shoulders, and Kim descended with clenched teeth.

No one took any notice of them, even though some of the Riverfolk ran past them only a few yards below. After a few moments, they reached solid ground again and—gasping for breath—ducked behind a large rock.

"Not bad," Jarrn praised, "at least for a fool like you."

Kim glared at him. "Once we get out of here," he promised, "I'll teach you some manners, little man."

Jarrn stuck out his tongue at Kim, grinned, and then abruptly turned serious again. "And how are we going to get over there without being seen?" He pointed at the cave entrance in the domed cavern's sidewall.

Kim's gaze lingered there for a moment, and then he resumed his survey of the cave. Although most of the Riverfolk had left the cavern, there still were plenty of them on the lakeshore . . . definitely too many for Kim's taste. "Actually, the key question is: How do we—and your friends—get back out afterward? And by the way," he said, "how many dwarves have been captured, anyway?"

"How should I know?" Jarrn spat out rudely. "Maybe only a handful, maybe hundreds."

Kim was shocked. "Hundreds?! There's no way we can liberate hundreds of prisoners!"

"No?" Jarrn flashed an angry look at him. "But we could have freed hundreds of *your* people, right?"

Suddenly, Jarrn shrank back in fright.

Half a second later, Kim became aware of movement behind him. He spun around.

It wasn't a Riverman. Kim breathed a sigh of relief. A small, spiny silhouette appeared on the gray rock. Shortly thereafter, a little voice piped up: "If you two argue any louder, you might as well stand up and say hello to the Riverfolk. You can be heard all the way on the other side of the mountain."

"Chunklet!" Kim exclaimed in relief. Then, he frowned. "What are you doing here? You should have stayed with the others."

"Didn't want to," Chunklet squeaked. With a look in Jarrn's direction, he added, "Besides, I don't care for those dwarves. This one is alone with you, but the others with Priwinn are in a pack of five."

"How is Gorg?" Kim asked quickly, before Jarrn could explode in protest.

"Don't worry about him. He thrashed a dozen men, and now he's playing catch with the rest."

"I hope he doesn't underestimate them," Kim said soberly.

Chunklet shook his head. "Not likely," he chuckled. "You should see how he's chasing them all over the place. . . . That doesn't mean that we have all the time in the world, though. Do you have a plan yet?" His gaze moved from Kim to Jarrn; without waiting for an answer, he sighed. "All right, I see you don't. Why did I even bother to ask?"

"If you're so smart," Jarrn snapped, "then tell us what we should do."

Chunklet blew a raspberry, rose up on his hind legs, and gazed over at the cave where the dwarves were held prisoner. "Wait here," he said. "I'll go see what the situation is over there."

Silently melting into the shadows until he was almost invisible, Chunklet slipped away and scurried across the cave without anyone seeing him. After only a few seconds, he reached the round opening in the rock and disappeared inside.

Full of concern, Kim kept looking after his little friend.

Chunklet didn't reappear for a good while, but then he scurried back to them, unseen.

"Well?" Jarrn asked impatiently.

"Your brothers are there," Chunklet replied. "Two or three dozen—I couldn't see precisely."

"And how many guards?" Kim wanted to know.

"None. Really, not a single one—only the dwarves. They're working as if possessed."

"And no one is watching them?" Kim couldn't believe it.

"They're chained," Chunklet explained. "Even if they wanted to, they couldn't escape."

Kim looked around, uncertain what to do. The excitement in the large cavern had subsided a little. More than half of the Riverfolk had disappeared, and those who had remained behind stood around in little groups, talking excitedly. With a little luck, the travelers could reach the cave entrance without being seen.

"Let's go," Jarrn murmured. "Sooner or later, they're going to stop chasing that big lug. We'll never have a better chance."

His heart pounding, Kim quickly headed toward the cave entrance—walking, not running. His clothing wasn't so very different from that of the Riverfolk, and he was tall for his age: At a cursory glance, he might pass for one of them. He wouldn't attract attention automatically unless he started running.

He was almost dying of fear by the time all three of them reached the cave entrance. It took incredible willpower not to glance back over his shoulder at the Riverfolk standing on the shore. A few times, he heard a suspicious sound or saw movement out of the corner of his eye that made him think their daring game was up.

But they were lucky. Completely unnoticed, the trio reached their destination. Kim stopped in surprise and looked around.

This cave was much larger than he had expected: a real hall with a low ceiling, supported by countless black pillars of granite and solid lava. Dozens of fires flickered. As Chunklet had said, nearly three dozen dwarves stood around the fire sites, forging and hammering with all their might. The room echoed from the pounding of heavy hammers, sparks flew up, and the heat was unbearable. White-hot iron hissed into sand molds or produced clouds of steam when plunged into cooling water.

"Those miserable swine!" Jarrn murmured with a shaky voice.

Kim understood when he took a closer look at the prisoners.

No dwarf he'd seen thus far was impressive, neat, tidy, or otherwise attractive—but this group was a pitiful lot. It was amazing that they could still stand on their feet and swing their heavy forge hammers. Most of them were naked except for dirty loincloths; they were so emaciated that they looked like skeletons someone had draped with worn-out, filthy skin. Their wasted little bodies shone with sweat. A black iron ring circled each dwarf's right foot, and a long chain bound together the rings. The chain disappeared into the wall at the back of the hall.

With an effort, Kim pulled himself together and beckoned to Jarrn. "Hurry now, before someone comes."

Up until then, they'd stood in the cave entrance, so the dwarves inside were mere silhouettes, at most. Now, the companions stepped into the flickering red light of countless fires. When the wretched creatures saw them, one after another, they lowered their tools and stared in amazement. Not a single dwarf said a word; a mixture of surprise and fear spread on the faces.

Eventually, one of the dwarves put down his hammer and walked as far as the chain on his leg allowed. "Jarrn?" he asked uncertainly. "Is it you?"

Jarrn made an annoyed gesture. "Quiet now," he said. "Where are the guards?"

"There aren't any guards," replied the dwarf. "The Riverfolk come every so often to bring new material or inspect the work. There's only the overseer, and he's asleep most of the time."

"Good," said Jarrn. "That makes things easier." He searched the walls. "Who has the key?"

"The overseer," replied the other dwarf, gesturing at the back wall of the forge. "His chamber is over there."

"We'll pay him a little visit," Jarrn said determinedly. "The rest of you—keep on working as if nothing has happened. The pirates can't notice what's going on. Otherwise, I'll end up keeping you company."

He was about to walk off, but Kim gripped his shoulder, holding him back. "What's going on?"

"We need the key for the chain," Jarrn said, brushing away Kim's hand.

"Why?" Kim asked, puzzled. He pointed at the heavy hammers and tools in the dwarves' hands. "There are enough tools here to break the chains."

Jarrn made a wry face and laughed scornfully. "What a fool you are," he said. "This chain comes from our forges in the eastern mountains. No tool in this world can break it."

They walked through the hall while the dwarves started hammering and pounding again. A short distance from the hole in the wall where the chain disappeared, they found a heavy, ironclad door. Kim cautiously opened it a crack and peeked inside. Dimly lit by a brazier full of glowing coal was a little chamber with a crude desk, a matching chair, and a low pallet covered with straw. A figure curled up on the straw, snoring loudly: the overseer.

With extreme care, Kim opened the door, gestured for Jarrn to keep quiet, and tiptoed into the room.

He looked around, fascinated. The chain ended directly over the sleeping man's bed, where it was fastened to an iron ring with an enormous padlock. The guard wore an oversized key on his belt.

With his heart thudding in his chest, Kim approached the bed, halted, and closely observed the sleeping man's face. He was bearded, broad-shouldered, and very coarse-looking. His mouth hung open, indicating that he was in a deep sleep. Nevertheless, Kim's hands shook as he reached for the man's belt, preparing to slip off the key.

Jarrn's arm flashed out, holding Kim back. "Stop!" he whispered. "I can do that better."

As quick and agile as a pickpocket, he slipped the key from the man's belt, grinned as he stepped back, and then walked to the lock. He was too short to reach it, so Kim wrapped his arms around Jarrn's hips and boosted him up. Just as silently as the dwarf had taken the key, he now opened the lock.

Unfortunately, their luck ran out.

The lock sprang open with a clank, and the heavy chain fell with such force on the overseer's body that he didn't have enough breath to scream out.

Kim and the dwarf stood there, paralyzed, staring into the overseer's wide eyes. Then, the man tossed the chain aside and sprang out of bed.

Kim hopped backward in fright as the overseer lunged for him. He managed to evade the grasping hands, but he lost his balance, stumbled awkwardly, and ended up falling over the chair. As he was falling, Kim saw Jarrn turn on his heels and, with a powerful leap, disappear out the door.

There was no time to think about the dwarf's betrayal. The overseer grabbed Kim by his collar and waistband and roughly yanked him into the air.

"Who are you?!" he yelled at Kim. "What are you doing here?"

These questions didn't really require an answer, for as the overseer was saying the words, he shook Kim so violently that no answer could have been possible, even if Kim had wanted to reply. Suddenly, the man stopped shaking Kim, and his eyes widened. For a heartbeat, he stared into Kim's face. Then, he spun around and looked at the ring and the open padlock in total shock, as if he just now truly understood what had happened.

"Treason!" he roared. "The prisoners!" The end of the chain already was moving like the tail of an iron snake. Clanking, it slid down from the bed and moved toward the hole in the wall. With another bellow of rage, the overseer dived for it—without releasing his grip on Kim, however. He missed. In the fraction of a second before he reached it, the chain disappeared through the wall. Outside in the forge, a triumphant cheer resounded.

"Treason!" the guard cried again. Furious, he stood up, stared at Kim, and raised his hand to strike. Instead of completing the movement, though, he twisted Kim's arm around, making Kim groan and bend over in pain. With his other hand, the man drew his sword from his belt—or at least he tried to. A sprightly black figure landed on the back of the overseer's neck, digging one hand into the man's face and pummeling him with the other—all the while screaming shrill curses.

The man stumbled and crashed into the table, trying to shake off his attacker; however, small, spindly figures appeared everywhere. Several grasped the overseer at the same time, wrestling him to the ground thanks to sheer numbers, although he defended himself with considerable strength. Before he knew it, he was trussed up with strips torn from his own clothes. Everything happened so fast that he didn't have time for even one last scream.

Kim stood up, wobbled, and rubbed his aching arm. "Thanks," he murmured when he spotted Jarrn among the dwarves. "That was close."

"You shouldn't have let him catch you, stupid," Jarrn replied, as much a loud mouth as ever.

This time, Kim smiled. "And I thought you were just going to abandon me."

Jarrn pursed his lips. "So he could beat you up and sound the alarm to the whole mountain?" He shook his head. "And besides, now we're even," he growled, speaking more to himself than to Kim.

Kim preferred not to think too hard about the meaning of those words and instead turned to exit the forge.

"Where are you going?" Jarrn called after him.

Kim pointed to the other side of the hall. "I'd rather not stay here," he said.

Jarrn mocked, "Imagine that. We can't get out that way, though: It's teeming with Riverfolk outside."

"Oh, is that so?" Kim replied angrily. "Should we wait here until they get bored and go home?"

At that, Jarrn stuck out his tongue at Kim, left him standing there, and turned to his brothers. "Half of you, keep working!" he ordered. "Make plenty of noise, so they'll think everything is the same as it always is in the forge. One of you, stand guard. The rest of you, come with me."

The dwarves obeyed—with so little dissent that Kim was very puzzled indeed. He'd never seen a dwarf do anything without complaining or making a spiteful remark. At least half the ragged creatures immediately walked to the fire and started making so much noise that the whole mountain reverberated. To Kim's astonishment, the others crowded into the overseer's little chamber and began to pound on the back wall with hammers and pickaxes.

Kim was astounded at the speed with which they dug into the mountain. Although none of the emaciated figures looked capable of even lifting a piece of bread—to say nothing of swinging one of the heavy tools—the granite broke up under their blows like rotten wood. Within a few minutes, there was a circular tunnel not quite three feet high; the dwarves hacked away as fast as the wind could blow.

Jarrn was amused when he saw Kim's dumbfounded expression, but he refrained from commenting and instead yelled at the dwarves in the forge and in the tunnel, encouraging them to work harder.

Kim watched, speechless, as the tunnel extended into the mountain with amazing speed. Already, the dwarves at the forefront no longer were visible. Their hammering and pounding sounded more and more muffled until, eventually, it was a barely noticeable knocking sound.

Then, a frightened shout resounded in the forge. Barely a second later, a dwarf rushed into the chamber and breathlessly gasped, "They're coming! The Riverfolk have noticed something!"

The other dwarves rushed in, as well, one after another, all equipped with hammers, pickaxes, or weapons they had forged themselves. Whether Kim desired it or not, he was carried into the tunnel on a tide of small, raggedy figures.

The passageway was so low that Kim couldn't run even if he stooped over. Instead, he had to crawl on his hands and knees. The dwarves who swarmed in behind him pushed and shoved him so much that he lost his balance more than once, falling flat on his face. Those following behind simply ran over him. Before long, he heard furious yelling at the end of the tunnel. When Kim looked back, he saw a broad, black silhouette, vainly trying to squeeze into the tiny passageway.

Then, Kim's groping hands encountered resistance. Before him was a massive rock wall. Kim realized he hadn't reached the end of the tunnel, though—he'd made it only as far as a right-hand turn, which the dwarves had created for some unknown reason. Gasping, he squeezed through the narrow gap, got back up as far as he could, and crawled a little bit farther.

Not one second later, something broke the rock wall with a metallic clatter. When Kim turned his head, he saw a broken arrowhead gleam in the little bit of light that came from the end of the tunnel. There was an angry shout, and then Kim saw a broad-shouldered silhouette hastily squeeze into the narrow tunnel. Luckily for Kim, his pursuer got stuck barely a yard in, and he was unable to move either forward or backward. Now, Kim was very glad the dwarves' tunnels were so low. . . .

XVII

Two days later, they saw sunlight again for the first time. As the eerie gray light of the mountain world gave way to pale moonlight shining through the cave entrance, Kim wasn't the only one who felt as if he'd just awakened from a long nightmare. An icy breeze hit him, making him shiver, and everyone quickened their pace. Not even the steep, rocky, debris-covered slope outside the cave entrance could slow them down. One after another, Kim and the dwarves tumbled down the slope; no one came away from the experience without scrapes and bruises, but that didn't seem to bother anyone. A general sigh of relief went through the group when they finally saw a real sky in place of a solidified-lava ceiling.

Jarrn, Kim, and the freed dwarves had wandered aimlessly through the labyrinth of rocks and caves before they'd encountered Priwinn and the others. For many additional hours, they'd anxiously expected the Riverfolk to find their tracks and follow them. Luckily, the dwarves had proven to be excellent guides. Although the Riverfolk very clearly had the advantage in this subterranean world, the dwarves were incomparably more familiar with it. They hadn't encountered any more members of pirate society.

The journey had been hard enough, even so. The eternal twilight had strained their nerves; they hadn't a thing to eat and only seldom found any water. As a result, they all were at the end of their strength. Even Gorg's movements had lost much of their buoyancy, and the giant had become quieter.

Kim was the last one to reach the foot of the rock pile. Exhausted, he sank down on a stone. Suddenly, he hardly could keep his eyes open. His eyelids drooped. His arms and legs seemed to be filled with lead and felt as if they would sink him to the ground. He tiredly looked around but couldn't make out anything except jumbled shadows and the glint of silvery moonlight reflected on damp grass.

The dwarves had promised to bring them close to the tree; at the moment, however, there was no sign of it, though they all looked far and wide.

Kim was much too sleepy to pursue that thought. They'd finally escaped from that dark labyrinth beneath the earth, and that was all that mattered.

The others were affected in the same way. Although the smaller children occasionally had started to cry during the day from hunger and exhaustion, Kim didn't hear a single word of complaint now. Considering that there were more than sixty people on this little spot in front of the rock pile—including the children, the dwarves, Kim, and his companions—it was eerily quiet.

Someone started a fire, and the crackling flames and the warmth dispelled the eerie atmosphere a little—but not entirely. Kim attributed this impression to his own exhaustion and despondency, but it also seemed as if something had accompanied them out of the dreadful caves.

All of a sudden, there was commotion near the edge of the forest. Kim looked up with heavy-lidded eyes and caught sight of Gorg.

Gorg must have continued on, unnoticed, right after they'd arrived at this place, for he now emerged from the forest carrying a dead buck over his shoulder. Kim was too tired to help, but Priwinn and some of the larger boys and girls quickly ran over to the giant and began gutting and butchering the buck. Soon, two huge spits of juicy meat turned over the flames, and the tempting smell of roasted meat made everyone's stomach growl.

The food and the feeling of relief lightened Kim's despondent mood a little. As he sat there—forcing himself with all his might to take little bites of the meat he'd been given and to chew each bite carefully instead of gulping everything down all at once—his gaze wandered over the many children who sat in a circle around the fire. Still, no words were spoken, only hungry smacking and chewing.

"What's the matter? Is something wrong?"

With great effort, Kim turned his head and looked at Priwinn's face. He hadn't noticed that the prince had sat down next to him. "You look as if you've just been through the worst defeat of your life."

"I'm just tired," Kim murmured.

"We all are," Priwinn replied, "but something is still bothering you—so, out with it."

Kim hesitated a moment, bit off another piece of meat in order to gain some time, and finally answered with a full mouth: "The children."

"What about them?" Priwinn asked. "We set them free. You're acting as if you disapprove."

"Nonsense!" Kim took a deep swallow. "But there are so few of them, and they're not the ones we were looking for."

"Every single life is important," Gorg said from Kim's other side.

"Yes, of course," Kim murmured. "I'm sorry. It's just . . ." He searched a moment for the right words before shaking his head, at a loss. "In the end, it was all in vain," he murmured. "Nothing has changed."

"And what were you expecting, dimwit?"

Kim didn't have to raise his eyes to know that Jarrn had joined them. Nevertheless, he glared at the dwarf. "I bet you know what's going on with the children who've disappeared," he said.

The dwarf looked at Kim in a way that Kim couldn't interpret. Then, Jarrn answered, "I bet I wouldn't tell you if I did know."

Priwinn jumped up, but Jarrn waved his hand and continued in a different tone of voice. "We kept our word. You're back. My brothers and I are going now."

Kim leaned back his head and searched the night sky. "The agreement was: You bring us to the big tree," he reminded Jarrn.

"We did," Jarrn replied. He pointed with his hand at the darkness behind him. "In the morning you'll see a hill. The tree is behind it."

"Wait a minute," Priwinn said. He stood up, signaled to Gorg with a movement of his head to keep an eye on Jarrn, and walked off. A few minutes later he came back, but he was no longer alone. Beside him was Eib, blue leafy boy.

"This dwarf claims that we're near your tree," Priwinn said, pointing at Jarrn. "Is that true?"

Eib looked around, unable to make up his mind. It took a long time before he replied, and when he did, his voice sounded very unsure. "I don't know," he admitted. "This seems . . . familiar. Maybe it's true."

Priwinn sighed and rolled his eyes.

Jarrn made a face again. "You're no wiser now than you were before," the dwarf said spitefully. "But you'll have to believe us, whether you like it or not. Besides, if we want to go, we will."

"Are you sure?" Gorg rumbled.

Jarrn chuckled maliciously. "Absolutely, numskull. We could have left you at any time. If you don't believe me, ask him." He pointed to Kim, who reluctantly nodded.

"So, why didn't you?" Priwinn asked.

"I gave you my word," Jarrn replied, insulted. "But the truce is over. We're going now. And the next time we meet, it's going to end differently than last time. That's a promise."

"You've got my word on that, too," Priwinn said, full of hate.

Kim turned away, depressed; he stepped back from the fire. The quarrel that had flared up between Priwinn and the dwarf showed him that nothing had changed. For a few brief moments, he'd let himself hope that the dangers they'd surmounted together might have turned enemies into friends—or at least allies. But that wasn't the case. When Kim went back to the fire, the dwarves already had vanished silently into the night, like ghosts.

They didn't leave until noon the next day, for the food and warmth of the fire gradually had its effect and they'd all fallen into a deep, exhausted sleep. It was late in the morning when they awoke.

They indeed saw the hill that Jarrn had mentioned, but it was much farther away than they'd expected, and the few hours of sleep and one meal they'd had were not nearly enough to fully restore their strength, so they were slow to leave their resting place. When they finally reached the top of the hill, the sun entered the last third of its daily journey.

The sky was blue on the other side of the hill. There were no branches and leaves arching across the sky—no green-tinted sunlight.

The tree wasn't there.

Kim stopped, disappointed. "He lied," he whispered. "The dwarves lied to us, Priwinn."

The Prince of the Steppe nodded grimly. "What did you expect?" he asked. "They probably led us on a wild goose chase. It will take us months—maybe years—to get back home."

"No, it won't," said a voice behind them. "We're there."

Something in Eib's voice frightened Kim to the core; when he turned around, he looked directly at the leafy boy's face, which had paled under the brown of his weathered bark skin. The leafy boy's eyes were black with horror, and his outstretched, trembling hand pointed to the east.

Kim looked down, following the path of the boy's outstretched arm.

And then, he saw the tree.

It had fallen.

Where an enormous construct of wood and foliage and frozen time once had stood, a splintered stump now jutted into the sky. Even though it still was ten times higher than the highest fortress tower Kim ever had seen, it was still pathetic in comparison to the tree that once was.

The trunk, which had broken into several parts, had toppled eastward—burying forests, meadows, streams, and entire hills beneath it. Far, far away, almost on the horizon, the crumpled treetop towered like a mountain ridge of green shadows.

It took them the rest of the day to reach the ruins of the tree. Kim had expected that the horror he'd experienced at the first sight of the enormous, collapsed structure would fade a little as they approached. The exact opposite occurred: The nearer they came, the more devastated he felt.

A steadily increasing uneasiness spread among the others. The only one completely calm on the outside was Eib. But Kim kept a close eye on him and very quickly saw that it wasn't true calm. Not the slightest emotion showed on Eib's face—it was as if his expression had suffered rigor mortis. He walked along without complaint, but his movements resembled a machine running without knowing why. When they arrived at the tree stump late at night and halted at the foot of the giant wooden staircase, Eib was the only one who didn't visibly react to the horrendous destruction.

It was very quiet. During the last hour, they'd marched single file, snaking around massive debris and detritus that littered the ground for miles. Broken branches as huge as a whole forest, giant fragments of the trunk as large as houses and towers, whole mountains of crushed foliage—all those obstacles forced them to take detours. The detours often hid tree stumps from their view. No matter their location, though, they hadn't heard the least bit of noise: not a single bird, not the softest rustling breeze. Nothing interrupted the deathly silence that spread across the land.

"What in the world happened?" Priwinn whispered, shaken to his core.

Of course, no one replied. No reply was necessary. *Basically,* Kim thought despondently, *it doesn't matter what exactly happened.*

The only thing that now counted was the fact that it *had* happened.

He slowly walked over and put his hand on the leafy boy's shoulder. Eib gave a start, as if he were waking up from a trance. With excruciating effort, he turned his head and looked at Kim; finally, Kim saw in the boy's eyes what he'd been waiting for the whole time: glistening tears.

Somehow, all the consoling words that Kim had prepared suddenly were gone. He couldn't say anything to make the boy feel better. He felt empty and shattered, too, like something inside him was as broken as that gigantic tree. Kim couldn't help Eib at this point; he himself was in need of help.

"Let's go." Priwinn pointed at the staircase that led up the stump. "Maybe someone is up there."

Eib replied with a shake of his head. "No."

Priwinn went up a few steps, stopped again, and then despondently came back down.

They were just about to rejoin the others when a rustling sound came from a broken branch. Suddenly, a gnarled figure with hair and clothes of green foliage stepped out.

"Oak!" Kim called out, running toward the man.

He stopped when he saw Oak's expression. Oak's eyes were as vacant and dark as Eib's, and his face didn't look weathered but *old:* ancient and excessively tired.

Priwinn, Gorg, and some of the older children also headed toward Oak; like Kim, they stopped some distance away.

When Oak looked up in slight surprise, Kim realized that Oak hadn't understood what had happened, up until now.

"It fell," the green man whispered. "It fell."

Kim was the first to pull himself together. He walked closer to the gnarled man. "Oak," he said softly. "What happened here? Tell us."

"It fell," the green man murmured again. "It . . . it simply fell over." It didn't seem that he'd heard Kim's words at all.

"How did that happen?" Priwinn asked, speaking louder than Kim and in a much sharper tone of voice.

"It fell," Oak said again, and then he shook his head, looked up, and whispered: "And it's our own fault."

Priwinn and Kim looked at each other.

"Your own fault?" the prince repeated. "Oak, please! Explain to us what happened here! The tree—this tree—it couldn't have just toppled over!"

"A storm," Oak just murmured. He appeared to be looking at Prince Priwinn, but his dark eyes really gazed into empty space. His voice grew softer and trembled as his memory of the terrible event threatened to overwhelm him. "There was a storm," he said then. "A bad storm."

"That's impossible," Kim objected. "This tree has survived thousands of storms."

"A storm," Oak repeated. "It . . . it just fell over."

Priwinn wanted to say something else, but Kim quickly put his hand on the prince's shoulder and shook his head. He realized they weren't going to get anything more out of Oak at the moment; it was impossible to talk with the man in his current condition.

Instead of trying to get answers out of him, Kim stepped up and reached out. Then, something unexpected happened: Oak stopped his ceaseless babbling, put his arms around Kim, and started to sob—silently and without any tears, but intensely.

Under any other circumstances, it would have been painfully embarrassing for Kim. He was just a boy, and Oak was a man of virtually unimaginable age. Yet, Kim now gave solace to the leafy man simply by holding him.

What Priwinn's words hadn't accomplished now happened naturally: Oak stood that way for quite a while, eventually calming down. Embarrassed, he pulled back from Kim and looked down, his gaze once again lucid—although still veiled with horror and fear. At least, he now recognized Kim.

"I'm sorry," he murmured. "I . . . I lost control of myself."

"That's all right," Kim said. "Could you . . . tell us what happened, Oak?"

Oak hesitated briefly before nodding. "It fell," he said. "Limb and the others were right. We destroyed it. There was a storm, like thousands of other storms in the past. But this time, the tree didn't survive. It was weakened. We wounded it in too many places. We cut out so much of its heart that it didn't have the strength to withstand the storm."

"Where are the others?" Priwinn whispered. "Are they . . . dead?"

Again, Oak waited a while before answering; while the man silently stared at the prince, Kim was afraid to hear the answer. Then, the leafy man shook his head soberly. "Many are dead," he said. "Hundreds, maybe thousands. The ones who are still alive have retreated to the branches." He pointed in the direction where the tree's huge crown merged with the horizon. "But they're going to die," he continued in a whisper. "The tree has fallen. Its branches will wither, and there is no other place where we can live."

"*You* are still alive, though!" Kim protested desperately. "And . . . and Eib survived in the Riverfolk's prison. You'll find a new place to live."

Oak looked at him and smiled, but it was a very sad expression. "I wish it were so," he said. "But there is no other place we can live except on our tree. We can be somewhere else for a while—but without our tree, our people will soon die out."

"That can't be!" Kim exclaimed. He felt anger so intense that it scared him. It was the kind of anger that wasn't directed at anyone: It burned in him solely because of the way everything was turning out. "You'll find another tree," he said hopefully. "Another homeland."

"Let it be, little hero," Gorg rumbled. "He's telling the truth. There's no other place where they can live. And there was just this one tree."

"Those damned dwarves!" Priwinn said with a trembling voice. "I swear I'm going to chase them and their damned iron men back to where they came from—even if it's the last thing I do."

At that, Oak suddenly shook his head. "It wasn't the dwarves, Prince Priwinn."

"Of course not," Priwinn said hotly. "Just their iron men, right?"

"It was not their fault," Oak repeated, emphasizing each word. "They weren't the ones who destroyed the tree. We did it ourselves. You warned us—you and your giant friend over there, Limb, and many others. We didn't listen to you, and now we have to pay for it."

"Someone else is going to pay even more," Priwinn insisted, but the leafy man soberly shook his head.

"Is there a higher price than the destruction of an entire people?"

This time, Priwinn had no answer.

They spent the night in the shadow of the enormous tree stump. There was enough dry wood for them to light a big fire, which protected them from the chilly night wind. Oak brought them some food: enough fruit and berries to fill all their growling stomachs. He gradually regained his composure as the evening progressed. Neither Kim nor any of the others attempted to broach the subject of that terrible event. However, after they finished eating and sat around the fire for a while, Oak brought it up on his own.

"I'm glad you're still alive and unharmed," he said, after Priwinn related their adventures in the Icy Wasteland and the Riverfolk's labyrinth. "We were all very worried after you disappeared."

"You didn't do anything bad to Limb and his friends, did you?" Priwinn worriedly asked.

Oak shook his head with a forgiving smile. "What kind of people do you think we are?" he asked. "Many were angry about what you did—especially when the dwarves showed up fewer than two weeks later, demanding compensation for the iron men you destroyed. But—"

Surprised, Priwinn interrupted him. "Two weeks?" he repeated. "But that's impossible."

Oak looked at him inquiringly and Priwinn exclaimed, "We just left a little over a week ago!"

"You've been gone almost half a year," Oak protested, puzzled.

Now, it was Priwinn's and Kim's turn to look at Oak in astonishment.

"Half a year?" Kim asked—checking if he'd heard correctly. "You're sure?"

Oak nodded and shrugged his shoulders. "Give or take a month, I suppose. Time does not interest us as much as it does you."

"The caves!" Gorg recalled.

All eyes turned to the giant; bewildered.

"The dwarves' caves," Gorg repeated. "There has to be a secret to them. It took us only two days to travel from the Castle at the End of the World to here. But it's a long way—very long. If someone went by foot, he definitely would travel for half a year, if not longer."

Oak nodded in agreement. "The dwarf folk have magic powers," he said.

"They're going to be in dire need of that power when I get my hands on them," Priwinn said savagely.

Oak looked at him reproachfully but refrained from replying. After another pause, he continued with his tale: "We didn't do anything to harm Limb and the others," he repeated. "We didn't listen to them, either. If only we had! Maybe back then, it wasn't yet too late. We were blind. It all seemed so easy: bigger houses, nicer clothes, better furniture—an easier life. They warned us that we would have to pay for it, and I think deep in our hearts we knew they were right."

Oak looked up. For a moment, that helpless expression of horror spread across his features again. "We didn't know it would happen so fast, though. We thought we would have plenty of time. We thought we would find a solution or stop in time . . . before the damage was too great. We were fools."

"It wasn't your fault," Priwinn insisted. "The dwarves made you confused. It's their magic. You succumbed to its temptation."

Oak looked as if he wanted to contradict Priwinn; then, he probably realized it was useless to argue with the prince about it. Silently shaking his head, he stared at the flames of the fire and left it at that.

An uncomfortable silence ensued, interrupted only by the crackling of the flames and sound of the wind as it rustled the foliage of the broken branches.

Eventually, Kim stood up and walked away from the others. He felt dejected and tired. Everything seemed so pointless. No matter what they did, no matter how much effort they expended, things always seemed worse—as if they were fighting on the side of their enemies.

Then again, maybe that wasn't right. Perhaps the real answer was that the enemies they sought didn't exist.

As Kim walked off, preoccupied with these thoughts, the ground beneath his feet grew marshy. Just in the nick of time, Kim realized that he was about to fall into a little lake. He stopped abruptly, looked at the water that shone like molten pitch in the moonlight, and encountered the reflection of his face.

At the very last moment, he recalled what Oak once had said about this lake. He immediately turned around to walk off, but he took only one step before an approaching figure emerged from the darkness ahead: Priwinn.

For a while, the two stood there silently. Kim simply didn't want to talk at the moment. Yet, he didn't want to be alone, either. He was overwhelmed by feelings of indecision and confusion. Those emotions were stronger than his horror over the tree's destruction.

Finally, the prince broke the oppressive silence. "Have you decided?" he asked.

Kim reluctantly turned around and looked at Priwinn in surprise. "Decided?"

"Yes," said Priwinn. "Which side you're on. Are you going to keep on watching our world die without doing anything?"

What is the prince trying to do? Kim thought. *Priwinn has to know the decision he's forcing me to make is so hard.*

"I . . . I can't," Kim whispered.

The prince's face darkened. His eyes flashed, and suddenly there was a steely edge to his voice that made Kim shiver. He hardly recognized his friend anymore. "Fine!" Priwinn said grimly. "Stay here then, or go back to Themistokles. Do whatever you want. I, at any rate, am going to take action, so this land isn't ruined for good."

"What are you going to do?" Kim asked softly, although he had a good idea what the answer would be.

"What we've already begun!" Priwinn answered passionately. "We're going to smash all these damned iron men to pieces—and everything else that comes from the dwarves."

"You can't win this war that way," Kim protested. "We don't know for sure that the dwarves are the ones ruining Magic Moon, Priwinn."

"Maybe you're right," the prince conceded. "I don't see any alternative, though. I listened to Themistokles and you. We went north, even though we knew full well that it would be useless. We've lost Rangarig. We barely missed being captured by the dwarves. What more do you want from me?"

"I don't know," Kim admitted in agony. "It's so . . . so terrible. Maybe the ones you're going to fight against are the inhabitants of this land—not just the dwarves."

"So, I'll have to defeat them, too," Priwinn said with determination. "I'm not alone, Kim. There are many who think the same way I do. And after what's happened here, more will join us." His voice took on an urgent tone. "If you were leading us, we would win—I'm sure of that."

"You're asking me to do the impossible," Kim cried in despair. "I can't take up the sword against Magic Moon itself!"

"If it has to happen . . ." Priwinn said urgently. "We're going to do what has to be done. We're going to destroy the iron men, and then we're going to take care of the dwarves."

"Even though you haven't proven their guilt?" Kim shuddered inside.

"Well, we have no other choice. Are we supposed to wait until this whole land is covered under a sheet of iron? Until every flower, every tree, every plant suffocates because there's no more air to breathe? Until every man and woman is forced to work in the dwarves' mines? Maybe the iron men and the dwarves aren't our real enemies, but they're the ones we can fight."

Kim didn't reply. He secretly understood Priwinn, but the logic of Priwinn's argument was flawed. Maybe he really would accomplish something by destroying every machine the dwarves made. And maybe, by driving away the dwarf folk, he might avert the catastrophes spreading across Magic Moon. *If that's victory,* Kim thought, *then the victory comes at too high a price.*

"Give me one more night," he whispered. "I'll tell you my answer early tomorrow morning."

Priwinn didn't merely seem disappointed; he looked at Kim with unconcealed anger. But he didn't say anything; instead, he stomped past Kim, clenching his fists, and stared into the lake. Suddenly, he gave a start, took another step forward, and bent over to look at his reflection.

"You'd better not do that," Kim said. "This lake is—"

"I know its secret," Priwinn rudely interrupted. "Probably better than you do. But look!"

Kim reluctantly looked down at the water, carefully avoiding his own reflection. Priwinn's face was reflected clearly on the still water; because the face wasn't his own, Kim saw it exactly as it looked in reality—narrow, with dark shadows of exhaustion and discouragement under the eyes, and very embittered. "Don't look," Kim implored once again.

Priwinn shook his head and held Kim when he tried to step away. "Look!" Priwinn said once again, pointing with his outstretched hand at his own image in the water. Then, he pulled his hand back, touched his cheeks with his fingertips, and gave a violent start as if he had received an electric shock.

"What's the matter?" Kim asked worriedly.

Instead of answering, Priwinn abruptly backed away from the shore of the enchanted lake, stopped, and raised both his hands to his cheeks. Curious, Kim stepped closer. When he looked at Priwinn by the pale light of the moon, he thought he saw a dark shadow on the prince's cheeks that hadn't been there before.

"Is that a beard?" Kim asked uncertainly.

Priwinn gasped. His eyes widened with horror. "I . . . I'm getting older," he whispered.

At first, Kim shrugged; after all, that happened to everyone. Then, he suddenly understood what Priwinn's words meant: "Your father . . ."

Priwinn's hands started to tremble. With unconcealed horror, he stared at Kim, felt his face once again with his fingertips, and held his hands up to his eyes as if he were expecting to see the wrinkled fingers of a very old man instead the hands of a boy. "I'm beginning to get older," he whispered again. "You know what that means!"

Kim nodded without saying anything.

Priwinn whispered, "My time as a prince is over, Kim. My father is dead."

They left Oak before the sun rose the next morning. Quite a few Tree People had joined them during the night, drawn by the light of the fire. They'd offered to take care of the children and bring them back to their parents—a suggestion that Kim and the other two travelers willingly accepted. Another surprise was in store for Kim when he opened his eyes: Stardust! Oak and his friends had taken care of the steed the whole time, and the magnificent animal seemed happy to see Kim again, just as Kim was delighted to see the steed. A horse also had been found for the Steppe rider, but there was no suitable mount for Gorg. When Oak, slightly embarrassed, had apologized for this, Gorg simply grinned and said he was faster than a horse, in any case.

After they lifted Chunklet and Sheera onto the horses' saddles, they bade farewell to everyone and rode off in a southeasterly direction. Priwinn barely had spoken a word since the previous evening, and Kim understood why all too well. He also accepted the fact that the only thing his friend wanted to do now was return to Caivallon as soon as possible. For that reason, he'd been surprised when Priwinn offered to accompany him part of the way. Caivallon and Gorywynn were in different directions. For Priwinn, it meant a detour of several days to ride with Kim until their paths absolutely had to part if Priwinn wanted to reach the Fortress of the Steppe.

Also, he never demanded to hear the decision that Kim had promised.

For days, they rode almost continuously toward the southeast. As before, Priwinn and Gorg avoided all settlements and sought out the most remote locations for their night quarters. They didn't talk with each other very much. Most of the time, Priwinn slumped in his saddle, barely moving, his eyes gazing into empty space. Several times, when Kim addressed the Steppe rider, Priwinn startled as if he'd been sleeping, regarding Kim with a confused expression. That required Kim to repeat his words. Kim tried to imagine what it must be like for Priwinn, but he couldn't do it. He'd never lost a close relative. It was one thing to talk about pain and to say he understood it . . . but during those days, as he rode next to Priwinn and looked at his rigid, expressionless face, Kim began to understand that this pain felt altogether different.

In the late afternoon of the third day, they crossed a series of hills. When they arrived at the top of the last hill, they saw that the flat land below extended in a broad plain. Priwinn halted his horse and looked toward the south with a puzzled frown. Kim, too, felt that something wasn't quite right. Unlike Priwinn, however, it took him a while to understand.

During their ride, they'd seen an arbitrary mix of meadows, forests, rocky terrain, streams, roads, small villages, and farms. Now, the landscape gradually turned into one geometric pattern. A dusty strip of road diagonally crossed the plain, like a grayish-brown line drawn with an enormous ruler. To the right and left of the road, the land was divided up in a checkerboard pattern of brown, black, and a huge variety of green tones—fields laid out in such rigid order that it almost hurt the eyes to look at them.

Priwinn didn't say a word, but his face looked grim. He released his horse's reins and pointed at a field right next to them. Well over half of it already was plowed. The earth had been sliced up in countless strips as wide as a handkerchief—in a pattern of perfectly straight, parallel lines. At the end of the last of these lines, there was a tiny, dull-gray object, pulled by a strange, metallic-colored . . . thing.

As they approached, slowly riding down the hillside, Kim saw that it was a farmer sitting on a plow and a horse. The farmer must have noticed them, too, because the plow team suddenly stopped moving. When the two travelers covered half the distance, the farmer climbed down and walked toward them. He wildly waved his arms. Only now did Kim realize that Priwinn hadn't ridden along the edge of the field or taken the narrow paths separating the rows; rather, he had led them directly across the freshly plowed furrows. They were still too far from the farmer to make out his words, but his furious signaling made it clear how angry he was.

"You there!" the man shouted, when he got closer. "Have you lost your minds? What do you think you're doing? Can't you do what everyone else—"

Suddenly, he stopped, lowered his arms, and looked at them with a gaping mouth and wide eyes. Kim wasn't quite sure what had provoked this frightened response in the farmer—the dull black armor that Priwinn now wore openly, or the sight of the giant, trotting several paces behind their horses. From far away, Gorg might have looked like a third, slightly oversized rider.

They reined in their horses when they got within a few feet of the farmer. The man continued to stare at the giant and didn't take any more notice of Kim or the prince. "Oh!" he eventually whispered. "You are . . ."

"What?" Gorg asked, squinting one eye and looking ready to pounce.

"Rather l-large," the farmer stuttered. He gulped a few times and tried to smile, failing miserably. His fear was unmistakable.

"Not in my opinion," Gorg retorted. "On the contrary, you are rather small."

Kim felt sorry for the man. Gorg was known for his practical jokes, but he wouldn't hurt a fly. Still, it was clear that the farmer was practically out of his mind with fear.

"You don't need to be afraid," Kim said to calm him down, while giving Gorg a pointed look. "We just happened to come by. We're sorry we rode through your field—aren't we, Priwinn?"

The Steppe rider ignored these words, instead turning around in his saddle and pointing at the farmer's vehicle. "I've never seen anything like that," he said to the man. "Will you show it to me?"

The farmer hesitated for a very brief moment. His gaze wandered over Priwinn's pitch-black armor, lingering on the sword at his side; then, he nodded in agreement and took the lead. Priwinn and Kim climbed out of their saddles and followed him. Kim was quite surprised when they got closer. The plow itself was normal, though very large and with unusually wide plowshares. In the end, though, it was just a plow. The only strange thing was the horse to which it was spanned.

It wasn't like any horse Kim had seen before; it resembled a horse in the same way that an iron colossus resembled a man. It had approximately the same shape as a horse, but it was too big and too massive—with too many overly sharp edges. There was a glowing green eye in the form of a narrow slit across the upper half of its metal-colored face.

"An iron horse!" Gorg exclaimed. The giant's hands tightened around an uprooted tree that he'd been carrying over his shoulder like a cudgel.

Kim shot an alarmed look at Gorg.

"Yes, my lord," the farmer said, ill at ease. Nevertheless, an unmistakable undertone of pride came into his voice when he continued: "It's impressive, isn't it?"

"Impressive?" Gorg made a face and the farmer turned pale.

Kim hastily stepped between them. "Where does it come from?" he asked the farmer.

The answer was just as he expected: "The dwarves. I got it a few weeks ago—together with the new plow. And now look how much soil I've turned already." Proudly, he gestured over the huge field extending before them. "All by myself. It normally takes me three months to do this much."

"Without any help?" Priwinn asked skeptically.

The farmer nodded proudly. He was gaining more confidence. "I had three farmhands until last winter," he replied. "Often, all three of us had to tighten our belts so we would feel full. Those days are over. I was able to let the farmhands go, and I'm still going to harvest more than in the last five years combined."

"Oh," said Gorg, "and what about your farmhands? How do they make a living now?"

The farmer looked at him, taken aback.

Kim walked a few steps behind the huge plow and studied the furrow.

This farm appeared exactly as Brobing's field did. The furrow was too deep. The huge plowshares hadn't turned over only the topsoil, but also the clay beneath. For one or two years, this field might produce twice as much as normal, and then it would be dead. The sight filled Kim with such rage that he considered becoming a rebel himself, just to destroy the plow.

"Do you have more of such . . . things on your farm?" Priwinn asked slyly and politely.

The farmer nodded proudly. "Two iron men," he said. Suddenly, he visibly started and looked first at Priwinn and next at Kim. "Please pardon me for being so inattentive," he said. "You must have come from far away—you must be hungry and exhausted. If a simple farmhouse is not too shabby for you, come with me and spend the night at our house."

Kim was surprised when his friend agreed to this proposal with a nod of his head. Up until now, they had been anxious to avoid such contact.

Priwinn unexpectedly said, "Thanks. We'd like to. My companions and I have come a long way, indeed, and we have at least an equally long road ahead of us."

Kim gave Priwinn an inquisitive look, but the King of the Steppe studiously ignored it and went back to his horse.

Gorg stood still for a moment longer, looking at the plow and the iron with an ominous expression. Eventually, however, he turned around and followed the farmer.

"Why did you accept his invitation?" Kim asked in a whisper after he'd climbed up on Stardust's back. "Up until now, we've made big detours around all villages."

Priwinn nodded grimly. "That was a mistake, maybe," he said. "If you don't talk to anyone, you don't find out anything." Frowning, he continued with a lower voice, speaking more to himself than to Kim. "An iron horse. That's new. I wonder what they'll think of next."

They followed the farmer across fields so uniformly laid out that they looked dead—even though quite a few of them were ready for harvest. The farm buildings gave the same impression as the farmer's fields. It was a small homestead with an impressive appearance: The courtyard of firmly compacted dirt had been swept so clean that a person could have eaten off it, and the two buildings arranged at right angles to each other were so freshly whitewashed that they glowed in the last light of the sun. Everything was well ordered and clean, like an oversized toy farmhouse instead of one that real people lived in.

Priwinn clearly took all this in just as carefully as Kim, and the expression on his face turned grim. Abruptly, he swung down out of the saddle and looked for somewhere to tie his horse's reins. Kim followed his lead. The farmer didn't fail to notice this. He quickly shook his head and clicked his tongue. Immediately, a giant, angular figure with a shining green eye walked out of the barn door.

Priwinn froze and Gorg winced. To Kim's astonishment, both remained motionless as the iron man took the reins—first, from Priwinn's horse; then, from Stardust—and led the animals into the barn with an even, stomping gait. At the last instant, Kim awoke from his trance, ran after Stardust, and plucked Chunklet from his mane. The little animal acquiesced without protest, making no sound when Kim put the creature on his shoulders and went back to the others. Fleetingly, it occurred to him that Chunklet had fallen silent during the past two days—compared to his previously normal, annoying talkativeness.

In the meantime, Sheera, too, had made himself comfortable on the giant's shoulders. However, he jumped down when Gorg bent far forward to enter the farmhouse. Purring, the cat rubbed up against the giant's legs before disappearing into the house. Barely a second later, he came dashing back out. Furious barking sounded from inside the house, and a large, shaggy dog tore after the cat, chasing him across the courtyard.

The farmer turned around in mid-stride and was about to call back the dog, but Gorg shook his head, which he then banged against the low ceiling of the entry hall, making the whole house creak. "Let him go," he said. "Sheera is more than able to take care of himself."

Kim walked through the small entry hall into the main room, followed by the farmer, Priwinn, and—with some difficulty—the stooping giant. As it turned out, their host had understated the bounty of his hospitality. Once his wife got over her initial fright at Gorg's appearance, she turned out to be very friendly, serving them a meal that satisfied even the giant's hunger. At least, Gorg was polite enough to say it did, after he demolished five loaves of bread, a cask of wine, and a whole wheel of cheese.

Chunklet was the only one who grumbled about the portions being too small—after he'd wolfed down the contents of Kim's plate for the third time without giving Kim a chance to taste even one of the delicious-smelling dishes. Laughing, the farmwife gave Kim a fourth helping. She was foolish enough to joke that Chunklet was welcome to retire to the house's pantry and eat there until he was full. Chunklet murmured his acceptance of this offer and vanished into the kitchen's adjoining pantry. Kim rightly suspected that the farmwife would regret her generosity the next morning.

Well, he thought, *we'll reimburse these good people for their hospitality.*

After they finished eating, the farmer pulled out a pouch of tobacco, stuffed his pipe, and then offered the pouch to his guests. Kim and the Steppe rider declined with thanks, but Gorg took a big snuff and handed back a completely empty pouch to the astonished farmer. Then, he sneezed, rattling the glassware on the table. He smiled apologetically and left the room with the remark that he wanted to stretch his legs a little. The farmer seemed very relieved to hear that, but Kim caught the meaningful look that Priwinn and the giant exchanged before Gorg—after banging his head against the door lintel again—slipped out of the house.

Kim sensed that something was going on between those two. In the past day, Priwinn had spoken with Gorg just as infrequently as he'd spoken with Kim. But the two friends didn't depend on words to make arrangements each other. *No,* Kim thought, *something is going on here. The two are keeping something secret from me.* He decided to broach that subject with the Steppe rider as soon as they were alone.

"That iron horse," Priwinn began, "is really amazing. I didn't even know there was such a thing."

"I didn't, either—until recently," replied the farmer, smiling as he took a puff on his pipe. "I bet you'll see them everywhere before long."

"Yes," Priwinn murmured. "I think so, too."

Obviously, the farmer understood these words differently than they were meant, because he blew a little cloud of blue smoke in the air and continued, sounding quite pleased with himself: "They're much stronger than real horses. They don't need to eat, don't need to sleep, and are never sick or skittish."

"And also," Kim suddenly heard himself bitterly saying to his own surprise, "they'll never fetch help if you're lying injured somewhere. They won't stop if you fall out of the saddle . . . or are defending yourself from a wolf or a bear."

For a moment, the farmer looked confused; then, he smiled as if Kim had said something very stupid. "Of course not," he said calmly. "I've seen your horse. It's a truly magnificent animal. The most beautiful one I've ever seen."

"That's right," Kim replied. "Stardust is my friend."

"I have a horse like that, too," the farmer said, still smiling in that strangely tolerant manner. "Oh, it's not quite as a beautiful as your Stardust and not nearly as well bred. We had a foal, too, until a few weeks ago."

"You did?"

The farmer nodded sadly. "It was stolen," he said. "One morning, I went into the barn and his stall was empty." He sighed, sadly shook his head, and then smiled again. "I still have the other one, though. I've had it for a long time and enjoy taking it out for a ride. I can do that more often now, because I have the iron horse. Before, my horse had to pull the plow or the heavy wagon—although he would much rather have run around in the pasture or galloped across the fields."

Kim looked at the farmer and, all at once, he felt a little naïve. Maybe he was, too. Maybe they both were. Possibly, they both were telling the truth; and possibly, they both were wrong to a certain extent.

For just a brief instant, Kim thought he knew the answer to all his questions and the way to avert the terrible danger to Magic Moon. Before he could grasp hold of the thought and put it into words, though, Priwinn said sharply, "And your farmhands are now free, too, aren't they? Free to do and not to do whatever they want. Free to starve, to sleep under the open skies in winter, and to—"

"You're wrong," the farmer interrupted. He still smiled, but his voice had an edge to it that made Kim look up in alarm.

"I saw to it that they found work and a place to live in the city," the man explained. "They're better off than in past years. Believe me, Prince Priwinn, they could have found better work a long time ago—work where they wouldn't have to starve and freeze every winter. They stayed with me out of loyalty, not out of desperation."

Priwinn looked at the farmer with a mixture of surprise and distrust. "Prince Priwinn?" he repeated warily. "How—"

"Let me save you the trouble," the farmer interrupted, taking his pipe out of his mouth. "I know who you are." He stared at the Steppe rider in silence, and then he pointed at Priwinn's metal garb with the chewed end of his pipe. "And I also know why you're wearing this armor."

"And you invited us into your house, anyway?" Kim asked in surprise.

"Why not?" the farmer countered. He kept his gaze leveled at Priwinn for a moment, and then he turned around to Kim. "I don't know who you are, son, but I do know who this young hothead is."

Priwinn winced at these words but didn't say anything. Kim felt that the farmer's words were not meant the way they sounded.

"I know that you're not a bad person, Prince Priwinn," the farmer continued, addressing the Steppe rider once again. "You're impetuous, but impetuosity is the prerogative of youth. At the same time, you're not unjust or cruel. I know I have nothing to fear from you."

Priwinn clenched his fist on the table so tightly that Kim could hear his knuckles cracking. The look he gave the farmer was as cold as ice. "Maybe you're wrong, farmer," he said.

The farmer shook his head, smiling. "Absolutely not. Maybe you're the one who's got it wrong, Prince Priwinn. I've heard about you and what you've been doing. Believe me, it's wrong. You're not helping anyone by marching through the land with your friends and destroying the iron men. Senseless destruction never does any good."

"We destroy only what's destroying Magic Moon," Priwinn replied.

The farmer was about to answer, but at that very moment, the faint cry of a child came through the door, and his wife quickly stood up and left the room.

The guests looked in that direction. "You have a child?" Priwinn asked.

The smile in the farmer's eyes vanished. He nodded very sadly. "A son," he replied. "He was born last winter and is the last one we still have."

Kim looked at him searchingly.

After a long, gloomy silence, the man continued: "We used to have two other children—a twelve-year-old son and an eleven-year-old daughter. Both disappeared last spring."

"And you've never heard from them again?" An expression briefly passed over Priwinn's face, one that almost horrified Kim. What he saw in his companion's expression wasn't sympathy or even pity but a look of satisfaction—as if Priwinn had heard exactly what he wanted to hear.

Kim no longer had the will to look the farmer in the eyes.

For a while, they sat together in uncomfortable silence. Then, they heard the house door bang open, followed by the clattering sound of heavy paws approaching the room. All eyes curiously turned toward the door, and Kim wasn't the only one surprised to see the dog that had chased Sheera out of the house now walking in alongside the cat.

The two animals looked very bedraggled, but they no longer gave the impression of being enemies. *Maybe they never were,* Kim thought.

As if the two animals' return was the signal he'd been waiting for, Chunklet sauntered out of the kitchen, jumped up on the table, and checked out the plates, sniffing for leftover food. He cleaned up what he found in no time. Then, he jumped back on Kim's shoulder, curled up into a fluffy feather ball—and burped so loudly that the farmer's pipe almost fell out of his mouth.

"That was good," Chunklet said appreciatively. "Please compliment your wife for the outstanding pantry, my good man."

"I'll do that," the farmer replied. "I'm glad it tasted good to you. You can eat as much as you like."

"I'll do that," Chunklet replied, burping again so loudly that Kim's ears rang. "As soon as there's something else to eat in there."

The farmer, who naturally had no idea that Chunklet wouldn't exaggerate on this subject, laughed heartily. "That's a funny fellow you have there," he said, addressing Kim. "Where did you get him?"

Kim was about to answer, but at that moment, the front door slammed closed, and the giant's heavy steps shook the house. A moment later, Gorg entered the room, bent over deeply.

Crying out, the farmer jumped up so abruptly that his chair tipped over. The pipe fell out of the corner of his mouth and clattered on the floor. Kim and Priwinn also sprang up from their chairs.

The head and shoulders of the iron horse were hanging over Gorg's left shoulder! With a single step, the giant crossed the room and threw the severed horse head onto the table.

The piece of furniture broke into pieces under the weight, and the farmer jumped back a step, gasping. His eyes almost popped out of their sockets as he stared at the smashed horse head.

Kim's gaze, too, moved from the horse head to the giant's face and back again. He was speechless.

He'd never seen Gorg so filled with hate. Never before had he seen such an expression—a wild, almost bestial flickering in his eyes, which made the giant terrifying. Gorg's hands were bleeding. His body was covered in sweat and trembled; his breathing was heavy and irregular.

"What . . . what have you done?" the farmer gasped. He stared at the giant, his eyes wide open; his face turned pale when he saw the hate in the giant's face. Then, the farmer retreated until his back bumped against the wall; he whispered once again, "What have you done?" He whirled around, let out a croaking, half-suppressed cry, and rushed toward the window.

Gorg grabbed the farmer, angrily jerked him back, and flung him at the wall so hard that he fell.

"If you're planning to call those two iron helpers, don't bother," he hissed furiously. "What's left of them is on the floor of your barn."

Priwinn gave the giant a surprised look. Now, Kim had no doubt that those two had been planning something exactly like this, but the seething hate in Gorg's eyes confused even Priwinn.

Probably drawn by the noise, the farmer's wife appeared in the doorway. She was carrying a small child in her arms; when she caught sight of her husband on the floor, she gave a little cry and ran over to him. Only when she bent down to help him up did she see the smashed table and what lay on top of it.

She froze. Kim saw the color drain from her face; all of a sudden, her hands began to shake so violently that Kim was afraid she would drop the child. But when he walked over to help her, she drew back in terror, quickly righted herself, and took a few steps to get out of his range.

"Wh-why have you done this?" she stammered. "We . . . we didn't do anything to hurt you. Why have you done this to us?"

"Don't worry," Priwinn said. He glanced at the giant's face and visibly pulled himself together. "We're not going to hurt you in any way."

Neither the farmer nor his wife seemed to hear his words. While the husband sat there, rigid and unmoving, staring vacantly at the crushed horse head, his wife began to tremble more intensely. Tears streamed down her face. When Kim tried to approach her, though, she cringed again and protectively clutched the baby to her breast. The child started to cry, and the woman's left hand caressed his face in a soothing motion.

With great effort, the farmer stood up. "This is the end," he said in a hushed voice. As he spoke, his lips barely moved and his gaze was fixed on the severed neck of the horse. On his face was an expression of such deep horror that Kim shuddered. "You . . . you've taken away everything from me," he murmured. "You've destroyed everything. Now, they're going to take my farmhouse and the land—everything. I'll have to work in the pits until I die."

"Don't worry," Priwinn said with a hard edge to his voice. "I'll reimburse you for the loss."

Neither the farmer nor his wife heard Priwinn's words.

"You've destroyed everything," the farmer moaned again. "We . . . we were friendly to you. We didn't do anything to hurt you. We . . . we wanted only to—"

"You'll understand later," Priwinn interrupted. "We had to do it, and we're going to keep on doing it. Everywhere. Until this curse ends!"

Kim felt a deep, painful emptiness. The crushed horse's head was just a piece of metal, but the sight of it horrified him as much as if it had been a real animal.

"They're going to take everything from me," the farmer whispered again.

"Nonsense," Priwinn replied. "How much did you have to pay for this horse and the two iron men?"

For the first time, the farmer pulled his eyes away from the table and looked at Priwinn again. His whole body began to tremble. "You don't understand," he murmured. "It's not the money. It's—"

"How much?" Priwinn almost screamed at him. "Tell me!"

With a trembling voice, the farmer said an amount and Priwinn reached in his satchel, counted out a handful of gold coins, and threw them at the farmer. "Here!" he said contemptuously. "That's more than enough to pay your debts!"

"It's . . . it's not the money!" the farmer moaned. "The dwarves, they . . . they severely punish people if their iron men are destroyed. They're going to send me to the pits! And they're going to take the farm from my wife and drive her away. Now . . . now, we've lost everything: first, the children and now, the farm, too!"

Priwinn looked at the farmer, stunned and dismayed. What he'd just heard was news to him, but he recovered quickly.

"Come with us," he said. "If you're afraid of the dwarves, then come with us to Caivallon. You'll be safe there. This nightmare will soon be over, and then you can go back to your farm. I'm going to liberate Magic Moon from these creatures!"

Again, it seemed as if the farmer didn't understand him. His gaze was directed at Priwinn's face, but he wasn't focused.

"We just wanted a little . . . a little prosperity, so we wouldn't have to go hungry or freeze, and so we would have fewer worries and enough for our children to eat. That's not too much to ask."

As suddenly as it had appeared, the anger vanished from Priwinn's face. He went to the farmer and put his hand on the man's shoulder. "I know," he said in a calm, almost gentle voice. He smiled encouragingly, bent over, and picked up the coins that he'd thrown at the farmer. "Take this," he said. "Take this gold and leave. It's enough to start anew somewhere else. Believe me, I know you had good intentions."

The farmer stared at the gold coins glittering in Priwinn's outstretched hand. He made a movement as if to reach for them, but he didn't complete the gesture. "What we wanted—was that too much to ask?" he asked.

"No," Priwinn replied sadly, "but the price is too high."

Kim couldn't continue listening. He felt like someone in the audience of a play in which all the actors kept saying the wrong lines, no matter how hard they tried. He abruptly turned around and rushed out of the room.

The sun had set while they'd been enjoying the farmer's hospitality; it was now dusk. With a soft cry, Chunklet hopped off Kim's shoulder and scuttled around the corner of the house, probably to assume his nocturnal form in peace. With sadness, Kim watched the little creature until it disappeared from view. Suddenly, this whole world reminded him of Chunklet. It seemed as if Magic Moon underwent a metamorphosis at sunset, changing from something indescribably beautiful and magical into something equally ugly and disgusting. Except now, the daytime might never return.

A considerable period of time went by while Kim stood there, lost in thought. When he heard footsteps, without looking, he knew it was Priwinn.

The Steppe rider walked up next to him, tried to catch his eye, and finally shrugged when he didn't succeed.

"I think he's calmed down again," Priwinn said.

Now, Kim faced him. "Why did he do that?" Kim said softly.

"Gorg?" Once again, Priwinn shrugged. "If he hadn't done it, then I would have," he said with a hard edge to his voice. "They have to be destroyed. There's no alternative."

Kim shuddered. *First Kelhim,* he thought, *then Rangarig, the ice giants, and finally, Gorg . . . Do only anger and malice remain when the magic is extinguished? And what is going on with Priwinn?* He took a long, careful look at Priwinn's no longer youthful face. *Is it possible that Priwinn has changed, too?*

For a moment, Kim thought he saw a hard, bitter expression on Priwinn's face. Priwinn was still the same person he knew, but even so . . . Once again, Kim was forcibly reminded of the words that Brobing had said so long ago: *"It's as if we were losing something, and we don't even know what."* That was it, exactly. Maybe what the prince had lost irretrievably was the secret of youth.

"You still owe me an answer," Priwinn suddenly said.

Kim looked at him, annoyed.

The Steppe rider gestured that he would explain: "Our ways are going to part, Kim," he continued. "Early tomorrow morning, at the latest. Before then, I need to know if you're on our side."

"This is absurd," Kim said tiredly. "If I don't decide in favor of your fight, Priwinn, we'll still be friends. I'm not on the other side, because I—"

Priwinn cut him off. "Are you going to join us?" There was such coldness in his voice that Kim didn't answer at all; he just stared at his friend, speechless.

Finally, he said in a quiet voice, "No."

Priwinn nodded, as if he'd expected that answer. "And what are you planning to do?"

"I don't know," Kim admitted. "I'm going to return to Gorywynn and talk with Themistokles."

Priwinn laughed bitterly. "You two are a perfect match," he said. "An old wizard who has forgotten everything and a young hero who has forgotten how to fight."

Kim said nothing. The words stung, and he sensed that Priwinn had wanted to hurt him. Kim also understood why things were this way, though—and he didn't hold it against the prince. Priwinn had lost his father, and he was watching his world fall apart, piece by piece, helpless to stop it.

If only to change the subject, he asked, "Are you going to take the farmer with you?"

"I think so," Priwinn replied. "The man hasn't made up his mind yet; but if he's telling the truth about the dwarves, then he can't stay here. He'll be safe in Caivallon. And later, when everything's over, he'll come back and work his farm again."

The last sentence, at least, didn't sound very confident. Kim wasn't certain there would be anything left for the farmer to return to.

XVIII

Before sunrise the next day, Chunklet and Kim said goodbye to the others and set out for Gorywynn on Stardust's back. Their parting was very cold, and Kim was glad when he finally steered the horse south, away from the farm. The farm family, who had spent the entire night packing their belongings and loading them onto a wooden cart, averted their eyes from him, making him feel as if he alone were responsible for their misfortune. Gorg said nothing, and Priwinn merely wished Kim good luck, suggesting that Gorg escort him part of the way, for safety's sake. The giant had stood quite close to them and must have heard what was said; however, he didn't react. Kim was relieved.

He had begun to fear Gorg. Just as Kelhim had changed from a friendly, magical animal into a dangerous beast, and Rangarig had transformed from a good-natured dragon into a deadly threat—something was happening to the giant. It had started the moment they reached the Castle at the End of the World and realized that the ice giants no longer existed. *Maybe this is Gorg's way of dying,* Kim thought, *and maybe the next time we see each other, Gorg won't be a warm-hearted giant but a creature just as cunning and dangerous as Kelhim.*

Kim followed Priwinn's advice and rode directly south. It was noon before he finally encountered a road. As Priwinn had instructed, he turned right. He rode for another hour before he took a rest break.

The farmers couldn't give him any provisions because Chunklet had devoured everything they'd had. However, Kim found enough fruit and berries to satisfy his hunger. Chunklet, for his part, disappeared into the forest for a while; when he came back, he burped so loudly and offensively that Kim didn't have to ask if he'd found something to eat.

After they traveled for another hour, Kim spotted a cloud of dust on the horizon. It quickly grew and turned into a group of at least twenty or thirty armed horsemen, galloping toward them at a fast pace. The sight of them made Kim uneasy, but it was too late to turn around and hope the riders hadn't seen him. Besides, he really hadn't a thing to fear. So, he reined in Stardust and waited until the riders reached him.

The group was larger than he'd originally thought—more than forty men, all armed to the teeth. There were some knights among them, sitting on armored horses. The man in the lead wore shiny, sharp-edged, silver armor, which covered everything except his face. It gave him an almost eerie resemblance to an iron man.

"Who are you?" he asked Kim in an unfriendly manner, after pressing his horse right up next to Stardust.

Kim's stallion nervously danced in place, on the verge of bolting. Kim had to use all his strength to keep the steed under control.

Kim gave his name, but there was no spark of recognition in the armored man's face. Kim was almost happy about that. He wasn't sure whether he was welcome in this land anymore.

"What are you doing here all alone?" the knight asked.

"I'm on my way to Gorywynn," Kim answered truthfully.

"For what purpose?"

"I'm looking for someone."

"All alone?" the man persisted skeptically. When Kim didn't make any reply, he continued: "A boy your age shouldn't be riding alone, especially not on such a long journey. If you're looking for someone, though, we're after the same thing. Maybe you can help us."

Kim cocked his head inquiringly, and the knight studied him with a thoughtful, suspicious look before he continued.

"We're looking for the rebels who are attacking farmers and destroying iron men. Did you happen to see them?"

"Rebels?" Kim was a little surprised at how skillfully he put a surprised tone in his voice. He shook his head.

"The word is they've been seen in the vicinity," the knight said. "The giant, Gorg; Priwinn, the son of the King of the Steppe; and a boy your age, who supposedly has a horribly ugly animal with him." The suspicion in his voice grew sharper, and Kim didn't fail to notice the man's right hand drifting downward, as if by chance, until it was on his belt, just a finger's breadth away from the hilt of his powerful sword.

"What are you hiding there under your shirt?"

Sending a silent prayer of thanks to heaven that it was bright daylight, Kim unbuttoned his shirt and pulled out Chunklet with his left hand. The werecreature, who had fallen asleep, woke up with an uneasy growl and softly expressed his displeasure.

The knight's eyes widened in astonishment. "What's that?" he asked, confounded.

Kim shrugged. "I have no idea," he said. "I found it here in the vicinity a few days ago. I think it's as dumb as can be, but it's very friendly—and very pretty, isn't it?"

"Yes, very," the knight said hesitantly. He looked Chunklet over for a long time; shaking his head, he said, "You do fit the description of the boy, but they told me the sight of his companion is enough to turn one's stomach. No, you're not him."

Kim had to exercise self-control to avoid letting out a sigh of relief.

Quickly stuffing the red-orange featherball back under his shirt, he made Stardust back up a couple of paces and prepared to ride on. At that point, when Stardust whinnied and tried to bolt, Kim discovered what was making the magnificent animal so panicked: The knight wasn't sitting on a horse. It did resemble a warhorse in the same way that the farmer's mechanical plow horse looked like a plow horse, but what Kim initially had taken for rough, steel-plate armor was, in fact, the creature's skin. The knight was sitting on an iron horse.

"What's the matter with you, boy?" the man said when he noticed Kim's dumbfounded expression. "You can go."

"Your . . . your animal," Kim stammered, no longer needing to feign astonishment.

"What about it?" the knight asked crossly. "Leave. We're in a hurry." He was about to ride on, but Kim held him back.

"One more question, sir."

The knight turned around in his saddle with obvious impatience. "What?"

"Those rebels you were talking about," Kim said. "Are they dangerous? I mean, should I be afraid of them?"

"It's always best to be wary of strangers. Make a note of that for the future," the knight said bluntly.

"What will you do with them if you catch them?" Kim persisted.

The knight's armor clanked as he shrugged his shoulders. "I don't believe that's any of your business, boy," he said. "We'll bring them to justice, though. And I can tell you one thing: I don't think they'll ever work off the damages in the mines. Their lives won't be long enough." He laughed before abruptly turning serious again. "You're awfully curious, boy!"

Once again, the silver knight intently examined him—and in a very unpleasant manner. Then, he had enough of it. Pulling hard on the reins, he made his iron horse take a sideways step. He was about to leave when commotion erupted among his companions.

Only now did Kim see that there were a number of other angular figures moving in among the three or four dozen mounted men. Amid all that armor and all those weapons and shields, the iron men hadn't caught his attention—but he'd caught theirs.

With a pounding heart, Kim watched one of the iron men walk up to the knight and lift his agile right hand. The knight leaned forward in the saddle, conferring with the iron figure. Though Kim never had heard any of the iron men talk—and he was certain that they were unable to do so—suddenly, he had an unpleasant feeling that the two were communicating.

"I've held you up for long enough, sir," he said hastily. "I have to be on my way." Kim turned Stardust all the way around and slapped the reins, but the silver knight quickly raised his hand and signaled a command. One of the other riders blocked Kim's way. At almost the same time, a second armored figure pushed in behind Stardust, preventing the stallion from moving either forward or backward.

"Just a moment," ordered the man in the silver armor.

His eyes passed over the iron man's expressionless metal face, and a very confused expression spread over his own features. Then, he turned around in the saddle to face Kim, looking him over once more from head to toe. "You never did tell me where you're from," he said, "or who you're looking for in Gorywynn."

"Why . . . why do you want to know that, sir?" Kim asked hesitantly.

"Answer the questions," the man commanded. His hand again moved toward the hilt of his sword.

Maneuvering as well as he could in the tight space, Kim turned Stardust around and rode the short distance back to the knight. His hand casually drifted down onto the saddle and moved toward the hilt of the dwarven dagger, which he'd hidden in the saddle bag. "I'm on my way to an old friend of my parents, who lives in Gorywynn," he claimed, while simultaneously guiding Stardust even closer to the iron horse. The stallion very reluctantly obeyed him. The fear Stardust had of his iron brother was unmistakable.

"What's the name of this friend?" the knight asked.

"Themistokles," Kim replied, smiling. Then, he quickly—but not too hastily—pulled the dwarven dagger from the saddle bag, bent forward, and plunged the sword into the iron horse's neck, all the way to the hilt. The iron horse collapsed as if hit by lightning, pinning down not only its rider, but also the iron man standing next to him. Two or three armed men cried out in surprise, and one rider tried to grab Kim from behind and pull him out of the saddle.

As quick as a flash, Kim leaned forward over Stardust's neck and swung the dagger around in a half circle, causing his assailant to jump back in terror. Then, he pulled on Stardust's reins as hard as he could.

The stallion reared up on his hind legs with a startled whinny. Kim clung to the saddle and Stardust's mane with all his strength, somehow managing to avoid being thrown off. He forced Stardust around so that his whirling hooves drove back another rider blocking the way behind Kim.

For a very brief moment, pandemonium reigned among the armed men. Everyone yelled and gesticulated; some horses panicked and tried to bolt. Three or four men attempted to charge Kim, but their fellow soldiers and the horses milling about obstructed them so much that they hardly could move.

Kim took advantage of the opportunity. Stardust's hooves had barely touched the ground when Kim gave the horse a powerful kick in his flanks. The faithful steed leaped forward, bringing Kim out of the riders' immediate reach. Amid sounds of splitting wood, Stardust crashed through the dry underbrush that bordered the road. Kim saw thorny branches tear his horse's coat, leaving bloody scratches on it, but Stardust didn't whinny in pain; instead, almost of his own volition, the horse took off in powerful strides, galloping at a right angle toward the road. Kim leaned far forward over the horse's neck, clinging to the animal's mane with both hands to keep from being knocked out of the saddle by the whipping branches that the horse raced through. At the same time, he turned his head and looked back at the road.

The knight in the silver armor still was trying to get out from under his collapsed iron horse, but six or seven of his companions had recovered from their surprise and set out in pursuit. Their horses might not have been as fast as Stardust, but they weren't much slower, either. Unlike Kim, these men mercilessly drove their animals forward.

Kim ducked low when a spear flew in his direction. It missed.

Evidently, it was all the same to his pursuers whether they brought him back unharmed, wounded, or dead.

Moving at a steady gallop, Stardust charged up one side of a hill and back down the other, jumped a narrow creek, and doubled back toward the right in order to get to a broad, flat, grassy plain. When they reached the open grass, Kim thought there was a chance of escape. Stardust was a magnificent animal that could leave any other horse behind—if only he had the chance to use his superior strength.

However, a quick glance over his shoulder showed Kim that his lead was dwindling. Two of his pursuers had separated from the rest and were coming steadily closer. One of the two raced along, deeply bent over his horse's neck. The other sat up straight in his saddle, twirling a net with little balls of wood fastened to its end. Kim still was trying to figure out the purpose of this odd contraption when the man let it go, and the net turned into a whirring shadow that shot toward him with breathtaking speed.

In a desperate move, Kim yanked his steed to the left. The net missed him by a hair and landed in the grass, but the sudden jerk was too much for Stardust. He lost his rhythm, stumbled, and caught himself at the last minute. He continued running, noticeably limping. The distance between Kim and his pursuers rapidly dwindled.

Kim might have gotten away if the ground in front of the steed hadn't opened up at that very moment, spewing out a half-dozen small figures wrapped in ragged black capes. Stardust jerked back with a frightened whinny, rearing up on his hind legs. Kim catapulted out of the saddle in a high arc. He somersaulted two or three times in the air before slamming into the base of a tree. He lay there, half-stunned.

His two mounted pursuers raced past him, carried forward by their own momentum. Kim tried to get up again, but he lacked the strength. He fell a second time, rolled heavily onto his side, and felt his consciousness begin to fade.

As if through a gray fog, he saw the little figures dance toward him—flat, black, faceless ghosts in black capes, reaching for him with spindly, dirty fingers. Then, one of the figures came up to him. The black face beneath the hood morphed into a narrow visage that reminded Kim of a bird of prey; Kim saw glittering eyes as hard as stone.

"I promised you we would see each other again, dimwit," Jarrn said.

That was the last thing Kim heard for a long, long time.

XIX

The fall must have been harder than Kim thought, because he barely could recall what happened afterward. Very vaguely—he wasn't even sure whether it was a real memory or just disturbing images that plagued him—he thought he remembered Jarrn and the silver knight arguing about his fate. If this argument really did take place, then the dwarf clearly had won it. In the endless hours—or perhaps days—that followed, the few times that Kim woke up in a fever, the world consisted of nothing but dark tunnels; endless caves; and the hard, metallic grip of the iron man that carried Kim in his arms. On a number of occasions he was awakened as the dwarves virtually force-fed him a little food. But before long, Kim woke on his own; when he did, he sensed that he was exceedingly far from the clearing.

His surroundings were a surprise. Kim knew he was in the dwarves' power, so he assumed that he'd ended up in a dark cave dungeon. However, he was lying on a wide, soft bed in a room with completely normal furniture.

Normal, that is, except that all the furniture—aside from the bed—was too small. Moreover, while the room had a door, it didn't have any windows. Light came from a torch in a skillfully forged fixture next to the door. It had burned almost to its end, and the wall above it had blackened with soot.

Kim cautiously sat up on his bed, lifting his hand to touch his head. He felt a taut, freshly applied bandage and became aware of mild pain. He hastily withdrew his fingers.

Carefully swinging his legs over the side of the bed, he sat up, looked around, and winced. As faint as it was, the flickering torchlight hurt his eyes. When he moved too quickly, his head started to pound in pain, as if a tiny dwarf were sitting inside his skull, enthusiastically beating on a kettle drum.

Kim wondered where he was. As the same time, he couldn't get rid of the feeling that he knew this place. It was . . . *No.*

He didn't know it for a fact, yet something told him with unshakable certainty that this wasn't the dwarf cave complex in the eastern mountains; rather, it was a place he'd been before.

This thought led to another one, which—in Kim's opinion—was more important: *How am I ever going to get out of here?*

Determined, he stood up, swayed for a moment, groaned as the dull thundering between his temples returned with a vengeance, and waited until the violent dizziness subsided. Then, he went to the door, stretched his hand out to the heavy forged metal handle, and shook it.

"You can pull on it until you're blue in the face," said a cranky voice behind him. "The bolt is made of dwarves' steel. Nothing can break it."

Kim turned around in surprise to see a small, ugly, prickly ball creep out from under the bed and stare at him with bulging, gooey eyes.

"I was starting to think you were never going to wake up," Chunklet complained.

Kim felt profound relief at the sight of his little companion. "Where did we end up, actually?" he asked.

Chunklet scuttled the rest of the way out from under the bed and jumped up onto the table, which wasn't much higher than Kim's knees. "With really nice people," Chunklet replied sarcastically.

"What?" Kim said, confused.

Chunklet nodded so vigorously that his spines moved like a sea urchin's in a stormy ocean. "Believe me," he said. "They're so hospitable that they don't want us to leave ever again."

Kim frowned but decided not to comment on that. He looked around the little chamber again, this time paying closer attention. "I know this place," he murmured. "This isn't a dwarf cave."

"No one said it was, did they?" Chunklet snapped. "Don't worry: There are plenty of dwarves here—a few more than you might like."

Kim went back to the bed and sat down. Inside his head, thoughts whirled about in wild confusion. Not for the first time, he felt that the answer to all his questions was very close—almost within his grasp. Not for the first time, the answer slipped away—like a fish in water when he tried to grab hold of it.

"How long have we been here?" he asked.

"Well," Chunklet said, "that's hard to say down here. In any case, I'm as hungry as if we'd been here a week."

Despite the seriousness of their situation, Kim had to smile. He could imagine vividly what Chunklet would have to say about dwarf-sized portions. "Have they treated you well?" he asked.

"Yes," Chunklet growled, "aside from the fact that they're obviously trying to starve me to death."

A key rattled on the other side of the door; three dwarves and a giant, angular iron man entered the chamber. Kim looked for a familiar face under the black hoods but didn't see one. The dwarves didn't seem surprised that he was awake and sitting on the edge of the bed.

Obviously, they'd kept him under observation the whole time.

"Come!" one of the dwarves ordered in a shrill voice. A forceful gesture added emphasis to his command; when Kim didn't stand up immediately, the iron man took a menacing step toward him.

Kim hastily jumped up.

"Where are you taking me?" he asked, as he and Chunklet left the chamber.

"To our king," replied the dwarf. He laughed derisively. "He's looking forward to seeing you. I hope you slept well. You'll be in dire need of what little brains you have if you want to get your neck out of the noose."

Kim stopped in surprise, but he quickly resumed walking when the iron man threateningly lifted his left hand.

"What do you mean by that?" Kim asked.

"They're going to sit in judgment over you."

"Sit in judgment?" Kim was completely confused. "What have I done?"

"They'll tell you soon enough," the dwarf jibed. "Hurry up. We've had to wait long enough for you to get your beauty rest."

Deeply confused, Kim quickened his pace, particularly in thanks to the fact that the iron man emphasized the dwarf's words with a rough shove.

Sit in judgment? Over me? He was stunned.

In the meantime, they walked down a long, windowless passageway, with walls made not of mountain rock but carefully placed, square black stones. Here and there, a heavy, semicircular oak door led off to the right or left; at regular intervals, burning torches on the walls filled the passageway with an eerie red light.

They went down a stairway and entered a similar corridor leading in the opposite direction. It occurred to Kim that both the doors and the height of the steps were normal size—not on a dwarf scale. He didn't see a window anywhere; however, various doors were open, allowing him to glance into the rooms as he passed by. This structure, which had the dimensions of a fortress, was situated either under the earth or constructed entirely without windows. That seemed absurd to Kim—until, all of a sudden, it struck him that, once before, he'd been in a black stone fortress with walls that had no windows! This realization hit him with such force that he stopped in mid-step and gasped in fright.

"What's the matter?" the dwarf asked suspiciously. "Don't try any tricks, boy!"

"Morgon!" Kim whispered. "This . . . this is Fortress Morgon!"

"So?"

Before Kim could give any further expression to his astonishment, the iron man gave him such a hard shove between his shoulders that he stumbled for a few steps. He would have fallen if he hadn't gripped the wall at the last minute. The last of his doubts vanished as soon as his fingers touched the black stone. He knew this eerie, disembodied coldness and this soul-piercing darkness: There was no doubt about it—this was Morgon, the fortress where the black wizard Boraas had launched his attack on Magic Moon.

Now that he knew where he was, Kim recognized everything down to the last detail. They climbed up the seemingly endless black stone spiral staircase, where he'd begun his escape back then. Next, they crossed several rooms that hadn't changed in all this time, finally stepping out onto one of the roofed parapets.

It was night. An icy wind howled around the battlements, making Kim shiver. The fortress courtyard loomed down below like a bottomless pit—and yet, Kim thought he saw movement there. Large, angular figures stomped this way and that, and flickering red firelight shone out of open doors.

To Kim's surprise, when they left the battlement and reentered the fortress, he was not led downward, where he knew Boraas' old throne was located; instead, he was taken up a steep staircase. When they reached the door at the top of the stairs, Kim's heart skipped a beat before pounding so hard that it hurt. He knew what lurked behind this door. If he'd had even a fraction of a second to react, he would've spun around and tried to escape—despite the dwarves and the iron man, whose claw was poised to grab him.

But the door swung wide as if opened by a ghost and, at the same moment, the iron man pushed him through the doorway. He fell on his knees. Horrified, Kim shut his eyes.

He knew where he was. This was the tower where the black mirror hung: the source of everything that was wrong and bad in Magic Moon. That terrible device once almost led to the destruction of the magical realm. One single look into it, and he would be lost.

Kim crouched there, unmoving, listening to his racing heart.

A familiar, mocking voice said, "You've been kneeling before me long enough, fool. Stand up!"

Kim didn't move. He knew he'd be lost if he opened his eyes. A single glance at the giant mirror opposite the door, and he'd turn into the worst enemy of this world and its inhabitants!

"I think our guest is still a little tired," the mocking voice continued. "Maybe someone could help him stand up."

Almost in the same instant, Kim felt a powerful steel hand grab him by the arm and jerk him up. He cried out in pain and involuntarily opened his eyes.

Powerless to stop it, his gaze fell on the wall across from him.

For an infinitesimally brief, terrible second, Kim expected that he'd be transformed, and that his mirror image would come to life and spread death and destruction among the inhabitants of Magic Moon. However, nothing happened. The black mirror didn't change him—it couldn't have, because it was no longer there. Where it used to hang, Kim saw a huge, gently curving pane of pale green glass, rounded at its four corners. Flickering strips of variously colored light rushed across the green glass, and he thought he saw confusing letters in an elaborate, alien script; however, the characters faded so quickly that he couldn't see them precisely. The mirror had disappeared. In its place now was something like a gigantically magnified image of a—

"This way, honored guest," the mocking voice said, breaking into his thoughts. "If you would be so kind as to grace us with your esteemed attention, we would be overjoyed."

With effort, Kim pulled his gaze away from the green glass and glanced at Jarrn, who perched on a huge, black wooden table, where a dozen other dwarves sat. The table and matching chairs obviously belonged to the previous inhabitant of this fortress, because none of the furniture was the right size for the dwarves. Jarrn's feet dangled a good foot and a half above the floor, and the top of the table would've made a good dance floor for his brothers.

Nevertheless, there was nothing ridiculous about the sight—quite the opposite. Kim suddenly sensed the menace that emanated from the dark-clothed dwarves.

He sullenly looked at Jarrn. "What's this about?"

"Oh," Jarrn said with feigned surprise. "Didn't anyone tell you, my friend? We're sitting in judgment over you."

"I can't imagine on what grounds," Kim replied.

"You'll find out soon enough."

Now that he'd overcome his fear, Kim's temper gradually began to rise. Defiantly, he walked toward Jarrn and stopped only when the iron man raised his hand in a threatening manner. "I demand an explanation!" he said.

"Why was I attacked and brought here? And what is this nonsense: You're going to pass judgment over me? You are going to tell me what all this means, or—better yet," he said, pointing at the dwarf who had brought him there, "this dwarf said your king was here. I demand to be brought before him."

Jarrn chuckled. "Your wish is my command," he said, standing up. At least, he tried to stand, but he forgot he was sitting on a chair that was too big for him. So, he plopped down one and a half feet, banging his chin on the edge of the table. Cursing, he clutched the armrests of the carved chair, scrambled back up onto the seat, and stared at Kim as if he were holding Kim personally responsible for his own awkwardness. Kim had a hard time suppressing a grin, but he managed, particularly because Jarrn had no sense of humor at the moment—not that he ever did.

"All right," Jarrn growled menacingly. "Here I am. What do you want to know?"

It took a while for Kim to realize the significance of these words. "You?!" he exclaimed in astonishment. "You're the king?"

"With your permission, yes," Jarrn snarled, spitting out a bloody fragment of a broken tooth.

Kim quickly overcame his surprise. "All the better," he said. "You'll be able to explain to me what all this means. Why have you kidnapped me? Why have you been pursuing me ever since I arrived in Magic Moon?"

Jarrn's eyes narrowed. "Maybe *because* you're in Magic Moon," he replied.

"But—"

The dwarf cut him off with an angry wave of his hand. "That's enough," he said sternly. "I have more important things to do than waste my time with you, you dunce. The proceedings are formally open!"

One of the dwarves pulled out a gavel from under his cape. It must've weighed at least three times as much as he did. He pounded the heavy oak tabletop so forcefully that a crack appeared in it.

Jarrn glared at the idiot before turning back to Kim. "You stand accused of various crimes—very serious crimes."

"Oh, is that right?" Kim said caustically. "Might I hear what they are?"

"Everything in its own good time," Jarrn replied crossly. "So, how do you plead—guilty?"

Kim's jaw dropped open and his eyes widened in amazement. "Guilty? I don't even know what I'm accused of!"

Jarrn sighed. "Clerk!" he said. "Note for the record: The accused is unreasonable and has insulted the court, which will result in a more severe penalty if he is found guilty."

"Hey!" Kim protested. "I—"

Once again, Jarrn cut him off. "Let no one accuse us dwarves of being unjust," he said. "You do not deserve this, but you will have the opportunity to defend yourself in a fair proceeding before this court. I assume you have no defense counsel?"

"No *what?!*" Kim groaned.

"Clerk!" Jarrn barked. "Note for the record: The court will assign someone to defend the accused." His gaze passed over the faces of the dwarves present. "Is there a volunteer?"

An uncomfortable silence spread throughout the room. Jarrn sighed. "All right, I will pick one," he said. He pointed at a particularly small and ugly dwarf. "You, there! You will defend the accused to the best of your ability!"

"Yes, but—" the dwarf started to say; he didn't get any farther, because Jarrn roared at him, "Counsel for the defense, you must respect this court, or you can share the fate of the accused!"

The dwarf shrank beneath his cape and didn't say another word for the rest of the proceeding.

"All right." Jarrn sat up straight in his chair with an air of satisfaction. "Once the information has been properly recorded, we can begin. So, you deny everything, defendant?"

"Maybe I would if I knew what I was being accused of . . ." Kim said, disconcerted.

The dwarves began to mutter and Jarrn rolled his eyes. "All right, fine," he sighed. "If you're absolutely determined to waste time . . . For one thing, there is the destruction of several of our iron men—"

"I was defending myself!" Kim protested.

Jarrn continued, unimpressed. "Then, there would be the attack against the King of the Dwarves—"

"How was I supposed to know who you are?" Kim said, defending himself.

"And finally, the destruction of our iron dragon," Jarrn concluded.

The dwarf's words literally left Kim speechless for a moment. "That—that wasn't my fault," he exclaimed, beside himself. "You were there! He attacked Rangarig and was destroyed in the process."

Something akin to pandemonium broke out among the dwarves. Some started to curse him, others booed and whistled, and a few cried out, "Put him in chains!" or "Throw him in the dungeon!"

Jarrn signaled to the dwarf with the gavel, who reestablished order with a loud knock that split the tabletop.

"Do you deny that the dragon was destroyed while we were pursuing you?" Jarrn asked, leaning forward and squeezing one eye shut.

"No, that's what happened," Kim said, "but I—"

"Exactly!" Jarrn interrupted triumphantly. "If you hadn't run away, we wouldn't have had to pursue you; consequently, the golden dragon wouldn't have attacked and destroyed our iron dragon." He turned to the other end of the table with a triumphant expression. "Clerk! Note for the record: The prisoner has confessed."

"That's not—" Kim started to say, only to be booed by the entire assembly. This time it took much longer for Jarrn to establish order, and the long table lost two of its many legs in the process.

"It would be smart of you to stop denying your guilt," Jarrn said. "Not that it would change the decision."

"Which is already established, I suspect," Kim murmured.

Jarrn looked at him, honestly puzzled. "Obviously," he said. "What else did you expect?"

Kim didn't know whether to laugh or cry. The whole situation seemed to him like a bizarre dream from which he couldn't wake up.

"Now that you finally seem to be reasonable," Jarrn continued, "we can proceed to the truly serious crime of which you are accused." He leaned forward and folded his hands on the table. Once again, he slipped off the chair, managing to grab the edge of the table only at the last second. "Do you admit it?"

Kim didn't even deign to give him an answer. He now was convinced that he was in a nightmare.

Jarrn rolled his eyes. "He does not confess," he said. "Counsel for the defense, your client is very imprudent. You should give him a talk so that he doesn't make his situation worse."

The counsel for the defense retreated beneath his hood and said nothing.

"So, what are you accusing me of?" Kim asked calmly.

"He's pulling our leg!" Jarrn snarled. "That is an outrageous insult to the court!"

Once again, there was an uproar among the dwarves. Some stood on the seats of their chairs and angrily shook their fists at Kim, others yelled curses and denunciations at him, and one took the glass in front of him and threw it in Kim's direction.

His voice screeching, Jarrn tried to regain order, but his words were lost in the commotion. So, he signaled the dwarf with the hammer.

The dwarf swung his tool in a high arc. The hammer crashed down on the table; two more of its legs folded under, and then the whole table collapsed with a crash. Jarrn, who had been leaning on his elbows, fell forward and got a bloody nose.

Cursing, he climbed back up on the chair and stared at Kim, full of hate. "You dispute that you came here and interfered in our affairs? You dispute that you took the side of the rebels, whose sole intention is to interfere with our business and ruin us?"

Kim was mystified. "I don't understand what you mean," he said helplessly. "I just—"

"Aha!" Jarrn cried at the top of his voice. "Clerk! Note that the accused has confessed!"

"I'm not going to say anything more," Kim said defiantly.

"Now, he's being stubborn, too!" Jarrn wildly waved his hands in the air. A couple of the dwarves next to him started raging again, and the dwarf at the end of the row of chairs raised his gavel. However, evidently he'd forgotten that the table was no longer there: The heavy tool sailed downward in a wide arc and demolished the leg of his chair. As the handle of the hammer flipped around, the dwarf executed a perfect somersault and landed precisely under his own collapsing chair.

"Your stubbornness will not help you at all," Jarrn cried angrily. "The evidence is overwhelming."

"What evidence?" Kim murmured.

"You came here and changed the course of things," Jarrn replied. "Things that are none of your business. It's your fault that we've lost a lot of business, and it's your fault that countless expensive tools have been destroyed. But it won't do you any good, you dunce—no more good than that little war your blockhead friends have unleashed."

"War?" Kim was shocked. "What war?"

"He's pretending he doesn't know anything!" Jarrn yelled, leaning so far forward that he fell out of his chair again. Kim's defense lawyer hastily jumped down from his chair and ran over to help his king up—in thanks, he earned a slap that sent him flying across the room. Jarrn stood up, smoothed the wrinkles on his crumpled cape, and pointed at the green pane on the wall behind him.

As soon as he did this, the dizzying succession of colors and strange letters extinguished, and Kim looked down on a map of Magic Moon from far above.

"If you absolutely must have proof, look there," Jarrn said venomously, "and then keep on denying it, if you dare!"

What Kim saw in the magic window put such a spell on him that he no longer heard the Dwarf King's words. The screen now showed mighty Caivallon and the Steppe riders. As if in time-lapse photography, Kim watched Priwinn, Gorg, and the farmers arrive at the fortress. A little later—probably days or weeks in the world out there—a vast number of Steppe riders marched out of Caivallon, heading south. The little army grew and grew. More and more men joined it.

They left a trail of destruction. Kim stopped counting the farms and villages through which Priwinn's mounted army marched, destroying all the men and horses of iron. He also stopped counting the number of dwarves who fled before the advancing army.

As Kim watched the slender figure in the pitch-black armor ride at the head of the army, he understood that Priwinn truly was no longer a prince. After his father's death, the young man had become King of the Steppe, and he'd carried out the plans he'd announced to the farmers that night. He had assembled not just a small team but a whole army, and he marched through the land with a sword in hand, using force to try to accomplish his goals.

As Themistokles had foretold, something else also had come true: the thing that Kim had feared the most. Not all the inhabitants of Magic Moon agreed with what Priwinn was doing—not by a long shot. Not all of them fled from the rebel army without a fight. The farther south the army went, the more resistance it encountered along the way. At first, there was minor hand-to-hand combat; then, there were skirmishes. Soon, that led to sieges where the inhabitants of a town closed their gates and manned the walls to defend themselves. Finally, the rebels were opposed by a second army of almost equal size. Kim watched with a mixture of horror and paralyzing disbelief as the two powerful armies moved toward each other like two giant beasts, each made of one hundred thousand parts. The image flickered out before they collided.

"Oh no!" he whispered, horrified. "What has he done?"

"Do you still want to dispute that you are to blame for all that?" Jarrn asked.

"But—I didn't want that!" Kim looked at the dwarf almost in horror. "Jarrn, you have to believe me! I tried to talk Priwinn out of it! You were—"

"Fiddlesticks!" Jarrn snapped. "None of this would have happened if you hadn't come and stuck your nose in our affairs."

Kim's voice was pleading. "Please, Jarrn! You can't have forgotten everything. We fought together against the Riverfolk. We survived because we helped each other! I saved your life and you saved mine."

"So what?" Jarrn spat contemptuously, but his aim was too shallow, and he hit the tip of his own foot. "Romantic fiddle-faddle! Why are you interfering in our affairs?"

"Your affairs?" Kim got angry again. "Maybe you're right, you damned dwarf! But do you know what? If your business consists of destroying Magic Moon, then I'm happy to interfere."

"Aha!" Jarrn cried. "He finally admits it! Clerk, note for the record that the accused has made a full confession!"

Kim stared at the dwarf, outraged. He had to exert all his willpower to keep from charging at Jarrn and twisting his spindly neck—regardless of what might happen as a result.

"Clerk!" Jarrn barked. "Read the judgment!"

"What judgment?" the clerk asked.

His king gave him a withering look. "It must be somewhere in your documents," he snarled.

While the clerk busily leafed through a stack of rumpled papers piled on his knees, Jarrn ambled over to Kim, condescendingly staring at him.

The fact that he had to lean his head back to do so didn't detract from the effect of his gaze. "You would have saved us all a lot of trouble, idiot, if you had come with me back then," he said.

"Why are you doing this?" Kim asked quietly. "Does it make you happy to hurt others?"

Suddenly, Jarrn sobered. All contempt and mockery disappeared from his gaze, and he looked at Kim in a way that made Kim's blood run cold. "We do only what people ask of us," he said. "When misfortune befalls you, it's in your nature to look for someone to blame. But we're not that way. We do only what we've been asked to do."

And then, the King of the Dwarves took a step backward, his face resuming the malicious expression so familiar to Kim. "Clerk!" Jarrn called. "Have you found the judgment yet?"

The dwarf still diligently rummaged through his papers; but then, with a triumphant shout, he pulled out a worn piece of parchment. "Here it is!" he cried. "It says . . ." He frowned and started again. "It says . . ." Frowning again, he looked at his king, slightly embarrassed. "Well, I can't read it. Whoever wrote this awful scribble ought to be ashamed."

Jarrn looked at each person in turn, challenging them. "Can anyone remember the judgment that we passed?" The dwarves lowered their gazes in embarrassment and pretended to be occupied with something else.

Jarrn grimaced again and shook his head. "Oh, forget it," he said. Then, indicating Kim with a tip of his head, he added, "Take him away."

XX

When Kim was led back out onto the parapet, it was the last time he saw the sky for a long, long while. Kim felt as if he were in a dream. The fact that a crazy band of dwarves had judged him already was strange in itself, but the idea that their judgment might have any influence on his life seemed absolutely ridiculous. Yet, an iron man held Kim's left wrist with pitiless strength, hauling him across the parapet—and Kim knew he truly was in trouble. Instead of reentering the main building, they tramped down the steep wooden stairs to the fortress courtyard. There, the iron man halted, his steel claw holding Kim's arm in its grasp.

A long time passed. The courtyard lay before them in ghostly black, and only occasionally did the shadow of an iron man or dwarf move past. Kim didn't hear a thing. The darkness absorbed not only almost all light but also all sound. The longer Kim stood there waiting for something to happen, the more he felt as if he were imprisoned in a giant underground cave. For a moment, he had to fight against the thought that perhaps *this* was his punishment: that he would stand here—chained to the immobile iron man—until he died of hunger, thirst, or exhaustion.

Of course, this thought arose only from his own fear. Jarrn wasn't that cruel. At the same time, Kim knew that he couldn't expect mercy from any of the dwarves. The better he got to know the dwarves, the more the diminutive folk confused him. He'd grown accustomed to Jarrn's effrontery, but what Kim had experienced in the tower chamber was too absurd. The dwarves seemed like a pack of out-of-control children—impudent, odious, bad-natured children. The thought that these people threatened the whole land—indeed, that they were causing the destruction of Magic Moon—seemed ridiculous to him.

Just when Kim started to wonder whether he'd been forgotten, the huge fortress gate creaked open; an enormous box-shaped wagon rolled into the courtyard, pulled by two iron horses. Kim's eyes widened when he could see the wagon better. The box shape was a cage with rusty bars as thick as his thumbs. A dozen boys and girls of various ages were locked inside. One of the larger boys pulled and shook the bars with all his strength. The other children apathetically sat on the straw strewn on the cage floor.

"So it *is* true," Kim murmured as the creaking wagon rolled past him.

"What do you mean, 'it *is* true'?" Chunklet asked.

Kim had almost forgotten that he was there, but the little creature had followed him like a loyal dog, making himself comfortable between the iron man's giant feet, where he'd found protection from the cold night wind. His gooey, bulging eyes looked back and forth from Kim to the cage.

Kim said despondently, "The dwarves are the ones who kidnapped the children." He sighed. For some reason he couldn't explain, he was disappointed.

"Priwinn and Gorg were right," he concluded bitterly.

Chunklet scuttled out from between the iron man's feet, ran behind the wagon for a few steps, and then turned around to run back to Kim. "So it seems," he confirmed. "They're children. They seem to be in bad shape."

"Priwinn needs to find out about this," Kim said. With all his strength, he tugged on the claw that tightly held his left arm, but the iron man's grip didn't loosen even a bit. "Help me!" Kim cried. With his free hand, he tried to bend back the giant's steel fingers, and Chunklet leaped up onto the iron colossus' arm and tried to pry open the giant's hand with teeth and claws. That only resulted in several broken fingernails and claws.

Finally, Kim gave up and sank to the ground. Chunklet hopped down from the iron arm.

Kim was silent for a long time while he contemplated his little companion's ugly nocturnal form. Chunklet was hardly bigger than a young cat; in the darkness, he was nearly invisible, even though he stood a yard in front of Kim.

"Do you think you can find the way back to Gorywynn?" Kim asked.

"What do you mean?" Chunklet asked cautiously.

"Because one of us has to go there," Kim replied, demonstratively shaking the steel giant's arm. "And the way things look, I'm not the one who can. So, how about it? Can you find the way?"

"I think so," Chunklet replied, "but I'm not going to abandon you."

"Rubbish!" Kim replied sternly. "Who do you benefit if you stay here? Not Priwinn, not Themistokles, and most certainly not me." With his head, he indicated the wagon behind him. "Nor those children over there or any of the others that have been kidnapped. You have to try to get out of here and cross the Shadowy Mountains."

"That will take much too long!" Chunklet pointed out. "By then, you could be long dead!"

"I don't think so," Kim replied, and he didn't say that merely to reassure Chunklet. "Be sensible, friend," he continued. "I know how brave you are. So, do what I say: Hide somewhere. Wait for a good opportunity and try to get out of here. You have to get through to Priwinn and the others and tell them what happened here. Then, seek out Themistokles . . ."

"An interesting idea," said a squeaky voice behind Kim.

Startled, Kim whirled around and found himself looking right at Jarrn's face. Under the cover of darkness, the King of the Dwarves had crept up silently. Now, he looked at Kim and the little animal with a mixture of anger and contempt.

"I'm afraid I can't allow that, though," he added mockingly, signaling a large group of dwarves to rush over and seize Chunklet.

The clumsy, slow-moving, spiny animal suddenly transformed into a whirling dervish, flitting past the dwarves' grasping hands at fantastic speed, wildly zigzagging from right to left, nipping any finger that came too close.

The dwarves' triumphant cries rapidly changed into a chorus of yelps and shrieks; quite a few of the little figures started hopping up and down, pulling long, needle-sharp spines from their fingers and faces. Jarrn, too, let out a furious scream and charged at Chunklet with widespread arms, but Chunklet made no attempt to evade him.

Quite the contrary: The creature suddenly stopped, spun around, and—with a shrill whistling sound—jumped into the air. Jarrn's furious bellow changed into a shrill scream as the prickly ball disappeared under his pointy hood. The dwarf's cape billowed for several seconds, quivering as if a hurricane raged beneath it. Then, Chunklet jumped out again and raced across the courtyard until he disappeared in the darkness. Three or four dwarves rushed after him, and at least one of them must have caught up with him, as a shrill cry of pain rang out.

The dwarf didn't return, and nothing was seen or heard of Chunklet, either. Kim wasn't very worried about that, though. Chunklet had proven thoroughly that he was capable of taking care of himself.

Jarrn picked himself up, groaned, and stumbled toward Kim. He was reeling, and it looked as if the king's face had encountered a berserk lawn mower. Where his skin wasn't cut, scratched, or scraped, it was stuck with the sharp ends of Chunklet's quills.

"Clever!" Jarrn snarled "Very, very clever." He threw back his hood and started to pull the quills out of his face with his pointy fingers. "But it won't do you any good," he continued with clenched teeth, suppressing moans of pain. "That porcupine has delusions of grandeur. We're going to catch him, never fear. The road to the west is long, and there are many dangers lurking along the way."

Kim preferred not to respond. He felt certain that Jarrn would be enraged at anything he said.

Clenching his teeth, Jarrn pulled the last spine from his face and lightly fingered his cheeks; then, frowning angrily, he gazed at the blood stuck to his fingertips. His expression didn't bode well.

"Go ahead, dimwit," Jarrn growled, insulted. "Laugh if you want. In any case, it will be the last time that you have anything to laugh about for a long while."

Angrily, he took a step backward, stumbled over the hem of his own cape, and landed roughly on the seat of his pants. The laughter that rose in Kim's throat got stuck there when he saw the expression on the Dwarf King's face.

Cursing, Jarrn picked himself up again and gestured, at which the iron man abruptly woke up from his rigid, immobile state and jerked Kim to his feet.

"Take him away!" Jarrn ordered. "Take him with those other brats—where he belongs!"

The iron man obediently turned around, but then Jarrn stopped him again. "One more thing, fool!" Jarrn said venomously. "Don't rejoice too soon. If your friends came here—which they definitely won't do, merely to rescue a dimwit like you—that won't do you any good." He laughed angrily. "You wanted to learn the secret of our forges? Now, you will. You're going to work in them, just like those other brats. You're going to pay for the damage you've caused. I swear, you're going to pay for it all, down to the last penny."

Kim and the other children left Fortress Morgon before that night was over. However, they were taken to a small, stuffy forge first. Sparks flew up around flickering fires. There, they were chained together: A heavy iron ring was fastened around Kim's right ankle, and a long chain was pulled through its eyebolt. At first, the chain seemed ridiculously thin to Kim, but then he recalled what Jarrn had told him about the dwarves' steel chain in the Riverfolk's cave. He didn't attempt to break the chain, although its individual links were barely thicker than twine.

In the meantime, Kim tried to start up a conversation with the other children—unsuccessfully. Almost all the children seemed detached, as if they were in some kind of trance. The only one who seemed awake was the boy who had been testing the bars of the cage. Either he didn't understand Kim's language, or he didn't want to answer, for his only response to Kim's questions consisted of angry looks and a threatening motion with his fist when Kim came too close to him.

So, chained together in this manner, they left Fortress Morgon in the wheeled cage. Two dwarf coachmen guided the dreadful vehicle down a narrow, winding path to the plains below. Any thought of escape or resistance was nipped in the bud by the presence of an iron man stomping behind the wagon.

They traveled in this manner through the dark forests, which that surrounded Morgon like an entangled wall, and then they stopped. At a signal from the dwarf, the iron man opened the cage and, with a clumsy gesture, ordered the inmates to climb out.

Another robot stepped out of the thicket. The iron giants picked up the two ends of the chain that linked the children's ankle rings. They pulled their captives through the thorny underbrush until, eventually, they arrived at the ruins of a dilapidated fortress tower in the middle of the forest.

A strange sort of fear crept over Kim when he saw the first iron man and the captives ahead slowly disappear in the blackness of the gateway. It was the same horrifying black that Kim had experienced in the Icy Wasteland, when they'd descended into the cave after Jarrn. Again, what lay before him wasn't simply darkness: it was like diving into a black, light-devouring lake that swallowed up souls. When it was Kim's turn to step into the tower, he felt that familiar, eerie shudder he'd experienced at the Castle at the End of the World.

Kim knew that the ice fortress wasn't the dwarves' own, exclusive realm—no more than Fortress Morgon belonged to them. Jarrn and his half-crazy followers might have selected the abandoned fortress as their headquarters because it was in an inaccessible location, easy to defend, and moreover, because there was no one left to claim it.

This realm, however . . . this belonged to them alone.

The tower had no floor. The door led immediately to a steep staircase. The first part consisted of packed dirt, and then the stairs were hewn out of the natural rock. In endless spirals, they wound deeper, deeper, and ever deeper into the earth. There was no light, just that eerie gray shimmer that Kim's eyes got more accustomed to the farther down they climbed. Upon entering the gloomy world of the dwarves, the children chained together ahead of him became pale and began to turn into flat, almost disembodied ghosts who moved in uncanny silence.

It seemed as if the stairs never would end. Kim tried to count the steps, but he soon gave up. At some point, he stopped thinking about anything at all. He needed every ounce of strength just to put one foot in front of the other.

The staircase terminated in a circular cavern. Its ceiling dripped water and its walls had countless openings. Flickering red firelight shone from many of the holes, and Kim heard the hammering and banging of tools mixed with creaking, thundering sounds. Kim's knees shook, and he felt so weak that he had to fight with all his might not to collapse on the spot. The other captives also staggered with exhaustion, but the two iron men mercilessly drove them forward. The robots roughly herded the children to one of the passages in the rock from which light glowed. On the other side of the opening was a huge underground room. Here, sparks flew as metal was forged and hammered over thousands of fires. Steel and white-hot liquid iron hissed; countless figures moved about, carrying large pieces of ore or baskets of tools. Kim couldn't take it all in at once.

Despite how depressed and exhausted he was, he noticed something at first glance: Only very, very few of those working there were children. Most of the busy figures here had tiny, spindly legs and wore tattered black cloaks. Kim rarely saw anyone who looked like his fellow captives. Without exception, however, the few children there had been assigned the hardest physical work.

If all the children who had vanished from Magic Moon were in the realm of the dwarves, then they were not in this part of the caves.

Before long, Kim found himself at one of the glowing forge fires.

He was forced to operate huge bellows that fanned the flames to an ever brighter glow. No one had taken the trouble to explain anything to him—and no one bothered to guard him or supervise his work. The chain on his foot was attached to a large rock, so he could take only two steps in any direction. If he didn't work the bellows hard enough, his workmate on the other side of the forge fire—a dwarf—would rebuke him and call him names. Kim's fellow captives were split up among the numerous sites, where they were assigned various tasks.

So passed the first of many days that Kim spent in the underground forges. On his first day, he worked the bellows until he thought he couldn't lift his arms. The dwarves, however, continued to work on without tiring; when Kim was too slow, one of the iron men roughly enforced the dwarf overseer's barked commands. When Kim finally was unchained and taken away, another captive immediately took his place at the bellows. The work continued without interruption.

At that point, Kim was so tired that he hardly noticed where he was going. The route went back to the round room with the countless openings, and he went to another, smaller cavern, where he was chained on the floor next to a wretched bed of straw. He was so tired that he fell asleep on the spot and didn't even notice when the dwarves appeared and brought the prisoners a meager meal.

Kim slept like a rock that night, without dreaming. However, the next morning, when he was shaken awake, he felt like he'd shut his eyes merely seconds before. Every single muscle in his body ached, and the dwarf who woke him had to pinch and punch him several times just to get him to rise from his pallet. Kim's stomach growled, and he was unbearably thirsty. When he told that to the dwarf, the little man laughed and stated that there had been food the evening before; if Kim was hungry, he would have to wait until he'd earned his food for today.

Kim wasn't led back to the bellows but was assigned the task of carrying large woven baskets of charcoal to the individual fires. After a short time, he was at the end of his strength, but there was no mercy. The louder he complained, the larger the baskets he had to carry. The slower he became, the more he was prodded.

Afterward, Kim didn't remember how he managed to survive. At some point, he probably reached a state of exhaustion in which he simply worked on without being conscious of what he was doing. After what seemed like eternity, he was brought back to the rock chamber and chained next to his sleeping quarters. Although he was more exhausted than the previous day, he forced himself to stay awake—because his stomach was aching from hunger. He sensed that he would need every bit of food he could get.

What the dwarves brought tasted disgusting, but Kim forced himself to eat all the unappetizing gray porridge, even asking for a second helping—a request, however, that produced only spiteful laughter.

When he allowed himself to sink down on his bed, Kim surveyed his surroundings for the first time. The room was nowhere near as huge as the adjoining forge, but it still was large enough to hold dozens of straw beds. The captives here were mostly boys and girls Kim's age, but there were also a few smaller children. Most of them seemed just as exhausted as Kim, for they fell asleep as soon as they wolfed down their porridge. Some, however, still sat on their beds, conversing with each other in soft voices. Kim heard words without really understanding them.

Then, he saw the boy who had been brought here in the wheeled cage. He sat not very far away, his legs drawn next to his body and his arms wrapped around his knees. Although he was looking directly at Kim, his eyes stared into empty space. Kim smiled at him, but the other boy's face didn't show the least reaction.

"Where are you from?" Kim asked him.

The boy lifted his head and looked at Kim in astonishment. Kim had to repeat his question two more times before the boy answered.

"From the west," the boy said finally. "My parents had a farm three days' ride west of Gorywynn."

"They *had* a farm?" Kim asked. "What do you mean by that?"

The boy looked at him in silence. At first, Kim interpreted the expression in his dark eyes as anger, but then he realized that it was deep, penetrating despair.

"The rebels," was all he murmured.

Kim was suddenly alert.

"King Priwinn's Steppe riders," the boy now blurted out. His voice sounded full of hate. "Have you ever heard of them?"

Kim nodded. Obviously, the boy didn't know who Kim was. It probably would be best if things stayed that way. "I've heard of them," Kim said cautiously. "They—they're fighting against the iron men and the dwarves, aren't they?"

"Against the dwarves?" The boy laughed bitterly. "I don't know about that. I just know that they fought against my father, his brother, and our farmhands."

"Priwinn's riders?" Kim asked skeptically. "I find that hard to believe."

"So don't," said the boy in an unfriendly way, lowering his eyes again.

"I'm sorry," Kim said, starting again. "I didn't mean to insult you. But I've heard that they don't hurt anyone; they just destroy the iron men."

The boy suddenly looked up. "You heard wrong!" he said angrily.

Kim was silent for a while. He felt responsible, if only because he hadn't succeeded in deterring Priwinn from his plan.

"What happened, then?" he asked quietly.

The boy continued to stare into empty space, and Kim resigned himself to the fact that he wouldn't get an answer—but the other boy started to tell his tale with a trembling voice:

"We heard that they were in the vicinity," he began. "They've raised an army, you see. They march through the land, plundering and robbing, and they're ruthless: They wreck anything made of iron—without asking who it belongs to. And people say there are more and more of them all the time."

Kim recalled what he had seen in the green glass pane. How much time had passed out there in Magic Moon?

"And your father had an iron man?" Kim said, picking up the conversation.

"Three," replied the boy. "And an iron horse. In the fall, we were supposed to get a plow that didn't need to be spanned to a horse."

"And you didn't want to turn them over," Kim guessed.

"Turn them over?" The boy laughed hysterically. "My father mortgaged the farmhouse and all our land so he could buy the iron men and that iron horse," he almost yelled. "Our farm always was big, but the soil there is poor and it takes a lot of hard work to get it to produce anything. My father was hoping to get more out of the land with the help of the iron men. But then came the Steppe riders. They wanted him to destroy the iron men; when he refused, they attacked him, tied him up, and made him watch while they destroyed the iron men."

Kim was deeply shaken. Despite everything he'd experienced, it was hard for him to believe the boy's words. At the same time, he sensed the kid was telling the truth.

"They said it had to be," the boy continued bitterly. "They said the iron men and everything else that came from the dwarves were ruining Magic Moon. But they're the ones who ruined *us*."

"They didn't hurt you, did they?" Kim asked, shocked.

The boy sadly shook his head. His eyes filled with tears, but not a single muscle moved on his face. "Isn't that enough?" he said. Then, he continued: "After everything was over, they untied him and told us all to join them. My father didn't want to, so he chased them from the farm. That same evening, we started to pack up our things in order to leave. But it was too late. As soon as the rebels left, the others appeared."

"What others?"

The boy shrugged his shoulders. "I don't know, armed men in silver-colored armor. Some of them were riding iron horses, and there were also iron men and dwarves with them. They surrounded the farmhouse and accused my father and his brother of being responsible for the loss of the iron men and the iron horse. Father tried to explain to them what had happened, but they didn't listen. They demanded the money that he owed the dwarves; when he didn't have it, they put him, his brother, and all the farmhands in chains, taking them away."

"And you?"

"I was supposed to go to the pits, too, but one of the dwarves said I was too young for that and couldn't do the work, so they brought me here."

Kim felt deep, honest sympathy for the boy. At the same time, he was confused. The story that the boy had told was different from the one he'd heard from Brobing and others. This boy hadn't magically disappeared from his parents' house but had been dragged off. As terrible as that was, it didn't solve the riddle of the missing children.

"What's your name?" Kim asked.

"Peer," replied the boy without looking up.

"The other children, Peer—" Kim continued cautiously, "—the ones that you came here with . . . were they kidnapped by the dwarves for the same reason?"

Peer shrugged. "Most of them. A few had the bad luck to be in our path, and one of the iron men simply grabbed them and put them in the cage. Why are you asking?"

"Just because," Kim quickly replied. "I'm just surprised that there are . . . so many."

Actually, it was exactly the opposite. Granted, the caves were huge and every child there was one child too many. Still, there were too few of them. If it was true that almost all the children of Magic Moon had already disappeared, then there should have been countless children here.

Kim slowly sank down on his bed and closed his eyes; although his limbs felt as heavy as lead, it took a long time—a very long time—before he was able to sleep.

Gradually, he learned all the tasks done in the dwarves' forge. Almost every day, he was assigned a new job, and each one seemed a little harder than the previous one. He carried coal, then ore—and finally, baskets of heavy wrought iron. He stoked the fires, mended tools, and hauled pieces of glowing-hot iron. He brought the dwarves water and handed them new hammers when the old ones had become red-hot from their incessant use.

Little by little, he also learned the other parts of the underground realm: In the complex network of caves were chambers where components created by the industrious dwarf smiths were assembled into huge, mysterious machines. Kim couldn't even guess the purpose of this equipment, but their sheer size and appearance frightened him to the core. At other work sites, the ore was delivered in huge chunks, which Kim and his fellow slaves had to break apart with heavy sledgehammers until the pieces were the correct shape for smelting.

At first, he felt like he would die from all the work. Every fiber of his body ached, and his fatigue seemed unendurable. But as bad as it was, Kim got used to it. His hands developed calluses; his body grew stronger. Despite the meager food, his muscles began to grow from the hard labor. Granted, he was tired to the point of falling over, but sometimes Peer and Kim sat together after dinner and talked.

Kim also got to know some of the other prisoners—not very many, though, and none as well as the boy from the west. There was no chance to talk while they were working. And because they always were chained to the same sleeping places, Kim could exchange a word with another child only if they were brought back to the same sleeping room. Yet, these few conversations with other kids revealed that Peer had been right: In most cases, the prisoners shared Peer's fate. Their fathers hadn't been able to pay for the iron men, Priwinn's Steppe riders had devastated their farms and left them vulnerable to the dwarves' revenge, or they simply were unfortunate enough to be caught in the wrong place at the wrong time. No one said that they simply had awakened here one morning. Everyone had logical reasons for being in the mines; not a single child had disappeared magically.

The dwarves were responsible for the fact that Magic Moon was suffocating under a blanket of black iron, but that hadn't a thing to do with the secret of the missing children.

Kim had stopped counting the days. He didn't know how long he'd been down there when Jarrn, the King of the Dwarves, paid him a visit. It was one evening after he and Peer had worked in the quarry cavern. Kim was tired in the extreme. He'd stretched out on the damp straw immediately after eating, but he wasn't asleep when a rough kick to his side made him bolt up. When he opened his eyes, Jarrn stood before him.

The King of the Dwarves took a precautionary step out of Kim's reach, but he grinned insolently. "So, dimwit," he started cheerfully, "how do you like it here with us?"

"Thanks for asking," Kim muttered angrily. "The food leaves something to be desired, but you have a truly nice selection of leisure-time activities. How did you know that I like sports so much?"

Jarrn laughed derisively. "I'm glad that you have a sense of humor about this," he said. "I made a special trip down here to make sure that our guest of honor is satisfied with his accommodations."

"Guest of honor?" Peer said, sitting up and looking at Kim in astonishment.

Jarrn nodded vigorously. "Oh, yes," he replied. "Didn't he tell you? He's going to stay here for an especially long time."

Kim gave the King of the Dwarves a pleading look, which triggered new mocking laughter. "I came to inform you that we have, in the meantime, calculated the damage that you are responsible for," he said. "Of course, only approximately—we can't determine the exact amount until we've stopped the handiwork of that out-of-control grass-eater."

"And? What figure did you arrive at?"

Jarrn acted as if he had to think it over hard for a minute. "As a rough estimate, I would say that you will work off the damage maybe in five or six hundred years," he said. "Excluding interest, of course. But I don't want to be petty. Let's say I come back in four hundred years, and we revisit the issue at that time."

"Is that supposed to be joke? I'm afraid I won't get to be quite that old."

Jarrn no longer laughed. He looked at Kim in a way that sent a shiver down Kim's spine. "I wouldn't be so sure about that," he said very softly and earnestly. "Here in our realm, you know, time does not pass. You will work here for five hundred years or for five thousand, if that's my will. As long as you stay in these caves, you'll never get older."

Kim was paralyzed with horror. He didn't doubt for a second that the dwarf was telling the truth. He already knew that time stood still in the dwarves' realm. Outside in Magic Moon, months had gone by while he lay unconscious in Fortress Morgon.

"Oh?" Jarrn asked maliciously. "Lost your sense of humor?"

Jarrn received no answer and, after he spent a while gloating over Kim's boundless horror, he took a step backward and raised his hand. A second dwarf appeared behind him. He carried a sack of coarse linen—in which, something struggled.

"And just so you won't get your hopes up only to be disappointed later," the King of the Dwarves continued, sneering, "I also have a special surprise for you here."

He untied the sack's knot and turned it upside down. A prickly, ugly creature fell out and rolled to the ground with a furious whistling sound.

"Chunklet!" Kim exclaimed in shock.

The werecreature whirled around and hissed angrily. When he recognized Kim, an expression of immense sadness entered his eyes.

"So, there you are," Jarrn said. "It was really hard to catch this four-legged little monster. Considering what he did to my people, I ought to give you an extra fifty years. But I'll let it go this time. Accept him as a gift and as company for the rest of the time you'll have to spend here."

With that, he turned around and walked away, roaring with laughter. After a few steps, he stopped to face Kim. "Oh, by the way," he said in a tone of voice as if this had just occurred to him. "You and your odious porcupine there," he said, pointing at Chunklet, "can spare yourselves the trouble of trying to escape. These caves have no exit—at least, none that you can use." Chuckling, he left.

It was quiet for a long time. Jarrn's appearance had awakened some of the other prisoners, causing them to sit up curiously, but no one said a word. The way they looked at Kim now made him feel very uneasy.

"Is it true?" Peer finally asked quietly.

"What?"

"What the dwarf said," Peer said. "That the Steppe riders are your friends."

Kim didn't like Peer's tone. He looked up and saw something in the boy's face that made him afraid.

"Yes," Kim confessed.

"You lied to me," Peer said. "You said you were my friend. But you lied to me from the beginning: You're on their side."

"No!" Kim helplessly shook his head and added in a quieter voice: "Or rather, yes—but not the way you think."

"Not the way I think?" Peer echoed. "How else, then? The King of the Steppe is your friend! I bet you secretly were laughing your head off when I told you what happened at our farm!"

"That's not true!" Kim protested. "Priwinn is my friend—that's right. But I never wanted him to do that. I tried to persuade him not to. Why do you think I'm here?"

"How should I know?" Peer retorted with bitter hostility.

Kim continued in the same tone of voice: "Because I parted from them, Peer. Because I wanted to try to find out the dwarves' secret *before* things turned out as they did."

The boy looked at him uncertainly. "The dwarves' secret?"

Kim swept his arms out in a gesture of helplessness. "I . . . I thought I could find out what happened to all the children, but I failed."

"What children?"

"The children who have disappeared from Magic Moon," Kim replied. "No one knows what—"

Peer interrupted him with an impatient gesture. "You don't have to tell me—I had three brothers who are no longer around."

It was Kim's turn to look at Peer in bewilderment. They had talked a lot in the past few weeks, and he'd gotten to know the boy well. Peer had told Kim many things about his life on the farm, but he'd never mentioned brothers and sisters. There was something else about the boy's words that alarmed Kim. *Three brothers* . . . Something about that seemed significant to Kim, but he couldn't say what.

"What does any of that have to do with the dwarves?" Peer asked.

"Nothing, I'm afraid," Kim said dejectedly. He sighed. "I'm a fool. I thought I could come here by myself and do what everyone else failed to do."

"Well," Peer said, "you'll have a long time to think about where you went wrong. Five hundred years should be enough."

"Surely you don't think I'm going to stay here," Kim said with resolve. "I don't know how, but I'm going to get out of here—and all of you will, too."

Peer laughed softly, not in the least amused. "Uh-huh," he said. "All we have to do is wait until our chains rust through and these rocks disintegrate."

"It wouldn't be the first time that I broke out from of a supposedly escape-proof prison," Kim said. "I'll do it again."

"I'm afraid," Chunklet piped up in very quiet voice, "it won't be quite so easy this time." He scuttled closer to give Peer an appraising look before rolling up next to Kim, his sharp quills poking through Kim's tattered shirt. "The dwarf was telling the truth. There's no way out of these caves."

"That's nonsense," Kim said crossly. "After all, we did come in here."

"In these caves, the passageways lead only inward—none lead out," Chunklet insisted. "Believe me, only the dwarves know the way out." He snuffled audibly. "Those dwarves with their magic. How do you think they caught me? Certainly not with their bare hands! It was their miserable tricks—I fell for them."

"Even so!" Kim shook his head. "I swear I'll find a way out—if I have to dig through the rock with my bare hands!"

Chunklet didn't respond. Secretly, Kim thought what sounded like determination in his voice actually was defiance and desperation.

XXI

An opportunity to escape did come, indeed—for a completely different reason than Kim thought. For the first several days after Jarrn's visit, he tried everything he could think of to get free of his chain. It was just as the Dwarf King had said back in the Riverfolk's caves: The thin, black links were impossible to pry open. No amount of strength and no tool that he used could scratch the dwarven steel—and he tried one tool after another. Even Chunklet's teeth, which nothing else could withstand, failed against this magic metal.

Chunklet made himself useful in another way, however: He could move about freely in the caves. The dwarves had tried to put him in chains, too, but the little creature had bitten and scratched with such ferocity that no one could hold him down. At the time, Kim wondered how Jarrn's henchmen had managed to catch Chunklet, but his spiny companion stubbornly refused to discuss this topic. Otherwise, though, the little creature was very eager to help.

Over time, Kim sent him to every part of the giant underground smithy—into every cavern, every passageway, and every chamber. He had Chunklet check out every cleft and every crack in the rock, always in search of a potential escape route. In the meantime, it appeared that the other captives gradually became friends with the spiny animal, who could be seen only in his ugly nocturnal form when he was locked up in the eternal twilight of the dwarves' subterranean world.

From Chunklet's reports, Kim found out that there was a part of the cave system that even the dwarves avoided. At the far end of the area where the ore was broken into smaller pieces, there were several passageways that the dwarves never entered. In fact, they apparently took a big detour around them. Kim didn't find out what went on there, because Chunklet steadfastly refused to investigate. Kim saw the fear in his eyes whenever they talked about that part of the labyrinth, so Kim stopped pressuring his friend. Clearly, something was there that Chunklet feared—and that was saying a lot!

As it turned out, however, this place offered an opportunity for escape.

One day, Kim, Peer, and a half-dozen other boys and girls were working with large sledgehammers, breaking up huge lumps of ore into smaller, more manageable pieces. These pieces then were crushed by a giant machine—a cogwheel three times the height of a grown man, complete with razor-sharp steel edges—until they were the right size for smelting. The kids had performed this work numerous times. It was the hardest job in the mines; nevertheless, it was the one that Kim found most tolerable, because he wasn't shackled to his workstation but instead linked to the others by a long, thin chain. The chain gave them all enough freedom of movement to take a few steps. On this day, he suddenly felt such a hard jerk on his foot that he almost lost his balance. Before he could whirl around, he heard a piercing, horrified shriek behind him.

When Kim saw what had happened, he also cried out in terror!

One of the other boys had come too close to the cogwheel, and his chain had slipped under the massive iron teeth. The giant wheel continued to turn relentlessly, and the chained boys slowly were pulled toward the apparatus' grinding teeth!

Kim dropped his hammer, grabbed the thin chain with both hands, and pulled on it with all his might. Peer and the other boys did the same. Desperately, they braced themselves, trying to find a handhold on large pieces of ore—but nothing helped! The chain started to cut into Kim's fingers like a thin knife, but he didn't release his grip: On the contrary, he pulled even harder. Nevertheless, the chain and the captives shackled to it continued to be drawn toward the giant wheel.

Kim watched in horror as the writhing, screaming captive inexorably approached the deadly cogwheel. The boy panicked and started thrashing like a madman, as if that might help. There were six feet left between him and the grinding teeth. . . and then four . . . and then two . . . finally, only a little more than one. One more tug of the machine, and the boy's foot would be cut off!

At the very last moment, the wheel suddenly came to grinding halt. The razor-sharp iron edge was only inches away from the unfortunate boy's foot. A very annoyed dwarf popped out from the other side of the machine, took in what had happened with a quick glance, and began to curse as he scurried toward them. The boy hadn't realized yet that he'd been saved; he still was screaming and flailing. When the dwarf tried to approach him, he struck the little man. The dwarf had to jump back to keep out of range.

"Help me!" the dwarf cried. "Hold down this maniac!"

Kim, Peer, and other kids did as the dwarf asked. At least for the moment, fear seemed to have robbed the boy of all reason. While they held his arms and legs, the dwarf pulled a huge key out from under his cloak and unlocked the chain's ring. Kim and the others hastily dragged the boy a short distance away from the huge cogwheel and waited until his panic had subsided before daring to let go of him.

In the meantime, the dwarf ranted: "You fools are too stupid to swing a hammer!" he yelled. "Look what this idiot has done! This will put us way behind schedule! You're all going to pay for it—that's a promise. There won't be anything to eat tonight—nothing tomorrow, either!"

Kim and Peer glanced at each other as the dwarf tugged on the end of the chain with both hands—completely in vain, for the chain had been pulled deep into the cogwheel's gears.

"It's broken!" screeched the dwarf, who was filled with rage over his stalled machine.

Kim and Peer glanced at each other again, exchanging meaningful looks. It was as if they'd agreed long ago what should be done in a moment like this. While the others looked on in surprise, they cautiously approached the dwarf and took up positions behind him.

"And there won't be anything to eat the day after tomorrow, either!" the dwarf scolded, tugging with all his strength on the hopelessly entangled chain. "And you'll all have to work double shifts, too—" He stopped mid-sentence.

Kim grabbed him by the neck and the seat of his pants and lifted the little man, literally leaving him breathless, while Peer almost casually extracted the key from his belt.

The dwarf's eyes widened in astonishment. "What are you doing?" he gasped. "Have you lost your mind? This isn't allowed!"

"I know," Peer said, smiling as he squatted down and unlocked the ring on his right foot. The chain rattled as it fell to the ground. The boy stood back up with an audible sigh of relief.

The dwarf breathed deeply, preparing to yell, but Kim smothered his cry.

Peer released Kim from the chain as well, and then he turned around to unlock the others. Soon, they all could move about freely for the first time in a long while.

But this newly won freedom was destined to last for only a few moments; as fast as they'd been, their attack on the dwarf hadn't gone unnoticed. From the other end of the cavern, shrill and angry voices raised the alarm.

Kim turned around; he saw a dozen dwarves charging toward them. They were accompanied by a giant iron man, who walked at a casual pace but still moved faster than the dwarves' rapid little steps.

"Run!" Kim yelled. "Scatter so they can't catch us so easily!"

Only one boy took his advice to heart and rushed off. The others remained where they were, behind Peer and Kim. Two or three grabbed huge hammers and resolutely stared at the dwarves and the iron colossus.

"We'll never get out of here, anyway," Peer said. A grim expression appeared on his face as his hands closed around the handle of the sledgehammer. "At least they'll remember us for a while."

Kim was about to get a weapon, too, but then he stopped. He knew there no sense in fighting. If they could overcome this one iron man, there still would be so many others down there that they couldn't handle them all. There had to be another way.

There was no time to think it over, however: The dwarves and their iron escort arrived on the scene, and things devolved into an uproar in front of the fateful cogwheel. The dwarves tried to wrestle their captives to the ground, but their strength was inadequate. The boys' and girls' muscles were steeled by heavy labor, and they defended themselves with stubborn rage. They slapped and cuffed and slugged and kicked. If the iron man hadn't intervened, it would have been a delightful free-for-all.

But the iron giant was deadly serious.

His huge shovel hand flung one of the captives against a rock wall; the boy now lay motionless and bleeding. One of the other kids swung his sledgehammer and delivered a terrible blow against the iron chest, but the colossus didn't waver. Instead, he spun around with astonishing speed, smashed the boy's hammer to pieces with a single blow, and broke the boy's arm. The robot's victim sank to his knees with a pained whimper, pressing his right hand to his chest.

Kim's thoughts raced. He knew that the dwarves wouldn't really hurt them: They were valuable laborers. However, the iron giant had no such inhibitions. His arms flailed among the children like a threshing machine, mowing them down. His steel claw snapped open and shut like a bear trap. Although struck with hammers again and again, he didn't seem to even notice, for he raged on relentlessly. The rebellion threatened to collapse as quickly as it had begun.

Kim ducked under the iron giant's whirling arm, stooped down to get the chain, and held its end tight. Scrambling to evade the giant's deadly blows, he ran circles around the iron man, wrapping the chain around the giant's legs.

The robot tried to catch Kim, but he couldn't snap the chain of dwarven steel. For the first time, the iron man was in danger of falling—but he caught himself. For a moment, he looked confused. His shining green eye briefly fixed on Kim before following the thin chain in Kim's hands down to his own legs. With a ponderous movement, he bent over, extended his agile right hand, and tried to loosen the knot. To Kim's immeasurable surprise, he almost succeeded.

Then, Kim jerked on the steel links with all his strength. The loop tightened around the iron legs; but at the same moment, the iron man's left hand grabbed the chain and held it with relentless strength. His right hand began the task of freeing his legs.

Suddenly, Kim had an idea. Quickly turning around, he beckoned Peer over and pressed the end of the chain in his hand. "Keep a good hold on it," he ordered. "Pull it as tight as you can."

Peer obeyed, although his expression indicated that he had no idea what that was supposed to accomplish. Kim took off, dashing around the cogwheel to where the dwarf with the key had first appeared.

A few dwarves tried to bar the way, but Kim simply plowed through them. Circling behind the cogwheel, he found what he'd been looking for: On the other side of the huge machine was an oversized, shining red lever!

Leaping forward, Kim grabbed the lever with both hands and pushed it down. The ground rumbled, and then the wheel slowly started moving again.

Howling with rage, the dwarves tried to push away Kim so they could turn off the machine. But sheer determination gave Kim almost superhuman strength for a short time. He fended off the attack until some of the other boys rushed to help him.

The dwarves quickly scattered. Although the kids had discarded their weapons after realizing they were useless against the iron man, their deep resentment of the dwarves gave them strength.

When Kim rushed back from behind the cogwheel, the situation had changed completely. Peer had let go of the chain—he'd had to, because it now was being reeled toward the giant machine. There was an unpleasant grinding sound, as if large pieces of the gear's teeth were breaking off. Along with the chain, the iron man was being pulled in, too.

The robot resisted with all his might. Sparks flew up from the rocky floor as he tried to brace his feet; and for a moment, the whole wheel vibrated as if it would break apart. Despite the iron man's tremendous strength, though, the colossus drew nearer and nearer until he was pulled into the gears of the machine.

A terrible splitting and crashing resounded. First, the feet; next, the legs; and then, the torso of the reddish-brown figure disappeared among the grinding teeth. The iron man reared up one last time, but then he went limp.

With a relieved sigh, Kim approached the motionless giant.

The narrow green eye glowed with a cold fire. The powerful hand jerked out and closed around Kim's foot like a trap snapping shut.

Kim cried out in fear and pain. He pulled away with all his might, but the iron man's grip held fast. The wheel still turned, and its razor-sharp gears continued to pull the colossus deeper into the machine's interior, all the while crushing the iron man apart. Kim was pulled along with it—no matter how desperately he resisted!

Only the head, shoulders, and a small part of the iron man's chest stuck out of the machine, but its murderous grip didn't loosen. Kim clawed the ground with his fingernails, trying to hold on. Peer rushed over and pulled Kim's arms with all his might, but even their combined strength wasn't enough. The iron man's right shoulder disappeared . . . and then, his head. Finally, the only part left was the hand that held onto Kim's foot.

Its grip had still not relaxed.

"Kim!" Peer yelled, his voice cracking. "Do something!"

But Kim couldn't do a thing. He continued toward the crushing maw of the machine. Before long, he would share the iron man's fate and be sawed into pieces.

Suddenly, a diminutive figure wrapped in a ragged black cape appeared next to Kim, roughly pushed aside Peer, and bent over Kim's foot. Kim couldn't see anything—but all of a sudden, his leg was free, barely a second before the iron man's fingers disappeared into the machine. . . .

With a deep sigh, Kim hastily backed away from the giant machine. His little rescuer looked at him, grinning—and then kicked him in the shin so hard that Kim recoiled with a cry of pain and hopped around on one foot.

While Peer and some of the other boys watched in astonishment as the little man disappeared again, dodging this way and that, Kim grabbed the key from Peer and ran to free the other captives. No one tried to stop him. The few dwarves who had escaped the wrath of their slaves had fled to safety.

It took only a short time before all the children were freed. Kim stuck the key under his belt. Twenty or thirty confused kids now crowded around Peer and him, looking at them expectantly.

"What now?" Peer asked, breathing hard. He gestured toward the exit with his head. "How are we going to manage it? They'll be all over us."

Kim nodded despondently. He, too, was well aware that their victory was temporary. Even if they succeeded in freeing all the other prisoners—which was by no means certain—they'd never get out. He hadn't forgotten what Jarrn and Chunklet had said about the way out of the labyrinth.

He looked around, searching for Chunklet. In the confusion, he'd lost sight of the little creature and, for a moment, he feared something dreadful had happened. Then, he discovered the little pincushion among three dwarves who sat on the ground, sobbing. They didn't dare move, for Chunklet would snarl and hiss if they so much as twitched an eyelid.

"Chunklet!" Kim said sharply. "Stop this nonsense. Come here."

The little animal seemed disappointed, because he hesitated before turning and moving toward Kim. One of the dwarves tried to take this opportunity to run away, and Chunklet scratched him across his hooked nose.

"That passageway that you were talking about," Kim said. "The one that even the dwarves are afraid of—where is it?"

Chunklet gave a frightened squeak.

"We have to get out of here somehow," Kim pressed impatiently. "Take us there. Hurry!"

"But . . . but I don't know where it leads," Chunklet stammered. "Maybe the passageway goes deeper into the earth."

"We'll have to take that chance," Kim said. He glanced around inquisitively. Despite the fear reflected on the other children's faces, everyone nodded with great determination. They couldn't go back now. Kim sensed every kid knew that. They would rather face an uncertain fate—or death in the bowels of the earth—than allow themselves to be shackled again.

"All right," Chunklet muttered to himself. "Come along."

He turned around and scurried off between the chunks of rock so quickly that Kim and the others were hard-pressed to follow him. They were very glad their guide had set such a pace, though, because a sea of black capes now filled the cavern entrance, brandishing knives, axes, and cudgels in their little arms. The dwarves howled furiously as they took chase.

A whole army of dwarves is charging at us, Kim thought fearfully, *and behind them, there are more than a few iron men!*

The farther they went into the cavern, the darker it became. The eternal gray light of the dwarf world remained, but the flickering firelight that transformed the workplaces into a never-ending sunset was left behind. Now and again, Kim glanced back over his shoulder and saw that the distance between them and their pursuers gradually dwindled. The iron men, in particular, advanced at an alarming pace. There were a great many of them—at least one iron giant, if not two, for every fugitive.

But they made it: Kim and Peer formed the rear, and they were still forty or fifty paces ahead of the iron men when Kim caught sight of a huge semicircular tunnel in the gloomy twilight up ahead. Chunklet darted into the tunnel with a shrill whistle, and the others followed—Kim and Peer arriving last.

As soon as Kim stepped into the tunnel, he understood what Chunklet had feared. It was palpably cooler in here than in the other caverns, and the gray light was less intense; the kids running in front of him were perceptible only as vague shapes. The sound of their footsteps eerily reflected off the stone walls, creating long, drawn-out echoes. It sounded like something evil—to Kim's ears, the echoes sounded like mocking laughter.

He tried to dismiss the thought and glanced back again. The iron men also had reached the tunnel, but they stopped at the entrance: A row of black shadows with glowing green eyes completely filled the semicircular opening. The dwarves pushed their way in between the huge legs, but they didn't enter the passageway, either. It was as if there were an invisible border inside the tunnel entrance, and neither the dwarves nor their fearsome helpers could cross it.

Suddenly, a voice called out. It screeched so shrilly and unpleasantly that Kim would never forget it for the rest of his life. "Stop, you fools! You're running toward death!"

Kim slowed down, coming to a halt. Peer and the others stopped, too.

"Come back!" the voice very forcefully cried.

The words echoed and distorted in an evil way. It was as if a broken voice whispered in a language they didn't understand.

Kim dismissed the thought and gestured with his head at the gray darkness behind them. "We have to go on," he said. "That's Jarrn. He's probably hatching some plot."

The boys and girls started moving again, but they no longer ran as quickly as before; Kim noticed a growing sense of unease spreading among the group. Obviously, Jarrn's words had their intended effect. They all were afraid of this huge, absolutely straight tunnel, which led directly into the mountain.

"Come back!" Jarrn screeched again when he realized that they weren't listening to him. "I won't punish you! Come . . . back . . . you . . ."

His voice grew fainter before fading away completely; but for a long time, Kim felt he could hear its echo.

Time and space couldn't be measured in this bleak part of the dwarves' world. No one could say how long they'd been walking or how far they'd come. Kim slowly counted to one thousand in his mind before he signaled for the others to stop.

He looked around, feeling uneasy. The other kids crowded together like of herd of anxious animals that sought one another's company for protection; all eyes were directed expectantly at him. Only now did he become conscious of the fact that the others automatically assumed he'd know what to do next.

Eventually, Kim solved his dilemma with a shrug and assumed a confident expression. "I think we're rid of them for now," he said. "So, let's go on. There's only one direction, after all."

Peer gave him a skeptical look. Kim thought things over for a moment before adding somewhat more quietly: "Maybe Jarrn is right. Who knows what dangers we'll face? This tunnel might lead deeper into the earth and have no exit. So, anyone who wants to go back can do so. I won't stop you, and I won't be mad at you, either."

No one moved. Kim waited a little longer, and then he said it again, this time in a very loud, strong voice, so that everyone could understand his words. "Anyone who wants to go back should do it. I'm certain that Jarrn will keep his word and not punish you."

After a while, two boys and a girl stepped forward. Kim saw the fear in their eyes and smiled at them encouragingly. "Go ahead and go," he said. "You three might be the only ones who have any sense."

He waited until they disappeared into the gray twilight. Then, he addressed the others again: "Listen, I can't promise you anything. I don't even know where this passageway goes. We might get hopelessly lost and starve to death or die of thirst or be killed in some other way. If you want to come along, you should know that it's a matter of life and death. So, what do you think?"

Again, some time went by, and then two more boys stepped forward and quickly headed back.

Kim once again looked at everyone. There were still more than forty children left, and the responsibility for all of them rested on Kim's shoulders. That thought was anything but pleasant. But no one gave any indication of wanting to return to the dwarves. With a heavy heart, Kim continued on, marching at the front of the little group of lost souls heading into the eternal twilight under the earth.

* * *

It seemed as if they wandered endlessly. The gray light and the unchanging nature of their surroundings fooled their senses, so Kim had his companions slowly count to five hundred, one after another, to approximate the passing of time. When they got to ten thousand—which meant they'd been walking for a good three hours—they arrived at a fork in the road. The tunnel split—one branch leading toward the right and the other heading left. Both paths were the same size and completely round, leading into the mountain like two giant tubes.

It wasn't easy to decide which branch to take. The tunnel on the right led farther into the mountain in the same direction they'd been traveling, while the tunnel on the left branched upward so steeply that making any progress on the smooth, glassy tunnel floor would require a great deal of strength. Kim decided in favor of the tunnel on the right; none of the others objected, but they grew quieter and more pensive. Kim sensed that the fear in their hearts was increasing rapidly. Something about this passageway was different. The gray light still was there, and it still was impossible to see more than ten or fifteen paces ahead. An endless, foggy void extinguished everything immediately behind them and grew before them no matter how quickly they walked. This tunnel was larger than the previous one. Its walls were smooth, as if they'd been polished carefully. Although the passage was very broad, after a while, the children moved in single file; their feet barely could find purchase on the round tunnel's curved floor.

They took a rest break, but not for long; they hadn't a thing to eat or drink and could make no fire for warmth. They were not moving, so the tunnel's clammy chill felt doubly cold. Hardly anyone spoke, and even the few whispered conversations trailed off the deeper they penetrated into the body of the earth. After a while, they arrived at another fork . . . and then another one . . . and another one still. They always took the right branch because Peer insisted that that way they couldn't get lost if they had to turn around for some reason.

Just as Kim thought that a little sleep would help them regain some strength, Peer abruptly stopped.

Kim stopped, too. "What's going on?"

"Shh," Peer said, closing his eyes and cocking his head to listen.

Kim held his breath and listened, but he couldn't hear anything. Only after some time had passed did Peer open his eyes again. He shrugged. "Nothing," he said. "I must have been mistaken."

Now, Kim felt intense unease. The eerie atmosphere hadn't lessened one bit since they'd escaped. As they trudged through the tunnels with their polished surfaces, the children got used to the worrisome interior of this labyrinth.

They hadn't gone farther than one hundred steps when Peer stopped again, this time frowning and pointing in front of Kim's feet.

Kim took a closer look. There was a dark spot on the ground—no larger than the palm of his hand. It was distinguishable from the surrounding ground only because it glistened as if it were damp. Kim ascertained that it was damp when he squatted down and cautiously extended his hand. Chunklet curiously sniffed the spot and jumped back with a disgusted sound. Kim made a face when he brought his fingertips to his nose.

This wasn't water but some kind of transparent, sticky, foul-smelling slime.

The spots grew more frequent the farther they went. At first, there were small drops here and there; soon, they encountered whole pools of the stinking, sticky liquid. They couldn't avoid the pools, because the tunnel floor, walls, and ceiling were smeared with this odd slime. *As if something had crept along here,*

Kim thought, shuddering. The slime reminded him of a huge snail trail—*but what kind of snail could completely fill a tunnel as tall as eight men standing on one another's shoulders?*

They counted to ten thousand a second time, and Kim wasn't the only one almost completely exhausted. The thought of lying down to sleep on this sticky, slimy ground made his stomach turn; but before long, they'd have no other choice—unless they wanted to keep on walking until the weakest among them collapsed.

Every step felt harder than the one before, and it seemed to Kim as if pulling his feet out of the sticky goo on floor cost him precious energy.

Chunklet even scrambled up onto Kim's shoulders to avoid the slime. Suddenly, the werecreature sniffed excitedly.

Kim turned his head to look at Chunklet, and although the pincushion didn't say anything, he excitedly moved his nose this way and that, catching a scent.

Kim sensed his fear. "What's going on?" he asked.

"There's . . . something down there," said Chunklet.

"What?"

Chunklet shrugged and shook his head at the same time, poking Kim in the cheek and temple with his sharp quills. "It's . . . coming closer."

"From what direction?" Kim cried.

Chunklet lifted a paw and pointed ahead. "From there."

Kim strained his eyes, staring into the darkness, but he didn't see anything. After a while, though, a ghastly feeling crept over him: Somewhere in this vast grayness, there was . . . something big and evil.

"We'd better turn around," Kim said. His heart pounded, and he had a hard time hiding his fear. They'd passed one of the branching tunnels a short while before, and Kim thought it best that they hide there.

None of the others objected, and so they turned around and retraced their path—much more quickly than they'd come.

Chunklet gave another start on Kim's shoulder and said with a squeaking voice, "You'd better hurry!"

That was all it took. All at once, their fatigue was forgotten. They took off running as fast as they could.

Already, Kim sensed something behind them in the darkness, coming closer and closer. He resisted the temptation to turn his head, instead concentrating on running as fast as he could.

Then, they heard it: The ground under their feet trembled, and the rocks vibrated with a rumbling, grating sound. It was as if something massive rolled toward them—or rather, as if the whole mountain undulated.

"Faster!" Kim yelled.

Their running turned into panicked flight. Kim and Peer fell back a few paces to grab one of the slower boys by the arms and drag him along. Kim inadvertently glanced behind him. What he saw made his heart race all the faster—with the force of an out-of-control pile driver. The darkness behind them awakened with seething life. A monstrous, formless mass rolled toward them—and for a fraction of a second, Kim had the feeling he was looking into two huge, angry, glowing red eyes.

He didn't take a second look, but he sped up so much that even Peer had a hard time keeping up. They dragged the other boy between them. Still, they made it only at the very last moment. The branch tunnel suddenly appeared before them out of the gray twilight, and Kim had just enough time to hurl himself inside, pulling Peer and the boy along with him. An avalanche thundered past them. The huge mass completely filled up the tunnel, shaking the entire mountain.

Kim fell down, finally letting go of the boy's hand, and rolled over. His heart hammering, he looked up.

Where the tunnel opening had been, there was now a quivering, seething, soft black mass, passing at a furious speed. Whatever it was, it had to be extremely long.

Kim felt a blast of air wash over him. It had a suffocating, rank odor, similar to the stench emanating from the slimy puddles—but one thousand times stronger and more ominous. He hastily crawled farther away from the tunnel entrance as a wave of the disgusting, transparent fluid slopped in, soaking his feet and pant legs.

The rumble had grown to a roar, and Kim couldn't tell whether it was the groaning mountain or the terrible monster outside.

"What *is* that?" Peer whispered after the rumbling and groaning had quieted down. The ground beneath them still shook gently.

Kim shrugged helplessly. "How should I know?" he whispered. "Maybe—no, that's impossible. Or maybe not . . . Could it be a worm? Or a snake?"

"A worm?" Peer's eyes widened in disbelief. "That thing was at least three hundred feet long!"

"Optimist!" Chunklet squeaked.

Kim unhappily stared at the tunnel opening. He sighed. "At least now we know what the dwarves were so afraid of!"

"Very comforting," Peer said, getting back on his feet. He had skinned his hands and knees when he fell, and now he examined the scrapes. He didn't say anything else, instead looking around, studying each person in turn. "Is anyone hurt?" he asked.

No one answered. But a few seconds later, when he asked if they wanted to go on, everyone was silent.

"Hey," he said in a vain attempt to sound encouraging, "I know you're afraid. I feel the same way. But we can't stay here."

"It's all right, Peer," Kim said. "We're tired. Maybe we should sleep a little."

"Here?" Peer shook his head in disgust. "In case you haven't noticed yet, this tunnel is just as slimy as the other one. An avalanche like that could happen here at any time."

"We have to sleep somewhere," Kim said tiredly. "Why not here? Besides," he added, not sounding very convinced, "this thing might be alone. Who says there are more?"

"Well," Peer sighed, frowning, "if there are, then I guess we'll notice, won't we?"

Kim sensed that it was best not to say anything more now. They all were exhausted to the point of irritability, and what they'd been through didn't necessarily help calm them down. Without another word, he turned around, searched in vain for a dry spot where he could stretch out, and lay down on the slimy ground to sleep.

His sleep was as restless as it was brief. Kim woke up when someone pulled on his nose powerfully and persistently. Confused, Kim lifted his hand to shoo away the person bothering him and promptly felt a painful bite on his forefinger. He opened his eyes with a start and found himself looking at a spiny creature crouched on the floor in front of his face, studying him with oozy, bulging eyes.

"What's going on?" Kim murmured, still very groggy.

"Not so loud," Chunklet whispered in a tone of voice that instantly made Kim awake and alert.

Hastily sitting up, he saw that all the others still slept. Even Peer, who offered to keep watch, had nodded off.

"Well?" Kim whispered.

"I've looked around a little," Chunklet replied.

"And?" Kim asked impatiently. "Don't make me pull every word from your ugly snout."

Chunklet's eyes crossed as he looked at his snout and murmured something. Then, he said, "I think I've found a way out."

"What?!" Kim sat up as straight as an arrow.

Startled out of his sleep, Peer sat up and blinked in confusion.

"I'm not sure," Chunklet whispered. "That's why I wanted only you to know. I walked a little way down the passage until I came to a new fork."

"And it leads out?" Kim asked excitedly.

"Not so quick. I said, I *think* it leads to the outside."

"You didn't make sure?" Peer joined in, frowning.

Chunklet shook his head. "No. But there was a fresh breeze, and I think I saw light."

"But you just think so. It's just a guess," Peer grumbled.

"Stop," Kim said. "We'll have to try." He quickly stood up, woke the others, and told them what Chunklet thought he'd discovered. Although there was great uncertainty, they all wanted to head down that corridor immediately.

They hadn't a thing to eat and there was no water, either; so, they left right away. They didn't have to go far: Barely three hundred paces past where they'd turned around the previous evening, another circular tunnel branched off to the right. They had taken a few steps before Kim believed he felt a breath of fresh air on his skin.

The thought that they had found a way out of this underground labyrinth spurred them on. Their steps were more energetic, and even their fear of the horrifying inhabitants of this tunnel system couldn't hold them back.

Before long, Kim saw a brighter area in the unnatural gray that surrounded them. They ran, ignoring additional branch passages. The vaguely brighter area indeed became a circle filled with rays of sunlight.

This sight gave them new strength. Instantly, all their fear and exhaustion was forgotten, and they covered the last stretch running full tilt—Peer and Kim in the lead.

If Peer hadn't grabbed Kim by the arm at the last minute and jerked him back, all would have been in vain. The radiant blue sky arching over the tunnel exit had made Kim forget all caution, and he would have plummeted into the depths before he'd realized it.

The sudden jerk made Kim lose his balance, and he fell flat on his face. Muttering angrily, he picked himself up and was about to yell at Peer, who just pointed ahead with his left hand. The tunnel ended in a vertical rock face that dropped away before ending in a lakeshore strewn with boulders and sharp pinnacles. It was a large, perfectly round lake that covered the floor of a rocky crater. The walls around the crater looked smooth and polished and were riddled with round holes. Kim groaned in disappointment. True, they had found an exit from this underground maze. However, it seemed that wouldn't help them much. The crater was as smooth as polished iron, and they couldn't see any place where they could climb down to the lakeshore below. That wouldn't have helped, anyway, because the cliff fell a good ninety feet down and rose ten times as high over their heads. This wasn't a crater but a giant, vertical shaft, driven down into the rock.

"End of the line," Peer murmured despondently as he looked up.

Instead of answering, Kim cautiously got down on his knees and leaned as far forward as he dared.

He got dizzy when he looked into the chasm, but he forced himself to scan the wall, foot by foot.

Not even a fly could have found a foothold on this cliff.

"Now what?" Peer asked apathetically.

Kim shrugged. "We *have* to get down there some way."

He looked at the lake. The water was a dark blue-black color, which indicated that it was very deep. The distance between the lakeshore and the foot of the wall was a good fifteen feet—maybe a little more. From this height, the distance couldn't be estimated accurately. Kim wasn't sure they could jump that distance. Not to mention the fact that he was a little nervous about jumping into the water from this height.

Kim stood up and turned to the others. "Take off your shirts," he said.

When Peer looked at him inquiringly, he explained: "If we knot them together, that might work as a rope we can climb down."

"That's impossible!" Peer said. "It'll never work!"

"Do you have a better idea?" Kim asked. "Then, do as I say," Kim continued. "We'll both hold the rope and the others will climb down it."

"Even if we don't break our necks in the process," Peer interjected again, "what's the use? We'll never get out of this hole!"

"At least we'll be out of this horrible tunnel," Kim retorted. He gestured at the lake. "Do you see all these holes in the wall? What do you think made them?"

Peer turned pale. Then, he stopped objecting; instead, he pulled his shirt over his head and started twisting. Kim, too, took off all his clothes except for his pants and knotted everything to the others' clothes. It took quite a while to tie everything together, and the result didn't exactly inspire confidence.

Kim and Peer took hold of one end, two strong boys took hold of the other end, and they all pulled. The knots tightened . . . and the rope held. It certainly could hold the weight of a single child. That was obvious.

"All right, let's go!" Kim commanded. "We'll take turns: two hold the rope, a third person climbs down." It took a long time before the first boy was ready to risk the perilous descent; once he'd survived it unscathed, though, the other boys and girls descended into the depths. Finally, the last one arrived on the rocky lakeshore, and only Peer and Kim remained in the tunnel exit.

Peer looked at Kim, at a loss for what to do.

Kim grabbed the rope tightly, spread his legs to try to get a firm footing, and nodded his head. "I think I can hold you if you don't writhe around too much."

Peer shook his head. "How will you get down?"

Kim tried to look as convincing as possible. "Don't worry," he said. "I'm going to jump."

Peer's eyebrows flew up in astonishment. "Jump?" he repeated incredulously. "Down there?"

"Sure," Kim replied. "Unless you happen to have a hammer and a strong hook with you so we can tie off the rope."

"You'll never make it!"

Kim grinned. "Shall I prove it to you right now? How would you get down, then?"

Peer leaned forward, looked down into the depths, and visibly shuddered. "No thanks," he said. He gripped the rope, hesitated once again, and looked at Kim inquiringly. "And you're not just saying that so that I'll climb down?" he asked to be sure.

"No!" Kim assured him, although he didn't feel entirely certain about that. "Now, do it. I don't want to spend the rest of the day here."

Peer wasn't fully convinced, but he did take hold of the rope, cautiously climbed over the edge, and descended using a hand-over-hand technique.

Afterward, Kim couldn't explain how he'd managed to support the other boy's weight all by himself. It felt like his arms were being pulled out of their sockets; after only a minute, Kim already had the feeling that his muscles would give out. He had to summon all his strength to force his way back up the slippery ground. Once, the rope started jerking in his hands so violently that it was a miracle he wasn't pulled over the cliff head first. Somehow, though, he managed to stay upright. Abruptly, the terrible strain ended, and Kim sank to his knees, gasping in exhaustion, his eyes closed. For a good while, he sat there, gasping for breath and waiting for the pain in his shoulders and wrists to subside.

His knees shook when he stood up and looked down at the others.

The group had formed a semicircle under the cave exit, and now they peered up at him. Kim heard Peer yell something, but he couldn't understand the words. Shuddering, he let his gaze wander over the lake. He felt terribly afraid.

He had no other choice, unless he wanted to return to the dwarves' caves for eternal slave labor—assuming the slimy monster didn't flatten him first.

With a resolute sigh, he stepped back, ran, and pushed off as hard as he could.

For endless, terrifying seconds, he was afraid he'd splatter on the lakeshore. Then, he heard many voices crying out beneath him.

He opened his eyes. His leap had carried him out past the stony shore in a perfect arc, and there was nothing beneath him but the dark-blue water of the lake, toward which he now dove.

His freefall lasted only a second or two—but in that time, Kim died a thousand deaths. Half a heartbeat before he hit the surface, he started to scream in fear. Then, he plopped into the water. He felt as if an invisible giant were pummeling him through a thick pane of glass. He plunged down through the water like a stone. Instinctively, he opened his mouth to scream and saw silvery bubbles of precious air rise up in front of his face.

He paddled with all his might—but kept plunging ever deeper. The surface of the lake was a reflective, silvery sky, immeasurably far above him. The force of the fall still pulled at him, yard after yard, until the pressure became unbearable. Finally, with desperate paddling and kicking, he managed to start back up.

His need for air caused him to panic. It felt like an iron ring clamped down on his chest. Although he rapidly approached the surface, Kim's strength was waning. In another second, he would try to breathe even if it meant he'd drown.

Then, he saw the shadow: It was an outline—a gliding impression in the dark blue. But something large created a pulsing wave, which made Kim whirl around like a top. That wave shot him upward, saving his life.

Gasping, Kim broke through the surface of the water and sucked air into his lungs. When he splashed back down and swallowed water, he coughed painfully. Hastily, he worked his way back up to the surface and gasped for breath, trying to get his wildly flailing limbs back under control. Then, he swam for the shore.

The shadow! He knew it had been there. It was gargantuan!

"Watch out!" he cried as he made for the shore with desperate strokes. "Save yourselves! There's something in the water!"

He didn't even know if Peer and the others understood him. Where were they supposed to run? There was just this lake and the fifteen-foot-wide strip of rock debris surrounding it.

Suddenly, the surface of the water churned, tossing Kim up and down. All at once, Peer and the others screamed in terror and ran every which way. For a fraction of a second, Kim saw an enormous shadow rise from the depths of the lake. Then, the whole lake exploded in a huge, frothy wave. It flung Kim into the air like a withered leaf. When he slammed back down into the water, boiling foam broke over him, and a monstrous roar blasted his ears, shaking the rocky cauldron. Gasping and spitting, he tried to swim away but immediately was pushed back underwater as a second large wave crashed over him.

A gigantic, shiny black monster raged behind him—and just as the previous day in the tunnel, Kim thought he felt the piercing gaze of two glowing red eyes.

With the last bit of strength he had, Kim worked his way to the shore. The previous wave had crashed against the cliff and had knocked everyone off their feet. Some children scrambled back up and now stood as if paralyzed, staring at a point on the lake behind Kim.

Utterly exhausted, Kim didn't turn around. He was only a couple of strokes from the shore, but he wasn't sure he'd make it.

Kim had an idea what was behind him. *I've been a fool,* he thought bitterly. *Why did I assume that the monster stayed in the mountain's interior?* The countless holes in the cliff should've been evidence enough. At least if they'd stayed inside the tunnels, the children could have hidden from the beast. Here, they were defenseless.

Exhausted, Kim reached the shore, crawled on his hands and knees for a short way on the rocky beach, and turned around.

His heart stopped when he saw what had emerged from the lake: giant, black, and as shiny as wet leather—a beast of unimaginable strength and malice. This wasn't the creature that had rolled through the labyrinth: It was the Tatzelwurm!

Spellbound, Kim stared at a head as big as a taxi. It towered over him as high as a church steeple. The Tatzelwurm—the biggest and most dangerous beast in Magic Moon. His glowing red eyes stared at Kim, full of unbridled hatred; spittle and foam dripped from his teeth.

Kim understood why the monster was no longer in his ancient realm: The dwarves had brought him to this eerie place in the heart of their empire—and that wasn't all. Around the creature's shiny black neck hung a ring of black iron, a good three feet wide, which attached to a chain of dwarven steel as thick as a man's arm.

The Tatzelwurm was a prisoner, just like them.

Still lying on his back, Kim inched farther up the shore, never once taking his eyes off the monster. The beast stared at him like it wanted to burn Kim's soul to a crisp.

This wasn't the first time that Kim had come face to face with that monster. Recognition flashed in the Tatzelwurm's giant eyes, as well—followed by a blazing, unquenchable hatred. With an enormous roar, the Tatzelwurm reared up; unfolded a pair of gigantic, leathery bat wings; and lifted off the surface of the water. His open mouth moved in Kim's direction.

Kim thought his time had come—when the chain suddenly tautened, and the Tatzelwurm jerked back into the water with an enormous splash. The subsequent wave tossed Kim a little farther onto the shore—thus, out of reach. The other children were knocked off their feet for a second time. Gasping, Kim sat up again, got up on his hands and knees, and wiped the water out of his eyes.

The Tatzelwurm thrashed and flailed. His wings whipped the water. His long, scaly tail struck the other side of the cliff like a crashing thunderclap. But the Tatzelwurm was powerless against the chain of dwarven steel.

The dragon raged on in this manner for quite some time, until he realized the futility of his efforts. Or perhaps, he merely became exhausted or disheartened. His eyes still blazed with hatred; his head bobbed back and forth, searching the shore with rapid, snakelike movements.

"You!" he thundered, causing the ground to shake. "You, over there! I have you to thank for all this!"

Peer and some of the other boys looked at Kim, who shrugged. He didn't know what the Tatzelwurm meant. Nevertheless, he stood up, took a few steps toward the lake, and then stopped a healthy distance away from the water, taking care that he didn't come within the chain's radius.

The Tatzelwurm reared up again when he saw Kim head toward him, straining against his chain with all the force he could muster. The ground shook, and chunks of stone broke away from the cliff, falling to the ground with a rumble. But the chain held fast and, after a few moments, he gave up again.

Kim studied the giant, shuddering. The monster was at least three times as large as Rangarig and filled with a kind of malevolence that compelled him to destroy everything that lived, moved, or breathed free. And yet . . . there was something else—something that hadn't been in this monster's gaze the first time they'd met.

Kim furrowed his brow in thought. *Is it possible?* he wondered. *Could that eerie transformation happening to everyone in Magic Moon also affect the Tatzelwurm?* Good and evil were differentiated more clearly in Magic Moon than where Kim came from. Here, good was simply good, and nothing else. Evil was simply evil—no ifs, ands or buts, without any gradations. *Yet, Kelhim, Rangarig, and Gorg had felt hatred and murderous feelings,* Kim thought, mulling it over. *Is it possible that this huge creature suddenly is capable of other feelings besides evil ones?*

For a long time, Kim stood on the bank, staring in silence at the Tatzelwurm—torn between wild fear and desperate hope. Finally, he took one step, which he knew brought him within reach of the beast's horrible fangs. The Tatzelwurm knew this, too, because he cocked his head to the side and speculatively looked at Kim. However, he didn't move. Perhaps he sensed a trap, or maybe he just wanted to wait until his victim was too close to flee.

"So, you know me," Kim said, addressing him.

The Tatzelwurm emitted a deep, vibrating rumble, whipping the water with his wings. "I hate you!" he hissed, looking like an enlarged snake.

"Why?" Kim asked.

The monster's gigantic eyes flashed in anger. "Everything was fine before you came!" he rumbled. "You and your damned golden dragon! After you, the black knights came. You defeated me!" the Tatzelwurm bellowed, rearing up again. "Then, all the others came. It never stopped. I had to fight—again and again and again. In the end, I grew old and tired."

"I . . . I'm sorry," Kim said truthfully. As evil as this creature was, it still had its place in creation. Kim actually felt guilty about the creature's fate, although he knew he'd had no other choice back then.

"You're *sorry?!*" the Tatzelwurm roared, pulling on his chain again. "Look at me! They put me in chains! Me, who never met his equal!"

"We're prisoners, too," Kim said simply.

The Tatzelwurm stopped raging and eyed Kim mistrustfully, looking slightly confused. "I don't see any chains!" he bellowed finally. "You're lying!"

Kim pulled his right pant leg up so that the dragon could see the iron ring on his ankle. "We sprang our chains," he said. "You can, too, if you really want to."

The surface of the lake instantly grew still. The Tatzelwurm stared at Kim. Then, with gliding, snakelike movements, he slowly drew nearer until his gigantic head was so close that Kim could touch him.

Kim almost died of fright, and everything within him screamed to run away. But he held up under the appraising red eyes, even though it felt like he was being vivisected. No secrets, lies, or thoughts of betrayal could be concealed from the Tatzelwurm's penetrating gaze.

"If you succeeded in springing these chains, then you must be stronger than I am," he said finally. "My strength wasn't enough."

Kim was about to answer when a little red-and-orange striped fluffball scurried up next to him. Chunklet squeaked as impudently as ever, "Hey, you there! Maybe you should flex your big muscles a little less and use that tiny brain of yours some more. Then, you'd be free for sure."

The Tatzelwurm blinked.

Kim wasn't sure whether the monster could see Chunklet; in his daylight form, Chunklet was no larger than the goop stuck in the corners of the dragon's eyes.

The Tatzelwurm rumbled: "Who is this pipsqueak?"

Chunklet replied with an insulting, impolite noise that caused the gigantic dragon's gaze to darken ominously.

"Don't take Chunklet seriously," Kim said hastily. "My friend doesn't mean it that way."

"Oh, I *do* mean it that way!" Chunklet protested.

Kim simply ignored him and tactfully continued with the Tatzelwurm. "We didn't force open these chains. No power in the world can spring them—they were forged by dwarves. But we—"

At that point, Kim fell silent. He stared at the Tatzelwurm with his mouth agape, and then his hand very slowly drifted down to his belt and closed around the iron key beneath it. Back in the ore chamber, he'd stuck the key in there and forgot about it.

"Yes?" rumbled the Tatzelwurm.

Kim was about to answer when someone shouted a warning. Kim looked up, tilting his head all the way back; he saw dozens of tiny figures in fluttering black capes lined up along the rim of the crater.

"Get out of there, dimwit!" Jarrn yelled down at him. "Or do you want to become dragon food?"

The Tatzelwurm's head jerked up, too. When he recognized the dwarf, his eyes blazed in anger, and he gave a terrible roar as he tried to devour his tormentor. Halfway there, the chain jerked him back, and once again the lake exploded in foam and boiling water. Kim and the others beat a hasty retreat from the lakeshore. Even so, the wave drenched them to the bones.

"You!" bellowed the Tatzelwurm. "Come down so I can rip you apart!"

Jarrn made a face and stuck his fingers in his ears until the roaring had dissipated. Then, he put his hands down, shook his head, and said calmly, "I wouldn't think of it, wormlet. If you want to eat someone, take the ones down there." Addressing Kim and the others, he smoothly continued: "You don't deserve it, but we'll get you out of here. Watch out down below."

Two of his dwarf companions threw down a rope ladder, which clattered against the wall as it unrolled. "Climb up!" Jarrn yelled. "Before he eats you alive."

Some of the boys actually did head toward the ladder, but the majority of the children didn't move.

Kim's gaze thoughtfully passed over the giant figure of the Tatzelwurm. The dragon appraised him coldly, and Kim couldn't interpret the expression in his fiery red eyes. Kim's hand closed around the key and pulled it out.

Jarrn screeched when he saw what Kim held in his fingers. "Are you mad?!" he yelled at the top of his lungs. "He'll kill you all—and us, too!"

Kim took another step toward the water. The Tatzelwurm cocked his head to the side and almost beseechingly looked at Kim. The blazing fire remained in his eyes, and Kim didn't forget for a second what a terrible monster he faced.

"Don't!" Jarrn howled. "He'll kill you all! It's a miracle you escaped his cousin, the Steinwurm. Do you want to test your luck?"

"If I free you," Kim said to the Tatzelwurm, "will you give me your word not to harm us?"

The Tatzelwurm was silent.

Kim hesitated for a moment. He took another step, raised his right hand with the key in it, and pointed with his other hand at the dwarves on the rim of the crater. "And you won't harm them, either? I'll open your chains, but you can't spill any blood."

"I'm supposed to spare their lives?" rumbled the Tatzelwurm. "They put me in chains and locked me in this forsaken place."

"And I will free you," Kim said earnestly. "At the price of their lives."

No one breathed. Even the Tatzelwurm was so confounded that he didn't answer immediately. Eventually, he moved very close and lowered his heavy head.

"They're your enemies, just as they are mine," he growled. "Why are you asking for their lives?"

"Because life is sacred," Kim replied. "And no one has the right to destroy it, no matter what the reason." He was silent for a moment, considering every word very carefully; he sensed that the fate of all Magic Moon might depend on what he said. "You're big, Tatzelwurm," he proclaimed. "You're the biggest and strongest creature I've ever seen. You have your powers in order to serve evil. Please, make an exception this one time: Help us."

"You?" The Tatzelwurm made a noise that sounded like a laugh. "You've lost your mind, pipsqueak! You all are my enemies!"

"No, we aren't," Kim replied. "Take us out of here, Tatzelwurm, and help us fight the true enemies of your world. Maybe then, everything will go back to how it was. You will live the way you used to—proud, fierce, and unchained."

After a while, Kim interpreted the Tatzelwurm's silence as consent.

Up above, on the cliff, Jarrn screeched as if he'd been impaled. "You madman!" he yelled. "What are you doing?"

Kim didn't listen to the dwarf. Instead, he walked into the water until the lake came up to his hips and he stood beside the Tatzelwurm's black neck. Slowly, Kim lifted his hand and stuck the key into the tiny padlock that bound the ring to its chain. Once more, he hesitated. One thousand reasons why it would be better for him to turn around shot through his head. However, he pulled himself together and snapped open the lock.

The Tatzelwurm reared up with a tremendous roar; spread out his wings, causing the foaming lake water to shoot upward again; and disappeared into the sky with a single, powerful thrust of his wings.

A surging wave hurled Kim and the others to the ground; by this time, they were used to it. When Kim stood up again, he saw the dwarves fleeing in total panic. Only Jarrn stood still, looking up in horror at the Tatzelwurm, who was now a tiny dot in the sky.

The Tatzelwurm didn't fly away, though. For a moment, he disappeared fully from their view—then, he returned, circling over the lake like a giant eagle. Suddenly, he spread out his leather wings to stop his descent.

Kim looked out at the lake, his heart pounding. For the very first time, he saw how absolutely enormous the dragon's body was. Unlike Rangarig, this dragon's body resembled a snake or a giant worm as he glided through the water toward the shore. He was so big that Kim wondered how he fit in Crater Lake.

The monster's foaming mouth gaped wide open; hatred still blazed in his eyes. Kim and the others retreated until their backs pressed against the smooth rock wall. For a few moments, Kim was convinced that Jarrn had been right, and Tatzelwurm was going to kill them.

The monster's head and neck grated along the gravel shore. His gaze fixed on Kim, and Kim thought it was like looking into hell. An inextinguishable rage burned in those glowing eyes—a rage directed at everything that existed. This creature had been created as the embodiment of hatred and destruction. And yet—Kim sensed something else inside the creature's heart. When the Tatzelwurm opened his mouth again, he didn't devour them.

"Everything will return to how it was?" he rumbled.

"I can't promise you that," Kim replied, "but we can try. Together, we might succeed."

The Tatzelwurm looked at him for a very long time, and Kim felt the silent struggle raging inside that huge head.

The Tatzelwurm growled, "All right, little hero. Let's try it."

Kim breathed a sigh of relief.

But a second later, he was convinced that he'd made a mistake, because the Tatzelwurm spread his wings and flew up to the crater's upper rim with a single powerful thrust. His wide, outstretched claws aimed at the Dwarf King, who stood paralyzed for a second before fleeing with a shrill scream.

"No!" Kim screamed in despair. "You can't do that!"

Screeching, Jarrn dodged to the side, trying to evade the dragon's outstretched claws, but he wasn't fast enough. The giant talons closed around him, enveloping his entire body.

Jarrn's horrified scream ceased as the Tatzelwurm powerfully beat his giant batlike wings, made a quarter turn over the crater, and then descended toward the lake in slow, tight spirals.

Thirty feet above the water, his forepaws opened; a howling black bundle fell into the water and disappeared with a splash.

Jarrn didn't seem to be injured. At least, he complained at the top of his lungs the second he bobbed back to water's surface. The Tatzelwurm flew in a circle a short distance above him, and the storm wind generated by his wings pushed the dwarf back underwater. However, it also drove him closer to the shore.

Kim started to run up to the king, but Jarrn had reached the shore on his own and now glared so angrily that Kim stopped in his tracks. Then, a panicked look appeared in Jarrn's eyes—for the Tatzelwurm had landed barely a body's length away from him, and the dragon looked ready to devour Jarrn for good.

"No!" Kim desperately screamed once again. "Don't do it!"

A miracle occurred. The Tatzelwurm's giant jaws gaped like a barn door with teeth, but he didn't snap his mouth shut.

Seconds went by; no one dared to breathe. Very, very slowly, the Tatzelwurm's huge head rose up again. Jarrn stumbled backward and plopped flat on his behind.

Ten minutes later, the dwarf and the children all climbed upon the shiny, black, serpentine body of the dragon, so he could carry them to freedom.

XXII

Despite his enormous strength, the Tatzelwurm couldn't carry the weight of so many passengers for more than two or three hours at a time. As a result, their westward flight was broken up into small stages. Each rest stop lasted longer than the previous one. All the while, feverish impatience plagued the children. No one knew how much time had passed while they'd been working inside the dwarves' caves, and no one had any idea what had happened beyond the Shadowy Mountains. The children wondered how their families were—whether they were free or still alive. However, Kim didn't dare push the Tatzelwurm faster.

Even after three days, Kim still didn't understand how he'd managed to get this giant, ill-tempered creature to help them. There was no sense in talking to the Tatzelwurm. The fact that he was helping them didn't mean that he suddenly was their friend—not by a long shot. He still was an evil dragon—so moody and unpredictable that everyone kept a healthy distance from him whenever they rested. Kim talked to him only when it was absolutely necessary. The closer they got to the mountains, the conversations between Kim and Peer grew briefer, as well; eventually, they stopped talking altogether. The fear of finding the land beyond the sky-high peaks of the Shadowy Mountains devastated by war darkened their mood like a storm cloud. Months might have passed—maybe even years. Maybe, it was too late to save anything.

Jarrn, whom they simply had taken along with them, was the only passenger in a good mood—in a manner of speaking. During the first few days of their journey, he'd hardly said a word, glaring at everyone silently. But after he got over his initial fright, he went back to his usual insolent, contentious manner. Whenever Kim tried to talk with him, he either said nothing or spewed out a selection of rude remarks, insults, and nasty comments.

This behavior didn't anger Kim. Despite everything, there was something about Jarrn's impudent, disrespectful nature that made it hard for Kim to resent the little man. Jarrn's comments did worry Kim, though—more than he was willing to admit to the others. Jarrn might be a loudmouth—or, to use one of the dwarf's favorite words, a dimwit—but he was no fool. There had to be a reason why he was chipper, despite being a captive en route to his greatest adversary.

Kim had a feeling that he wouldn't like this reason.

On the fourth day of their journey, they reached the Shadowy Mountains. There was enough daylight left for three or more hours of flight, but the Tatzelwurm started descending, regardless. He looked for a place to rest for the night, and Kim didn't try to dissuade him. The Shadowy Mountains were too high to fly over. No one knew how high they really were; many said the ice-encrusted peaks went all the way up to space. If the Tatzelwurm was to succeed in flying over those mountains, he needed every ounce of strength he possessed.

No one slept very well that night. Kim tossed and turned, waking suddenly when he felt someone staring at him.

He wasn't mistaken. A small figure in a dirty black cape sat cross-legged beside him, staring down at his face. They'd shackled Jarrn with a dwarf chain and fastened the other end to the Tatzelwurm's neck ring, so the dwarf could move about but had no way to escape. Kim thus far had been very careful to stay out of the king's reach whenever it was time to sleep.

On this particular evening, however, he hadn't taken such precaution. Realizing with horror how easy it would have been for Jarrn to get free, he immediately lowered his hand to his belt.

The key still was there.

"Never fear, blockhead," Jarrn said. "If I had wanted to escape, I wouldn't be here still—and you definitely wouldn't have woken up."

"I can believe that," Kim grumbled, sitting up halfway. "When it comes to stealing and cheating, you dwarves get the prize."

Jarrn looked taken aback. "Who says that?" he asked. "We don't cheat anyone, and we don't steal, either. We're just businessmen."

"Yes," Kim replied, "but I don't care for the kind of business you do."

His words came out less kindly than he'd intended, and he realized that his rudeness was a result of his own embarrassment. He had been unjust to Jarrn.

It was strange. The better he got to know Jarrn, the harder it was for him to get mad at the dwarf. They were on different sides, true, but the dwarf wasn't a cheater. Even so, it did seem as if the little man knew more than he said. That made Kim furious, because it was like Jarrn secretly was laughing at him.

"Let me sleep," Kim growled. "We have a hard day ahead of us tomorrow." With that, he turned over and went back to his restless slumber.

Unlike the previous days, no one was eager to get going the next morning. They all were very quiet, and their faces clearly reflected their fear. When Kim once again asked who wanted to continue along, no one answered. Eventually, they all climbed upon the Tatzelwurm's back, and the dragon commenced his ascent.

The gray of dawn was beneath them; they emerged into sunshine that hadn't reached the land below yet—but instead of getting warmer, it became cold at first . . . and then, bitterly cold . . . and then, freezing. Kim's skin had goose bumps from the chill, and his breath froze into gray steam.

The Tatzelwurm continued his upward spiral over the Shadowy Mountains; meanwhile, his shivering passengers banded together for warmth. It didn't help much. An icy wind cut through their clothes like a knife. The air was frosty, and glittering ice covered the entire mountain chain like suffocating armor.

The Tatzelwurm circled higher and higher. The initial mountain peaks were behind them—but higher, blacker mountains remained. The icy air burned Kim's throat, and he hardly could move his hands.

Farther and farther up they continued. Kim saw a glacier that's peak was lost somewhere up in the dark-blue sky. The wind now cut through them. It made Kim's eyes tear, and the teardrops froze on his cheeks. A thin, crackling sheet of ice formed on the Tatzelwurm's coarse hide.

The flying dragon's movements gradually lost vigor and grace. He still climbed—but not as quickly and effortlessly. Meanwhile, more mountains stretched ahead of them. Beyond each peak was another glacier, and Kim wondered whether they were lost. The air grew thinner, making it hard for them to breathe.

Finally, the inevitable happened: The Tatzelwurm began to lose altitude. He beat his wings, exerting his enormous muscles as powerfully as he could, but nothing helped. The thin air couldn't carry his body anymore; the weight of his passengers and the ice building up on his skin was simply too much for him.

Kim felt a surge of fear when he looked down past the dragon's wings and saw sharp rocks and ice-encrusted ridges. There was no safe patch of land to give the Tatzelwurm a rest. Suddenly, Jarrn leaned forward and cried, "Go left! See the mountain with the cleft in the peak? Fly to the left of it!"

Although the howling wind and whooshing dragon wings almost drowned out Jarrn's voice, the Tatzelwurm understood, changing course as directed. He lurched. Kim acutely sensed how hard it was for the Tatzelwurm to maintain altitude. Time and again, he had to work his way back up with slow strokes of his wings. Sometimes, they came so close to mountain peaks that Kim expected one of the razor-sharp ridges to slice open the dragon's belly, plunging them all to their deaths.

Somehow, they made it. The Tatzelwurm groaned at every stroke of his wings, as if the movement cost him unparalleled effort; the children struggled to suppress a whimper from the pain and cold. The tips of their fingers and toes felt dead, and the icy cold gradually crept into their bodies, freezing their insides. As they glided past the mountain that Jarrn had pointed out, they came so close that the giant dragon's outspread wings almost touched the cliffs.

Jarrn pointed to the left, screaming at the top of his lungs; again, the Tatzelwurm followed his commands.

The dragon turned left, barely missing a razor-sharp ice ridge as he dipped down into a gorge. Quite suddenly, it was over: The mountains grew farther apart, and the panorama of a broad, sunlit land replaced the icy, rocky terrain.

Kim shuddered when he saw how high they were flying. It was impossible to tell the forests from the meadows. The rivers looked like thin, silvery hairs, glittering in the sun.

Suddenly, he felt the Tatzelwurm's strength give out. The giant creature groaned and tipped sideways, causing them all to grab hold of one another as they slid over. At the last possible moment, the dragon recovered his balance and started to dive. The wind howled, practically sweeping the children off the Tatzelwurm's back. The land rushed toward them.

Before long, they could make out towns, villages, farms, roads, and streets. Then, the Tatzelwurm flew so close to the ground that his wings lopped off several treetops. He smacked down with terrific force, bounced back into the air like a stone skipping over water, and then crashed to the ground a second time. His enormous body plowed a deep furrow in the ground, and his outstretched wings ripped up bushes and trees before he finally jolted to a stop.

The impact flung the children in a high arc, and they landed in the grass.

Hours later, they still were miserably cold. Kim gradually felt all the scratches and bruises and bumps that he got thanks to the crash. It was a miracle that no one was seriously hurt—not even Jarrn, who remained tied to the dragon. The chain had brought Jarrn's fall to a sudden, rough stop, however.

Kim was concerned only about the Tatzelwurm. True, the dragon was alive—his chest moved with labored, heavy breath. Sometimes, he opened his eyes and looked about vacantly, but he didn't react when Kim talked to him.

Although the sun shone down from the sky, they gathered wood and dry foliage for a warm fire. Kim worried about the younger children getting frostbite.

Kim felt as if he'd frozen into a block of ice. He held his hands so close to the fire that the hot flames almost touched his fingers. Chunklet slipped in next to the glowing embers, shivering. Jarrn wrapped his arms around his chest, and his teeth chattered.

After a while, the dwarf pulled his hand out from under his cloak and grasped the chain on his foot. They'd released the chain from the Tatzelwurm's neck and fastened it around a tree trunk so the dwarf could sit by the fire but not run away.

"When are you going to unlock this thing?" he asked. "I helped you. You're on the other side of the mountains, aren't you?"

"So?" Kim asked.

"So? So!" the dwarf repeated. "Why don't you set me free, then? Didn't I show you the way?"

"Yes, sure," Kim replied. "But only to save your own life—right?"

Jarrn gave him a furious look.

Kim didn't want to release the dwarf. Jarrn had been a little too happy the night before. No—the dwarf knew something, and Kim wasn't going to release him until he found out his secret.

"You're planning to take me to those grass-eaters."

"Yes," Kim replied without looking at the dwarf.

"They'll kill me," Jarrn said gloomily.

"No, they won't," Kim countered. "I give you my word that no Steppe rider will touch a single hair on your head—"

"Someone's coming," Peer interrupted, pointing. Kim looked over the crackling flames of the fire and saw two tiny dots along the ridge of a hill.

Riders.

The two faraway figures stood on the ridge for quite some time. A blazing campfire on a warm summer day was astonishing enough, but the sight of the Tatzelwurm lying motionless in the grass would have given anyone pause. Eventually, the two figures approached the fire.

Kim, Peer, and a few other boys walked toward them, shivering.

They saw a man and a woman dressed in coarse, heavy leather and metal. Each was armed with a longsword and a bow, and each wore a quiver filled with arrows on their backs. Obviously, they were warriors.

The man rode off to the side so that he could keep an eye on the children by the fire—and the Tatzelwurm, too, of course. The woman steered her horse close to Kim and Peer, silently staring down at them from her saddle.

"Who are you?" Her voice didn't sound very friendly.

Kim introduced himself and Peer before pointing at his companions, who stood around the fire, their teeth chattering. "These are our friends," he said. "We—"

He hesitated. He didn't know anything about these strangers. There were only two of them, but they were both armed and didn't seem inhibited about using their weapons. They hadn't said who they were, either. "We also have a dwarf with us," he said, carefully choosing his words.

The woman's face darkened, and her hand quickly moved to grip the hilt of her sword.

"A dwarf?" she asked sharply. "What kind of business do you have with those vermin?"

"Nothing," Kim quickly assured her. "We all escaped from their mines. We had to take this one along with us."

The woman's hand let go of the sword hilt. "Escaped?" she asked skeptically. "You're trying to pull my leg, boy. No one has ever succeeded in doing that."

"Ask the dwarf if you don't believe us," Peer said irritably.

"We wouldn't have made it, either," Kim added quickly, "if the Tatzelwurm hadn't helped us."

He pointed at the motionless dragon while keeping an alert eye on the woman. Her gaze passed over the giant dragon. Kim feverishly considered who she might be and whether she was an enemy. It made him sick to have to think in those terms. *What has happened to this land, that people have to be so careful about what they say to strangers?*

"The Tatzelwurm?" murmured the woman. "Is that him?" Swinging out of the saddle, the woman said, "I've heard about him. But they said he was dead. The word was that the iron men killed him."

"They just took him away," Kim explained. "He was imprisoned, but we were able to free him."

This didn't remove the doubt on the woman's face. "You?" She gave the half-starved children a contemptuous look. "You're saying you managed to do what even we couldn't?"

"We were lucky."

After dismounting from his horse, the man approached in silence, a stern, distrustful look on his face. Kim worried that their landing spot might spell their doom.

The woman intently studied the faces of the boys and girls. Meanwhile, the man stared at the dwarf, his gaze full of hostility, before he abruptly turned toward the Tatzelwurm. He kept a good distance away, but he showed no fear—merely caution, despite the fact that the creature was big enough to kill him simply by accidentally moving the wrong way.

"All right, boy," the woman said after the warrior returned to her side. "Tell your story."

Kim told it, carefully observing their reactions. He explained about his capture, the time in the dwarves' forge, and their great escape. The strangers listened without interrupting. When he told about their flight over the Shadowy Mountains, however, the woman frowned skeptically. After Kim finished, she was silent for a while. Then, she said, "And now you're heading west, to join Priwinn's army?"

"I don't know anything about an army," Kim said cautiously. "We just heard that he's on his way to Gorywynn."

"You might say so," said the woman, who still hadn't revealed her name. "King Priwinn and his Steppe riders have been victorious almost everywhere. The dwarves have retreated to Gorywynn, and it will be hard work to get them out of there, especially because the Riverfolk and a lot of other rabble raised an army that marches on Gorywynn."

Kim looked at her in shock, and the woman nodded somberly. "A huge army. My companion and I, by the way, are also on our way west to join Priwinn's forces."

The warriors exchanged a look. "You can come with us," she said. "I wouldn't advise you to keep traveling on this . . . thing. If the story you told is true, then maybe he did help you this far. But you shouldn't press your luck. It would be better to take off while he is exhausted. When he wakes up, he could kill you."

"That's the first sensible thing I've heard today," Jarrn said, volunteering his opinion, but then immediately fell silent again when he noticed the icy look the woman gave him.

"You're wrong, my lady," Kim said firmly.

"Listen, boy!" the woman urged him. "That thing is a monster. It thinks and acts differently than you might expect. Be sensible and heed me."

Kim pondered the woman's words—not because he thought she might be right. Kim knew he wasn't mistaken about the Tatzelwurm. As evil and angry as the Tatzelwurm was, the dragon would never lie. He didn't even know what the word "lie" meant—violence, certainly, but lies and deceit were foreign to him. In any case, a creature like the Tatzelwurm had no need to lie to anyone.

"We have to get to Gorywynn by the fastest route," Kim said finally. "And we have to hurry. Maybe we can still keep the worst from happening."

"What?" the woman asked derisively.

"The big battle that you were talking about," Kim explained. "It can't come to that."

The woman laughed softly. "How does a boy like you intend to prevent something like that?"

"I don't know," Kim replied honestly. "I also don't know if I'll succeed, but I have to try." He gave the woman and her companion a thoughtful look. "Maybe you could take the other children." He indicated the boys and girls gathered by the fire. "We'll be faster if only three of us fly on the Tatzelwurm."

"You're really planning to go to Gorywynn with this monster?" the woman asked in astonishment. Then, she shrugged her shoulders. "Whatever you say. We were heading for the nearest town to replenish our supplies. We'd be happy to take the others along. We'll find someone there who can make sure that they all get back to their parents," she promised.

Kim and Peer said goodbye to their companions. Chunklet stayed with Kim—and, of course, Jarrn had no choice but to come along.

It took the Tatzelwurm the rest of the day and night to recover from his previous exertion; they didn't continue their westward flight until the sun rose the following morning. Despite his furious protests, Jarrn once again was chained to the ring around the dragon's neck. Kim now had another reason for taking the dwarf along with them: Neither the woman nor her silent escort had said anything about Jarrn, but Kim was well aware of the hostile, appraising looks they'd given the dwarf. He wasn't sure that they'd let Jarrn live, even if he were a prisoner under their protection.

The travelers no longer flew as high or as fast as they had over the Shadowy Mountains, but they still made great speed. The Tatzelwurm had recovered now and rarely stopped to catch his breath. They rested at night. No one approached the monster anymore. Instead, every living being in a wide circumference fled wherever the Tatzelwurm appeared. After two days, they were halfway to Gorywynn, and Kim hoped they would arrive in time to—

Well, to do what, actually?

He didn't like to admit this to himself, but he had no idea what to do. Of course, he would see Priwinn and the others. But how was he going to prevent this catastrophic war? How could he keep Magic Moon from drowning in a sea of blood and tears? He had come to help, but everything had gotten worse. He'd traveled from one end of Magic Moon to the other, and it hadn't done any good. He hadn't come one step closer to solving the mystery of the missing children.

On the third day of their journey, the Tatzelwurm became restless. He fidgeted, and his powerful head continually twitched left and right, searching for something. Kim asked him several times what he was looking for but got no answer.

By noon, they flew over a burning farmstead. The Tatzelwurm soared so high in the sky that Kim saw only a tiny glowing spot on the ground. However, they noticed the smoke, and Kim ordered the Tatzelwurm to turn around. He had to repeat himself three times, but the Tatzelwurm finally complied, reluctantly descending in slow spirals.

Kim attentively studied the scene below. The dragon's shadow passed over the burning farmhouse three times, and Kim saw a number of people duck down in fear, running off in sheer panic when they realized where the dragon would land.

Only a gray-haired man and a slender boy about Kim's age held their ground as the travelers landed. Paralyzed by fear, they stood there as Kim told the Tatzelwurm to wait one hundred yards away from the burning barn. He ran the rest of the way on foot.

The man and the boy looked at him blankly. The boy's left hand was badly burned, and some of his hair also was singed, but he didn't seem to feel the pain. His face was pale, and his lips trembled. The older man was probably his father, Kim guessed.

Dispensing with long explanations, Kim bluntly asked, "What happened?"

"Who are you?" the man promptly asked back.

Kim made an impatient gesture with his hand. "That doesn't matter at the moment. You don't need to be afraid of me. What's going on here? Did the iron men do this?"

He saw the boy recoil. The man replied, "No. It was . . ." He hesitated, glancing anxiously at the Tatzelwurm, and then he continued, ". . . a dragon."

"A dragon?" Kim repeated, shocked.

The man nodded a couple of times. "Yes, a dragon," he confirmed. "It wasn't as large as the one you're riding. Nor was it black, but—"

"But a golden color?" Kim excitedly interrupted.

"Yes." The fear in the man's face gradually gave way to dull, deep despair. "How did you know that?"

"I didn't know it," Kim whispered, horrified.

Rangarig! The news was like a slap in the face. Rangarig had caused this horrible devastation—no doubt about it. There was only one golden dragon in Magic Moon.

"What happened before that?" he asked softly. "What did you do to anger him so much?"

"What did we do?" Suddenly, the farmer started laughing hysterically, as if he were on the verge of madness. "What did we do? How did you get that idea? We didn't do a thing. He . . . just came and attacked us. Almost all my cattle have burned to death, and it's a miracle that none of us were killed. He's been ravaging these parts for a long time; until now, we'd always been spared."

Kim said nothing consoling or encouraging; instead, he turned around without saying a word and went back to Peer and the Tatzelwurm.

"What's going on?" Peer asked impatiently when Kim climbed up on the Tatzelwurm's back. The other boy's voice sounded concerned; he'd seen the shaken look on Kim's face.

"Rangarig," Kim murmured.

Peer frowned. During their captivity, Kim had told him all about the golden dragon—the adventures that they'd been through together and also how Rangarig had saved his life more than once.

"The . . . the golden dragon?" he asked incredulously.

Kim nodded.

Peer wanted to say something, but the Tatzelwurm's body quivered. He curved around his snakelike neck so he could see his passengers.

His red eyes blazed. "Rangarig?!" he thundered. "He's here?"

Kim felt a surge of fear. Suddenly, he saw the Tatzelwurm's restlessness in a completely different light. He understood the terrible danger they were in now. What a frightening prospect: By chance, Rangarig the golden dragon, the scourge of the countryside, had met up with his old archenemy, the Tatzelwurm. Perhaps, it wasn't chance after all. Perhaps, like two forces of nature irresistibly attracted to each other, these two different but similar beings had to find each other to cancel each other out.

"He's no longer what he once was," Kim said hastily. "No more than you are."

"He's my enemy. That's enough." The Tatzelwurm didn't speak loudly, and there was no anger in his voice—nothing threatening. It was precisely this cold objectivity that frightened Kim to the core.

"Nonsense!" Chunklet squeaked. Moving quickly, he scrabbled out from Kim's shirt and onto his shoulder. "You're talking nonsense, old friend," he continued. "Fine, he's your enemy. So? You can kill each other. That's all you can do, though."

"If it's destined to be, then so be it," gravely replied the Tatzelwurm.

"Oh, yes. That's typical for a blockhead like you. Muscles like a mountain, but a brain as big as a walnut. You two are going to bash in each other's skulls, but you don't care about anything else that happens. Everything else can go to the dogs."

Kim held his breath when he heard the way Chunklet spoke to the Tatzelwurm. Amazingly, the dragon didn't get angry. Instead, he thoughtfully regarded the little creature for a very long time. Then, with a sudden movement, he turned his head, abruptly spread his wings, and shot back up into the sky without warning.

XXIII

They finally approached Gorywynn—the crystalline heart of Magic Moon. More than once on their flight, Kim thought he saw a flash of gold on the distant horizon; it never came any closer, though, so Kim wasn't sure if it was really there or he'd just imagined it. The Tatzelwurm remained nervous and irritable, but nothing else happened. In any case, if the golden flash was indeed Rangarig, the Tatzelwurm made no attempt to change course and charge at his hated enemy. Kim had no idea if this was due to Chunklet's sermon.

Late in the afternoon of the fourth day, Kim saw flickering red lights from countless campfires. Peer had noticed, too. Even Jarrn emerged from his persistent brooding, shading his eyes with his hand in order to see better.

Kim's heart began to beat faster. For a while now, the terrain had seemed familiar to him, and that meant they were nearing the crystal city. But what was the significance of this firelight? Had they come too late?

"Is that Gorywynn?" Peer asked, as if he'd read Kim's thoughts.

Kim shrugged unhappily. "I don't know," he said, although he knew better.

Peer squinted. "That has to be Gorywynn," he said. "I recognize the river and that chain of hills back there. Where is all the smoke coming from?"

Tatzelwurm approached the crystal city—however, the rainbow-colored walls and towers barely were recognizable because a dense veil of dust and smoke darkened everything. The red sparks turned out to be the light of countless fires that burned in a wide swath around the city. Before they reached Gorywynn, Kim heard a dull thundering and roaring sound, like the pounding of distant ocean waves on the sand.

"They . . . they're fighting!" Peer whispered, horrified. "Those are Priwinn's Steppe riders!" He turned around and stared at Kim with wide eyes. "We've come too late."

Kim didn't reply. From up on the Tatzelwurm, he peered down at the huge encampment, spellbound. There were tens of thousands—maybe hundreds of thousands—of warriors, assembled in two huge armies. From this great height, it was impossible to tell friend from foe, but Kim saw that the two armies were approximately the same size. The decisive battle already had begun!

At Kim's command, the Tatzelwurm descended so they could see more details. Kim realized that Priwinn's Steppe riders and their allies were besieging Gorywynn, and the Riverfolk and their vassals that occupied the city had formed a defensive line around it. Kim and Peer had come just as Priwinn stormed the city.

"No!" Kim whispered in dismay. "We have to stop them."

Kim tried, but he was unable to locate the King of the Steppe among the huge throng of soldiers. Even if he'd found Priwinn, what could he have done?

He wouldn't lay down his sword and order his troops to retreat because I asked him to, Kim thought desperately.

The Tatzelwurm took a wide turn to make another sweep of the battlefield. The first time, they'd flown over so quickly that people down below had noticed only the huge shadow and thunderous sound of the dragon's wings. Now, more and more faces turned to the sky; despite the noise below, Kim could make out a multitude of voices crying out in horror as both armies recognized the Tatzelwurm. They forgot the battle for a moment. A wave of panic followed in the dragon's wake. Everywhere, the battle came to a halt. For a second, the warriors' shrill cries of terror were the only sounds. As the travelers swept past the army a second time, Kim ordered the Tatzelwurm to fly slow and low.

The third time they approached the battlefield outside the crystal walls, Kim found what he was looking for: There at the forefront, where knights and foot soldiers had collided with unrelenting force, he caught sight of his friend's dull black armor. Next to Priwinn, towering over everyone, stood a figure armed with a huge cudgel: Gorg.

As if the dragon's third pass were a signal, the battle resumed with undiminished intensity. The armies collided with devastating violence; the clashing of weapons, howls of rage, and cries of pain rang out. Priwinn's army had the upper hand. Slowly but surely, the Riverfolk and their allies were driven back toward the crystal walls—no matter how stubbornly they defended themselves. Steppe riders weren't their only opponents. In among the leather-clad men of Caivallon, Kim recognized members of many other peoples. To his astonishment, there were even Tree People among them!

Who would have thought that such peace-loving people were capable of fighting? Yet, he caught sight of more of them, as if they'd come to avenge the death of their tree. That made it painfully clear to Kim how high a price the peoples of Magic Moon paid to follow Priwinn's path.

The Tatzelwurm circled close. An occasional spear or arrow struck him, bouncing off without any effect. Kim sensed that the dragon was getting restless. His huge talons snatched at empty air as if he lusted after something to rip to shreds. Kim didn't know how long the Tatzelwurm could keep himself under control. He was a monster, after all—the most dangerous beast in Magic Moon. They'd been allies up until now, but that didn't mean the Tatzelwurm wouldn't return to his true nature amid all this killing, blood, and battle.

Suddenly, Kim forgot all his fears about the Tatzelwurm. The Steppe riders' army had formed a wedge that advanced toward Gorywynn's gates. The enemy army parted before them. What appeared to the riders down below like a retreat of the Riverfolk seemed completely different from on high. Kim saw that the Riverfolk were retreating to reassemble close behind the riders. It was a trap, Kim realized in horror. Obviously, the Riverfolk had recognized the King of the Steppe and were trying to bring him under their power. It seemed they would succeed.

"Priwinn!" Kim yelled as loud as he could. "Watch out! It's a trap!"

Priwinn didn't hear his words. The pirates completed their encircling movement, and the divided battle line now re-formed behind Priwinn and his knights.

The Riverfolk began an all-out attack. Priwinn and his companions defended themselves against the superior force with courage born of desperation. Three or four combatants would charge toward a Steppe rider, but often the Steppe rider was the victor.

Gorg raged among his attackers like a madman, mowing down dozens at a time with his enormous cudgel. But even the greatest courage and the greatest strength inevitably would fail against the superiority of numbers—and so it was. For every Riverman who lay defeated, three more materialized: The number of men that Priwinn and his few companions faced grew continually. They streamed in from all directions, strengthening the ring around the King of the Steppe. No matter how desperately Priwinn's army tried to break through their enemy's ranks to come to the aid of their leader, they didn't succeed. One after another, Priwinn's companions fell from their saddles. Finally, only the King of the Steppe and the giant Gorg were left. They defended themselves back to back, with Gorg protected by his superhuman strength and Priwinn saved by his magic armor.

Kim cried out loudly, threw himself forward, and kicked the Tatzelwurm's flanks as if to spur on a battle steed. The Tatzelwurm responded. Maybe Kim's cry was the order he'd been waiting for, because the Tatzelwurm let out a monstrous roar, unfolded his wings to their full extent, and dived down on the Riverfolk's army with outstretched claws and a gaping maw. Behind Kim, Peer screamed something that Kim didn't understand; Chunklet whistled shrilly in terror and ducked back under Kim's shirt; and Jarrn shrieked in fear, pulling his hood over his face. Kim barely noticed any of that. The Tatzelwurm plunged from the sky like an attacking falcon, diving in among the Riverfolk.

His claws knocked men and horses aside, and his beating wings swept dozens of riders from their saddles. Like a tornado sweeping across a field, he plowed through the pirates' army, heading straight toward Gorg and Priwinn. The Riverfolk fled in sheer panic, but the Tatzelwurm left behind a swath of death and destruction along the warriors' frontlines. Like a black demon, he swept forward, barely three feet above the ground—clawing and biting and snapping. Riders who had managed to escape his claws were knocked from their saddles by the hurricane-force wind his beating wings created.

Gorg and Priwinn now noticed the dragon rushing toward them, and Kim saw the giant's eyes widen in disbelief when he recognized Kim on the back of the enormous beast. Kim sensed that the Tatzelwurm wouldn't stop. They already were near, but the dragon increased his speed. He no longer distinguished friend from foe, shredding everything in his path.

"Go back!" Kim yelled to his friends. "Save yourselves!"

Priwinn stood there, shocked. He lowered his sword and looked at the raging monster, completely stunned. At the very last moment, when Kim was convinced that Priwinn would be run over, the king saved himself by leaping to the side, escaping the dragon's grasping claws by an inch.

Gorg was less lucky. He, too, woke from his trance and tried to get out of the way, but he moved too slowly. One of the dragon's huge wings struck him, catapulting him high in the air. Gorg smashed against the city wall.

The dragon would not calm down. He roared loudly and wildly, thrashing his wings violently—then, he slammed into the closed city gate. The planks were as thick as a grown man, but the collision broke them like matchsticks, and the gate collapsed with a crash. Kim and Peer were tossed off the monster's back. As Kim fell to the ground, he saw the dragon rear up and shake; then, the beast rolled helplessly until he slammed against the crystal wall.

Stunned, Kim rose to a kneeling position. His head hurt terribly. As if through a gray fog, he saw a figure running toward him. He had a fleeting impression of black metal, leather, animal pelts; he saw the flash of a sword; he sensed it was one of the Riverfolk.

With a frightened whistle, Chunklet popped out from under Kim's shirt and scurried to safety, and the mere sight of the werecreature astonished the charging pirate so much that he hesitated for a second.

Before Kim had time to gather his wits, the pirate tightened his grip on his sword and charged.

Kim dodged to the side, and the Riverman's sword struck the crystal wall behind him, sending sparks flying. Kim rolled, came back onto his feet, and blindly charged.

The Riverman was bigger and stronger, but Kim's attack took him by surprise. Clutching each other, they fell to the ground, rolled several yards, and then separated again.

Kim tried to turn around, but the river pirate was much faster. With a triumphant yell, he raised his sword, and Kim saw the deadly blade flash.

The mortal blow never came. Instead, a red featherball shot toward the man, slammed against his neck with a strangely soft noise, and bit down.

The river pirate stumbled, more from shock than anything. Reaching behind his back, he pulled Chunklet off his neck and flung away the little critter.

The distraction served its purpose: Kim sprang up and kicked the man off balance. The warrior cried out, fell, and dropped his sword. A yellow and green arrow whizzed past Kim and pierced the river pirate.

Kim hastily turned around, looking for Chunklet. The little werecreature scurried toward him, staggering. He was unharmed but seemed a little dazed.

"Are you all right?" Kim asked.

"Of course," replied Chunklet. "It will take more than one of those fish-eaters to make me afraid."

The battle was in full fury. The Tatzelwurm's attack had turned the tide, however. Everywhere Kim looked, Riverfolk tried to save themselves by fleeing. Priwinn's riders pitilessly cut them down. What had started as a stubborn struggle for access to the city had now turned into a free-for-all. The mighty river pirates began to scatter in all directions.

Without quite realizing how it had happened, Kim found himself in the middle of the battle, a sword in hand. The Tatzelwurm still raged among the Riverfolk like a black demon. All around him, the battle continued with undiminished fury.

A Riverman suddenly appeared out of the smoke in front of Kim, who gave the attacker a painful cut in his thigh and kicked him to the ground.

The man dropped his weapon and doubled over.

Kim frantically looked around for Priwinn and the giant, but couldn't see them anywhere in the general melee. Alternately fighting and dodging, he worked his way toward the smashed gate, where the bitterest fighting took place.

The Riverfolk who hadn't been able to escape now tried to retreat behind the city walls, but their pursuers wouldn't let up. The arched crystal gateway magnified battle cries and the clash of weapons. Kim defended himself fiercely, but he was concerned by the pirates storming Gorywynn with weapons in hand. Everything was turned on its head. The good had become bad, and the bad had become good. Who could tell right from wrong?

Then, he caught sight of Priwinn. The King of the Steppe had raised his sword again, leading his men to pursue their retreating enemy.

Kim shouted Priwinn's name several times, but the din of battle drowned out his voice. Although he soon threw caution to the wind and thrashed about as wildly as the others, he didn't manage to get closer to Priwinn. The Riverfolk had formed up on the other side of the wall to make their last stand. As a result, a roiling mass of men piled in front of the gate.

Finally, the Rivermen's defense weakened, and hundreds of voices cried out in triumph. The attackers stormed into Gorywynn, carrying Kim along with them.

An inner voice warned him that this was wrong, and that they should throw down their swords and end this battle. But another part of him suddenly felt furious anger at the Riverfolk and their allies; at that moment, his anger was stronger than the voice of reason. Before long, Kim found himself fighting at the forefront, wielding his sword as skillfully, confidently, and quickly as he'd done in the battle against Borass' black riders.

The resistance collapsed the minute Kim stood at the King of the Steppe's side. Kim's inhibitions had been swept away. He felt no compunctions. Indeed, it didn't even occur to him that he could be injured or killed in this battle. The sword in his hand gave him a feeling of power and invulnerability—the same feeling, as intoxicating as it was deceptive, that all the soldiers felt during the battle.

Priwinn parried an enemy's sword thrust, made some breathing room for himself by swinging his magical weapon, and flipped up the visor of his helmet. His face shone with sweat, but his eyes twinkled brightly when he saw Kim. "I knew you'd come," he said.

"Where's Gorg?" Kim cried. "Is he still alive?"

Priwinn shrugged. "I think so," he replied. "He's not hurt easily."

"I'll go see!" Chunklet cried. He hopped down from Kim's shoulder and disappeared into the tumult before Kim could stop him. Almost at the same moment, a large black shadow with yellow eyes separated from Priwinn: It was Sheera, who now joined Chunklet.

Priwinn and Kim were attacked again; they had to defend themselves, shoulder to shoulder, with bitter resolve. The Rivermen realized that they'd lost the battle, but they seemed intent on dragging down their enemies with them. They now attacked with no regard for their own lives, exacting a terrible toll from the advancing Steppe riders.

An organized battle line no longer existed. Instead, clusters of men got caught up in bitter hand-to-hand fighting. Kim tried several times to get Priwinn to stop so they could talk, but Priwinn didn't want to listen. The young king fought as if he were intoxicated. His sword sliced through equipment, smashing weapons and shields and armor. Kim's horror grew at the sight.

This was the second time they'd fought side by side in a battle for the survival of Magic Moon. Yet, this time, it was different—different in a terrible way. The battle against Boraas' black riders hadn't been any less serious or deadly than this one, but there had been a fundamental difference: In the battle for Gorywynn that time, they'd been the defenders against evil. Now . . .

The last flare-up gradually subsided. More and more Steppe riders and their allies pushed through the shattered gate and overran the enemy. Finally, gasping for breath, Kim lowered his sword and stood still. His heart raced. Sweat coated his face and clothing; he bled from a dozen harmless cuts and jabs he wasn't aware of until now. Weakness crept into his body, transforming his limbs into lead.

But it wasn't over yet. Exhausted, he turned to Priwinn, wanting to talk, but Priwinn cut him off.

"Themistokles!" the Steppe rider exclaimed. "We have to get to him. If they take him prisoner, then it was all for nothing!"

Tired though he was, Kim realized that Priwinn was right. Without a doubt, the Riverfolk would try to get Themistokles in their power. Although the wizard had become old and weak, he still was considered a powerful, dangerous wizard. Undoubtedly, they also knew that he was their last bargaining chip—a means to apply pressure, which wouldn't bring them victory but might gain them more favorable conditions for withdrawal.

Yes, Themistokles was in great danger. For that reason, Kim joined the Steppe riders as they stormed into the proud fortress.

The battle ended just inside the gate, but the deeper they penetrated into the maze of little streets, the more often lone fighters tried to delay them. Priwinn cleared a path, protected and almost invulnerable thanks to his armor. By the time they reached the palace, their energy level had dropped. A last, bitter struggle ensued when two dozen river pirates charged them. They overcame this final barrier, as well.

Priwinn and Kim rushed up the glass staircase to the wizard's tower. Kim had expected to encounter fierce resistance again, but the fortress now seemed dead. Here and there, they saw traces of the Riverfolk: a sword heedlessly cast aside, a forgotten piece of clothing, and a shoe lying in the middle of a step. But no one obstructed the way to the tower.

When they arrived at the top of the stairs, however, two Rivermen guarded Themistokles' door, their weapons raised. Between them—like a nightmare of polished steel—stood the gigantic figure of an iron man.

"Not one step closer," said one of the men. His gaze moved back and forth between Kim and the King of the Steppe.

"Not one step, King Priwinn—otherwise, we'll kill the wizard."

The other one added, "If you don't believe us, look!" He pushed open the door.

Both young men cried out in horror.

Themistokles sat in his chair beside the window, but they hardly recognized the trembling old man, with long strands of hair falling over his wrinkled face, his sad eyes, and his drooped shoulders. A black chain of dwarven steel bound him to his chair. An iron man stood behind the chair, his powerful left hand extending toward Themistokles in a menacing gesture. His eerie green eye seemed to glare scornfully toward the doorway.

"What is the meaning of this?!" Priwinn asked sharply, obediently lowering his sword at the same time. "You know that you've lost."

"Maybe so," one of the men replied calmly. "Or maybe not, as you see." He shrugged and continued in the same relaxed tone of voice: "It depends on what value you place on the wizard's life."

Kim took a step backward, so he was standing directly behind Priwinn. The guard looked at him mistrustfully but returned his full attention to Priwinn's face.

Kim managed to whisper into Priwinn's ear without moving his lips in the least: "Keep them here somehow. I'll be right back."

Then, he slowly backed away until he felt the first stair under his feet. He ran down the tower staircase—taking two, three, and four steps at a time—and dashed out of the palace.

As fast as he could, he raced back to gate. He was so exhausted that he stumbled and fell several times; it was hard for him to get back up and continue running. His heart hurt, and he was afraid he might collapse. Nevertheless, every second was precious and could make the difference between the wizard's life or death.

It wasn't the guards that Kim feared so much as Priwinn! Kim had seen the expression in Priwinn's eyes when he'd looked at the chained wizard.

Kim knew that the King of the Steppe would do a great many things to save Themistokles' life—but he wouldn't give up his victory for it!

Staggering more than running, Kim shot out of the city gate and looked around. To his immense relief, he discovered the Tatzelwurm in the same place where he'd last seen the dragon.

The Tatzelwurm's fiery red eyes looked down, full of hate, at the people standing in a cautiously wide circle around him. They stared up at him with a mixture of fear and curiosity. Occasionally, he uttered a deep rumbling growl and bared his teeth.

Kim stumbled again, fell on his knees, and remained there with his eyes closed until he had the strength to stand up. Staggering like a drunkard, he fought his way through the onlookers. A hand reached out and tried to pull him back, but Kim kept on running, despite a chorus of dismayed voices.

The dragon's head jerked around. For a moment, his eyes reflected nothing but pure bloodlust; then, he recognized Kim, and the bottomless hate in his gaze turned to anger and confusion—and something like reproach, which Kim didn't understand but which made him feel guilty.

When he came closer, Kim saw that the dragon was wounded. The Tatzelwurm's thick hide couldn't withstand the bombardment of stones, spears, and arrows forever; he bled from countless wounds—a few of which were very serious. One of his wings hung down as if he no longer had the strength to fold it. But Kim didn't give any more thought to that. Instead, he ran directly between the Tatzelwurm's forepaws, bounded onto the dragon's back, and bent over a whimpering, cowering bundle.

Kim felt a sharp pain in his chest when he saw the piteous state of the Dwarf King. Unlike Peer and Kim, Jarrn hadn't been flung off the dragon, because he'd been chained to its neck. The dwarf had felt the full, terrible impact when the Tatzelwurm had smashed into the city gate. At first, Kim feared the dwarf was dead; Jarrn didn't move at all when Kim turned him over and pulled back his hood. But then, Jarrn opened his eyes with great effort; blinked at Kim without recognizing him; and gave a soft, tortured groan.

"I'm sorry," Kim murmured, meaning it sincerely. Although Jarrn might have been responsible for much of the misfortune in Magic Moon, at the same time, Kim had the feeling that the Dwarf King perhaps was the most innocent of all. He dismissed this random thought, reached under his belt, and pulled out the key. His hands trembled slightly as he unlocked the chain around Jarrn's foot, and the dwarf groaned in pain when Kim carefully stood him up.

"It's going to be all right, Jarrn," he said, walking the length of the Tatzelwurm's back with the dwarf in his arms. He looked for a place where he could climb down without losing his balance. "We'll fix you up. But first, you have to help us."

"Help?" Jarrn groaned. "You're . . . actually . . . as daft . . . as I always thought. What should I help you with?"

Kim didn't bother to answer; he climbed down and ran back the way he came. Rows of onlookers parted before him as he charged toward the city with the dwarf in his arms. He reached the gate unchallenged, crossed the great square, and headed to the fortress for a second time.

He was on the verge of exhaustion, so overcome with fatigue that he had to lean against a wall to recover his strength several times. Once, he even dropped Jarrn. The dwarf plopped onto the glassy pavement with a dull thud and immediately began to complain. Gasping, Kim picked him up again and stumbled on. When he reached the entrance to the palace, a grim-looking Steppe rider walked toward him, wanting to take the dwarf from him. However, Kim shook his head and brushed past the man.

Step by step, he worked his way up the enormous spiral staircase to the tower chamber. Kim already could hear the voices. He couldn't understand what was said, but it sounded like an exchange of sharp words.

He gently set down Jarrn, sank down next on the glass step, and buried his face in his hands for a moment.

"What now?" Jarrn asked. Something in his voice made Kim look up.

The dwarf stood before him, grinning, suddenly quite vigorous and lively. His cape hung in tatters and his skin had scrapes and scratches, but the sardonic grin on his face was almost cheerful, and his dark eyes surveyed Kim with malicious glee.

"You . . . you can walk?" Kim whispered faintly.

"Of course I can walk," Jarrn replied. He hopped in place and raised both arms over his head to prove it. "Nothing's wrong with me. I feel great. It will take more than that slug with delusions of grandeur to kill me."

"And you let me carry you the whole way?" Kim murmured. He didn't even have the strength to be angry. "Why didn't you tell me you could walk?"

"You didn't ask me, did you?" Jarrn snapped back. "I thought you were enjoying it."

Kim suppressed the angry retort on the tip of his tongue. It didn't really matter. Jarrn's short legs would have been too slow in any case.

"I need your help, Jarrn."

"My help?" Jarrn chuckled. "I already told you: You're crazy."

"I'm serious, Jarrn," Kim continued. "Themistokles' life is at stake."

The dwarf blinked. "His life?"

"The Riverfolk have him in their power." He nodded. "They know that they can't escape. I think they'll do something desperate if Priwinn doesn't give in to their demands."

"He won't," Jarrn said, suddenly very serious.

"That's what I'm afraid of, too," Kim replied tiredly. "He's changed so much, Jarrn. He's become hard. Sometimes, I barely recognize him."

"So, what can I do?" Jarrn asked. "The Riverfolk don't obey me any more than they obey you. They're not our friends—or have you forgotten already?"

"No," Kim replied, "but they have two iron men with them. How did that happen?"

"Iron men?" Jarrn's left eyebrow lifted in surprise. "They have iron men?"

The dwarf looked shocked and a little concerned, it seemed to Kim. Only now, when he saw the astonishment on Jarrn's face, did it occur to Kim that he hadn't seen a single iron man in the Riverfolk's army. One of those iron giants would have equaled one hundred of Priwinn's riders.

"Help us, Jarrn," Kim begged. "I promise you your freedom. I'll let you go as soon as Themistokles is safe. You have my word."

"I don't think your word is worth much at the moment," Jarrn snapped. "Why should I help you? Do you know what you've done? Do you know how much damage you've caused us? More than that crazy grass-eater and all his friends combined!"

Kim felt such despair that his eyes filled with tears. "Please, Jarrn," he begged. "You . . . you can ask anything you want. As far as I am concerned, I can return with you as your prisoner, and I give you my word of honor that I won't try to escape again. But help save Themistokles: He's not your enemy."

For a long time, Jarrn looked at Kim. The dwarf's gaze sent a chill down his back. Most of the time, the Dwarf King behaved spitefully, maliciously, or childishly—like all his subjects. Other times, Kim could see wisdom in Jarrn's face.

"All right," Jarrn finally agreed. "But I'm not doing it for you—and definitely not for that crazy grass-eater up there. I'm doing it only for Themistokles. Afterward, I'll be free and go on my way?"

"You have my word on that," Kim confirmed. He stood up and continued on, but Jarrn shook his head.

"Wait here a moment," he said. "I have to . . . go a different way. If they see me, they'll immediately know what's going on and they'll kill the wizard. I know these Riverfolk. They're a crude, villainous people. They destroy what they can't have—that's their way."

Kim nodded tiredly. "I'll wait here," he said. "I'll count to thirty. Slowly. Will that be enough time?"

"Better count to fifty," Jarrn said. "If you can count that high."

"I'll try." Kim gathered his energy for a tired smile—but he was too astonished to do anything but gape: Jarrn suddenly disappeared. The dwarf simply dissolved into thin air. Kim eventually realized that Jarrn had moved too fast for his eyes to follow.

Kim shook his head. Then, trembling with impatience, he forced himself to count calmly to fifty. When he was done, he took two or three deep breaths, straightened his shoulders, and went up the stairs.

The scene hadn't changed: The two Riverfolk and the iron man still stood in front of the door; Priwinn, who was now surrounded by eight or ten of his Steppe riders, stood on the other side of the corridor, glaring at them, his eyes full of hate. When he heard Kim's steps, he broke off mid-word. He wrinkled his brow inquiringly, and an annoyed expression appeared on his face when Kim didn't respond.

Then, he abruptly turned back to the two Rivermen and raised his hand in a command. "All right: decide. Free passage for you and for the ones who are still inside the walls *if* you give up your arms and deliver the iron men to us. We demand the destruction of all the machines the dwarves have built for you."

"Never," the Riverman replied. "By your leave, King Priwinn—you've won the battle, not the war."

"You're asking us to let you go and trust your word that you won't come back and try to avenge this defeat?" Priwinn's laugh had a hard edge. "You're crazy! Give up your weapons and turn over those creatures and you can go. Otherwise, you can't."

"Then, the wizard will die," the Riverman replied earnestly.

"That may well be," Priwinn answered very gravely. "But I'm not going to wager the fate of my entire people in order to save one life. If it were my own life, I wouldn't decide any different."

Kim's blood ran cold when he heard those words. This was no longer the cheerful, fun-loving boy that he'd known. Priwinn had become a man—a harsh man.

"Your time is running out," Priwinn continued when the Rivermen didn't reply. "Decide, or—"

"Or what?" the Riverman asked.

Priwinn slowly pulled his sword from his belt. All his companions did the same. The two Rivermen suddenly faced a dozen unsheathed blades.

Kim thought he saw a shadowy movement behind the door.

With tremendous effort, he forced himself not to react. He was sure that he'd seen something, though. A second later, he saw it again. And then, he caught sight of Jarrn, who stepped out from behind the wizard's chair and now stared at the iron man guarding Themistokles.

Something in the green eye flickered. Then, the iron figure bent down and grabbed the chain that bound Themistokles, pulling on it with all his strength.

The robot wasn't strong enough to break dwarven steel, but the chair on which the wizard sat collapsed with a crash, and Themistokles fell heavily to the ground.

The two Rivermen whirled around in shock. Their iron companion raised his sword. Everything happened so fast that Kim couldn't follow it all.

With a loud cry, Priwinn charged forward and pierced the iron man with his magic sword. The King of the Steppe's companions set upon the two Rivermen so quickly that they couldn't defend themselves. Within a short time, they lay on the ground, pinned down by strong arms. Meanwhile, Priwinn jumped over the fallen iron man and dashed toward Themistokles.

Kim ran over to the wizard while Priwinn gave another blood-curdling yell, raised his sword high, and charged toward the second iron man. With a frightened, shocked look, the Dwarf King raised his arms high and tried to block the way; Priwinn simply ran over him, swung his blade, and decapitated the iron colossus with a single blow. The figure crashed to the floor and lay motionless.

In the meantime, Kim knelt down next to Themistokles. The old man groaned softly but didn't seem seriously hurt by his fall. He was weak and incalculably tired. With eyes full of exhaustion and grief, he looked at Kim as if he knew that his life was coming to an end. The sight almost broke Kim's heart.

It wasn't anything that the Riverfolk had done to Themistokles. It was like what Rangarig had told Kim so many months ago: The magic of this world was dying, and so the life of their oldest and most powerful wizard also approached its end.

"What's wrong with him?" Priwinn asked, very agitated. "Is he wounded? Did they hurt him?"

"No," Kim whispered. He slowly shook his head, stood, and helped Themistokles up. Priwinn wanted to help, but Kim brushed aside his hand and lifted up the old man's fragile body all by himself.

Themistokles seemed to weigh almost nothing now. Although he'd been a tall man, he didn't seem to weigh as much as the Dwarf King. Kim's eyes filled with tears as he gently carried Themistokles over to the simple bed next to the door. Kim laid down the old man.

"What's wrong with him?" Priwinn asked again. His voice sounded sharp. When Kim didn't answer this time, either, Priwinn grabbed him by the shoulder and roughly turned him around.

Kim brushed aside his hand and glared at him. "He's dying, you fool!" he said in fury. "Don't you see?"

Priwinn turned as white as a sheet and bent down to look at the wizard's face. Kim also stepped closer to the bed.

Themistokles opened his eyes and smiled very weakly. His voice was as soft as a whisper. "Not yet, little hero," he said, smiling. "My time is running out, but things have not yet reached that point. Our world is dying, and I am dying along with it, but there still is a way to save it. You helped us once, Kim. Do it again."

"How?" Kim asked in despair. "I . . . I've tried everything. I would give my life if that would do any good."

"Sometimes . . . one life is not enough," Themistokles whispered sadly. "Help them, Kim. You are the only one who can still do it. I'm too weak."

With that, he closed his eyes. His breathing became shallow and quiet. He'd fallen into a deep, deep sleep—from which he might never awaken.

* * *

Although the battle had been decided, isolated skirmishes were fought all night long. Groups of Riverfolk had taken up positions in the city lanes and defended themselves with stubborn tenacity, although they'd realized there was nothing to gain by it.

Gradually, however, the clash of weaponry grew fainter, and other sounds filled the city: the clatter of horse hooves on the glass pavement, the laughter of men celebrating, the crackling of large campfires . . . The army was too huge for all the men to find quarters in houses, so they camped out on the streets. Footsteps soon echoed in the fortress, as well, because Priwinn and his generals had chosen it for their headquarters.

Kim took little notice of any of this. He sat next to Themistokles' bed, holding the old man's slender, wrinkled hand as he waited for the wizard to awaken. Sometimes, he was alone; sometimes, there were Steppe riders or Tree People with him. Once or twice, Priwinn came in and questioned Kim, never receiving an answer.

Kim didn't rouse from his brooding until long after midnight, when a noise outside the door startled him. A moment later, the King of the Steppe walked in, followed by a broad-shouldered figure, who held a writhing, flailing dwarf in his left hand and a hollering boy in his right.

A red featherball sat on his left shoulder, and Sheera's slender black figure slipped into the room between his legs.

"Gorg!" Kim exclaimed in relief. "You're alive!"

"Well," Chunklet said, impudent as usual, "It was a close call. If I hadn't come at the right time, they would've gotten him."

The giant grinned. He set the boy down on the ground in front of Kim. "Of course I'm alive," the giant said. "What did you think?"

"This boy says he's with you." Priwinn pointed at Peer. "Is that right?"

"He's my friend," Kim confirmed.

Peer stared at the King of the Steppe, his eyes filled with hate. Suddenly, Kim recalled what Peer had told him on their first evening in the dwarves' caves.

Kim gave Peer an conspiratorial look and stood up. "He helped me escape," he continued. "I probably wouldn't have managed it without him."

Priwinn studied the boy with an unfriendly look.

Kim turned around and looked up at Gorg, who still held the writhing dwarf in his left hand.

"Put him down, Gorg," he said.

The giant exchanged looks with Priwinn, a question in his eyes, before he did as Kim asked. He set Jarrn on the ground but kept a firm hand on the dwarf's shoulder.

Spewing invectives, Jarrn tried to pry off the giant's fingers—of course, with no success at all.

"Let him go," Kim said.

"What?" Priwinn repeated incredulously.

Kim nodded, indicating Jarrn with a motion of his head. "I promised him his freedom," he said. "If he hadn't helped, Themistokles might be dead now."

"Nonsense!" Priwinn said. "We would have overpowered those scoundrels somehow. You want to let him go? Are you crazy? Do you know who he is?"

"Yes," said Kim, nodding. "The King of the Dwarves."

"Precisely!" Priwinn exclaimed almost triumphantly. "We hardly could hope for a more valuable captive. It was smart of you to bring him along. He'll be very useful to us."

"I gave him my word," Kim said sadly.

"That was a little premature, perhaps," Priwinn said coldly. "I'm sorry—but he stays here. It's not over yet, Kim. The Riverman was right. We've won a battle, but not the war."

"What do you mean?"

"We've reclaimed Gorywynn and driven out the pirates' army," Priwinn replied, "but that doesn't mean we've won—just the opposite." His face darkened. "I'm afraid the worst still lies ahead."

Shocked, Kim glanced at the dwarf. Jarrn coldly studied the King of the Steppe, but Kim also noticed a thin, malicious glint in his eyes. Kim remembered the apparently inexplicable joyfulness that Jarrn had displayed in response to his own capture. Priwinn was right. It wasn't over.

"You mean they're going to come back?" he asked.

"The Riverfolk?" Priwinn shook his head. "Not likely. Their noses got bloodied and they'll need a long time to recover. But for the last several days, our spies have sent reports about an army on its way here. Unless there's a miracle, it'll be here by sundown."

"What kind of an army?" Peer asked.

Priwinn looked at the boy as if he wondered whether Peer was worthy of an answer. Then, he shrugged his shoulders and said, addressing Kim rather than Peer, "Iron men."

"Iron men?!" Kim recoiled as if he'd been hit. He looked at Jarrn with wide eyes. "Is that true?" he whispered.

Jarrn grinned with evil joy. "Did you think we were going to stand by and watch while you destroy everything we've built, dimwit?"

"How many are there?" Kim shuddered.

"Thousands," Gorg volunteered.

Priwinn added, "All the ones that escaped us and probably all the new ones the dwarves have built in their forges. You were there, Kim. You should know better than we do how many there are."

Kim just shook his head. "I didn't see a single one," he said. "They must've sent them away or made them somewhere else."

The dwarf's eyes twinkled as if Kim had said something extremely funny. He grinned more broadly than ever, but he didn't say a word.

"Then, it was all for nothing," Kim whispered despondently.

Priwinn shook his head. "Not at all," he said. "We won the first battle; now that you're here, we'll win the second one, too. And if you can continue to keep the Tatzelwurm under control, then our prospects are good."

Kim had related the tale of the Tatzelwurm's escape, but Priwinn obviously hadn't understood the nature of Kim's relationship with the evil dragon. Kim doubted they'd be victorious. Although the Tatzelwurm was a valuable ally because of his enormous physical strength, the giant dragon wasn't invulnerable—as this battle had shown. Moreover, the iron men already had defeated the Tatzelwurm once.

Kim sadly looked down at the bed where the wizard slept. If only Themistokles were awake. If only he would open his eyes and tell Kim what to do. Everything was so confusing.

Despondent, Kim looked at the dwarf. "Is that why you're in such a good mood?" he asked.

Gorg tightened his grip on Jarrn's shoulder and the dwarf grimaced in pain. "Well? Answer him."

Jarrn chuckled spitefully even as Gorg's powerful hand turned him toward Kim. The dwarf wisely held his tongue.

Priwinn clenched his fists and took a step toward the dwarf. "Don't rejoice too soon, dwarf," he said; then, gesturing in Gorg's direction, "Lock him up somewhere, Gorg. Get twenty of our best and bravest warriors to guard him."

The giant did as Priwinn ordered.

For a while, an uncomfortable silence spread. Priwinn looked at Kim, and Kim sensed that his friend was waiting for him to say or do something in particular. But he couldn't force himself to do it. It was a moment of truth, and if Kim made the wrong decision now . . .

Priwinn unbuckled his sword belt and laid it on the table in front of Kim. After a moment's hesitation, he placed his helmet next to the belt. "That belongs to you," he said.

Kim shook his head.

"You already decided a long time ago," Priwinn said with a slightly sad smile. He came closer, put his hand on Kim's shoulder, and gravely looked into Kim's eyes. "Don't think I don't understand you. It breaks my heart that I have to take up arms against my own people. But there's no other choice."

"I can't," Kim said softly. He wasn't entirely convinced by his own words.

"You already have," Priwinn replied. "This evening in the battle for Gorywynn—didn't you join the fight? And when you and your friend here escaped from the dwarves' caves, didn't you fight your way to freedom?"

"That was different," Kim murmured.

"Was it?" Priwinn asked softly. "Was it really?"

Kim didn't know how to answer. After a while, the King of the Steppe turned away and, without another word, took off the rest of his armor and laid it on the table. "It belongs to you," he said again. "Tomorrow morning, when the sun rises, you will wear it and lead us in the final battle."

XXIV

Kim had a nightmare that night. The city was vastly overcrowded and he didn't want to leave Themistokles alone, so Kim had asked to have two beds brought to the tower chamber for him and Peer. They'd talked for a long time before Kim reluctantly stretched out on his bed and closed his eyes. As soon as he drifted into a restless sleep, he started dreaming.

He saw himself lying on this bed, staring up into the darkness. Chunklet laid next to him, curled up into a little pinball, snoring so loudly that the walls shook. But Kim and Chunklet were no longer alone: a little figure wrapped in a tattered black cape stood at the foot of his bed, looking at him with a strange expression. There was no point in asking how Jarrn had managed to elude Priwinn's guards. Kim felt no fear, because he knew that this was a dream and Jarrn hadn't come to do him any harm. Next to Kim, Chunklet raised his head and sleepily blinked his eyes. He felt the tiny creature start to tremble.

For a while, Kim stared at the dwarf, who returned his gaze in a troubling way.

In the dream, Kim stood up, walked past the dwarf, and looked around the room. Peer's and the old wizard's soft, steady breathing were the only sounds that he heard. Red light came in from the fires burning outside, but the warriors' laughing voices had faded away. Deep night had settled over Gorywynn, and any soldiers who didn't have guard duty used the time to recover for the final battle.

Something called to Kim.

At first, he thought it was Jarrn, but the Dwarf King stood silently with the same strange, knowing look on his face. Kim realized he actually hadn't heard the call. Rather, it was like something had touched his soul: something cold and foreign but also familiar and protective.

His gaze passed Themistokles, whose eyes remained closed. It wasn't the wizard's magic that he sensed.

Kim's gaze now lingered on the small table where Priwinn had left the sword, helmet, and armor. He instantly knew this equipment had called him. A voice from his own past told of heroic deeds and brave battles, whispering to him that magic still was there, as strong and irresistible as before—indeed, one hundred times stronger in his own hand than in Priwinn's, for this equipment once had belonged to Kim.

Kim shuddered. In one small corner of his mind, he realized that it was the lure of power—the knowledge of the armor's invincibility and the black blade's deadly sharpness, which once had helped to save this land from a terrible danger. Nothing could withstand this weapon, and nothing could pierce this armor. If he put it on, he'd be invincible.

He tried with all his might to resist the urge, but it was as if his hands no longer belonged to him. Slowly, he picked up the breastplate; the black iron leg and arm armor; and finally, the sturdy chain mail gloves—caressing them, one after another. The armor had to weigh at least one hundred pounds, maybe more. But instead of feeling its weight, each piece increased Kim's strength. With every black iron plate that he fastened to his body, he became increasingly certain of his invulnerability and invincibility. As a last step, he reached for the notched black sword, and a wave of prickling, irresistible energy streamed through him.

A part of Kim knew what he was doing was wrong. This wasn't the energy of goodness—not really. It was the temptation of power, the evil attractiveness of violence, and the lust for destruction and annihilation.

Unfortunately, the part of his mind that knew all this had grown weak.

Kim had tried everything. He'd rushed from one defeat to the next, worked riddle after riddle, and exposed himself to a multitude of dangers in order to solve the terrible secret linked to the fate of Magic Moon—but he was farther from the solution than ever. *Should I give up?* Was that what Themistokles had meant when he'd said that the price of one life was sometimes not enough . . . ?

Kim gladly would have given his life to save Magic Moon. But that was true of all Priwinn's men, as well. Too many already had died for that.

Perhaps his fate wasn't to die but to commit a wrong deed—something that Kim knew would lead to more harm and evil. Yet, he no longer had a choice. After everything he and Priwinn had tried, violence was the only option.

"Do you really believe that?"

Still dreaming, Kim turned to Jarrn and replied, "I don't know. I . . . I just don't know, Jarrn." He wasn't surprised at all that the Dwarf King had read his thoughts.

"You're a fool," Jarrn said earnestly. His voice had none of its usual malice; rather, it expressed an ancient wisdom, which Kim had previously detected in him. His words made Kim shudder.

Kim waited for the dwarf to continue, but Jarrn just looked at him before slowly walking over to Peer's bed.

Kim watched, full of curiosity, as Jarrn's fingertips swiftly flew over Peer's forehead and temples. The boy restlessly moved in his sleep. Then, the dwarf stepped back, looked at Kim one more time, and turned toward the door. He walked through it without opening it, and that was as it should be—in a dream.

It was strange that Kim had that thought. He was fully aware that he was dreaming. Normally, people didn't realize they were in a dream. He wondered if he'd convinced himself that he was dreaming because otherwise everything would have been unbearable.

Then, something happened that convinced Kim that he was in a dream: A trumpeting cry pierced the night; when Kim looked out the window, he saw Tatzelwurm's silhouette circle the lake. He wasn't alone; a second, smaller shadow soared beside him. It was a dragon shimmering gold in color. There was nothing aggressive about their flight patterns.

Rangarig and the Tatzelwurm had been enemies since the beginning of creation. Why weren't they charging with the intent to annihilate each other?

At this point, Kim thought he understood what the dream was trying to tell him: If Rangarig and the Tatzelwurm had overcome their ancient enmity in order to fight together against the enemies of Magic Moon, couldn't he? For a while, Kim watched their spiraling flight until they sank down on the field outside the city gate, disappearing from Kim's view. Then, a noise coming from the bed made him suddenly alert.

It wasn't Themistokles. Secretly, Kim had hoped the wizard had sent him this dream. But the old man lay motionless on the bed, still sleeping. Peer, however, looked around with jerky, confused movements.

For a moment, he gazed directly at Kim with vacant eyes. Indeed, it seemed that the boy wasn't aware of Kim at all. Very slowly, Peer stood up from the bed; his face appeared as if the boy were asleep still.

As Jarrn had done before, Peer stood for a moment at Kim's bed. Then, he turned around and walked toward the door with steady, measured footsteps.

Like the dwarf, he simply walked through the massive wooden door as if it were just an illusion. After a moment of hesitation, Kim slipped his sword into the leather sheath on his belt and followed his friend. Like Peer and the dwarf before him, Kim didn't bother to reach for the door handle. . . .

Dream or not—Kim bumped into the door so hard that he almost fell to the ground. Puzzled, he lifted his hand to his bruised forehead and gently touched the big bump forming there. Then, he stared at the closed door and shook his head, perplexed. What a crazy dream! Obviously, everyone in this dream could behave however they liked—except for him!

That made him curious. A strange sort of excitement took hold of him. Hastily, Kim pressed down on the door handle, pulled open the door, and rushed out into the corridor. Peer already had descended quite a few steps down the staircase and almost had disappeared from view. Kim immediately caught up with him and fell into the same tempo as the sleepwalking youth, two paces behind. He doubted that Peer would have noticed him if he walked beside the boy—or tried to detain Peer—but Kim wasn't willing to risk it.

Slowly, they descended the enormous spiral staircase to the castle's entrance hall. There, Peer turned to the left—toward one of the narrow side doors that led to the servants' quarters. Kim and Priwinn had walked through that door before, on their way to Themistokles.

The hall was filled with people. Many soldiers lay on the bare floor, using blankets and saddles as pillows. Some still were awake, talking with each other softly. When Kim walked past them, one of these men sprang to his feet in surprise.

"My lord!" he shouted. "What . . . ?" A puzzled expression spread over his face when he saw Kim wearing the black helmet. Almost immediately, this expression turned to mistrust and anger. "Who are you?" he asked sharply. "What do you think you're doing, putting on this armor, boy?"

Kim was too surprised to answer. He didn't move when the man extended his hand, grabbed him roughly by the shoulder, and began to shake him.

"Speak up!"

Kim hastily glanced at Peer. The boy almost had reached the doorway. There was no time to argue with this man, so he lifted his arm to brush away the warrior's hand. The man's grip strengthened, and he shook Kim harder.

"You'd better answer, boy!" he bellowed.

Now, others had walked over to them, curious. Deciding he'd had enough—especially because Peer had walked through the closed door and disappeared that very second—Kim roughly brushed aside the man's hand—and cried out when the man immediately responded by slapping Kim in the face. Even though the black helmet absorbed most of the blow, Kim still stumbled backward and fell to the ground, flat on his back.

Dull pain shot through the back of his head; it was so intense that he saw red veils before his eyes. Worse, he'd bitten his tongue and now could taste salty blood. Stunned, he groaned when the man roughly pulled him up.

Before another blow could strike Kim, a sharp voice rang out: "What's going on there?"

Kim blinked as he recognized the figure rushing toward him, zigzagging through the sleeping warriors. It had been so long since he'd seen Priwinn wear his native clothing that the sight seemed odd to Kim. There was something else about the entire situation that frightened him to the core.

"What's going on here?" Priwinn repeated his question, and then he stopped when he recognized Kim. The young king looked dumbfounded; then, an expression of joyful surprise spread over his face.

"Kim!" he shouted. "So, you've decided!"

Is this still a dream?

Priwinn whirled around and yelled at the man who had grabbed Kim. "Let him go, you fool! Right now! Don't you know who that is? It's Kim!"

Obviously, Kim's name was familiar to the man: He hastily released Kim and turned as white as a sheet.

Priwinn quickly walked up to Kim and draped his arm over Kim's shoulder. "I'm glad you decided. Can you imagine?! Rangarig is back and he's normal again! He and the Tatzelwurm want to join us in the fight against the iron men! Now, everything will be all right!"

This isn't a dream, Kim thought hysterically. Hastily, he brushed off Priwinn's hand and pointed to the door that Peer had gone through. "Peer . . ." he whispered.

Priwinn looked at Kim inquiringly. "What about him?"

"He . . . he just . . . walked past here," Kim murmured.

"Pardon, my lord, but you must be mistaken," said the man who had hit Kim just seconds ago. "No one walked past here."

Kim's head snapped around. "Are you sure?" he gasped.

"Absolutely, my lord," replied the man in a small voice. "You were the only one here. That's why I was confused. You seemed . . . in a trance . . ."

"What is that supposed to mean?" Priwinn interrupted. "What—"

Kim stopped listening. *They didn't see Peer! None of these men saw Peer. I'm the only one.* Kim suddenly felt certain what that meant. *It isn't a dream! This is reality!*

Without bothering to listen to Priwinn or anyone else, he tore away and rushed after his friend. In a few strides, he reached the portal and shook the door until he realized it was locked. Priwinn yelled something to him, but Kim didn't understand what he'd said. Instead, he pulled out his sword and brought it down on the lock with all his strength. The glass lock shattered, and then the whole door fell into thousand pieces. Kim rushed through, heedless of Priwinn's surprised shouts and the soldiers' trampling feet behind him.

Behind the shattered door was a long, dusty passageway that hadn't been used for a long time. There were several doors, all open, so as Kim ran by, he glanced into the rooms, looking for Peer. He was marginally aware of Priwinn rushing down the corridor behind him, repeatedly asking Kim to stop or at least explain what was going on. But Kim just ran faster, until he reached the end of the corridor and stood before another locked door. This time, he had to strike two or three times with his sword before the lock gave way and he could force open the door with his shoulder. Behind him, Priwinn's steps came closer, but Kim didn't pay any attention.

He also was aware of something shooting past his legs and disappearing in the gray twilight before him. It was Sheera. Chunklet jumped off Kim's shoulder and followed the cat with surprising alacrity. Obviously, both animals saw well even in poor light.

Ahead of Kim, the first steps of a narrow staircase wound down into the earth in tight spirals. A half-inch thick layer of dust indicated that no one had gone down this way for a long time. There were no fresh tracks; yet, Kim was certain that Peer had gone this way. He raced down the stairs as fast as he could, often slipping on the smooth treads and bracing himself against the walls. Once, he fell and tumbled down the stairs a good distance, without seriously injuring himself.

After Kim stood up, complete stillness fell around him. Priwinn's excited cries had faded away, along with the sounds of footsteps. Kim must have run faster and farther than he'd realized. Only now did he feel how hard his lungs worked and how much his knees trembled. All at once, it occurred to him that his surroundings had changed in an extremely eerie way: The walls, ceiling, and steps still were made of glass, but the glass no longer captured the colors of the rainbow.

A milky, translucent veil surrounded Kim—as if he now moved through a world of solidified fog. There was a musty smell in the air. The dust on the next step down was ankle-deep and completely untouched. Kim guessed that he must be deep, deep inside the earth; he almost could feel the enormous weight of the fortress overhead.

His anxiety gradually mounted. Until now, he'd been too agitated to think about things; now, it occurred to him how huge the vaulted foundations of Gorywynn were: so huge that a whole army could hide in them, definitely large enough for a person to get lost forever.

Where is Peer?

Kim wasn't sure he was going the right way. Maybe the boy had taken a turn somewhere, or Kim had overlooked a door or a side passage. Maybe he was going deeper in this labyrinth of glass stairways and tunnels only to be lost and forgotten.

Despite these worries, Kim started moving again, although at a slower pace.

It seemed like the stairs would never end. Step by step, Kim descended into the glassy inner workings of the magical city; his surroundings gradually changed as he advanced. The dream world of glass and colored light turned into a nightmare of frozen fog and glimmering gray. Kim felt afraid. When he finally reached the bottom of the staircase, he had given up trying to figure out how deep under the city he was.

Ahead of him lay a crystal hall, which was filled with the same eerie gray light as the dwarves' caves.

Chunklet and Sheera had stopped just inside the entrance and frozen in place. Kim could sense their fear as they looked into the empty glass cavern.

No, it wasn't completely empty: Something jutted out in the middle of the hall—so far away that Kim sensed it more than saw it in the leaden twilight. It was as black as night and resembled a giant stone cube.

Its appearance reminded Kim of an altar, except that it was bigger than a house and so heavy that it had cracked the glass floor beneath it. Standing before it was a slender figure with black hair.

"Peer!" Kim yelled. The walls of the desolate hall threw back his words as a distorted, mocking echo.

Peer didn't respond. He slowly turned and walked to the left side of the cube, where a narrow stairway led to its top.

Kim called out to him again. Instead of waiting to see if Peer understood him, he started running as fast as he could. By the time Kim arrived at the foot of the stairs and stopped briefly to catch his breath, Peer almost had reached the flat surface of the gigantic cube. The next time Kim looked up, the stairs were empty.

Kim shouted a third time to Peer. Then, he ran up the stone steps without considering what might await him. When Kim sprang up onto the cube's surface, the dark-haired boy stood motionless before him. Peer was ten or twelve paces away, standing precisely in the middle of the giant cube.

Now, Kim knew for certain that it was an altar.

Peer looked at Kim with strangely sad eyes. Shocked, Kim stopped in mid-movement. Peer smiled sadly and lifted his right hand as if to wave goodbye. Yes, it was a farewell—for as soon as Peer lowered his hand, something terrible happened—quickly and without any drama. Kim watched, breathless with horror.

The foggy gray light concentrated around Peer until he resembled a silhouette behind a curtain of cottony vapor. His body swam before Kim's eyes. It became blurry and flat like a shadow, with outlines that faded into the gray light.

When the gray light dispersed after a few seconds, Kim no longer stood across from the black-haired boy; he was replaced by a huge, angular iron man, with a single, glowing green eye. Kim wanted to scream, but his throat closed up with terror. He stood there, gaping, so paralyzed by fear that he forgot to breathe.

The iron man, too, stood motionless, looking down at Kim through his glowing eye slit. At that moment, Kim felt defenseless. If the iron man had grabbed him, Kim wouldn't have attempted escape.

But the iron giant didn't attack. Instead, he plodded past Kim, awkwardly moved back down the altar's steps, and turned right. Once more, he stopped, slowly turned his huge head, and looked up at Kim. Although it was impossible—because, after all, his face was made of iron and therefore incapable of any movement—it seemed as if the iron man wore an expression of extraordinary sorrow. The robot turned away, walking off with heavy footsteps.

Kim watched until the iron man disappeared in the gray twilight of the hall. It took a long, long time before Kim revived from the shock and set off on the return trip to the castle.

XXV

The sun already had risen by the time Kim had returned. He realized now that the catacombs belonged to the dwarves' realm, where time obeyed other laws. The palace's entrance hall was empty, and Kim didn't encounter anyone in the courtyard, either. An eerie silence had spread over Gorywynn. Although a cloudless sky arched over the towers, Kim's whole body shivered from the cold. He felt tired—more tired than ever before.

The journey back had been long and difficult, but the weakness in his limbs didn't come from that exertion. His exhaustion had deeper roots. Perhaps for the first time in his life, he understood what true discouragement entailed—a situation without exit, where every decision was wrong, and everything he did turned against him. They had lost. The battle had been hopeless from the very beginning. Deep within him, Kim had sensed this the whole time. A paralyzing agony that words hardly could describe seized Kim, but he wasn't surprised. It felt . . . inevitable.

Kim headed for the city gate. On the way, he once again was struck by the eerie silence that blanketed Gorywynn. It was unlikely that anyone in this city had slept much the previous night, so Kim hadn't expected to see a typical, bustling morning. However, no one was in the streets at all. It was as if everything had been swept clean. The houses were abandoned: Nothing moved behind any of the windows, no door was open, not even the slightest sound could be heard. For a few moments, Kim wondered if he were the last living thing left in Magic Moon. Maybe they'd all transformed into iron.

Kim finally saw the others, including Steppe riders and Tree People. Without exception, the men streaming toward the gate were soldiers. Beyond the gate, Kim could see a huge, seething crowd. He heard a dull thundering, like the sound of distant surf, and the occasional screech from the Tatzelwurm or Rangarig. Nevertheless, it was calm. The horses' hoof beats sounded muffled and unnaturally quiet. Even the wind, which normally sounded like a crystal harp when it blew around the battlements of Gorywynn, was still.

The whole world is holding its breath, Kim thought with a shudder.

When he walked through the gate, he saw what had taken place outside.

Where the battle between Priwinn's army and the Riverfolk had raged the night before, now hundreds of riders and foot soldiers marched in endless rows: Priwinn's army now was reinforced by thousands and thousands of other Magic Moon inhabitants who had come to stand by the new king of Caivallon. Above them, the two immense dragons cast long shadows. The two monsters circled, screeching and flapping their wings as if they hardly could wait to attack their hated enemy.

Kim saw the enemy army. In preparation for its attack on Gorywynn, the enemy ranks had formed barely a stone's throw from Priwinn's army.

Riverfolk who had escaped from Priwinn's men the evening before were among the enemy troops, but they were not the only ones—not by any means. In among the leather and ironclad figures, Kim saw countless smaller, spindly shapes, wearing tattered black capes. The dwarves stood among their iron men—an unimaginably huge number of iron men. The robots assembled in an immense, black, glittering mass. For every soldier who had joined Priwinn and the two dragons, there was at least one iron man: one for every child who had disappeared from their parents' houses, one for every tear that a father or mother had shed. Magic Moon's children had returned to exact the price their parents owed for their fate.

Perhaps it was cruel destiny that the battle ignited at the exact moment Kim stepped out of the gate. There was no signal, no sign. From one moment to the next, the two huge armies shook off the calm and charged toward each other. The battle cries of countless voices shattered the eerie silence. The armies collided with a terrible thudding sound.

In a single, concerted movement, the dragons swung up high in the sky before plunging own on the enemy army with their claws and teeth at the ready. Although the attackers had superior numbers and fighting power, Priwinn's riders drove them back—if only because of the force of their headlong charge.

Crying out in horror, Kim started running. Although he barely was one hundred yards away from Priwinn's army, he felt as if he hardly moved at all. Only a few seconds passed before he reached the first men; the battle already had flared up in full fury. Dead and wounded piled up on both sides, and Kim knew that every drop of blood spilled would make everything worse—everybody struck down by Priwinn and his men would strengthen their adversaries' resolve, and every victory they achieved inevitably would seal their own downfall.

Kim desperately called Priwinn's name again and again, but his voice was lost in the clamor of the battle. As soon as he reached the army, he got stuck in the middle of dozens of men and horses. Although the riders recognized his black armor and tried to make way, everyone had crowded together too closely. Kim kept calling out to Priwinn in vain. Finally, desperate to make faster headway, he simply pulled one of the men off his horse and sprang into the saddle.

The battle raged at full intensity. The air filled with so much dust and smoke that Kim hardly could see a few yards ahead of him. The ground shook from the collision of the armed forces, and the men fought with the determination of those who knew their only options were victory or death.

"Priwinn!" Kim yelled, as loud as he could. "Where are you?"

He shouted five or six times but didn't count on getting an answer. Suddenly, a huge, broad-shouldered figure emerged from the dust, and a moment later the King of the Steppe appeared beside the giant. Priwinn already was exhausted and bled from small wounds on his forehead and shoulder, but he wore an expression of grim determination on his face.

"Kim!" Priwinn shouted in relief. "Finally! Where have you been?" He cut off Kim's attempted reply with a hasty gesture, immediately continuing: "Never mind—it doesn't matter now. Come here, ride next to me! When my men see you, they'll take heart! We can do it!"

The thuds and crashes all around him drowned out Kim's voice. The defenders of Gorywynn wavered and began to fall back, for the Rivermen merely had led one part of the enemy army, and iron men now stomped toward Gorywynn like an avalanche of steel. Kim guided his horse close enough to Priwinn to try and make himself understood—but even in that short time, a dozen men fell.

The iron men carried no weapons, but they swept everyone to the ground with their fearsome arms, trampling over anyone who couldn't run away fast enough. The Steppe riders fiercely defended themselves. Gorg and the two dragons were not the only ones attacking the robots. Many of the other fighters were quite capable of injuring the iron giants: some had swords and daggers of dwarven steel, which they'd taken as booty from captives or stolen from forges and mines. Sometimes, ten or more warriors would charge one of the steel giants. Despite the iron man's superior strength, they would bring him down through sheer numbers. These desperate attacks exacted a terrible toll, however.

"Stop!" Kim cried. "Priwinn, call them back! You can't fight them!"

Priwinn stared at Kim as if he'd gone insane. "What do you mean?"

"You can't do it!" Kim repeated. "Th-they're the children!"

Priwinn's eyes widened. A stunned expression appeared on Gorg's face, followed a second later by a look of deep horror.

"What do you mean?" Priwinn muttered again.

"The iron men," Kim said. "They're the children who've disappeared, Priwinn. They've been transformed—do you understand?"

Slowly, the King of the Steppe lowered his sword. His eyes were dark with torment; he didn't blink. His face puckered as if he were suffering from unbearable pain. "You . . . you're lying," he stammered. "That . . . that can't be true."

Priwinn really wasn't accusing Kim of lying. Like Gorg, as soon as he heard Kim's words, he clearly recognized the truth. Again, seconds passed in which Priwinn simply sat in his saddle and looked at Kim. Then, he slowly turned around. With inexpressible difficulty, he gave the signal to retreat. "Stop!" he shouted. "Don't touch the iron men!"

The men in his immediate vicinity lowered their weapons and looked at their king in confusion, but the rest had not heard the order. Everywhere Kim looked, the battled raged. Their army was driven back, but the Riverfolk and the iron men also had suffered terrible losses. Only the dwarves didn't participate much in the battle. Instead, they flitted between iron giants' legs with astonishing dexterity, avoiding any confrontation.

"Retreat!" Priwinn shouted once again. "Stop! I command you!"

Again, only a few men obeyed. The rest were driven back by the Riverfolk and their steel comrades. More of Priwinn's men fell under the pirates' swords and spears. Kim noticed something else, as well: When the iron men didn't have to defend themselves, they didn't kill their adversaries, instead holding them with their terrible claws.

"Stop!" Kim now shouted, as well, as loud as he could. "Don't fight against them! They are your children!"

What Priwinn's command had failed to do, these words accomplished. Suddenly, more fighters lowered their weapons and reined in their horses. As they stared at the approaching army of iron giants, an expression of unbelievable horror replaced the hatred and anger on their faces. They weren't the only ones who forgot the battle for a moment. Kim saw that everyone froze right where they stood, trying to process this new information.

"They're your children!" Kim yelled once again. "Don't fight against them!"

As loud as his voice was, it didn't carry very far. However, the men repeated this message, and the word spread as fast as the wind. Warriors who were fighting with an iron man instantly withdrew from combat. Men who had raised their swords and daggers for a blow lowered their arms. Even the two dragons suddenly swung high into the air and circled the field.

"Retreat!" Priwinn shouted with a voice that carried far. "Fall back to Gorywynn!"

The fighters obeyed. The well-ordered retreat turned into a headlong flight, however. The Riverfolk quickly overcame their surprise, and the iron men never paused in their advance but plodded on with the relentless momentum of machines. As Priwinn's huge army fell back to the city, many of the Steppe riders were trampled underfoot. Kim, Priwinn, and Gorg were carried along. As they approached the gate, Kim realized the terrible irony of their situation. The previous evening, Kim's appearance had turned the tide in Priwinn's favor and led to victory. Now, Kim brought with him a crushing defeat. The iron men couldn't move very fast, so they fell behind a short distance. The Riverfolk pursued the fleeing soldiers; because they were hopelessly outnumbered, however, they didn't dare attack the army without their steel comrades. Even so, some fighting broke out between the Riverfolk and the Steppe riders, simply because the city gate wasn't wide enough to allow the retreating men to pass through.

Kim, Priwinn, and Gorg were among the last to enter the city. The giant's superhuman strength and Kim's protective black armor allowed the pair to hold off the attackers until the last men had withdrawn to the city. As soon as all the others made it inside, iron men arrived. Gorg and Kim quickly retreated, as well.

Utter chaos followed: a foretaste of the end of the world, more terrible than could be imagined. The iron men stormed through the gate without the slightest pause. The Riverfolk flooded in after them, eager to avenge their previous defeat. As the Riverfolk had done the evening before, Priwinn's warriors now sought shelter and hiding places in the city's maze of lanes. The iron men entered all the houses and searched every street, corner, and courtyard. They seized the city's defenders and held their prisoners in firm, inescapable, iron grips.

Kim and the others continually were forced backward; their numbers steadily dwindled. Eventually, they stood before the palace gates, vanquished men awaiting the final onslaught.

"What now?" Priwinn asked. He was bathed in sweat and wore an expression of complete discouragement. He stared at Kim, pleading with his eyes. "What now, Kim? What's the point of all this?"

Kim looked around in despair. There were maybe one hundred of them left: the sad remainder of a mighty army that had set out to rescue Magic Moon. Now, a superior force inexorably advanced upon them.

Kim gave no reply; Priwinn had not expected any, either. The young king suddenly sprang out of his saddle and rushed into the palace. After a brief hesitation, both Kim and Gorg followed him; meanwhile, the little group of defeated soldiers banded together in front of the gate to buy them some time. Kim glanced over his shoulder and saw that the men no longer defended themselves. They drew their weapons only if soldiers attacked them. The defenders walked toward the iron men with empty hands and didn't resist as the robots seized them. The iron giants were delayed because they had to carry away their prisoners.

In the meantime, Priwinn reached the staircase. He ran up the stairs by leaps and bounds. Kim and the giant followed him, but the young Steppe rider ran so quickly that they had a hard time keeping up with him. They were barely halfway up the stairs when they heard the stomping of heavy iron feet and the pirates' triumphant cries.

Kim's strength almost gave out before he reached the tower chamber. With a last-ditch effort, he dragged himself across the room and sank to his knees beside Themistokles' bed.

Priwinn, who had arrived before him, now grabbed Themistokles by the shoulders and wildly shook him.

"Themistokles!" he yelled. "Wake up! I beg of you, wake up!"

Sheera and Chunklet, who crouched on the wizard's bed, also tried to rouse the wizard.

But the old man didn't move. As Priwinn desperately shook him, the wizard's head lolled from side to side and his face contorted, as if in pain. But his eyes remained closed, and Kim knew that he wouldn't awaken—perhaps not ever again.

Finally, Kim used gentle force to push aside Priwinn's hand. "Let him be," he said softly. "He can't help us—not anymore."

Priwinn raised his fist as if he intended to hit Kim. His face contorted and his eyes filled with tears. But his anger wasn't directed at Kim, and his tears were from helplessness, not rage.

"It's over," Kim murmured. Tiredly, he stood up and gave the sleeping wizard one final look. Then, he pulled his sword out of its sheath. He laid it on the table in the exact position he'd found it—in the dream that wasn't a dream.

"That was very wise of you, my boy."

Kim slowly turned around and looked at a large man with a closely trimmed, black beard. He wore the standard clothing of the Riverfolk, but a silver band encircled his head, leading Kim to assume that he was a king or the head of the army. The man's eyes were hard but not as cruel as Kim had feared, and his face was that of a strong man not without mercy.

"And you, King Priwinn," the stranger continued, "should follow the example of your friend and lower your weapon. It's over."

Priwinn stared at the man without speaking. Then, his lips trembled and his hand gripped the hilt of the sword so tightly that his skin turned white. "Never!" he said softly. "Maybe you've won, but I'll never surrender. I'd rather die!"

He raised his sword high and charged at the stranger.

In a flash, Gorg pulled Priwinn back and wrested away the sword. He threw the blade at the wall with such force that it broke. Then, he gently set his friend back on the ground and shook his head. "Let it be, Priwinn," he said softly. "He's right. It's over. Your death won't do anyone any good."

With a cry of despair, Priwinn turned around and started hammering on the giant's chest with both hands. Gorg didn't defend himself but simply stood there, looking sad. After a few moments, Priwinn stopped hitting him. With slumped shoulders, he stepped back, continuing to sob.

"Kill me," he said. "Do as you like."

"We don't want your death, King Priwinn," said the other man. He smiled in a strangely tolerant, forgiving manner. "That was never our intention. We just want to live life as we choose. We didn't take up arms until you tried to force your kind of happiness on us."

He took another step forward to make room for an iron man. Then, he bent over Themistokles' bed and thoughtfully looked down at the old man. "So, that is Themistokles. I've heard a lot about him."

"He's dying," Kim said quietly.

"I'm sorry," replied the King of the Riverfolk. He sounded sincere. "However, he is an old man," he continued, "and he has lived a long life—much longer than any of us. His time is past. The magic is fading away; with it, the wizards must fade away, as well."

"And the future belongs to men like you, right?" Priwinn said bitterly.

"Maybe," the king replied. "Time will tell."

Kim walked over to the window, looked out, and said without turning around, "You have no future."

He knew he'd astonished the others, but Kim continued in the same quiet tone of voice, still refusing to look at them: "Look outside, and then you'll know what's left of your future. You've sold it for a little extra comfort and prosperity."

Priwinn was silent, but the Riverman said, "You're embittered, boy. I've heard about you. I know who you are. Believe me, I understand how you feel.

You once saved this world and you thought you could do it again. But you're wrong. You may be able to defeat the strongest enemy, but you can't stop the progress of the world."

Now, Kim did turn around.

An iron man entered the room and Jarrn followed close behind, as if he'd been waiting for this moment. Perhaps he'd been standing outside, listening.

"You don't believe me?" Kim asked tiredly. He pointed at the dwarf. "Ask him."

The Riverman turned his head, frowning in puzzlement. Priwinn also looked down at the Dwarf King.

Jarrn peered up at Kim, blinking his eyes. "What do you mean by that?" he asked innocently.

"Don't bother," Kim said. "I know the secret. I saw what happened to Peer."

"What is that supposed to mean, dwarf?" the Riverman asked suspiciously.

Jarrn shrugged irritably. "I have no idea what he's talking about," he snapped. "He's crazy! Don't believe a word he says."

"The iron men," Kim said. "You all believed that the dwarves used magical powers to forge them from ore, like all their weapons and tools. Well, that's not true." He turned to Jarrn with a challenging gesture. "Is it, Jarrn?"

Jarrn reluctantly muttered, "That depends."

"Don't speak in riddles, dwarf!" the Riverman said sharply.

Jarrn glared at him. "Showing off again, dirt bag? We have a contract, if I recall correctly. Maybe you could comply with it this time, for a change."

"That's not an answer," the Riverman said, unperturbed. Suddenly, he frowned as if something had occurred to him. He turned to Kim. "What did you mean when you said 'they're your children'?"

Jarrn began to shuffle his feet.

Kim was silent for a while; then, he said, "A while ago, you were talking about the future," Kim finally began, "and who it belongs to. You forgot one thing: Your children are the future. You gambled them both away—your children and your world. Whoever wins this war won't rejoice over the victory for long."

"He's feverish, delirious," Jarrn said sharply. "Don't believe a word he says."

But the Riverman gestured for Kim to continue speaking.

"You said it yourself—remember?" Kim continued. "You took up arms because you want to live your lives as you please. Priwinn took the wrong path, but yours isn't any better. You won, but for whom? This is the land of magic and fantasy; if both fade away, then Magic Moon will fade away, as well. You've sacrificed your children and your world."

"That's . . . nonsense," the Riverman now objected, but his voice sounded uncertain. "You're talking like this fool from Caivallon, who hates everything that the dwarves do and everyone who trades with them. We didn't want this war. All we wanted was a better life for us and our children."

"The road you've taken is wrong," Kim insisted calmly. "You're killing your world so that you can live in ease. You're using up everything that was meant for the generations after you, and you're destroying the land where others who are not yet born are supposed to live. That's why many children have gone. You think you can create a better world? You're building a world full of . . . things that make your life easier. Wide iron roads, where your wagons can move faster; rivers that flow in a manner that pleases you; machines that do your work for you . . ."

"And what's wrong with that?" Jarrn piped up.

"Nothing," Kim said, "as long as you don't harm others—as long as you don't take more than you give. That's not what you did, though. Your hearts have become as hard as the iron of your machines. While you've focused on prosperity, you've lost the only thing you truly possessed: your future. Where are your children?" He pointed at the window behind him. "Look outside. There they are. Some are dead. They are the collective price that you must pay for your prosperity."

"Is that true?" the River King asked, addressing Jarrn.

The dwarf shuffled his feet again; after a while, he reluctantly shrugged his shoulders. "It wasn't my idea," he grumbled.

The Riverman's face darkened, but Kim restrained him with a gesture. "Let him be," he said. "He's telling the truth." Kim smiled when Jarrn lifted his head and looked at him incredulously. "The dwarves are not to blame," he said with finality.

"Not to blame?!" Priwinn shouted. "They're the ones who made the iron men, and you're saying they're not to blame?!"

"You still don't understand," Kim murmured sadly. "The dwarves aren't the ones who created the iron men. *You* created them yourselves—and you created the dwarves along with them. You were the ones who summoned the dwarves, not the other way around. Themistokles told us that, don't you remember? The dwarves didn't appear until they were needed—by you, by everyone who summoned them. The dwarves are as you created them."

Everything in the chamber grew still. Finally, Priwinn slumped down on a chair and, with a deep sigh, buried his face in his hands. "Then, it's all over," he groaned. "Our fight was in vain. Nothing can save us now."

Suddenly, Kim felt as if something invisible moved through the room—a breath of disembodied warmth . . . a fleeting bit of the old magic that once had filled the crystal fortress. At the same moment, Themistokles opened his eyes.

Kim was about to rush over; but when Themistokles' gaze met his, he stopped.

"Themistokles!" Priwinn exclaimed, jumping up. The King of the Riverfolk also turned around in surprise. The look he gave the wizard showed respect and something like admiration.

"The boy is right," Themistokles said abruptly. Although he looked just as weak and tired as before, his voice sounded restored to normal—as if all the knowledge of his thousands of years had returned to him. "What he says is true, Priwinn," said the wizard. "You chose the wrong path. No one can conquer fate with weapons. And you, King of the Riverfolk," he continued, addressing the Riverman, "also took the wrong path. You're killing the world on which your lives depend; for that, the world will kill you. You've lost the power of dreams and, therefore, your future. For what is the future, except our dreams? What are we, if not the dreams of those who came before us? You're blind, and you didn't understand what you were doing. Some of our children sensed it and fled to other worlds—but they won't survive there. The ones who stayed paid the price for the sins of their fathers. You've won the war. Magic Moon belongs to you. There is no one left who can contest your right to it. But tell me—what good is victory if there is no one to inherit it? The future of this world will not belong to you; it will belong to your machines. Machines have no dreams."

The Riverman was silent. A stricken expression spread across his face; he looked at the robot next to him. The iron colossus gazed out from his glowing green eye slit, and it seemed to Kim as if the two dissimilar beings somehow were communicating.

"Then, is it as the Steppe rider says?" whispered the Riverman. "Is everything lost? Is it true we have no future left?"

"Not on the path you're taking," replied Themistokles. "Not until you understand this fact and live accordingly: You can't take more from a world than you give to it."

No one moved. Indeed, no one breathed. It was as if time itself stood still. Very slowly, the King of the Riverfolk pulled his sword from his belt and laid it on the little table next to Kim's weapon.

After a few more seconds, King Priwinn also stood up, bent down to get the broken hilt of his own blade, and laid it next to the other two.

Kim saw only sadness and a plea for forgiveness in the Riverman's eyes—and the presence of a tiny, desperate hope that it wasn't too late.

It wasn't. For when the Riverman looked at the iron man, a golden ray of sunshine streamed through the window: a shimmering, gentle beam enveloped the iron figure in bright light. The iron colossus faded into a shadow. For a short time, he stood there without any recognizable shape.

Then, where the robot had been, the figure of a boy about twelve years old appeared; he was clad in the leather and iron garb of the Riverfolk.

The Riverman cried out, leaped forward, and wrapped his son in his arms. In the hallway, a second and third cry could be heard, and Kim knew that the same thing had happened there.

Kim thought about how this transformation would repeat throughout the land—in the fortress, in the courtyard, in the city, and everywhere that people understood what a terrible price they'd paid for an illusion. Now enlightened, they could embrace the children once lost.

When Kim turned back to Themistokles, the wizard was no longer a dying old man, but the familiar, majestic, benevolent wizard. Kim saw a man with a timeless face, long white hair, a wavy beard, and eyes that had seen eternity. Themistokles knew the pettiness and meaninglessness of everything that humans did—and he also understood the great responsibility that each individual bore for these actions.

On his last day in Gorywynn—Kim had sensed that it was the last one when he opened his eyes that morning—he stood on the palace's glass balcony with Themistokles, Priwinn, and Chunklet. They looked down at the city.

Kim felt a little sad, but not bitterly so. He knew, after all, that although he would leave Magic Moon, he'd never lose the land of dreams. Much time had passed since that day when the fate of this enchanted world had improved. Much had happened in that time. Although they might not be friends, the Riverfolk and the other peoples of Magic Moon developed good neighborly relations and soon had realized that they benefited everyone.

Almost everywhere in the land, the iron men had disappeared, and most of the missing children had returned to their families. To Kim's and Themistokles' great sorrow, not all of them did. On some farms, in some villages, and throughout some cities, the occasional robot still could be seen at work—for some people's hearts had grown so hard that they were incapable of doing anything differently. But every day, there were fewer of the robots and, as Themistokles had ensured, not a single new one was created.

Kim and Priwinn had visited with their friends everywhere in the land, rejoicing with them over the future they'd regained. Kim had seen Peer again and also had spent some time in Caivallon. He saw the Fortress of the Steppe that Priwinn now ruled over as king. Priwinn was no longer an eternal youth: He was a young man who would always remain Kim's friend.

Kim had visited Brobing and Jara and, with a heavy heart, returned Stardust to them. Stardust had been meant for Torum, and Torum was back again. Much work still lay ahead for everyone. The wounds that the inhabitants of Magic Moon had inflicted on their world wouldn't heal on their own. Remedying these errors would take incomparably more effort and energy than the original destruction cost. Yet, Kim knew their efforts would succeed. Now that they had a future again, the people of Magic Moon had something to live for. Perhaps, they would learn from the mistakes of the past. Perhaps, there never again would be a time when iron horses plowed the fields and children disappeared because dreams had been abandoned and hearts had turned to stone.

When Kim sensed his stay in Magic Moon was coming to an end, he asked Priwinn to guide him to Gorywynn so that he could bid farewell to Themistokles. The new king of Caivallon had turned over his duties to a deputy so he could accompany his friend.

To Kim's pleasant surprise, they rode Rangarig, the golden dragon, who had returned to his old self (as had the Tatzelwurm, by the way, who was now back in his northern lake, spewing venom and gall whenever anyone approached). Now, Kim stood high above the towers of Gorywynn, looking down on the structures of glass that captured and reflected light. They spoke of various things, but both Themistokles and Priwinn sensed Kim's inevitable departure, and both men were filled with sadness and melancholy. Sheera restlessly rubbed against their legs as they simply stood together in comfortable, familiar silence.

Of course, Chunklet—who was as brazenly outspoken as always—complained that he was hungry. Kim could well understand that: Chunklet's last meal had been only two hours before. The poor fellow must have been close to starvation.

"Are you coming back?" Priwinn suddenly asked.

Kim shrugged. "I hope so," he said. Then, to his own surprise, he heard himself add: "Maybe I shouldn't."

"Why not?" Priwinn looked up in surprise.

"Well, I've been here only when . . . something bad has happened," Kim said haltingly. "Why is it that I come to the realm of fantasy only when it's in danger?"

Priwinn looked perplexed, but Themistokles smiled and gently shook his head. "It's typical of humans that they don't really appreciate what they have until it appears they might lose it. The world of fantasy is always there, though. It is inside you, just as you are inside this world. You simply don't notice it."

Kim mulled over these words for a while and eventually understood what Themistokles meant.

Smiling, he went back into the adjacent room in the tower chamber, where they'd last met with the King of the Riverfolk. All three swords still lay untouched on the table. They would remain untouched—the two intact swords crossed over the broken blade—as a symbol that weapons were not a solution, and that no enmity was so great that it couldn't be overcome.

Kim was a little sad as he thought about Jarrn, the Dwarf King. The dwarves had disappeared along with the iron men, and Kim felt a bit sorry for those feisty little people who'd endured everyone's hostility. Maybe they still existed somewhere and would come back some day to forge other useful things that would help other people instead of cause them harm. Kim turned around to ask Themistokles about that . . . but the wall, the glass balcony, and the sky above Gorywynn had disappeared. In their place he found himself in a small room. Grayish light poked through half-drawn blinds.

Startled, he whirled around and bumped into something that rattled. Kim cautiously extended his hand and felt cold, smooth glass.

He heard rustling noises, and then a little light switched on. His sister's sleepy face rose up from her pillow, and she blinked at him. "What do you want?" Becky complained. "Let me sleep. What are you doing here, anyway?" She shut her eyes and went back to sleep before Kim had time to answer—which he definitely wouldn't have done, in any case.

He was back home. In his confused state, he noted that he was standing exactly where it had all begun—in his sister's room, right next to the terrarium where two tiny red- and green-patterned lizards flitted back and forth, startled when Kim accidentally had bumped into their home.

It was strange. He felt no disappointment at all. The only thing he felt was a slight bit of melancholy. Perhaps, it really was as Themistokles had said: Magic Moon was within him, just as he was always there. Carefully, so as not to awaken Rebecca again, Kim tiptoed to the door, opened it, and walked out into the hallway.

Nighttime was almost over. The gray light of dawn already had spread to the stairway. He heard the muffled voices of his parents down on the first floor. Kim wanted to go back to his room but realized he couldn't sleep, so he turned toward the stairs.

When he climbed halfway down, he heard his father talking to someone on the telephone. Kim walked into the living room just as his father put down the receiver. Dad was surprised to see Kim up at this early hour—and completely dressed, too. But he didn't comment on it. Instead, Dad just exchanged a surprised look with Kim's mother, and then he motioned to the telephone.

"Do you know who that was?" he said.

Kim had a general idea, but he shook his head and feigned ignorance.

"It was the police." Dad's face darkened. He probably was thinking of the scene from the night before. Luckily, his voice sounded more surprised than angry when he continued: "The inspector wanted to come back this afternoon to ask you a few questions."

"What about?" Kim asked. "Did something happen?"

His father shrugged. "My guess is they don't really know. It seems that the boy from the hospital has disappeared, though. Inspector Gerber was of the opinion that you might be able to tell him something about that. But you can't, can you?"

"Of course not," Kim hastened to assure him.

"That's exactly what I told him, too," Dad said, giving him a searching look. "I told him that you don't have anything else to tell him, and that he would be wasting his time. I think he realized that. In any case, he's not going to bother us from now on. But this whole thing is definitely strange," he added, almost expectantly, when Kim breathed a sigh of relief. "Do you remember what the professor said? That they had picked up several of these kids who had no memory and apparently couldn't talk?"

Kim nodded. *What's Dad getting at?*

"Well," his father continued with a shrug and another searching look, "it seems they've all disappeared without a trace."

"That's weird," Kim said, "but what does that have to do with me?"

"Precisely," Dad replied. "Oh well," he sighed. "They'll find an explanation, sooner or later."

Kim felt absolutely sure that wouldn't happen, but he refrained from saying so. Instead, he sat down on the empty chair between his father and mother, reached for the glass of milk waiting for him, and said softly, "Sure, if they have enough imagination." He smiled.

His father looked at him in surprise but said nothing. It was as if he sensed that something was happening in Kim—a part of growing up that needed no discussion.

Oddly enough, Kim could feel his father's anger change into a combination of bewilderment and a kind of understanding. Was it possible that a part of Magic Moon was inside Kim's father and mother—and in that unpleasant inspector, too? Perhaps, there was a little fantasy somewhere inside every person.

Kim heard a truck pull up right next to their house. He exchanged a surprised look with his parents.

"The new neighbors," his mother said. "The house next door was sold, you know. The new family is moving in today."

Kim had a sudden urge to go outside and look at the people who would live next door. He looked at his father, who gave a silent nod, and then he rushed outside.

Despite the early hour, it was already warm. The sun shone in a cloudless sky, and something joyful and carefree filled the air. Almost as if an invisible shadow had been removed from the world.

Kim dismissed this thought and studied the huge truck that parked just a few yards away. Two movers in blue overalls were opening up the large doors at the back of the van. There was no one else in sight. Then, a battered Mercedes turned the corner and stopped behind the moving van. A man and a woman got out and started talking with the movers.

Kim gave them a fleeting look. His entire attention was directed at the slender, dark-haired boy getting out of the car.

The boy was Kim's age but a good bit taller; although Kim was sure he'd never seen the kid before in his life, it felt like they were very old friends. How strange!

Stranger yet, the boy seemed sense the same connection, for he suddenly paused and looked at Kim with a slightly puzzled frown.

Finally, Kim steeled himself and walked over to the boy. It was hard for him to address the other kid.

"Hello," he said.

"Hello," the boy said back. "Have we met before?"

"I . . . don't think so," Kim said hesitantly. "You're the new neighbors, aren't you?"

The boy nodded. "Yes. What's your name?"

"Kim. What's yours?"

The boy stared at him as if he had heard something astonishing. Then, he said, "Peter."

He stepped back to make room for a smaller boy to get out of the car. This kid also had black hair. "That's my brother, Jared," he added and grinned. "Ugly little cuss, but otherwise quite nice."

Jared got out of the car, bristling with indignation. He turned in a circle, surveying the neighborhood. Kim noticed the small boy held a leash in his spindly fingers. Kim gulped when he saw the creature waddle on crooked legs.

If that was a dog, it was definitely the ugliest one Kim had ever seen. Well, Kim thought it was a dog—he wasn't quite sure.

"Good-looking pooch, huh? I see you think so, too." Peter laughed softly. "But the two of them stick to each other like bread and butter. They sort of fit each other, don't you think?"

Kim didn't reply. Spellbound, he stared at the little dog, which waddled up to him.

The dog sniffed Kim's tennis shoes with interest, and then chomped down on Kim's toe.

Whining, he looked up at Kim and slobbered all over Kim's pants. His eyes clearly reflected one thing: hunger!

Kim was too astonished to move. When the dampness soaked through his pants, he quickly jumped back.

Jared grinned with malicious joy. "Hi, dimwit," he said.

POP
FICTION